DEADLY OBSESSION

APRIL HUNT

FOREVER
New York Boston

Copyright © 2019 by April Schwartz

Excerpt from *Lethal Redemption* copyright © 2019 by April Schwartz

Cover illustration and design by Elizabeth Turner Stokes. Cover copyright © 2019 by Hachette Book Group, Inc.

Forever
Hachette Book Group
1290 Avenue of the Americas, New York, NY 10104
read-forever.com
twitter.com/readforeverpub

First Edition: April 2019

Forever is an imprint of Grand Central Publishing. The Forever name and logo are trademarks of Hachette Book Group, Inc.

The publisher is not responsible for websites (or their content) that are not owned by the publisher.

The Hachette Speakers Bureau provides a wide range of authors for speaking events. To find out more, go to www.hachettespeakersbureau.com or call (866) 376-6591.

ISBNs: 978-1-5387-6333-9 (mass market), 978-1-5387-6335-3 (ebook)

Printed in the United States of America

OPM

10 9 8 7 6 5 4 3 2 1

To the "G" family…
Hero [he-ro]:
Is an ordinary individual who finds the
strength to persevere and endure in
spite of overwhelming odds.

—Christopher Reeve

ACKNOWLEDGMENTS

It's always a little nerve-wracking diving into a new world. New characters. New personalities. New struggles and motivations. But there's always a lot of excitement...and a lot of people who put their all into each word.

To my family, who have quickly learned that "Deadline Time" means a lot of take-out chicken wings and pizza—and don't complain.

My super-agent. Sarah E. Younger...as always, you don't simply look out for my career, but my sanity. My true champion! My editor, Madeleine Colavita—I love that you love my characters as much as I do! (You can name my sexy heroes ANY day of the week;-)) Everyone at Forever, I'm so glad to have you all on this crazy ride. Even with all the work that goes into bringing each book to life, you make it seem so effortless.

My #GirlsWriteNite crew: Tif Marcelo, Annie Rains, Rachel Lacey, and Sidney Halston. You help me keep the words flowing, sometimes by pulling me out of a plot hole that I'd accidentally stumbled into. To all my Agency Sisters, YOU ROCK! #TeamSarah all the way!

To all the readers, THANK YOU! You're one of the reasons I do what I do. Keep reading! Keep reviewing! And keep love alive!

And to all the heroes out there, whether you wear a military insignia, teach a class of seven-year-olds, or work long, twelve-hour shifts taking care of families while being apart from your own...YOU. ARE. APPRECIATED.

AUTHOR'S NOTE

Before there was a Knox, before there was a Cupid Killer, before a plot outline for *Deadly Obsession* existed, I knew Zoey's struggle intimately.

As a healthcare professional, I see it way too often.

As a friend, I've witnessed it firsthand.

No grouping of words or any written story could come close to describing the challenges faced by families with a child diagnosed with a Congenital Heart Defect (CHD). The strength, love, and pure, unwavering faith that they put in one another—and in a higher power—astounds me to this day.

I chose to have Zoey live with a CHD to make her vulnerable on an entirely different scale. Congenital Heart Defects aren't something that can be willed away. They're constant. They're chronic. And according to March of Dimes, they affect one in one hundred births. That's 40,000 babies per year in the United States alone.

Living with the vulnerability and uncertainty of a CHD drastically changes the emotional reactions of those affected, and can alter every daily decision from the small to the large.

Zoey's struggles and her dreams for the future barely shed a light on life with a CHD. But now that you've read her story, you'll be able to make that light shine a little brighter.

All my best,
April

DEADLY OBSESSION

PROLOGUE

A low, groaning whimper turned his head toward the corner of the dimly lit room. Huddled in a ball on the soiled mattress, his latest disappointment rocked to and fro, an empty shell of what she'd once been.

There wasn't a single sign of the woman who'd caught his attention two short weeks ago. Sallow and brittle, her skin sagged off her petite frame, and her eyes, previously a radiant blue, had long since dimmed into a vacant stare.

How in the hell could he have ever confused His Heart's beauty with the creature cowering in front of him?

This brought him to an even dozen. Twelve failures. Twelve imposters who'd believed they could mask the gritty dirt beneath their shiny façades. Twelve women of whom he'd disposed, and who'd driven his goal further from reach.

That goal: to re-create the pure, magical connection that he'd experienced with His Heart.

"You shouldn't have pretended." Fueled by a flash of white-hot rage, he grasped the heavy chain by his feet and yanked. The pathetic form attached to the other end jolted three inches closer. "You shouldn't have pretended to be something you're not."

"I'm s-sorry." Each feeble attempt to claw her way back into her corner gouged the plastic ties on her wrists deeper into her flesh. "Please let me go."

He tugged again, gaining another two inches. This time, her body melted into a puddle on the floor, every ounce of defiance, gone. Finally.

Two long days of prolonged stubbornness, and they were nearly finished.

He dropped the chain and stalked to the powder-blue dress carefully hanging on the rack, ready to be used in the next phase. Slowly, he trailed his fingers over the silken material, and closed his eyes. So soft. So pure.

Just like His Heart.

She'd faced adversity and had come out on top, was as strong as She was beautiful. She was resilient. She was his, no matter how much time passed or how much distance separated them.

With the image of Her in his mind, forgiveness swept through him, and with it, a wave of calm. He turned back to the shackled specimen on the floor. "In Her name, I will mend you and gift you a second chance..."

Hope flickered across the woman's face as she mistook his words.

They always did.

Deep in the recesses of his pocket, his fingers bumped against the syringe that he'd carefully filled less than a half hour ago. Its pale yellow liquid bubbled as he rolled it against the pads of his fingers.

The imposter's eyes locked on to the two-inch

needle, and in one final display of defiance, she screamed.

No one would hear her. No one would come to her rescue. And once his slate was wiped clean, he'd start over.

Next time, he'd get it right. Or he'd simply try again.

CHAPTER ONE

Chin up. Shoulders back. Breathe. Do not puke on the crime scene.

At her last position running the Washington, DC, crime lab, Zoey Wright had never needed a peppy mantra. There wasn't much that was nausea-inducing about Petri dishes and microfibers. But thirty minutes into her first on-site homicide and she'd already hit an even two dozen mental replays.

Repetition wasn't working.

Lieutenant Mason side-eyed her as they shouldered their way through a thick crowd of onlookers. "You look like you're going to blow any second, kid. If you need to go around the corner and puke, do it now. But you damn well better not contaminate my crime scene."

"I'm good." Zoey breathed in through her nose and out through her mouth.

The sixty-year-old police veteran lifted his bushy white eyebrows. "So good that you're the exact shade of green my wife made me paint our kitchen last week? Don't kid a kidder, Wright. If it gets too much for you, go take a breather. No one will think any less of you."

If she let an acute case of nerves derail years of hard

work and her position as DC's only civilian crime scene investigator, *she'd* think less of herself. Not to mention the ammunition it would provide her hotshot detective brother in his quest to get her to return to the lab—if she'd told Cade about her job switch-a-roo in the first place.

She'd given herself until next week to break the news, but this assignment bumped the deadline up to tonight. As head of the Special Crimes Task Force Cade could—and would—turn the corner at any second.

Zoey cursed the ill-timed bacon maple doughnut that she'd inhaled on the ride from the station to M Street and spotted her brother's truck among the squad cars and unmarked police vehicles lining both sides of the street.

At one in the morning, most family-run businesses had long since closed, which meant the gathering crowd had come from the dance club down the block. Anyone who lived, worked, or played in the District during the last six months knew a police turnout of this magnitude meant one thing.

Another victim.

"Do you have any words of wisdom to lay on me before we get there?" Zoey tugged their collection cart behind her, giving it a little extra oomph when it lodged into a crater-sized crack.

"Yep. Don't inhale food fifteen minutes before being called to a homicide."

Zoey's glare fired off a small chuckle. She took the good-natured barb and followed the older man to the yellow police tape that cordoned off the alley from the rest of the world.

"You make sure everyone stayed out of our scene, Reed?" Mason stopped in front of the officer stationed at the mouth of the alley.

"Only ones who've been down that way besides your people is the guy who called it in. He's giving his statement to Detective Wright now," Officer Scott Reed mentioned her brother.

Zoey swung her gaze around, expecting Cade to pop up at any second. When he didn't show, she released a small sigh of relief...until Mason ducked beneath the rope, leaving her alone with Scott.

She'd barely cleared the tape when Scott stepped into her path. His tall frame and wrestler's build made him impossible to ignore, as did the gaze he skimmed over her body. It slid over her three times before his mouth lifted into a grin *he* probably thought sexy.

She considered it creepy.

Scott shifted a little closer. "You're all over the place these days, aren't you? I tried calling you a few times after our date. I even left a couple messages."

"Really? Huh." Zoey pushed her glasses back onto her nose, a nervous habit she'd acquired in grade school. "I've been having problems with my phone holding voicemails hostage. I'm looking into another model."

And another phone number. That "date" had been the worst she'd ever been on—and thanks to a romance app and one too many blind setups, she'd been on a handful of doozies.

"Maybe we can catch up tonight when this circus is all over. What do you say? You. Me. We can grab a bottle of wine and head back to my place...or yours. I'm not particular." Scott flashed her a suggestive wink. "We can have fun at either place, I'm sure."

Zoey barely suppressed a disgusted grunt. "Sorry, but I'm going to be here for a while. You know how thorough Mason likes to be. It's going to be a long night."

"Okay, sure. Maybe next time."

Unless they stepped into the Twilight Zone, there wouldn't *be* a next time. Someone's family member wouldn't make it home for another dinner or pose for this year's holiday card. One life ended meant dozens— and more—would never be the same, and he stood there, sensing an opportunity to fill a few empty hours—and her pants.

Before Scott made another play, she hustled over to where the lieutenant waited.

Mason chuckled as she approached. "Finalize your plans?"

"Thanks for the save. You could've thrown me a life jacket, a T-bone, or *something*...but no, you practically fed me to the wolves...er, wolf."

"Figured you'd gotten yourself into that mess all alone and that you'd get yourself out. But I can't deny being curious how the hell that happened. I always thought you were the smart Wright sibling."

"It happened because I hadn't been on a date in far longer than I'm admitting aloud. It was *one* time, and I barely made it out of my apartment before I realized I'd made a mistake. Trust me, it's not going to happen again. I've proclaimed a moratorium on romance. It's career first from this point on."

"What did Romeo do to make you see the error of your ways?"

"Ogled the rear end of my sixty-year-old neighbor before we'd even made it to the car. Then the waitress's legs at the restaurant. And I don't want to know what went through his mind when he stared at the boobs of the barely-legal ticket-taker at the movies."

"What an ass." Mason snorted.

"Not going to disagree with you."

At five foot three, Zoey didn't possess the lithe body of a runway model, and her B cup had more wiggle room than she'd like. Girl-next-door *cute*. That's how one coworker had described her eclectic style to another. It wasn't a term with which every twenty-seven-year-old woman wanted to be linked, but it didn't bother her enough to give up her vintage Monkees T-shirts either.

Zoey fidgeted with her shirt collar. As it did whenever she contemplated wearing something more revealing than neck-high cotton, the healed scar over her breastbone itched.

Those six inches of puckered skin definitely weren't *cute*.

Their debut appearance came with her first open-heart surgery when she was mere days old. A rerun surgery before her first birthday darkened them. Following a third operation at the age of seven, the scar widened, and then after she hit puberty, and underwent a fourth, it thickened.

Last year's emergent heart valve replacement brought her open-heart surgery grand total to a whopping *five*.

Five times her chest had been cracked open. Five layers of gnarled, angry scar tissue loitered between her breasts, a physical reminder she'd skipped pajama parties and Spin the Bottle, and went straight to responsibility-laden adulthood.

Number five had been her wake-up call because some born with Tetralogy of Fallot didn't get a sixth chance.

Shedding the crime lab's cold isolation and joining scene investigation was the first step in redefining life on her own terms. Having lost his son a few years ago to a chronic illness, Mason got that, and had been a big reason why she'd stepped so far out of her comfort zone.

But the calm, laid-back man who'd taken a chance on her wasn't in that alley. The second they reached the site, he started barking orders. Crime scene techs bustled around the perimeter, not willing to incur his wrath for being too slow—or worse, sloppy.

Within the hour, the small four-flapped tent set off to the left would be filled with detectives and forensic scientists, all members of the task force who couldn't do their job until Zoey and Mason finished theirs.

She pulled the collection cart away from pedestrian foot traffic and kicked the wheel lock into position. On her right, a generator hummed to life. Overhead lights blinked once before flooding the entire alley into pseudo-daylight.

Zoey's lungs froze.

Having worked the string of homicides for the last six months in the lab, she thought she'd be okay, but pictures and written reports had nothing on the dark reality that rooted her feet to the ground.

Laid out on a pristine white blanket, as if her killer had wanted to make her comfortable, was the young victim. Her sleek blond hair had been meticulously brushed and fanned out over her shoulders; the wounds on her wrists, carefully bandaged.

The killer staged her resting place like he'd done the others—far enough from people so as to avoid detection himself, close enough for the woman to be discovered quickly.

"Wright." Mason's voice ripped Zoey from her trance. He watched her carefully, no annoyance or judgment on his face. Only concern. "You okay?"

Zoey forced her returning midnight snack back down her throat and let out a slow breath. "Yeah. It took me by surprise. I'm sorry."

"Hell, you don't need to apologize. When shit like this stops making your stomach roll it's time to get the fuck out...pardon my language."

"Do you apologize to all your trainees for swearing?"

"Not a damn one."

"Then don't start with me. Tonight, I'm the newbie grunt. Put me to work."

Mason didn't need to be told twice. He tilted his head in a slight nod and then immediately snapped orders. In the field, she wasn't Detective Cade Wright's little sister. She was the woman who'd hopefully replace Mason as lead CSI when he retired in a few years.

"You know the drill." Mason tossed her a Tyvek suit and gestured to the far right corner. "We start outside and work our way in. You photograph, drop a placard when needed, and log. Watch where you're stepping. Once that's all done, we'll start back at square one and begin the collection. Questions?"

"Not a one." Zoey shook her head.

Mason threw a fierce glare to the hovering technicians. "If any of you even think about doing something helpful, *don't*. Unless Wright or I give you the okay to breathe, you hold your breath. If you can't follow that simple rule, get off my scene now. Am I clear?"

"Yes, sir," a chorus of affirmations sounded around them.

Zoey secured her hair into a low ponytail, and after tugging her suit over her shorts and T-shirt, she donned her plastic booties. Satisfied she looked enough like a condom and wouldn't bring any contaminants into the crime scene, she grabbed her camera and got to work.

Picture. Placard. Log. Move onward. With her camera in hand, Zoey lost herself in the methodical pattern of canvassing and documenting, repetitive movements that never ceased to put her mind at ease. Before long, she stood two feet away from the victim.

Zoey counted to a long, drawn-out ten, then forced herself to examine the reason DCPD informally dubbed the monster responsible the Beltway Cupid Killer.

The *etching*.

Its top curves barely peeked out above the blue dress's sweetheart neckline, but it was there—a perfectly symmetrical heart carved into the flesh over the victim's sternum. Even without the medical examiner's report, she knew it would be the lone disfigurement other than bruised wrists and a single needle mark.

"I am so sorry this happened to you." Zoey battled welling tears.

Around her own age, or maybe a few years younger, the woman could've been a teacher or a nurse, maybe a college student from down the block like the last three victims had been.

No matter who she'd been in her life, she didn't deserve to have her hopes and dreams cut short. *This* was the difficult part of the job. There was no rewinding time and stepping in *before* someone got hurt.

There was only picking up the pieces and praying that one of those fragments helped put a loved one's mind at ease.

Mason crouched on the other side. "I always come in hoping to God that it's not another one."

Zoey chiseled her dry tongue off the roof of her mouth. "I didn't come across a purse or an ID. Did you?"

"Nah. Didn't expect to since he didn't leave them behind at the other scenes. The bastard's nothing if not predictable. We'll find out who she is and make sure to notify next of kin." The sky rumbled off in the distance. Mason glanced up and cursed. "That storm's coming in fast. We need to get this entire scene covered because I'll be damned if I'm going let a single strand of evidence wash away."

"I'll go get the tents," Zoey volunteered.

She backtracked toward the safe zone, careful not to disturb anything in the process. Less than five seconds into the arduous task of tugging off her protective gear, a familiar tingle formed at the base of her neck.

Her *Knox-dar*.

The strange, shiver-like phenomenon occurred whenever Knox Steele stood in close proximity, a sad reminder of the embarrassing level of interest she had for Cade's best friend. But it wasn't possible.

Knox hadn't stepped foot in DC in years—over two, to be exact.

"You're a little far from the lab, aren't you, angel? You get lost?"

Zoey's hand stalled on her zipper.

That voice. The impossible became reality because Knox Steele's low, husky baritone couldn't be replicated—except by the Knox who visited in her dreams.

Zoey turned on reflex, and came face-to-face with the man himself.

Sexily rumpled, Knox's dark hair curled over his ears as if he'd rolled out of bed a few minutes ago. Heavily worn blue jeans hung off his trim waist, and a leather jacket and dark cotton tee emphasized his broad chest and even wider shoulders.

Her heart stumbled into a double-time beat, and warmth rushed to her cheeks—and all points south. Under normal circumstances, she'd be ecstatic to realize her feminine parts hadn't dried up and turned to dust.

But there wasn't anything normal about Knox's presence, or the way his alert focus conjured life into her usually dormant libido.

Standing less than three feet away from her teenage fantasy, she'd never been more aware of the fact that with her Tyvek suit zipped to her chin and the hood pulled over her limp blond hair, she could've played the principal part in a live-action sex ed presentation. Knox, all six foot three inches of him, looked as if he'd stepped straight off the pages of *Bad Boy Weekly*.

She bumped her glasses onto the bridge of her nose even though they hadn't yet fallen, and forcefully put her attention back to shedding her suit. "I'm right where I'm supposed to be."

"You sure about that? This doesn't look like the crime lab—or your bed. Does Cade know you're here?"

"Are you sure about where *you* are? In case your cell doesn't have a map app, you're in DC. Thought you should know since you've made it your life's mission to avoid this place like the plague."

The muscle in Knox's jaw ticked wildly. If he'd been someone else, she'd apologize for hitting a nerve. Not with him. A former US Army Ranger like her brother, he could take that and a lot more.

"Hey, Wright!" Mason's voice shouted, garnering her attention. The older police officer pointed to the sky. "Put a little hustle into it!"

Saved by the grumpy lieutenant.

Without another word, or a glance at Knox, Zoey deposited her suit into a large collection bag—in case any crucial evidence managed to stick on to her person—and handed it over to the tech to put with the others.

Walking back toward the CSI van, she fumed.

Unlike the rest of his brothers, Knox hadn't returned home after his discharge two years ago. He'd wiped his hands clean of everyone, not even gifting them an occasional I'm-Not-Dead text. And now he was going to stand there, naughty smirk in place, and make comments about her life decisions?

No thank you.

The Zoey Knox had known two long years ago *would've* been tucked into her bed, sound asleep, with her cat, Snuggles, curled next to her pillow. But last year, she vowed that if her bum heart kept throwing obstacles into her daily routine, the least she could do was enjoy life in between the chaos.

Her heart worked fine now, nearly all textbook characteristics of Tetralogy of Fallot resolved. Things that had at one time been a trial were now second nature. She even maintained a healthy exercise routine, and because of her once-a-week self-defense class, could *almost* throw larger assailants over her shoulder and onto the mats.

But that was something he wouldn't have known.

Because he hadn't been around.

Cue mic drop.

Zoey possessed a strength she'd never known before—and yet after one prolonged glance from the eldest Steele brother, breathing ceased being an automatic physical response.

She needed distance to pull her head back on straight.

She needed time to collect her thoughts—and keep down her food.

She needed Knox Steele messing up her life like she needed another hole in her heart.

CHAPTER TWO

Stay. The fuck. Away.

Knox repeated those words in his head again and again, but they didn't take. His focus was superglued onto Zoey as she hightailed it away from him, and hell if he couldn't look away.

He'd screwed up the second he mentioned Cade. It shouldn't have come as a surprise. Messing up was what he excelled at, a fact of which his brothers and cousin Grace would no doubt remind him the second he walked into Steele Ops headquarters.

Cade had already filleted him with his own tirade. A few hours ago, before plying him with more lasagna than an entire platoon could digest, his mom shared some choice words with him too, and with the promise of more in the future.

He just wasn't used to dodging shade thrown by little Zoey Wright.

Knox fished his cell from his pocket and checked the time. One forty-five in the morning.

Thanks to an impromptu shortcut through an alley and his superpower as a trouble magnet, he was officially three hours late meeting up with Liam. Even if he left now, it would take another hour to cross the river into Old Town Alexandria.

For him, that was fine. He didn't sleep much these days. But his brothers—Ryder especially—got damn cranky if they didn't get their full eight. They wouldn't give a rat's ass if he'd stumbled onto a dead body or the winning Mega Ball ticket. The risk of thrown punches dropped dramatically if he waited until the morning for their in-person reunion.

He shot off a quick change-of-plans text to Liam and pocketed his phone. Across the street, Zoey had already stacked two tents onto a cart and was struggling with a third.

He jogged over to relieve her of the heavy bulk. "Let me help."

"I have it covered." Her face dotted with a fine dew, Zoey yanked again, and this time, placed the third tent with the others.

He reached out to grab the next one and got a glare in return.

"You can't help yourself, can you?" Zoey scowled.

"You want to do this yourself?"

"I'm pretty sure I said something to that exact effect, yes."

He lifted his hands in mock surrender and leaned against the back of the van to enjoy the show. "Fine. Go ahead, Rambo."

Zoey's T-shirt, sporting a cartoonish logo from an old television show, lifted, exposing her belly button as she maneuvered the bulky tent into position. "There. Another one down. *Without* assistance."

She shot him a smug smile that nearly had him swallowing his tongue.

Pink-cheeked and lightly breathless from exertion, she looked as if someone had just taken her in a good, hard kiss. *Lucky imaginary bastard.* In his pants, his cock twitched out a warning, and he quickly diverted his gaze to a less dangerous attribute.

Or so he'd thought.

The physical warning got stronger as he studied Zoey's expressive blue eyes. Amplified behind black-rimmed glasses, they showcased each and every one of her feelings. Without fail. Without filter.

Liam, one quarter of the Steele brigade, had once said that Zoey didn't realize how hot she was, which made her even hotter. At the time, Knox hadn't been inclined to think that way about his best friend's little sister. Hell, he'd known her since she rocked the block on her pink-tasseled tricycle.

Now, as she stood in front of him with legs a mile long despite her petite frame, he couldn't help but agree with his youngest brother—and imagine what those legs would feel like wrapped around his waist.

"Fudge it all to hell and back." Zoey's softly muttered curse pulled Knox's thoughts out of the gutter and back to reality.

The last tent crashed to the ground, barely missing her toes. This time, he wasn't taking no for an answer. "I'll get it."

"I almost had it," she said in way of refusal.

"And almost lost a few digits too." He cupped her slender shoulders and eased her off to the side.

"Did I ask for your help?" She shot her annoyance up at him through her long golden lashes.

"Nope." Not swayed by her world-class glare, he easily stacked the last tent on top of the others and remained standing in her direct path.

Hands braced on her slender hips and sapphire eyes probably plotting his downfall, Zoey resembled a pissed-off fairy—except this fairy would bite if provoked. That same fiery spark came to the surface when she dealt with Cade or any of Knox's brothers, but for some reason, dampened around him—until now.

This Zoey wasn't running in the opposite direction.

Knox, challenged by her flame of annoyance, folded his arms across his chest. "So you're in crime scene now. That's a hell of a lot different than the lab. I didn't even realize the District hired civilians."

"I guess desperate times call for desperate measures." Zoey tucked a stray lock of blond hair behind her ear, downplaying her skills.

"I'm sure you weren't hired out of desperation, angel. You're damn smart, and someone's actually intelligent enough to realize it. But I'm surprised Cade wasn't spewing off about it. He usually can't shut up about stuff like this."

Her attention shifted away as she grabbed the cart and tugged it around him.

Knox stuffed his hands into his pockets and boldly followed. "Ah, beautiful avoidance tactic. I'm impressed."

"Then you're impressed too easily," she tossed back at him.

"He doesn't know about the transfer, does he? You

realize that he's running lead on the task force, right? How long do you think you're going to be able to keep him in the dark?"

"Until I can't. He's my brother, not my boss. I don't have to ask for Cade's permission, and I sure as heck don't have to waste my time explaining my actions to you."

"Didn't say that you did. I just think he'd have a few things to say about his baby sister hanging out in dark alleyways in the middle of the night."

"Damn straight I do," Cade's voice growled.

He stood at the mouth of the alley and waited for their approach, his eyes darkening with a mixture of fury and exhaustion—and locked on his sister.

Not much riled his best friend—and fellow former Ranger—but Zoey's safety did.

"Saw Mason a few minutes ago. Had a nice chat, and he couldn't help but brag about his new wingman. Or is it wing-woman?"

Zoey came to a hesitant stop. "He was bragging?"

"Please tell me that he doesn't know what he's talking about, Zo."

"Depends on what he told you. But he's a pretty smart guy."

"Why the hell would you leave the Dungeon?"

"Because people call it *the Dungeon*. The longer I stay in the lab, the more my soul shrivels and withers away. Pretty soon I won't have one. I need a change."

"Then get a new haircut, but you don't switch jobs so you're close to the shit that happens in this city."

Her eyes narrowed into thin slits. "Did you seriously tell me to get a haircut?"

Knox snorted on a chuckle and was immediately rewarded with a murderous glare. "You have something to say? Again?"

He raised his hands. "Not saying a word, angel."

"Good." Zoey turned back to Cade. "As much fun as I'm having discussing this with you, I have work to do. If I'm not back at the scene with these tents in five seconds, Mason's going to roll heads down the alley like bowling balls. I'd like to make sure that mine isn't one of them— because I'm not getting a new haircut *or* a new job."

She tugged on the cart. Knox stepped aside with less than an inch to spare before she ran him over. He swallowed a chuckle as he watched her denim-clad ass strut away.

"You're so fucking lucky you got brothers," Cade muttered.

"Not so sure my brothers would agree with you. She's...different."

His friend scrubbed a palm over his face. "That's putting it mildly. Ever since the scare last year she's been doing her best to turn me prematurely gray. I actually contemplated buying that comb-in crap last week."

Knox remembered Cade's panicked voicemail as if it had been yesterday. Hell, it sent him into a tailspin too.

He'd abruptly quit the shipping yard where he'd been picking up a few odd hours fixing yachts for the well-to-dos and fishermen alike, and hustled to DC. No reunions. No side trips. His one stop had been Georgetown Hospital—and Zoey's bedside.

To this day, no one knew he'd been in town. He'd sweet-talked the night nurse into letting him stay long enough to make sure Zoey was on the upswing, and then he disappeared before first light.

Zoey Wright may not have caused his two-year absence from DC, but he couldn't deny that she was one of the reasons why he'd returned. Plagued with nightmares every time he closed his eyes, he experienced brief glimmers of peace when he thought about her smile, or the slight pink of her cheeks when she got embarrassed.

Knox didn't deserve peace. He didn't deserve Zoey. He didn't deserve to be back in his family's lives.

Yet there he stood.

For now.

* * *

From the dark recess of the building, he watched.

What started as gratification over a loophole closed quickly morphed to the warm tingle of anticipation. Less than ten feet away, His Heart stood like a bright, shining beacon.

She'd come to him.

Finally.

For years, She'd been a constant in his life . . . a steadfast pillar in a world of wavering disappointments. Her eyes. Her smile. Her laughter. He knew them all like his own, and he knew what life was like without them.

He'd never again take Her presence for granted.

Soaking up the sight of Her, he re-familiarized himself with the gentle sway of Her hips. Her hair, pulled away from Her face, revealed the tender arch of Her neck. Even from this distance, Her skin glowed with the softness he could practically feel beneath his fingertips.

She turned toward him, and he held his breath, expecting the gentle curl of Her smile. Instead, a frown marred Her delicate features. The sight of it tore apart his insides.

He'd caused that. Selfishly worrying about what he needed, he hadn't thought about Her.

All this time he'd been trying to duplicate their magical connection with others when he should've been trying to reignite it with Her. It was the reason why none of the others had worked.

They. Weren't. Her.

Shifting in the shadows, he vowed to do whatever was necessary to bring His Heart back into his life. Sacrifices would have to be made, but he'd been raised to believe that with success, came some loss.

He'd fix the damage he'd caused, and prove that his love and devotion knew no boundaries.

Her heart. Her body. Her life.

They were his to love and protect.

Until the end of time.

Or until the end of them.

CHAPTER
THREE

Knox pulled his refurbished motor sailor alongside the riverside dock and tied the *Angel Eyes* to the only cleat that didn't look about to fall into the Potomac. Seventy percent convinced his floating apartment wouldn't drift toward the Chesapeake, he jumped out and faced Steele Ops' new home.

He had to credit his brothers for their creativity. Built in the mid-nineteenth century, the Keaton Jailhouse was an Old Town Alexandria landmark. Aged gray stone rose up from the riverside foundation in a massive three-story structure with accented arched windows and four castle-like turrets nestling each corner.

Construction equipment littered the grounds, evidence of the remodel happening inside, which according to Liam's last text, was about 80 percent complete. They'd spent years dreaming the particulars required to start their own private security firm...and there she stood in all her cobwebbed, gothic glory.

As Knox climbed the steps, two distinct voices drifted onto the rotunda. He pushed the back door open and soaked in the sight of his two younger brothers hovering over the wood plank in front of them.

Arms folded across his chest, Ryder shook his head

in disgust. "You're holding the saw like a moron. I'm telling you right now, I refuse to sew your hand back on after you cut the damn thing off. Hell, I'm not even going to staunch the bleeding."

Liam threw Ryder a dark scowl. "Like I'd be stupid enough to let you near a life-threatening injury. Those Marines may have trusted you with their asses, but I'm smart. I joined the Navy."

Ryder scoffed, not one to give up or give in. "Navy Intelligence. You didn't exactly swim with the big fishes."

"You're right. The *big fishes* wouldn't be half as effective if they didn't have brains like me telling them what to do and when to breathe."

Knox's mouth twitched with the familiarity of the mutual branch-bashing. It was a family tradition nearly as old as time itself. "Why are you guys still having this argument? Everyone knows the Rangers are the only ones that get shit done. Everyone else is just playing soldier."

Both heads snapped his way.

Hair floppy and hanging over his eyeglasses-framed blue eyes, Liam embraced his Navy retirement with both hands while Ryder, the most recent of the quartet to get his civilian status, clung to the Marine cropped buzz to which he'd become accustomed. They had different personalities, served different military branches, but wore the same damn look.

Surprise.

"You actually came." Liam didn't bother hiding his shock.

"I didn't get an automatic fist to the jaw, so I guess that means I'm welcome inside?" Knox joked dryly.

Ryder snorted. "Roman's downstairs. I'm sure he'd be more than happy to pick up our dropped ball."

Knox didn't doubt that one bit.

A year younger than himself, Roman had been his co-conspirator growing up. They'd hatched schemes against Liam and Ryder and sent more than one teacher into early retirement. More times than Knox could count, their mother threatened them with bread and water rations and military school paperwork—which she never would've gone through with, and they both knew it.

They'd stayed close through separate boot camps and during overseas duty stations. After the IED explosion that took the bottom third of Roman's left leg, Knox's commanding officer threw his ass on the first cargo flight to Germany so he could be at his brother's side.

No one fucked with the Steele brothers because to mess with one was to deal with them all.

And then Knox screwed up.

There wasn't a doubt in his mind that Roman would throw a punch first and ask questions later. It's what he would do if the situations had been reversed.

Knox scanned the room to avoid the varied emotions on his brothers' faces.

While still a hazard zone, the indoor lobby looked a hell of a lot better than the outside grounds. "You guys have done a good job on this place."

Liam tossed the saw on the makeshift table. "Are you kidding me right now?"

Ryder looked ready to break Knox's no thrown punches observation. "We haven't seen your sorry ass in two years and your first comment to us is going to be about our carpentry skills?"

"What do you want me to say?"

"That you're an asshole."

He nodded. "Fair enough. I'm an ass."

"And that even though you're the oldest, you're a dumb fuck."

Knox cocked up an eyebrow, but conceded. "I'm not known for making the best decisions, that's for sure."

Ryder snuck a glance at a suspiciously quiet Liam and muttered, "All your agreeing isn't making this easy."

"Making what easy?"

"Staying pissed off at you."

Knox remained still while Ryder closed the distance and wrapped him in a bone-crushing bro-hug. "Are you trying to crack my ribs or my spine?"

Ry pounded on his back for good measure. "Either. Is it working?"

"No. It kind of tickles."

Ryder chuckled, giving him one last squeeze before backing away with a sly smirk. "Why couldn't you have gotten all weak and frumpy these last few years?"

"I figured I'd leave that to you," Knox teased.

"It's my turn." Liam stalked over.

Knox, lowering his guard and opening his arms, didn't see the punch coming until pain exploded up the side of his face. He stumbled back a few steps. "What the hell?"

"Did *that* tickle?" Liam waited in front of him, arms folded across his wide chest. The man may be a genius behind a computer, but he wasn't a lightweight.

Knox rubbed his jaw and the speck of blood that collected at the corner of his mouth. "Shit. No, that didn't tickle."

"Good. Now bring it in, you dumb bastard." Liam pulled him into his second hug in as many minutes. "You couldn't just breeze into town quietly, huh? You had to stumble into DC's very own hornets' nest?"

"Giving a statement to Cade wasn't exactly how I planned to spend my night. Neither was a dark-alley reunion with Zoey."

Liam pulled back, grinning. "And how'd that go?"

"Pretty sure the only reason she didn't lay me flat on the ground was because we were surrounded by cops."

"Then you're a lucky dumb bastard."

Laying eyes on his brothers for the first time in over two years, Knox felt his chest swell with emotion. The feeling was foreign to him. He'd gotten damn good at distancing himself from others and uncomfortable situations. *Too good* at it.

Work. Exercise. Sleep. And repeat.

He'd been on autopilot for the last two years, surviving instead of living. It took Cade's phone call last year and Zoey's health scare to wake him the hell up. But just because his eyes had been opened didn't mean his problems were instantly solved.

He was still trying to work that shit out, and why he hooked the boat to his truck and drove up from North Carolina. There'd no doubt be a hell of a lot more mixed feelings to come—both from him and his brothers. Definitely from his mother. It was the risk he took in returning home, even if the reunion was temporary.

Knox pulled back and gestured to the lobby. "You're outfitting the first three floors to be Iron Bars Distillery, right?"

Liam nodded and glanced around at their handiwork. "Third floor will be offices, second floor for events. We're standing in the lounge and tasting room, where people can sample the week's brews."

"And no one will know what's lurking beneath their feet." Knox smirked. "I'm impressed. You're well on your way without me."

"Yeah, but that's not the point, is it?" Ryder interjected.

"No. No, it's not," Knox agreed. They'd had plans and he'd given them all a big middle finger by staying away as long as he had. "But I'm here now."

"And how long is that going to last?" another voice echoed through the large room.

Roman, hands shoved deep in his pockets, stepped through the back door. Black hair brushing his collar and dark stubble covering his jaw, he looked more like a musician than a former Special Forces operator. His dark gray eyes—their father's eyes—locked him in a hard stare.

"Roman," Liam said carefully, "take it easy."

"Taking the easy route is our older brother's territory. So what's it going to be, Knox? You here for a week? Two? How long are we going to be graced with your presence?"

"I'm here for as long as it takes to get you guys up and running. One week. One month, or three. Whatever you need."

Ryder asked first, "You mean you're not staying?"

Knox wanted to say yes with every ounce of his being. He missed his family. He'd missed DC and all its little quirks. He missed the life he'd had when he'd lived here. But family came first...and the best thing he could do for his brothers was stay the hell out of their business—literally.

"An old buddy of mine started a celebrity bodyguard service out in California. He offered me a job and I'm going to give it a whirl."

"A Bodyguard to the Stars?" Liam's mouth dropped. He looked more than a little horrified at the prospect. "Are you freakin' kidding me?"

"Nope. But he's given me an open start date, so you guys have me for as long as you need."

Roman scoffed. "We *don't* need, so you can go ahead and make the cross-country drive ahead of schedule."

"Want and need are two entirely different things, Ro. You may not *want* me here, but it looks like you could use an extra pair of hands around this place." Knox held his stance, fully expecting a second shot to the jaw as Roman stalked closer.

Instead, he stopped an inch away, face harder than Knox ever remembered seeing before. "There's no *may* about it. Steele Ops isn't here to relieve your guilt for being a fucking coward."

"Good to know...but I'm not here out of guilt," Knox lied.

"And I'm not here to make your life easy."

"Didn't think you were, brother."

"*Brother?*" Roman's fists balled up at his sides, and he jutted his chin toward Ryder and Liam. "My brothers live by their word. Funny how all of us followed the plan except the one who actually thought it all up. Don't you think that's a bit ironic?"

Knox didn't back down from Roman's barely controlled fury. It wasn't anything he hadn't lectured himself about a million times over already. Steele Ops had been his brainchild before he'd even left the Army, and by talking it up on every furlough and R & R weekend, he'd quickly gotten his brothers on board with the idea.

And then he'd jumped the metaphorical ship.

"Do you want to know why Steele Ops isn't already open for business?" Roman demanded. "Because two years ago... hell, one year ago, I erroneously believed that you'd come to your senses. Good thing I finally came to mine or else we'd all still be sitting on our asses twiddling our damn thumbs. I don't care why you're here, just stay out of my way while you are."

Roman pushed him aside with his shoulder and slammed the back door as he left. The windows rattled precariously in their frames, and the floor shook.

"That went unexpectedly well. Not a drop of blood spilled," Liam joked.

"Uh..." Knox touched his busted lip.

"Oh yeah. Sorry about that. Kinda. Okay, not in the least." Chuckling, Liam dropped an arm over Knox's shoulder. "A bodyguard service? Seriously?"

Knox shrugged, making his brother sigh.

"Fine. Guess we'll just have to hope that we can change your mind with a tour of the underbelly. We have a private security wonderland right beneath our feet, man. Sleeping quarters. Ops center. Gym. You name it and it's down there. And we made sure to keep as much of the prisoners' quarters as we could...for ambiance."

Ryder smirked. "And for those times when we can't take Liam for another second and want to lock his ass in a jail cell. I mean, how many times have we wished we could do that?"

They all laughed.

For the first time in two years, the weight on Knox's shoulders lightened. It didn't change the endgame, though. He couldn't stay.

Once upon a time, when the pressure had been on, he'd let down good men who'd relied on him to make the hard—and best—calls. He'd failed his unit. He'd failed an entire damn operating base. Hell would freeze over before he let himself fail his brothers too.

CHAPTER
FOUR

Mid-stride and in front of an impatient taxi, Zoey's three-inch heel caught on a pothole. She stumbled, righting her balance a split second before hitting that point of no return.

The waiting cabbie laid on his horn.

"Sorry! Sorry!" She ignored the obscene gesture he flipped up as she shimmied her high-heeled boot out of the crack. "If you're going to be a jerk, then I'm *not* sorry."

Working the crime scene until the wee morning hours and crashing hard afterward, Zoey had spent the rest of her rare day off practice-walking. And it hadn't done much good. Chances were high that by the end of the night she'd end up in an emergency room with a broken bone, or at the very least, a concussion—and she'd have no one to blame but herself.

And Grace.

If not for her best friend's excitement, Zoey would've backpedaled the second her costume idea for O'Malley's March Madness Monday fell from her lips.

Safely on the opposite sidewalk, Zoey glanced around to see if anyone had caught her near catastrophic tumble.

Two teen girls talked animatedly with each other

despite having their heads bowed over their phones, and in front of her, an older man in an expensive suit shamed all power-walkers. Only the young college-aged kid on her left had seemed to notice. His grin widened as he dropped a leering gaze to her chest.

"I need to learn to keep my mouth shut." She fisted her coat closed and kept her focus on the Irish pub now less than twenty yards away.

There was still time to change her mind, turn at the next block and lose herself in the crowd that took advantage of the unseasonably warm April night. People had come out to the Wharf in droves, some in the posh, popular restaurants, others shopping in the quaint boutiques that abutted the Potomac River.

O'Malley's stuck out like a sore, but well-loved, thumb. Rudy, the owner, bragged that the pub was his little piece of Ireland in the Americas. Its aged plate-glass windows contrasted with the lush, shiny new businesses around it. The heavy oak-and-iron door stood open, spilling a U2 song out into the walkway, and with it, a burst of laughter.

By the sound of it, all of DC had come out to watch the Hoyas clinch the national championship, and Rudy's added promise of one free drink per costumed patron didn't hurt either.

A lot of people.

A lot of alcohol.

A lot of opportunity to make a fool of herself.

Zoey's pajamas practically called her name from across town.

"Do it, Zoey, and I'll chase you down and drag you

back by your ponytail." Grace's warning obliterated any hope of an escape.

Five inches taller than Zoey's own five feet three, Grace Steele stood out in any crowd with her brown silky hair and dark eyes. She could've donned the cover of a fashion magazine and been world famous, but instead, somewhere in the depth of her small black clutch were FBI credentials and probably Magdalena, her trusty Magnum .22.

Both her profession and the fact that she'd spent her teenage years living in a house with four oversized male cousins made her a formidable person to everyone except Zoey.

Grace pushed off the brick wall beneath the blinking O'Malley's sign. "What the hell are you wearing? A trench coat?"

"It's a *suit* jacket. And I'm wearing it because the temperature's supposed to drop tonight and I knew I'd probably have to park light-years away."

"You're still an awful liar. Hand it over." Grace fought off a smile as she held out her hand and wiggled her fingers. "You'd save us both a lot of aggravation and time by remembering that I'm not the type to take no for an answer."

Isn't that the truth? Since they met at the ages of eleven and thirteen, Grace had possessed a knack for talking Zoey into things. Pranks. Outfits. Going to parties. Since Grace had been there for an obscene amount of her procedures and hospitalizations, Zoey didn't often put up much of a struggle.

Friends didn't come any better.

With a heavy sigh, she reluctantly handed over her last layer of defense. "As my best friend, it's your sworn duty to tell me when I've had a monumentally bad idea. You slacked on the job."

"Are you uncomfortable?"

"Yes!"

"You want to go back to your apartment, change into flannels, and cuddle on the couch with your sadistic cat?"

"Firstly, Snuggles isn't sadistic. He has social anxiety, which I can totally relate to...and secondly, I wouldn't mind going home." Through the pub's stained-glass window, Zoey eyed the sea of bodies crammed inside and cringed. "It looks like all of the District came out and brought along friends."

"And why wouldn't they? The Hoyas are about to win the championship, and Rudy's doling out free drinks. I've missed a million event nights at O'Malley's, Zoey. You wouldn't deprive me of a walk down memory lane, would you?"

"As much as you wouldn't hold out on me about Knox visiting town."

Grace's sly smirk told Zoey all she needed to know.

"Run into my cousin already, did you?" Linking her arm through Zoey's, Grace steered them to the door. "With all the crap going on around town right now, people need an excuse to let loose—and that includes you. O'Malley's is built-in happy fun."

"Do I look like I'm having fun?" To emphasize her point, Zoey tilted her mouth down in an exaggerated frown.

Grace laughed. "No, which means this wasn't a bad idea...it was a *brilliant* one. What did you tell me after your open-heart last year? When you woke up from anesthesia?"

"I don't know. I was still groggy. I can only go by what you *claim* transpired."

"You told me that you were ready to try new things...put yourself out there for the world to see and be the Zoey you were always meant to be."

"Well, I'm definitely out there." Zoey adjusted her skimpy tank top and the bulky costume necklace that draped between her breasts, and more importantly, covered her scar. "Speaking of, I told you I was running late. Why were you waiting outside?"

"I needed fresh air," Grace said way too quickly. She avoided eye contact, a dead giveaway she held something back.

"*Now* who's lying?" Zoey teased. "Are you, a big bad FBI profiler, *that* afraid of being alone with my brother? I can only assume by the little twitch in your eye that he's here?"

"I do not have a twitch. I've been trained to be twitch-less."

With a smirk, Zoey pointed. "See. It's there again. Left eye. Twitch."

Since she'd returned to DC three weeks ago to help with the Cupid Killer case, Grace had done her best not to be alone with her childhood sweetheart. Even after more than ten years, Zoey still wasn't sure what happened to end things between them. When asked, Grace usually shrugged and said *Life*.

Cade didn't answer at all.

"You want to know why I was lying in wait? Because I knew you'd talk yourself into going home once you realized Knox was inside." Zoey froze, and in realizing she'd gotten her payback, Grace grinned. "Did I forget to tell you that I mentioned tonight's outing to Knox? All I had to say was O'Malley's, and he and the guys got this special twinkle in their eyes. Are you sure I didn't tell you they were going to be here?"

"I'm pretty sure I would've remembered."

She *definitely* would've remembered, and Grace was right—she wouldn't have left her apartment if she'd known O'Malley's would be taken over by the Steele boys—er, *men*.

Zoey glanced at the pub. As kids, they'd all spent countless afternoons in Rudy's back room, shooting pool and playing darts until the old Irishman had to kick them out and open for the night. But now, right in front of her eyes, a cloud of impending doom hovered over their old hangout.

Grace tossed Zoey's words back at her. "What's wrong? Afraid of being around my *cousin*?"

"No. I like Ryder and Roman fine, and you know I have a soft spot for Liam."

Grace's freaky power of observation—and Zoey's sudden jolt of nerves—had her best friend grinning ear to ear. "You know damn well they weren't the cousin I meant."

She did, although she wasn't about to admit it. Out of their close-knit group, Grace was the only person privy to her far-fetched teenage Knox fantasies, and only because she'd sobbed on Grace's shoulder more than once. His high school dating years had been particularly brutal, a close second to when he left home for boot-camp.

Grace tugged her into the pub and forced her into facing her fears. Heads immediately turned in their direction.

Zoey's hands itched to snatch back her coat because Buffy and Faith—circa leather-clad, feuding Slayers—had been her not-so-brilliant costume idea. Little leather jackets. Butt-hugging pants. Skimpy tanks. High-heeled boots. They'd gone all out. But while Grace pulled off the Faith ensemble as if it were her typical everyday outfit, Zoey felt like she'd raided a dress-up closet.

She returned a wave from one of the station's forensic lab techs, and mentally cursed when the hem of both her spaghetti-strapped top and her leather jacket lifted well above her belly button. She yanked them back to her waist, and then out came the Boobage Twins. Another sharp tug up, and hello stomach—*again*.

Grace pushed her hands away, failing to suppress a chuckle. "Will you stop? You're going to yank the stitching apart and then you're going to be *really* un-comfortable."

"I could always zip the jacket. Oh that's right." Zoey slid her a stink-eye. "I can't because someone made me buy the one that's two sizes too small. I couldn't zip it unless I rewind time eighteen years."

Zoey ignored Grace's warning and adjusted her top. Why couldn't the Buffster's signature style be yoga pants and a long-sleeve Henley? For two hours, she'd planted herself in front of a mirror, forcing life into her hair. And contacts? *Ha!* No fewer than three pairs had been sacrificed to her sink drain—the reason behind why she still sported her un-Buffy-like frames.

"One hour." Zoey scanned for a spot in which to lie low until she could make a clean break. "I'm giving it one hour and then I'm going home to my flannel pj's and sadistic cat—I mean, cat."

"Two," Grace countered.

"One hour and fifteen minutes."

Grace's dark eyes narrowed, and she pointed her slender finger in Zoey's direction like a schoolteacher. "One and a half. Final offer. But that means no hiding in the back corner. Do you hear me?"

She heard. That didn't mean she'd listen.

With a final warning, Grace strutted to the bar to get them drinks. Left alone, Zoey weaved her way through the crowd.

Due to O'Malley's close proximity to Precinct Five, cops filled the neighborhood pub on any given night of the week, but March Madness brought them out in droves. Some wore obvious costumes in the hope of eluding Rudy's wrath, and those dressed in plainclothes had probably gotten off shift or were about to head in.

Zoey fumbled her way to the edge of the dance floor, her eyes locked on the far back corner of the room. With a little bit of luck and this massive crowd, she'd survive her one and a half hours without a Knox sighting.

Ten feet from her destination, Scott Reed paused his conversation with his friend and ran his gaze up her body.

His smirk shifted from cocky Neanderthal to lecherous pervert, making her long for a hot, soapy shower.

"And this night just keeps on giving," Zoey muttered, and steered right, praying her heels cooperated.

Focused on her new destination past the pool tables, Zoey didn't see the brick wall that stepped out in front of her. She collided hard, her teeth rattling from impact, and braced for a harsh ass-landing.

Firm arms banded around her waist and quickly tugged her into a familiar scent of spice and pine.

Brushing her nose against soft cotton fabric, Zoey inhaled, and failed to withhold a sigh.

"Did you just sniff me?" A deep, humor-laced voice vibrated her yummy-scented wall.

Not a wall. A chest. A hard, *Knox*-like chest.

Zoey forced her eyes up and grimaced as they collided with Knox Steele's twin dark pools. "No. Maybe. I mean...absolutely not."

Knox's eyes crinkled as if he tried—and failed—to withhold a smirk. "You're not sure if you smelled me?"

"I didn't. I tried to—"

"Knock me down?"

On instinct, her gaze traveled to his mouth. Curled up a little higher on the left, his lips had starred in more Knox-inspired fantasies than she could count. If they possessed the power they did in her dreams, they needed to come with a warning label. An ice-cold shower wouldn't be a bad idea either.

Zoey wished for a super speedy hour and a half. "I didn't sniff you or try to knock you down. I was making—"

"An escape." His attention shot over her shoulder and latched on to Reed.

Of course he noticed. Not much got past him. On the rare occasions when she'd let Grace drag her to a high school party, it was usually Knox who sniffed out their location like a human hunting dog.

Scott stopped in his tracks, second-guessing his approach now that she stood in Knox's arms.

Literally.

Thickly muscled with a sprinkle of dark hair, Knox's arms held her flush against him despite the fact she'd long since found her equilibrium. Their continued closeness emphasized the juxtaposition between his rock-hard planes and her soft round swells.

"Do I need to take that bastard's head off his shoulders?" Knox drilled a menacing glare across the room.

"You can't dismember someone for being a horn dog."

His attention snapped back to her, voice dropping to a deadly growl. "What the fuck did he do?"

Crap. She hadn't realized she'd said that aloud.

Already having a top-notch internal protector alarm thanks to her brother, Zoey intervened quickly. "Didn't abide by the basic principal of *I will not stare at another woman's rear end while I'm on a date*. It's enough to avoid him, not turn him into the Headless Horseman."

Knox's gaze drifted to Scott and back, his mouth pinched in a tight line. A few tense seconds later, he slowly dropped his hands. Zoey felt the loss immediately... but not for long.

Unlike with Scott's attention, Knox's slow perusal of her body conjured an army of butterflies and not to mention, goose bumps. She opened her mouth to explain the atypical leather outfit, but was abruptly cut off by the two solid arms lifting her off the ground from behind.

"Is that a piece of wood shoved into your pants or you happy to see me?" a low, baritone voice teased with familiarity.

"Liam! Seriously, I haven't changed so much in a week that I like being airborne."

"Oh, come on now, blondie. If you're going to dress as Buff, you best be prepared to play the part." Knox's younger brother returned her to the ground and flashed her his signature crooked smirk. She couldn't help but laugh.

With a birthday a month apart from her own, he'd always been the Steele—other than Grace—she'd been closest to. Like the rest of his brothers, he'd left home after school and joined the military. But unlike Knox, he'd immediately returned after his discharge, and dove right back into DC life as if he'd never been away.

She scratched his scruffy jaw. "You have dirt growing here or something."

Liam ran his hand over his days' old stubble. "Just trying it out. I hear women dig a guy who looks rough around the edges."

"We also like guys who look as though they've bathed recently," Zoey teased.

Liam clutched his chest, feigning being wounded. "Harsh, blondie. Real harsh. And to think I came over here to save you from Sir Growls A Lot."

Their attention turned to an unamused Knox. He glanced between Zoey and Liam, and momentarily to his brother's arm still wrapped around her waist.

Grace chose that moment to bound up, handing Zoey a tall glass filled to the brim with a golden, slushy mixture. "You almost got a Bloody Grace instead of a Rudy Special. He accidentally served me before that pixie-hair brunette and I thought she was going to stab me in the eye with her umbrella straw."

"Maiming by cocktail. I guess stranger things have happened." Momentarily forgetting her friend's love of strong drinks, Zoey took a long sip.

Her eyes teared as the alcohol burned its way down her throat. "What's in this thing? Gasoline?"

Grace shrugged and sipped her own concoction. "I lost count after Rudy grabbed the fourth bottle. It's not half bad after you get past the first sip."

"You mean if you *survive* the first sip."

Grace slid her attention toward Knox. She let out a small squeal and wrapped him into a tight hug. "It's my favorite cousin!"

Knox chuckled. "I'd be flattered if you didn't call every single one of my asshole brothers your favorite."

Grace pulled away, laughing. "Well, yeah. But with you I mean it."

"Standing right here, cuz," Liam protested with a smirk on his face.

Grace waved him off. "I can't believe that all the Steele men are in one place. I'm sad that I'll be leaving once we catch this Cupid Killer. I'd like to have a first row seat to you lot knocking DC on its ass again."

"You could always stick around..."

Grace laughed until she sucked in a sharp, wheezing breath. "I love your sense of humor, Liam. Let's switch the conversation from fantasy to reality and take a moment to talk about how incredibly sexy Zoey looks in those leather pants." She not so subtly elbowed Zoey in the side. "And look at that, Zo. He's practically the Angel to your Buffy. It's like kismet."

Zoey choked on her drink mid-swallow. *When had she taken another sip?*

"Hate to break it to you, but I'm as far from an angel as they come." Knox's folded arms stretched his black shirt across his chest.

Zoey's mouth dried despite her cocktail.

He was right. He looked nothing like an angel—at least not one that wore white robes and a golden halo. A fallen angel wouldn't be so much of a stretch. Killer body—*check*. Talented, callus-roughened hands—she didn't know firsthand, but probably *check*. And a wicked gleam of the eye that promised untold pleasure to anyone brave enough to fall into their depths—there was no way that wasn't a check too.

Seriously, her libido could go back to sleep anytime now.

"Good information to have, but I mean *the* Angel." Grace ignored the fingers Zoey dug into her arm. "Sex on legs, mysterious, broody vampire who'd love nothing more than to sink his fangs—among other body parts—into Buffy."

Knox's gaze shifted toward Zoey.

Mortified over the mental picture Grace invoked,

she couldn't meet it. His reaction could fall into two categories—humor or disgust. Zoey didn't want to witness either.

Wondering if her police connections could help her avoid a murder charge, she searched for the nearest distraction. *Liam.* "You said Ryder and Roman are here too?"

"Hell yeah they are. Wait till they get a look at you. Just beware of Ro, because unlike me threatening Knox with a muzzle, we had to buy one for Ro on the way over."

"What did you do?"

"Wasn't me this time." Liam's blue eyes danced with amusement as he patted Knox hard on the back. "That honor goes entirely to this guy right here."

Zoey lost her battle not to look at Knox. "And what did *you* do?"

"I'm breathing."

She blinked, not expecting that response.

Knox wasn't known for his slew of inappropriate jokes and horrendously bad timing. He and Roman had always been the more serious brothers. But those two simple words, combined with his impossible-to-read expression, put him smack on top of the brooding tier.

Liam, oblivious to his older brother's tension, chuckled. "Or it could be that he finally showed. Or that he didn't stay away. Hell, it could be that he's leaving to go play with celebrities instead of joining Stee—ah, I mean, Iron Bars. Who the hell knows what gets Ro's boxers in a twist these days."

"You're leaving?" The question slipped from Zoey's mouth.

Knox's face remained blank slate. "New opportunities and all."

"Guess we should count ourselves blessed that you made us a pit stop then, huh?"

Her words surprised more than herself. Grace's brown eyes widened, and Liam hid a chuckle behind a cough. Knox, on the other hand, didn't look the least bit amused. The mouth that had been curled upward earlier pressed into a tight line.

An apology hovered on her lips, but she swallowed it.

Probably for the first time in *ever*, she stood firmly in pro-Roman territory when it came to Knox's reappearance.

A lot had happened in two years. She wasn't so self-important to think that she deserved daily phone calls, or even bi-monthly check-ins. But a card would've been nice to wake up to following surgery. Or heck, even an email.

Knox had been Cade's best friend, but he'd been her sexy, libido-waking friend too. At least that's what she'd thought.

But friends didn't play disappearing acts that lasted two years. They didn't return and jump back into things as if they'd never been away. And they didn't dream about what the other one looked like naked.

That last one may have been her, but it didn't matter.

It was one more thing friends weren't supposed to do.

CHAPTER FIVE

Grace and Knox followed Zoey and Liam at a slower pace. Zoey knew because her Knox-dar tingled the back of her neck, and didn't waver once as Liam navigated her through the thick O'Malley's crowd and toward the pub's back room.

Four antique pool tables stood sentry, all different in style and varying in age. Ryder and Roman stood by their regular table, a late nineteenth-century Brunswick, and argued back and forth while shooting an occasional glance at the balls' layout.

Life had been boring until the Steele boys started trickling back home.

"Neither one of you is right, so go ahead and hug it out." Zoey injected herself into their argument, grinning. "The rational choice is the blue solid into the left corner pocket. If you try anything else, you may as well put your feet up and let the other team go again."

Ryder dropped a massive arm around her shoulder, and tugged her into a side hug that lifted her feet. "Finally! A voice of reason! We're switching things up and I call dibs on Zo."

She laughed. "What is it with you Steeles and making me airborne?"

"If you didn't want us picking you off the ground, then you should've grown a few more inches." The former Marine slowly returned her to the ground. "Besides, it's in our genes to sweep gorgeous women off their feet."

She rolled her eyes and turned to Roman, who was standing noticeably apart from the group.

"You're not going to pick me up like an airplane too, are you?" Zoey joked.

Roman's lips faintly twitched. "No airplane."

His eyes screamed *do not approach*, but Zoey didn't listen because Liam was right. The Steeles and Wrights were basically one big—and obnoxiously loud—family.

Pretending his scowl didn't exist, she wrapped her arms around his waist in a tight hug. "You should probably know that I'm not letting go until you hug me back. It's okay. I've got all night. But just so you know, I have a freakishly small bladder. Things could get pretty awkward in about an hour."

Just when she thought she'd have to make good on her threat, his arms settled awkwardly around her and squeezed. "Hey, sweet pea."

Grace leaned against the wall, a smirk on her face. "If I was a lesser woman, I'd be greatly offended right now. Zoey gets *three* hugs. More because a Roman hug is like triple the points. You know what? Forget it. I *am* offended."

"That's what you get for coming back here without drinks." Ryder snitched her cocktail and took a sip. He grimaced and quickly handed it back. "Never mind. You probably would've brought us whatever fruity crap you have right there."

Everyone laughed. Even Roman chuckled, and a sneak over Zoey's shoulder saw the sight of it had gained Knox's attention too.

"Shit-on-a-stick." Grace pushed off the wall, her head swiveling around the room like a penned animal. "Don't hate me, Zo, but I have to make myself scarce. I'll come back when the coast is clear."

"What do you mean—" Zoey hadn't gotten out the rest of her sentence before Grace disappeared into the crowd and the reason for her departure stepped beside Knox.

Cade's blue eyes tracked her friend's exit across the room with hawk-like precision. "Where's Gracie going?"

"Bathroom. When a woman's gotta go, we gotta go." Zoey compounded the lie with another sip of her drink. This time, it slid down a heck of a lot easier.

Cade assessed her in a critical once-over, going through a quick metamorphosis of facial expressions before landing on one that looked like painful realization. "Are you supposed to be a dominatrix or something?"

Liam burst out laughing, earning him a glower from Cade.

Zoey forgot all about her shirt and propped a hand on her hip. "I'll tell you what I'm dressed as if you tell me what you did to my best friend."

"I don't know what you're talking about." His jaw muscle flexed, his only tell on record, and only when it involved Grace.

"You're seriously going to stand there and lie to me?

We both know that Grace isn't exactly an exercise enthusiast and yet she hustled away as if she were running bases at Nationals Park."

"Thought you said she had to use the ladies' room."

Zoey avoided replying by taking another long pull of her drink. "It's been nice chatting with all of you about secret reasons for staying in town, and your lack of hygiene, but I apparently have a dom outfit to try out and I'm not about to do so with anyone *here*."

She stormed away, putting a little extra sway into her hips. A warm, pleasant buzz slid through her body before she braved a glance over her shoulder. Her gaze collided with Knox's, nearly making her trip.

In all her years, she couldn't recall ever once being the recipient of Knox's Lust Gaze. Pity? Yes. Annoyance? Yep. Humor? Often. But desire? *No way*.

It could've been a trick of the lighting, or her exuberant alcohol consumption. Heck, it could've been a side effect from smacking her head against her washing machine a few days ago. No matter how Knox's heated look came to be, it fired her blood—among other body parts.

Zoey found Grace hiding amid a group of young rookie cops, and held out her empty glass. "I need another. Stat."

Grace's surprise switched to a chuckle. "Yeah, me too, although I expect for entirely different reasons."

"Having nostalgia sex with my brother is driving you to drink?"

Grace gasped, her face losing its color. "How did you find out? *Did he tell you?* Oh, my God. I'm going to *kill* him."

Zoey giggled. "He didn't tell me. *You* did just now. After the next refill, we're dancing until Rudy either tosses us out on our rear ends, or until I trip over these heels and fall on my butt myself. Whichever comes first."

"Now that sounds like a plan." Grinning, Grace grabbed her hand.

Zoey took great care in everything she did. Her diet was fairly balanced with the occasional indulgences. Sleep was her best friend—besides Grace. And she took her medications like a good congenital heart defect patient.

Dancing in mile-high heels while under the influence of Rudy Specials was the first idea Zoey had had that didn't involve doing the *responsible* thing.

And she kind of liked it.

A lot.

* * *

Zoey lifted her hands above her head and swiveled her hips to the beat of the music. The inch of bare skin between the top of her pants and bottom hem of her shirt turned into four, and when she *really* reached, Knox—along with every male in the place—glimpsed the bottom swell of a lace-covered breast.

It was the sweetest kind of torture, one he barely pulled his eyes away from except to shoot his Ranger scowl toward anyone who looked stupid—and horny enough—to make a move in her direction. In thirty minutes, he'd scared off no fewer than four guys and was now in a warning stare-down with a fifth.

A few feet away, Liam and Ryder flirted unabashedly with a set of brunettes, and Roman had used Zoey's departure to make his own mysterious exit, disappearing in the crowd. Some things never changed.

Knox trashed his warm beer and casually diverted his attention to his best friend. "So, have you given Roman's offer any thought? Liam said they've asked you. Multiple times."

Cade scoffed. "And I've turned them down. Multiple times. I'm going to tell you the same thing I told your brothers...I appreciate the job offer, but I'm not interested."

"So you say. But I saw your face when we helped Logan Callahan in Vegas. You can't tell me you don't miss the thrill of going on a mission."

"Says the man who's trading in a tactical belt for a tiara. How did that conversation go over, by the way?" Cade sipped his beer and smirked.

Knox released a subdued laugh. "About as well as expected. Now stop trying to change the subject. Why did you turn Roman down?"

"Because missions never happen close to home, and someone's ass is always on the line. *This* is where I need to be, man."

Knox followed Cade's attention to Zoey.

He got it. Family was everything. There wasn't any mountain he wouldn't climb or bullet he wouldn't dodge in front of for his brothers or Grace—and Zoey too. Cade was the same. The only difference between the two of them was that Cade didn't have a lot of shit to make up for.

"Zoey's a grown woman."

"She's not a woman. She's my sister." At Knox's pointed silence, he added, "Yeah, I know it doesn't make sense, but it is what it is. Zoey's different. There are special circumstances."

"Has she been having problems?" Knox unknowingly held his breath as he waited for the answer.

His gaze flickered to the dance floor where she danced with his cousin. At first glance, or hell, the sixth, no one would think Zoey had gone through hell on earth for most of her life. She leaned close to Grace to hear something she'd said, her sleek ponytail brushing over her slender shoulders, and then laughed. The sound drifted their way over the loud music, making Knox's insides clench.

There wasn't anything better than her laugh except for, maybe, her smile. And he still couldn't get the image of her last night out of his head, all pissed off and ready for a fight. He liked that spark in her eye, and had started seeing it shine through her shell when she hit sixteen . . . right around the time he began envying Liam for his and Zoey's close friendship.

Nothing good would've come from Knox acting on his interest for his best friend's baby sister. Cade would've given him the ultimate beat-down, and immediately after, his brothers would've gladly joined in the fun. Hell, Knox would've tried to find ways to pummel his own damn self.

For Knox, Army life had meant more than protecting his country. It meant short, sporadic visits home in which he got to keep Zoey Wright in his life without ruining hers.

"Are you going to answer the damn question?" Knox demanded, suddenly needing to know she was okay more than he needed his next breath. "Zoey hasn't had any more setbacks, has she?"

His friend's brow lifted. Knox settled before Cade called him out on his outburst. "No. Samuel's given her a clean bill of health."

"Samuel? Wasn't that her doc since the beginning? I thought he retired or something."

Cade shot him a curious look. "And how the hell did you know that?"

"I was in North Carolina repairing boats. I wasn't dead."

His friend smirked knowingly. *Asshole.* "Uh-huh. Well, the father retired, but the son still runs the practice. He's the one who performed her surgery last year."

Knox vaguely remembered seeing the young cardiologist on his brief visit last year. "If he's given her a clean bill of health, what's holding you back?"

"She'd had a clean bill last year too, and we know how that turned out. I'm not chancing something happening and me being unable to get to her."

"So nothing's wrong." The knot that had fisted in Knox's chest released. "We're talking the Keaton Jailhouse. How much closer do you want to get? You're as much a brother to me as my own family, man. I want you in on this."

Like Grace did when she fired up her psychology mumbo jumbo, Cade studied him hard without saying a word. Two peas in a damn pod, although they wouldn't admit it. A man's thoughts weren't safe around either one of them.

"Stop trying to get a read on me," Knox warned his longtime friend.

"What makes you think that's what I'm doing?"

"Because it's the only time you're quiet. I want what's best for you, pure and simple. Your talents are wasted on the DCPD."

Cade smirked. "Certain talents, maybe, but not my talent for smelling bullshit a mile away. If you want someone on the inside who's going to watch your brothers' asses, maybe that someone should be you."

Knox threw him a scowl but Cade didn't flinch. "We've been through this before. I'm not what's best for them."

"I think they'd disagree."

Knox snorted. "Not Roman. He'll click his heels together the second I leave town. Maybe even dance a jig."

"Then you're an even bigger fool than he is. I get that shit went down overseas. I don't need to be a mind reader to get that much. People may have gotten hurt. Decisions maybe could've been made differently. I'm not going to beat the details out of you. But it's not a failure. Failure comes when you let the past dictate your future."

"You sound like a fortune cookie," Knox grumbled.

But he couldn't argue against logic.

Avoiding home may have been the asshole thing to do, but better to be an ass than responsible for the death of your entire family. He wished he'd made the decision to leave the Rangers before his half-ass decisions cost good soldiers their lives.

To this day, he still couldn't pinpoint the exact moment his last mission had turned because it hadn't been a single decision that he'd fucked up, but a cascade effect that resulted in his unit staying out in the field a lot longer than planned.

If he'd stuck to the original mission guide after their visit to that Iraqi village, their forward operating base wouldn't have been left vulnerable to an insurgent attack. Team Five would've been there to intervene, return fire, and grind those insurgents' bones to dust.

Lives saved. Day over.

Instead, there'd been way too many losses. No way in hell was he anxious for a repeat occurrence. The California job put his skills to use, but with the highest stakes being an overzealous fan waiting for an autograph.

"You want me to give Steele Ops serious consideration?" Cade's eyes twinkled with familiar mischief.

"You know I do," Knox admitted carefully.

"Then I have two stipulations. The first, go with me to meet Roman's fund guy." At Knox's blank expression, he chuckled. "You really have been out of the loop, haven't you? You can't be surprised that they reached out to someone with a bulkier purse. All four of you could've saved every penny from the time you entered boot camp, invested big, and there'd still be no way in hell you'd save enough to get the distillery off the ground, much less two businesses."

It made sense. They'd once talked about joining with

a silent partner who had nothing better to do with his money. "And what's the second stipulation?"

Cade's grin left a bad taste in Knox's mouth. "Nothing that's not already in your wheelhouse considering your talent with the ladies. I signed on to teach a self-defense class down at the community center but this BCK case is kicking my ass. I need someone to take it off my plate—the class, not the case."

"Teaching a class and going to a meeting."

Cade nodded. "And I'll give Steele Ops serious consideration. No bullshit."

Knox didn't need to think about it. "Deal."

Twin laughs drew their attention to the dance floor. Cade groaned and Knox, transfixed by the slow sway of Zoey's slender hips, shifted uncomfortably in his pants.

Cade groaned. "Fucking crime scene investigation. Can you believe that shit? I bust my ass every day making sure Zoey's safe and she gets a job that puts her right in the middle of DC's first serial killer case in thirty years."

"Hasn't she been working the Cupid case in the lab since day one?"

"In the Dungeon with her high-strung assistant. Being on scene is a hell of a lot different from hanging out in that windowless hole in the ground."

"From what I saw last night, she handled it pretty well. Did a hell of a lot better than you did when our unit got called to that butcher house outside of Baghdad."

Cade's face blanched. "You had to bring that shit up?"

"No, *you* brought it up." Knox faked a shudder. "I

still can't eat cheese nachos because of that image—and hell, the *sounds*."

"So my little sis is a hard-ass, but I'm still worried. Working this case twenty-four/seven, I'm not going to be as reachable as usual. And Mom's been having health issues herself lately, so Zoey isn't going to bug her with anything." Cade yanked a hand through his hair. "It couldn't be a worse time for her to make a change like this."

"It's not like she doesn't have people she can go to if she needs them." *Like him*—although she'd be more likely to run *from* him than toward him. "There's nothing my mom and brothers wouldn't do for her, and Grace is back in town. I know she's working the case too, but those two may as well be sisters."

Knox's gaze strayed to the dance floor. He'd never been more aware of how *un*related he was to Zoey than at that moment. She'd slipped out of her tiny red leather jacket, revealing an entire canvas of milky white skin that he itched to touch.

Fuckin-A.

"I'll help keep an eye on her," Knox heard himself offer. "I'm pretty much making my own schedule these days, so I got the time."

Cade followed his gaze across the room. "I got to be honest, man. Your offer to watch over my baby sister is one of the things I'm having difficulty with . . . considering how adept you were at watching her ass walk away a few minutes ago."

He couldn't deny it. He wasn't sure if he wanted to, and that posed a huge problem. Zoey may not be sixteen anymore, but she was still his best friend's baby sister, and an honorary member of his own family.

Knox shrugged and prayed to hell he nailed looking indifferent. "It's been a while. At this point, I could probably get horny staring at a bowl of ice cream."

"Then go buy a pint of mint chocolate chip and stop eye-fucking my sister." Cade's cell rang and he glanced at the caller ID. "I'm going to have to head out. It's the station."

He cast a sharp frown toward Zoey and Grace. Oblivious to their growing admiration squad, the two women danced and laughed. "I swear, she's going to be the death of me."

"Which one?" Knox teased.

"Bastard." Cade chuckled before locking his attention to the left of the dance floor. He glared at the tall, cocky kid who'd openly gawked at Zoey earlier. "Fucking Scott Reed. It takes a special asshole to make me want to punch him without him *doing* anything."

It thrilled Knox to know he and Cade shared their intense dislike of the guy. "I've been keeping an eye on him for a while now. Don't worry. I'll make sure your girls get home safe."

"Thanks, man. I owe you a solid."

After Cade left, Knox worked his way across the room, finding a spot with an unobstructed view of Zoey and Grace.

In the course of an hour, no fewer than six guys approached the dancing duo with twinkles of hope in their eyes, and walked away, dejected.

Zoey appeared oblivious to her long line of admirers,

and it didn't surprise him one bit. Unlike his ex, Francine, who wasn't beyond using her looks to her advantage, Zoey hadn't the faintest clue how she turned heads.

She danced, unafraid of how she looked, and enjoyed spending time with her friend. If anyone deserved a bit of fun, it was her. It wasn't long until he found himself grinning, silently cheering her on from a distance.

CHAPTER
SIX

An hour and three Rudy Specials later, it became apparent that despite Zoey being a lot of things, one thing she *wasn't* was someone able to hold her liquor. One more pink drink and Knox would be carrying her home on his shoulder.

He approached the bar and flagged Rudy.

"'Bout bloody time ya came to say hello," the old owner scolded in his thick Irish brogue. He dragged Knox halfway over the counter and into a short man-hug. "How the hell ya been doin', boy?"

"Good. Just been a little preoccupied tonight, Rudy. Sorry." Knox leaned against the countertop. "How's life been treating you?"

"Oh, can't complain much. This ole body still gets me round." Rudy's glance shifted toward the middle of the dance floor. "I may be an ole man, but me eyesight's as good as it was when I was a wee one. You're playing watchdog tonight, eh?"

"Trying. But your specials are making my job pretty damn hard." On cue, Zoey and Grace performed a synchronized dance move that looked suspiciously like something that belonged in an eighties dance flick. He swallowed a chuckle. "See what I mean."

"Aye, and me specials do pack quite the wallop, but I can't take all the credit for *that*. I have a policy of one Rudy special per customer. After that first drink, I switched me good booze with fruit punch. Humor danced around the corner of Rudy's mouth. "They've been drinkin' the equivalent of juice for the last hour and a half."

"You mean this is them sober?" Knox busted out a laugh.

"'Tis the power of persuasion." The older man's attention slid back over Knox's shoulder. "But your job's 'bout to get a wee bit more difficult even with me *mock*tails."

Knox turned around and immediately zeroed in on Zoey, dancing alone. Reed slipped in behind her, his hands settling low on her hips as he whispered into her ear. She twisted sideways in a clear attempt to disengage herself from his hold, and the asshat's hand shot out, latching on to her arm.

"Fucking hell." Knox pushed away from the bar.

"Try not to break me furniture," Rudy hollered after him.

"I'll settle for breaking bones."

Knox reached them in ten strides, quick enough to hear Zoey tell Reed what he could do with his sexually explicit offer.

"Is the music too loud for you to hear properly? Take your hands off her and walk the hell away," Knox growled his warning.

The punk threw him a glassy-eyed glare but didn't relinquish his grip. "Who the fuck died and made you her keeper? Back the fuck off. I'm trying to collect the happy ending that I didn't get on our date."

Horror-stricken by his vulgar assumption, Zoey's eyes widened. "Sorry to break the news to you, buddy, but you were never getting a happy ending. Not in this reality or any other."

"You and I both know the direction we were headed, sweetheart. But in case you need a reminder." Reed reached around to her ass and squeezed.

Knox bunched his fist, ready to either break the bastard's nose or his arm. He didn't much care which body part. Zoey beat him into action.

"My ass is not yours to touch!" With a mighty roar, she stomped a dagger-like heel onto his foot.

Reed howled, hopping back. "What the fuck? You little—"

Knox fisted the bastard's shirt and hauled him to his toes. "Think twice before you finish that sentence."

Knox sensed his three brothers on his six before he saw them. Ryder looked cautious but prepped for action, and Roman, back from wherever he'd disappeared to, stood alert, looking ready to rip off Reed's head himself.

Liam warned Knox quietly, "Not like he doesn't deserve an old-fashioned ass-whooping, but there's an entire crowd of DC cops watching right now. Can't exactly slip out of an assault charge if you pound his nose to dust in front of dozens of witnesses."

"What-the-fuck-ever." Reed slurred his words. "I went for it in the first place because I figured the precinct's social reject was a sure thing. Didn't realize her legs had been sealed shut at birth."

"On second thought, we'll figure something out." Liam's lip curled into a snarl.

Knox whipped his fist back, prepping for contact, when Zoey's hand clamped down on his arm. "Stop."

"Let go, angel."

Her grip firmed, and her voice dropped to a bare whisper. "*Please*. It's not worth it."

Both the plea and her touch stopped Knox cold. Bottom lip caught between her teeth, she peered at him through her long lashes, her cheeks a bright shade of red.

Knox wanted to punch the idiot even more for embarrassing her. Against his better judgment, he dropped Reed back to his feet. The guy swayed before slewing another string of curses and hightailing it across the room to his friends.

Conversations slowly resumed and the dance floor re-filled with bodies.

Zoey wouldn't look at him, her gaze focused on her feet. He cupped her chin and nudged her face up.

Uncertainty dimmed her pretty blue eyes and made him want to go after Reed for putting it there. "Ignore the asshole."

"I second that," Grace's voice chimed in. His cousin pulled her from his arms and into a hug. "I am so sorry, Zo. I didn't realize the vulture would descend the moment I left you alone."

Zoey waved off the apology. "Don't be silly. We can't be attached at the hip. And it's not like I didn't prepare myself for this before I put on this ridiculous outfit." She glanced down the front of her body and cringed. "I do kind of look like a reject."

"No, you don't," Knox growled.

Both women's attention—and his brothers'—shot to him, but Grace masked a smile behind a nod. "You're right. She doesn't. Reed wouldn't know natural beauty if it smacked him on his Cro-Mag forehead. Forget him."

Zoey's smile wavered. "Thanks, to both of you. My ego will survive the hit, but I think this is a sign that I'm meant to go home."

She spun into a turn. Inches before she collided with the dancing couple next to them, Knox caught her elbow. "You're not getting behind the wheel of a car, angel. I'll take you home."

"What?" Her blue eyes whipped toward him, panic plastered all over her face as she shook her head. Glasses sliding down her nose, she looked like a sexy librarian. "No. No-no-no. I'm fine."

"You had how many Rudy Specials?"

She rolled her eyes. "Please. I think we all know Rudy's been giving us juice and soda for the last hour if not longer. I'm okay."

"Do you really want to chance it?"

She nibbled her bottom lip, deep in thought. "Grace can give me a ride home."

Grace grimaced. "Uh, sorry, but I took the Red Line here. I was either going to take it back to the hotel or hit Liam up for a ride."

Liam agreed. "I can play chauffer for both of you. I don't mind in the least."

Knox already vetoed that idea. "That would be going way out of your way. Zoey's place is practically on the way to mine. It's not a big deal."

Knox half expected Zoey to decline his offer. That she had to think about it so intently bothered him. Although not a people person, he hadn't achieved beastly ogre status yet, and even considered himself on pretty good behavior for most of the night.

The incident with Reed couldn't be used against him. That jerk would've incited a monk to break a vow of nonviolence.

Zoey's small nod of agreement released a breath he hadn't known he'd been holding. As she exchanged goodbyes with his brothers and Grace, he waited, and then let her lead the way to the exit.

A faint breeze drifted in from the Wharf, cooling the temperature a good few degrees. Knox palmed the small of Zoey's back and guided her right. "We need to make a quick stop at my place."

Her feet froze. "Your place? Why would you take me to your place?"

"Because I walked here, and to take you home, I need my truck keys—not to mention, my truck. It's right near the marina."

"The keys to my apartment are in my car, which is at the parking garage. I can grab them and meet you near—"

"That's not going to happen. We'll go together to get your keys and then walk back to my place." He cast a glance to her fuck-me boots. "Can you walk without killing yourself on those stilts?"

She huffed a snort as she changed direction toward the garage. "I'll have you know, I've walked in these things through four loads of laundry *and* a grocery trip and didn't stumble once—at least not one that counted."

Knox chuckled at her sudden burst of sass. "And how many times didn't count?"

She ignored him, and he chuckled louder.

He'd been home less than twenty-four hours and couldn't keep track of how many times he'd smiled. And not so coincidentally, most of them revolved around the woman in front of him. It was her superpower along with her crazy smarts. Both abilities were sexy as hell.

Zoey walked in a mostly straight line, only wobbling when they stepped off the curb. The more the parking garage came into view, the more the carefree, no-filter Zoey disappeared. Her posture stiffened, a far cry from the fluid way she'd danced back at O'Malley's. And her blue eyes, which had been bright with laughter, were guarded.

Knox liked silence. He liked hearing himself think—but something nagged him ever since he'd hauled that jerk off of her. "What made you go out with Reed? From what I hear, his reputation is colorful enough to travel through the entire DC Metro area."

"It's not something that someone like you would understand," Zoey murmured.

Knox supported her elbow as they cleared another curb and stepped into the garage's first level. "What's that supposed to mean?"

"Like you don't know."

"Pretend I don't and tell me." He braced himself for an explanation he wouldn't like.

She flung her hand up and down the length of his body. "Because you're you."

"Still not grasping it, angel."

"You're Knox Steele. Alpha Man. Women flock to the dark and mysterious type like starved bears to a honey hive, and please don't insult my intelligence by telling me that you have a stagnant dating life. Remember, I was there all through your teenage years. I witnessed the revolving door firsthand. And I highly doubt it slowed after adding a military uniform to the mix."

"I wouldn't exactly call it dating." Knox never hated the truth so much in his life.

He didn't *date*. He met women. Sometimes they had sex. And then they both moved on. The one time he'd made an attempt at something more, it ended in a catastrophic failure. And when he'd left the Army, he didn't have the right head space for any kind of social commitments. He still didn't, or it wouldn't have taken him so long to come home, and he wouldn't be dragging his damn feet over heading out to California.

"So *sex* life," Zoey clarified with a roll of her eyes. "The point is, you can afford to be choosy because you are a walking sex dream to any woman with a heartbeat. I, on the other hand, can't be so picky."

Knox stopped dead in his tracks and gently tugged her around to face him. "Care to run that by me again, angel?"

"Why do you keep calling me angel?"

"Repeat what you said and explain to me what the hell it's supposed to mean." He purposefully ignored her question. "You can't seriously believe the stuff that little shithead spouted off about."

"What's there to explain?" Zoey's eyebrows lifted. "To everyone around me, I'm either the sick girl who practically lived in the hospital or the woman whose brother threatens bamboo shoot torture if anyone looks at me even the slightest bit cross-eyed. That's a whole lot of obstacles for someone like me."

Knox hated the way she phrased that last bit. Worse than defeat, it felt more like...resignation. And it wasn't the first time he'd sensed it.

With their slight difference in age, he hadn't been on the playground with her, but he'd pulled her into more than a few hugs when she'd come home crying about being left out of playgroups formed by the other kids.

In middle school came gym class and communal locker rooms, and pre-teen taunting. Girls had latched on to her difference—and her scar—and they'd been relentless in their teasing. Knox had only been around through a portion of her high school years prior to leaving for the Army, but in that time, he'd threatened a fair share of stupid jerks just like Scott Reed.

But in the short time Knox had been back home, he hadn't once gotten a glimpse of that shy, uncertain girl whose only goal was to keep her head down and survive.

Until now.

"Someone *like you*?" Knox forced himself to ask.

"Do I need to spell it out for you?"

"Evidently, yes."

"I'm a blender," she stated, like he should know what

she meant. "There's nothing about me that stands out. I blend with the crowd. I melt into the background. I'm a backup singer. I—"

"I disagree."

"Oh, you're right. Being legally blind without my glasses makes me stand out from the rest of the population." Sarcasm dripped off her words as she stalked ahead of him down the next aisle.

He wanted to point out all the ways she didn't blend. *Melt into the background?* No way in fucking hell. When she migrated into his eyesight, tearing his focus away from her became next to impossible.

Zoey blew out an exasperated sigh and muttered under her breath as she unlocked her car and leaned half her body into the front seat. The other half, clad in delicious red leather, stuck out as she searched her console.

Knox closed his eyes and recited a mental prayer for strength. *He should've let Liam have the honors of taking her home.*

"Gotcha!" Zoey climbed out and dangled her keys. "Now you can fulfill your protective duty, as sworn *by* you, *to* my brother. Let the babysitting commence."

"Do I look like a teenage girl?"

Her gaze tracked over him in an assessing once-over. Knox felt every last bit of her silent scrutiny, and even mentally ordered his junior to stay the hell down when it twitched in his pants. She nibbled on her bottom lip, the sight nearly making him groan aloud.

"No," she finally admitted. "At least not like any of the babysitters my mom used to hire. But that doesn't change the fact that you *are* one."

"And what makes you think that?"

"Because I know Cade. There's no way he left O'Malley's without making you take a blood oath or something."

"I volunteered my services. There was no oath giving or blood taking."

Zoey openly stared, a million questions floating around in her eyes. "Why would you subject yourself to babysitting duty when you could be taking home any gorgeous woman of your choosing?"

"That's what I'm doing."

When his meaning sunk in, Zoey's cheeks went from pale pink to fuchsia. Zoey Wright, during any given moment, epitomized the term *gorgeous*. But flustered Zoey stole the breath from his lungs.

He couldn't help himself any longer. Slowly reaching out, allowing time for her to pull away, he tucked a wayward strand of blond hair behind her ear. Her creamy skin felt as soft as it looked, and he had to stop himself from touching it again.

He hadn't said what he did to make her feel better. He'd spoken the truth.

There had only been one woman he'd thought about taking home.

And she stood in front of him, nibbling the corner of her lush, pink-glossed mouth, and making him think about things that would make Cade threaten him with a hell of a lot more than bamboo shoots.

CHAPTER SEVEN

Time alone with Knox meant trouble. Time alone at *his* place spelled catastrophe, and not to mention increased the likelihood of making a fool out of herself—well, *more* of a fool because that ship set sail back at the pub.

Zoey knew it. The screaming voices in her head were aware of it too. But that one lone voice? The loudest one? That little bugger enjoyed Knox's hand on the small of her back so much it had her leaning *into* it.

After collecting her keys, they'd headed back the way they came. The loud chaos of the Wharf slowly shifted to their backs. Small white porch lanterns blinked off the floating figures in front of them.

Boats.

Zoey adjusted her glasses. "You live in Sunrise Marina? On a boat?"

"Nah. In a high-rise." Knox smirked. "Yes, a boat. A motorsailer. It's a lot more peaceful on the water than it is on land."

"And by peaceful, you mean that you don't have nosy neighbors cornering you in the hallway and asking to borrow sugar?"

"Or throwing obnoxious parties. Or having scream-to-the-heavens sex. Although I don't mind the latter so much if I'm an active participant." Knox gifted her a quick wink.

Her cheeks heated as a naked Knox flashed into her imagination. She'd never seen him in the buff, but thanks to the Steeles living across the street, and driveway basketball, she'd been blessed with firsthand glimpses of the grand evolution of Knox's chest—and other attributes.

But to see former-Ranger Knox in his full naked glory?

She'd combust on the spot. Heck, the mental image of it alone caused her forehead to break out in a warm sweat. To avoid bursting into flames, she grabbed on to the nearest thought. "Cindy must be over the moon that her boys are home."

"She is. I'm just afraid she's putting in too much hope that it'll be permanent."

"Ah. That's right. What did Liam say you were leaving to do? Play with Hollywood celebrities?"

"Let me guess... you don't approve of it either?"

She shrugged. "You don't need my permission. And logically, it makes more sense than what your brothers are doing. They're not exactly desk people and yet they're opening a business, which, from what I hear, involves a lot of paperwork."

"No, but they're drinks people, and besides Roman, they're social butterflies. A distillery and beer garden will be like a playground for them."

"When you put it that way..."

At the base of the white-lit gangway, Knox turned toward her, his face a mask of calm shadows... except for his eyes. They studied her carefully, their intensity making her squirm. "What do you really think about me leaving, angel?"

For some reason, the answer seemed important to him, which didn't make sense. He'd been living the last two years making his own decisions without worrying about what anyone in the family would say or think.

"Why does it matter?" she asked carefully. "You already took the job, didn't you? And it's your life. I'm not going to tell someone else what they should or shouldn't do with what's theirs."

He didn't move. "But?"

She forced herself to meet his gaze. "I think you're using the job—which I'm sure is a legit offer—as an excuse to be anywhere but here. And I'm pretty sure I'm not the only one who thinks that... and resents it."

Zoey thought she'd offended him. He stood quiet, as if digesting her words. Finally, he tipped his chin in a faint nod. "Fair enough."

She waited for more and when nothing came... "That's it? No *you're right*, or *sorry*."

"You *are* right, and I'm sorry about that."

"But you're still going to leave."

"It's for the best. Trust me."

As she tried figuring out what to do with that statement, Knox gestured to the narrow walkway leading from the dock to the boat deck behind him. "This is me. Think you can manage the ramp without falling into the river?"

Zoey's eyes tracked the length of the precarious bridge. She'd have better luck crossing it if it were a wet, spinning log and she wore oiled shoes. "Just... *go*."

She shooed him ahead of her and kicked off her boots before following at a much slower pace. By the time he reached the deck, she'd barely hit the halfway point.

He waited on the other end, a smirk playing at the corners of his mouth. "Should I have opted for the three-foot width?"

"Six feet wouldn't make me feel comfortable."

At three-quarters of the way across, he plucked her off the bridge and placed her safely inside the boat. Heat radiated off his body, filling the less than one-inch gap between them. Goose bumps erupted over her arms, worsening as the breeze swept in from the Potomac River.

Zoey reluctantly eased away from his hold before he noticed the effect his touch had on her, and she immediately missed his warmth. She distracted herself from the acute loss by inspecting the boat. "I don't know a lot about boats, but I recognize gorgeous when I see it. This is impressive."

"It took a hell of a lot of elbow grease to get her to this point, but the end result was well worth the effort."

She looked at him, surprised. "You built this?"

"From scratch? Hell no. I bought her off an elderly couple a few years back and restored her in my free time. I finished her a week ago."

"Is that what took you so long to come back? You were waiting until it was finished?" Zoey didn't realize how her words sounded until they'd left her mouth. Or maybe she did.

Knox didn't answer, instead saying gruffly, "My keys

are below deck. You can come down and look around, or you can wait here. I won't be long."

She tilted her face to the cloudless night sky. "I'll stay here and enjoy the stars." *And avoid putting her foot in her mouth again.*

"Don't fall overboard." He gestured toward a cushioned bench. "Maybe you should sit until I get back."

Zoey plopped down on the seat and caught Knox's satisfied nod. "I'm not sitting because you told me to sit. I'm just trying to get the feeling back in my toes."

"Sweetheart, I don't care why you're sitting as long as it means I'm not fishing you out of the river."

Zoey wrinkled her nose at his back and watched him disappear below deck. Yawning, she tucked her legs beneath her body and got comfy. Her eyes drooped closed until something brushed her cheek once, then twice.

With an irritated huff, she batted at the offending nuisance. "Go away. Sleeping."

"I can see that." A husky voice cut through her dream state. "But you need to wake up, sleepyhead. Stay curled up like that much longer and you're not going to be able to move for a week."

Zoey peeled open her eyes and came nose to nose with Knox. She jumped, startled, and crashed the top of her head into his chin with a loud crack.

"Oh, my God. I'm so sorry."

"No worries. I didn't need a movable jaw anyway." Knox slid his jaw side to side, barely hiding a grimace. "Shit. Your brother wasn't lying when he said you're hardheaded."

"Ha. Ha. And to think I almost cared about hurting

you." Zoey ambled to her feet, but on her first step, her legs gave out, attacked by pins and needles.

Despite having been assaulted by her hard head, Knox quickly banded a supportive arm around her waist. "You okay?"

"Sea legs. I didn't mean to maul you."

Knox's watch ticked, emphasizing the sudden awkward silence. Her hands automatically flexed on his arms. That same scent of pine and spice invaded her nose, and she took another involuntary whiff.

"Are you going to deny smelling me now?" His chest vibrated with his husky question.

Zoey forced a lump down her dry throat. "No. You smell really, really good."

Knox's gaze flickered down to her mouth, stealing her breath. A rush of thoughts and choices swirled through her head in one jumbled mess. It was difficult to pick out any single one... except the desperate need to feel his lips against hers.

"We should get you home," Knox announced.

But he didn't move.

Neither did Zoey. Her heart thumped hard behind her sternum, and led her to making a very un-Zoey-like decision.

For as long as she could remember, she'd always played things safe, did the smart, responsible thing, and kept her distance from anything that could end in crushing disappointment.

Stepping so far out of her comfort zone as to kiss Knox Steele definitely risked a severe, crushing blow to her pride. But suddenly, she didn't care.

Skating her palms from his biceps to his broad shoulders, she admitted, "I don't think I'm ready to go home."

Knox sucked in a slow, deep breath. "This isn't a smart idea, angel. For a hell of a lot of reasons."

"Like bamboo shoots?"

"And at least a dozen more."

"I'm sick and tired of always doing the smart thing, Knox." Zoey's subconscious spoke its piece...aloud.

"You've been drinking."

"*Mocktails*. Glorified fruit punch without a speck of alcohol in them. And the one drink I had was metabolized a *long* time ago. Would you like me to calculate the exact time it became a non-issue?" She couldn't blame alcohol if this backfired on her in a stupendous way.

Zoey swallowed her nerves. Lifting onto her toes, she brushed her lips against Knox's once, then twice before taking his bottom lip in a gentle nibble.

He didn't kiss her back.

He didn't deepen the embrace.

She'd scared the man immobile.

A tsunami of embarrassment flooded over her as she un-fused her lips from his. She'd barely taken a breath when something snapped...changed. Like the veracity of a lightning strike, one large hand slipped into her hair, and hungrily guided her mouth back for a claiming of his own.

Suddenly, Zoey was pressed up against Knox's hard chest, her fingers clutching his shoulders like a lifeline. She couldn't feel enough...touch enough. This had been one of her best-kept fantasies for so long and she was finally experiencing it.

And enjoying the heck out of it.

Knox's tongue swept against hers and she was more than happy to reciprocate. She returned his enthusiasm with her own, standing in the middle of his boat, oblivious to the world around them.

This was him *devouring* her.

This was her devouring *him*.

This was heady, in-the-heat-of-the-moment lust… and the most uncontrolled thrill she'd ever experienced in her life.

Desperate for more physical contact, Zoey pushed her hips against Knox. The hand not locking their mouths together dropped to her rear end, and held her close enough to feel the growing bulge pushing against her stomach.

In one moment, Knox's hands and body surrounded her. And in the next, nothing but cool evening air caressed her skin. As abruptly as their embrace started, it ended.

Knox, chest rising and falling hard, studied her carefully from three feet away. "This was a mistake, Zoey. I'm sorry. This shouldn't have happened."

Zoey's throat closed, making it hard to speak. She tugged her shirt back to her waist and counted to five. "You have nothing to be sorry about. I'm pretty sure I started it."

"And I'm ending it." Knox lasered her with a dark look she knew all too well. *Regret*. "I'm not sticking around."

"Pretty sure I didn't ask you to." The second he opened his mouth to interject, she raised her hand. "It was a kiss, Knox. Not a marriage proposal, or a request to father my children. It happened, and it's over."

"You're not going to let me explain?"

"No. Because there's nothing that needs an explanation."

"Men like me don't mess around with women like you for a *reason*. It doesn't make sense, angel."

His words slapped her across the face.

She blinked, hoping she'd heard wrong, but his tightly pinched expression told her that she hadn't. Grinding her teeth together, she lifted her chin and forced eye contact. "You're right. You're abso-freaking-lutely right. I don't know what was going through my head."

Zoey grabbed her purse, and tucking her boots under her arm, stalked toward the gangway.

"Zoey, wait."

At the foot of the narrow bridge, anger zipped her back around. Knox stood less than a foot away, following.

"You want to know something, Knox Steele?" She drilled an accusatory finger into the center of his chest. "Women like *me* don't need men like *you*. What *I* need is a grown-ass adult man. Not a watered-down man-baby who's so threatened by the idea of being around the people who care about him that he hides behind a job offer that doesn't make sense."

"That's what you really think, huh?"

"Yes! And while I'm dishing out honesty, I'm disappointed in you for even entertaining the idea, much less going through with it. Because the Knox Steele *I* remember was *fearless*—and I'm not talking about when he put on his uniform. He didn't let anything stand in the way of something he truly wanted. *That's the man I thought I was kissing.* But thank you for clearing up that little misunderstanding."

Right now, the honesty felt damn good, but Zoey wasn't sure she'd feel the same in an hour. She needed distance, and maybe a brain scan. She *definitely* needed to steer clear of the eldest Steele.

Her cheeks as hot as the sun, she rushed over the gangway, making it halfway across before stubbing her big toe on a raised lip. She stumbled, catching herself on the railing, but as she pushed herself upright, a faint snap evaporated all relief.

Balance lost, she teetered toward open air, her startled scream—and cursing of Knox's name—washed away by the murky water of the Potomac River.

* * *

Knox grabbed the life preserver tied to the aft, and rushed to the side of the boat, prepped to dive into the Potomac, clothes, boots, and all. A round of PG-rated curses slowly returned his heart to its normal position.

Zoey treaded water two feet out from the hull...wet, but *safe*.

He propped his arms on the broken railing. "I told you to stop."

Zoey's blue eyes snapped to him. Her blond hair plastered to her head, she spewed water like a geyser, forcing him to swallow a chuckle. "And I don't hang around where I'm obviously not wanted."

"I never said you weren't wanted, angel." Far from

it. The physical pain he'd experienced pulling away from her still seared his insides, and, he expected, would until they picked up where they left off.

Which couldn't happen no matter how much he wanted it to.

Zoey slipped past all his lines of defense, a skill she'd had for as long as he could remember. And she did it without even trying. Hell, all she had to do was be in close proximity and he was half ready to give up any pretense he had of control.

She let out a disbelieving grunt. "Aren't you going to help me get out?"

He rubbed his stubbled chin. "I suppose I could. But a grown-ass woman should be able to get herself out of this little jam without help from a watered-down manbaby like me. Right?"

If she had the power to skewer him with a glare, he'd be dead and falling over the railing right after her.

Mumbling under her breath, she collected her floating boots and swam to the ladder attached to the dock—and then the joke was on him.

Holy mother of God.

Knox's smile evaporated. Wet leather encased Zoey's perfect backside like a second skin, and her doublelayered tank did little to hide the lacy black bra beneath. His tongue dried to the roof of his mouth, and his body, suddenly all too alert, nearly combusted by the time she stepped onto the deck.

Tossing a dripping purse over her shoulder, Zoey threw him an eat-shit-and-die scowl and gave him a prime view of her ass as she stalked away.

"Where the hell are you going?" he called out.

"Home."

He followed at a leisurely pace. "You're going to hoof it all the way back to your condo? Barefoot?"

"I'll call a Lyft."

"With what? The cell that's probably floating in a pool of water in your purse? And even if it works, do you think that they're going to let a woman soaked in river water into their car? Come back to the boat, angel. I'll get you dry clothes, and then I'll drive you home myself."

"I'll be fine, thank you."

Knox growled at her renewed stubbornness. Enough was enough. Pissed at him or not, she'd be safer alone with him for a few minutes longer than out there by herself traversing the nighttime streets of DC.

He dodged in front of her, dropped his shoulder, and scooped her into a fireman's carry. One wide palm anchored on her luscious derriere, he walked back toward his boat.

"Put me down!" Zoey smacked a small fist against his ass, first by accident, and then with more intent. "I mean it, Knox! I am fully capable of walking on my own two feet!"

"Says the woman who fell into the Potomac. Keep struggling and you may find your sweet ass back in the river."

She gasped. "You wouldn't dare."

"You've known me for a long time, angel. When have I ever made hollow threats?"

Never. She and Grace learned that the hard way

when they'd snuck out to a frat party that they had no business attending. To this day, he didn't regret a single bruised knuckle or the severe tongue-lashing he'd gotten from his Army recruiter. Those frat boy horn dogs deserved every ounce of hell that he and Cade had rained down on them.

Zoey stopped wiggling, making the rest of the trek to his living quarters below deck that much easier. Once there, he returned her to her feet and nodded toward the bathroom. "While you go shower the river off you, I'll find something for you to wear that won't fall right off."

Her gaze bounced from the exit to the bathroom, and back.

"You're wet. You're shoeless. And I have nothing but time on my hands," Knox warned. "I could play cat and mouse all damn night if you want."

Zoey released an unladylike growl and disappeared into his bathroom, slamming the door closed behind her. As the shower started, Knox closed his eyes and tried erasing the mental image of her shimmying out of her nearly see-through clothes . . . of using his soap . . . of drying off with his towel.

Bad fucking idea, Steele.

Ignoring the sudden tightness in his pants, he gathered dirty dishes and dumped them in the sink. That done, he scrounged in his drawers, finding an old set of gym clothes, and set them outside the bathroom door.

Twenty minutes later, he stepped out of his bedroom to find Zoey curled on his sofa, asleep, her hand pillowed beneath her cheek. She looked too peaceful to move, much less wake up.

He covered her with the throw on the back of the couch and sat his ass in the spring-broken chair two feet away. Oh, he had a perfectly good bed in the back, comfy as hell with the right firm to soft ratio.

But he didn't want to leave Zoey out here alone.

And no way in hell was he prepared to attempt to dissect *that*.

* * *

He watched from the lot as the dark-haired guy from the bar man-handled His Heart below deck. Movement shifted behind the drape-covered windows in an intimate shadow performance with two distinct actors.

His Heart.

And Knox Steele.

With every window that went dark, his fingers tightened on the steering wheel until pain shot from his cracking knuckles to his wrists. His control had steadily disintegrated since the scene at the Irish pub.

He'd been forced to watch then too.

But it was too early to make his move. As much as it pained him to admit, neither of them was ready. It wasn't their time.

Yet.

He jerked back onto the street and headed to a place he knew as well as his own. No detours. No traffic. No tolls to avoid. It wasn't long before he pulled into the familiar lot, one devoid of streetlights and cameras, and parked in the far back corner.

No one would question him. No one would stop

him. They never did. He put people at ease, winning their trust without effort. It was a gift that had served him well through the years, and one in which he took a great deal of pride.

He tossed his duffel bag over his shoulder and treaded quietly along the winding path, bypassing his favorite oak perch. On the occasion that he needed a quick glimpse into Her world, it served its purpose well. But this time, a glimpse wouldn't do.

He needed to surround himself in Her essence.

She needed to become part of his day.

As her vivid blue door came into view, tingles zipped down his spine. But it was nothing compared to the euphoria that washed over him when he stepped into Her apartment.

Gaining access had been ridiculously easy...a well-placed smile here, and a coy chuckle there. The complex manager hadn't questioned his interest in the Kingsbrooke apartment community, trusting him enough to leave him alone for the few minutes it had taken him to copy her master key.

He had that lovely woman to thank for each and every one of his visits.

From the flowery fragrance that hung in the air to the yellow-painted walls and decorative artwork, His Heart could be found in every inch of the small apartment. The bookshelves, filled with knickknacks and leather-bound books, showcased not only her love of literature, but family.

He set his bag on the table and was rewarded with a low, rumbling growl. His Heart's furry behemoth slinked out from behind the couch, golden eyes locked on him in distrust.

"We're both looking out for Her, aren't we?" He dug into his pocket and pulled out a handful of treats. As expected, the feline gobbled them up and turned away, leaving him to do the job for which he'd come.

One by one, he pulled the cameras from his bag. Discreet but high-functioning, they'd serve their purpose to watch over Her when he couldn't. It was something he'd contemplated on previous visits, but hadn't followed through with until tonight. Seeing what happened at the marina only solidified the urgent need for their use.

The kitchen. The living room. He worked through the apartment until he reached the bedroom. Running his hand over the lilac comforter, he bypassed the unused side and climbed into the spot that She'd claimed as Her own.

"Ah. My Heart." He burrowed his nose into her pillow, her lingering scent firming his cock.

Dropping his hand to his zipper, he groaned.

She'd lain in this exact spot mere hours ago...

Asleep, her body undulating in slow, languid movements...

Skin caressing the soft sheets...

As the mental images of His Heart played in his head, he rubbed his palm over his hardening bulge. It twitched, urging him to rub faster.

"Soon, My Heart." He arched his hips up into his palm. "Soon you'll realize that only I can give you what you deserve... and only you can give me what I need."

Each breath fell from his lips in heavy pants. Sweat

dotted his forehead. His cock, rigid and heavy in the throes of lust, throbbed until with a loud grunt of release, he came in a series of violent bursts.

Panting through the last rolls of pleasure, he lay there, hesitant to leave, though knowing he had no choice. He secured the last camera, and before calling it a night, looked for a few tokens to complement the ones he'd taken last time.

In Her small jewelry box, he chose a pair of earrings and a silver necklace. While contemplating a third trinket, his gaze locked on to a photograph tucked off to the side.

In it, both His Heart's smile and her sparkling blue eyes were directed toward the man whose arm draped her shoulders.

Knox Steele.

Picking up the jewelry box, he hurled it against the wall. Wooden pieces splintered apart, spilling both the box's contents and his hard-fought control.

He tossed. He destroyed. He obliterated everything in his path, removing himself from the situation—and Her apartment—only when his destruction crunched beneath his feet.

This time, he detoured from his usual route home.

Closed businesses and dark, well-kept townhomes transformed to dirtied streets and sleeping homeless. Trash bags had been heaped into piles on every corner, and a rat, caught in his headlight beam, scurried into the sewer.

At a stop light, his car caught the attention of the two women outside the late-night convenience store.

His gaze bypassed the brunette immediately . . . and held on the blonde.

Her shy smile transformed to one of wicked promise as she approached his window. "What are you up to tonight, sweetheart?"

"Looking for you."

CHAPTER EIGHT

Every inch of Zoey's body ached. Legs. Back. Butt. Pain this severe while lying down meant *nothing* good would come from moving, but her distended bladder had long since reached DEFCON 1 status.

One sneeze, cough, or unexpected laugh and there was no going back.

"Here goes nothing."

She shifted, realizing too late that she'd rolled onto thin air, and landed, rear-down, on a hard, unforgiving floor.

She blinked her blurry vision into focus. Shadows slowly formed into dark, mismatched furniture, and a small ray of light slinked through the blinds, showcasing the sleeping man sprawled awkwardly in a plush chair catty-corner from where she lay.

As if delivered via freight train, Zoey's memories from the night slammed back—O'Malley's. Reed. Knox. The kiss. *Her dip into the Potomac.*

"Next time Grace mutters the word *party*, she's dead," Zoey mumbled to herself before remembering she wasn't alone.

Wincing, she got to her feet and trudged to the bathroom as quietly as she could. She immediately regretted glancing in the mirror. Her glasses, askew on her nose, emphasized the smudged black mascara framing her puffy eyes. Her hair, knotted and sticking up in varying directions, could've housed a family of rats.

She combed out the clumps with her fingers as best she could, and then attacked the Picasso on her face until her skin glowed. Next, she helped herself to the toothpaste resting on the sink and tried working a miracle with a small dollop and her finger. Finally satisfied that her breath wouldn't render anyone unconscious, she tiptoed back into the living room and thought about her options.

Staying wasn't one of them.

Staying meant *talking* and rehashing the embarrassment of Knox sticking her back on the friend-zone shelf—or more accurately, the never-in-a-million-years shelf. There wasn't any other possible scenario. She hadn't miraculously morphed into the type of woman Knox Steele *messed around with*.

Zoey couldn't bring herself to put on her river-soaked costume, and her phone, still dripping water, was useless. She called a Lyft from Knox's cell, and didn't breathe easier until the driver pulled up in front of Veronica, her much loved and worldly VW Beetle. Thirty minutes later, and she was home.

Zoey loved her community. Its mixture of up-and-coming youth and old-town history created a blended environment where everything was a short walk away. Neighbors knew neighbors, and for the most part, were always quick to lend a hand. Her back corner location kept her out of the chaos, but close enough that she could make social connections if she wanted.

She turned the corner onto her private landing and nearly got trampled by a four-foot-ten-inch tornado.

House coat thrown over a long nightgown and curlers rolled into her hair, Mrs. Shott, the elderly complex manager, wrapped her in a bone-crushing hug. "Oh! Thank the sweet Lord that you're okay! You *are* okay, dear, aren't you? I think my freshly dyed Vixen Red went straight back to white!"

Zoey returned her hug and gently pulled away. "Why wouldn't I be okay?"

Her gaze drifted over her landlady's shoulder to where her front door stood ajar. Her kitchen chairs lay in pieces. Her couch, which she'd purchased two months ago, had been slashed into shreds, its stuffing littering the room like an indoor snow scene. From inside, an angry meow echoed from the destruction.

"Snuggles!" Zoey cried.

As if she'd conjured his presence, her Maine Coon sashayed out the front door, his fluffy tail held high, and gave her a blameful glare. She picked up all twenty-two pounds of him and ignored his howl of protest as she turned toward Mrs. Shott. "I don't understand. What happened?"

"I came by to see if you'd be interested in a blind date with my beautician's son—a good boy who needs someone to look past his oddities and give him a chance. I saw the door open and the mess inside. I didn't know what to do. All those police shows say never to go inside."

"And you didn't, did you?" Zoey asked, concerned.

"Goodness no. I hustled back to my place and called the police."

A few seconds later, sirens wailed in the distance, the noise growing louder as two cruisers pulled into the lot. Squad cars meant uniformed police. Beat cops. No fire-breathing older brother wielding his shiny detective's badge.

Maybe miracles did happen.

As small as it was, she'd take it.

* * *

Training had taught Knox to sleep with one ear always listening, and a half of an eye always open. Yet this morning, Zoey had evaded detection as if she were trained by the Grand Master Ninja himself. By the time he pulled his truck to the curb outside Iron Bars, he still wasn't sure if he was thankful for her disappearance or pissed.

He'd been right when he told her their kiss shouldn't have happened—Rudy's doctored *mock*tails or not. He had no business starting anything with anyone.

He wasn't staying.

The second Steele Ops was fully up and running, he'd start the next chapter of his life, one that didn't involve dark extractions or a thirty-yard sprint through unmarked land mines. No one would lose their life at a red-carpet premier.

A headache blossomed under Knox's right temple just thinking about spoiled actresses and ego-laden pop stars, but he'd buy a value-sized bottle of ibuprofen and deal with it. A perpetual migraine was better than letting down anyone who was important to him.

Or worse—making a decision that could get them killed. If he was responsible for their downfall, he'd never be able to live with himself. This way, they may be pissed at him, but they'd be alive to hold their grudge.

Knox balanced the carrier of travel coffees and followed the sound of voices to the bottom dregs of the distillery. The heavy iron door, not yet linked to retinal scans and biometrics, stood open, showcasing the circular epicenter of Steele Ops.

Liam leaned back in a chair, legs kicked out in front of him, and immediately locked in on his target. "Please tell me those are from Perk Up."

"Perk Up?" Knox deadpanned. "I thought you texted me Stir It Up."

Liam narrowed his eyes and grumbled. "I knew I should've texted you a sixth time."

With a small grin, Knox plopped Liam's favorite coffee next to his booted feet. "Perk Up's black roast…as requested. How are things coming along here?"

"A friend of mine's coming in today to help me work on the wiring and circuit boards. I want to make sure we have more than enough juice for all the firepower we're going to have down here. By the time we're done, we'll be able to run NASA from our basement."

Knox snort-laughed. "Maybe we should settle for Steele Ops and let the rocket professionals do their own thing."

Roman walked into the room, his limp a bit more pronounced than usual. On seeing Knox, he straightened. "Back again, huh? You've broken a record."

"Couldn't wait to see your smiling face." Knox held out a coffee. "All yours."

If anyone needed it, he did. Dark circles framed his red-rimmed eyes. He either hadn't yet gone to bed, or had already been up for hours. He took the offered coffee, and pushing Liam's feet off the table, leaned his ass in their place.

Ryder stepped out from a back room, red-faced and sweaty from a workout in the gym. "The gang's all here...and with caffeine."

"Speaking of the gang," Knox started, "Cade promised to consider that job offer."

Roman looked doubtful. "How did you pull that off?"

Knox shrugged. "I bartered. But he agreed to meet with your fund guy...whoever the hell that may be."

"Hogan Wilcox."

Knox paused over his coffee, his interest piqued. "As in the former Joint Chief of Staff Hogan Wilcox?"

"The one and only."

"And how the hell did you pull *that* off?" Knox turned Roman's words back at him.

"Not much to pull. He heard about us through the grapevine and made the initial approach. He's retired and loaded with money to spare. I wasn't going to turn away no-strings greenery."

"And you're sure it's without strings?"

Roman's frown deepened. "What do you care anyway? Strings or not, you won't be here to deal with it. And as for Cade, it's good he's considering joining, but I'm not holding my breath. It would mean putting an end to his Zoey-smothering."

All three of them looked at Roman with varying WTF looks, darkening his already grim demeanor. "Why are you all looking at me like that when I'm right? Zo's what? Thirty?"

"Twenty-seven, asshole," Liam corrected. "Same as me."

"Twenty-seven. Thirty. Whatever. She's an adult with the good sense to go after what she wants and not take the road traveled by chicken-shits. He could learn a thing or two from her." Roman gave Knox a pointed look. "He's not the only one."

Three years ago, Knox would've fought back... definitely with his words, quite possibly with a headlock. Instead, he let the dig slide. "So you'll set up the meet for us?"

Roman gave a slight nod. "I'll make the call and see what I can put together. But I'm warning you right now, don't go burning any bridges for us. We got a good thing going with Wilcox and I don't want you fucking it up."

"No pyrotechnics. Got it."

Roman turned on his heel and disappeared as suddenly as he'd showed.

Liam cleared his throat. "He's warming up to you. Before you know it, you'll be cruising the club circuit for women together. I can just feel it."

Knox snorted. Neither he nor Roman had been clubbers when they'd been the appropriate age, much less now in their thirties. And yeah, that scene with Ro could've been a hell of a lot worse, but he wasn't printing matching T-shirts just yet.

Or maybe ever.

One thing Roman Steele had was a long, unforgiving memory.

Knox gestured to the stack of files sitting on the desk. "Are those possible recruits? Because let's face it, this is going to have to be a lot more than a three-man show."

"Could be five if you and Cade pulled your heads out of your asses." At Knox's glare, Ryder chuckled, raising his hands in mock surrender. "Just sayin'."

"Don't."

Liam tossed open the first manila file. "Here's possibility number one. Hunter 'Tank' Dawson. Even though he's Roman's friend, I like him. Special Forces with a fondness for invisible extractions. The man's a Cajun ninja. Smart as hell. I met him a few times. Good guy and eager to dive into the civilian front once his time's up."

Knox flipped through the history. "Looks good on paper."

Ryder smirked. "We thought so too, which is why he's making an appearance on his next furlough. Should be here within the week."

Knox trashed his now cold coffee. "Sounds good. Just don't go making promises. Until we're one hundred percent, we're not running any ops. No ops means no paychecks."

"*We?*" Liam teased.

"*You*," Knox corrected. "But since we share a last name, I don't want some special forces ghost chasing me down because you assholes made false promises."

Liam and Ryder both smirked.

"Sure." Ryder didn't look the least bit convinced.

Hell, Knox wasn't either. It slipped out easily and without any thought. His cell rang, distracting him from reading any further into his comment. The screen flashed with Cade's number. "What's up, man?"

"I need to cash in on that favor to watch after Zoey—and now."

Knox's blood froze, his sudden stillness alerting his brothers. "What's wrong?"

"Something happened at her place and with traffic, I'm not getting there anytime soon."

Knox already had in his keys in his hand as he headed out the door, his brothers calling after him. "Text me the address. I'm on my way."

CHAPTER
NINE

Zoey's morning luck shifted when she noticed her friend and former Miss USA contestant, Natasha James, climb out of her squad car with her partner, Deacon Black. But her luck didn't last long. After hustling her into her landlady's apartment, Nat unceremoniously told her to stay put while they checked things out.

That was forty-five minutes ago.

Trapped in Mrs. Shott's bathroom, Snuggles clawed at the door with gusto, stopping only to let out a wail of displeasure. Zoey felt like joining him. There was nothing worse than not knowing…except maybe listening to Mrs. Shott's extensive list on all the good qualities of her beautician's misunderstood son.

A heavy knock on the front door finally stopped the path she'd worn into her landlady's carpet. "About freakin' time."

Zoey flung it open, expecting an apologetic Nat with an update. Instead, she came nose to chest with a grim-faced Knox. Her traitorous heart fluttered before realization set in. "What are you doing here? Oh. Silly me. *Cade*."

Knox cocked his head to the side, studying her hard. "He's on his way. Are you okay?"

"Am I okay knowing that someone went full-on rockstar temper tantrum on my apartment? No."

"You know that's not what I meant, angel."

Zoey took a deep breath and reminded herself that Knox wasn't the source of her annoyance—at least not in regards to the break-in. "I'm fine. Evidently the party happened when I was out. But now that it seems to have broken up…"

She sidestepped him, but he blocked her exit with his oversized body. "It's kind of difficult to go back to my place with you standing in my way."

"You should put that off until someone comes in to clean the place up."

"What sense does that make? How do we know if anything was taken unless I look around?"

"All the big-ticket items are still there—TV, stereo, laptop. What's left, you don't need to see."

"I need to see because it's *my* apartment." Before she said, or did, something she'd regret later, she pushed past Knox and ignored the call of her name as she navigated the outdoor path to her condo.

"Morning, blondie." Liam popped around the corner with a taller, broader Steele by his side. *Roman.*

"Cripes! You guys replicate like wet mogwais."

Roman's wrinkled his brow in confusion. "Mogwhat?"

"Never mind." Evidently not everyone was as a big a fan of eighties horror as she was.

Liam dropped an arm over her shoulder and gently attempted to turn her away from the door that Roman now stood solidly in front of. "Why don't we go to that diner around the corner and grab breakfast? Knox only fed me coffee this morning and my stomach's growling like a damn lion."

Zoey frowned at the obvious Steele joint effort to keep her from her own apartment. "You'll have to wait a little longer."

Her self-defense classes paid off. She ducked out of his side hold and spun back toward her door, where she executed a quick side skip to avoid Roman's bulky frame. She nearly cheered with her successful evasion until she stepped into her foyer.

The way they'd all acted, she expected it to look as if someone had trashed it with a wrecking ball.

It looked *worse*.

Her overturned kitchen table was split into two pieces, no good for anything except kindling. Once gloriously filled, her bookshelf stood empty, its contents shredded and lobbed across the room. Knickknacks lay in shattered pieces on the ground, mixed with the stuffing that had been pulled from the couch cushions.

Carefully choosing her footing, Zoey headed toward the back room and hoped that she'd find *something* that hadn't been destroyed.

"Zoey, wait! Hold on one damn minute!" Knox's voice barked from behind her.

Glass crunched beneath her Buffy boots as she stepped into her once decently organized bedroom. Her hand flew to her mouth. "Oh my God. There isn't anything that hasn't been touched."

Her closet hung open and empty, and judging by the shredded pile of rags littering the floor, not so much as a single sweater survived. Her bed suffered the same fate as the sofa, sheets ripped and metal springs protruding from its carcass.

A wall of warmth coated her back a second before Knox's hand dropped onto her shoulder. "I'm sorry, angel."

She battled back a well of emotions. "Unless you're the one with a Freddy Krueger fetish, there's nothing for *you* to be sorry about."

"Doesn't mean that I don't wish this didn't happen."

"Where is she? Where the hell's my sister?" Cade stormed into her bedroom with Liam, Roman, and Ryder hot on his heels. He barely glanced around the room before locking his sights on Zoey, then Knox, who'd taken a subtle step away. "What's been done so far? Has anyone been sent out to canvass the area? And what about witnesses? Have we put out a BOLO on any suspicious vehicles yet?"

"How would Knox know—?"

"There weren't any witnesses," Knox interrupted Zoey. "The unit across the corridor's been empty for about a month and the neighbors upstairs are on vacation. By the time the call came through to dispatch, the perps were probably long gone."

"Did you join the DCPD sometime since, oh, *yesterday*?"

Knox looked her directly in the eye, his expression unreadable. "Cade called and here I am."

"Too bad that didn't work anytime in the last two years."

For a few seconds, no one spoke. Then something

clicked and Cade's face turned even redder. "Wait a damn minute. Why the hell would you wait to call this in?"

All eyes focused on her.

Shrugging off Cade's skepticism came easy. She'd had years of fine-tuning the skill. But the Steele brothers, standing side by side, made her uneasily shift her feet. Liam looked slightly confused, and Ryder, curious. But Roman?

Roman's calculating gaze took in her appearance...and her clothes, before snapping up to her in a hard stare.

Nerves sucked the moisture from her throat. She cleared it, wincing at the sudden dryness. "It was my landlady who made the call. I wasn't home."

"Where were you? With Gr—" Cade went quiet for the first time since he arrived. His eyes narrowed on what Roman had already noticed. "Who the hell's clothes are you wearing?"

Zoey's Knox-dar kicked into full blast, bypassing warm tingle and zipping straight to heat-of-the-sun inferno.

She ignored the question, and prayed her voice sounded as firm as her resolve to erase the last eight hours. "I wasn't here when someone forced their way inside my apartment. That's a *good* thing."

"There isn't any sign of a forced entry," Knox added.

Zoey waved her hand toward what used to be her belongings. "All my ruined things say otherwise."

"Every window was locked from the inside; the sliding glass door too. And there aren't any jimmy marks on the front door, which means whoever forced their way inside didn't have to work too hard."

Cade's head whipped toward Zoey. "Why didn't you send out housewarming invites that say *the door's unlocked, come on in*?"

Zoey ground her teeth. "I did *not* leave the door unlocked."

"Yeah? Then explain to me how this happened."

"I don't know how this happened, but I always lock my door. I even lock up when I go around the corner to get my mail!"

Five stern faces stared at her, unconvinced. But it was the truth. The sticky top dead bolt didn't catch at the first twist, and so she always turned it twice, and then checked the doorknob for good measure. Before heading to O'Malley's, she recalled with perfect clarity having done the same thing.

Her apartment had been sealed *tight*.

Cade, unsmiling and thoughtful, finally broke out with the expected suggestion. "You're staying with me for a few days. I'm not comfortable with you being here by yourself. Now that someone's been inside, it's obvious that you're a single woman living alone. There's nothing preventing them from coming back."

"Not happening." Zoey lifted her chin in a show of defiance. "A few days here. A week another time. If I were a random citizen, would you be telling me to pack what's left of my stuff and move?"

This was about a lot more than sleeping on her brother's couch. Conceding now made it easier to give in later when something a lot more important was on the line.

Cade gritted his teeth. "You're not a random citizen. You're my baby sister."

"Your *adult* sister who has no intentions of taking up room on her brother's couch." Zoey squeezed his hand affectionately. "I'll change my locks if it makes you feel better, and I'll even check into getting a security system. But I am not relocating my entire life because of a random case of bad luck."

Cade waited nearly a half minute before nodding reluctantly. "Fine. But I'm not letting any guy with a white van and a toolbox put locks on your doors."

"I'll do it," Liam interjected. "I don't have anywhere to be for a few hours."

Zoey shook her head. "I can't ask you to do that for me."

Ryder snorted. "Tech stuff is how he relaxes. You'll be lucky if there's not some kind of DNA scanner on your front door to go along with new locks. No saliva, no entry."

Liam looked appalled. "Saliva? What do you take me for? A barbarian? This isn't the twentieth century."

Zoey ushered them out of her bedroom. "I don't care if it takes saliva, my eyeball, or analyzes my breath. I just need you all to go so I can get ready for work."

Knox tossed her a surprised look. "Your place was burglarized and you're headed to the station?"

"Vandalized," she corrected. "You were right. It doesn't look as if anything was taken. I have a task force meeting this morning, and side note, Cade, so do you."

Knox didn't look thrilled. None of them did, but she corralled them into the living room and closed the bedroom door behind them. Slinking to the ground, she blew a stray lock of hair from her eye.

With her booted foot, she nudged away what used to be her favorite cardigan. What clothes hadn't been shredded had been handled by *someone*. No way could she bring herself to put anything on, not without multiple washings and a few gallons of heavy-duty bleach.

Zoey grabbed a pair of hard-soled slippers that had somehow thwarted the mutilation process, and returned to a Wright and Steele-free living room. The same couldn't be said for the parking lot. Although three of the Steeles were nowhere in sight, Knox and Cade stood near her car, talking in hushed tones.

Zoey turned in the opposite direction and spotted Nat and Deacon about to climb into their squad car.

"Nat!" Waving, she hustled across the lot. "Are you guys going back to the station?"

"We are. You want a lift?"

"Definitely. The sooner, the better." Zoey climbed into the back seat and glanced over her shoulder.

"Why do I feel like we could be charged with aiding and abetting?" Nat followed her line of sight and whistled. "Whoa. I haven't seen a man stare that hard at a woman in...well, ever. Are you sure you don't want to stay behind and talk to him? Because he sure as hell looks like he wants to speak with you."

Zoey ripped her gaze away from Knox's twenty-yard penetrating stare and buckled her seat belt. "I've never been more positive about anything in my life."

CHAPTER
TEN

In fifteen minutes, Zoey would officially be considered late to the Cupid Killer Task Force meeting. She needed to finish typing one last report, make copies, and hopefully change into something that didn't scream *I didn't sleep in my own bed last night*.

A second after she hit the save button, a shopping bag plopped onto her desk.

"You realize that you owe me a highly detailed explanation about this mayday call, right? It's not every day—or *any* day—that you entrust me with what to put on your body. It has my imagination running wild." Grace's brown eyes lit up with all the possibilities, and judging by her grin, none of them were G-rated.

Not that Knox's clothes didn't smell divine—and like him—but the last thing Zoey needed was someone like Marie from dispatch announcing she sported a walk-of-shame ensemble. If she was to become office gossip, she wanted to have *earned* the title.

Zoey peeked into the bag and dropped a loud kiss on Grace's cheek. "You brought me real clothes."

"What did you think I'd bring you? A ball gown? The black capris are probably going to be pants on you, but the blouse is pretty versatile and the tennis shoes are on the bottom."

"I don't know how to repay you." Zoey clutched the bag to her chest and hightailed it to the locker room, Grace close on her heels.

A few officers were in varying states of mid-dress when they arrived. Grace waited until the last one left and started her interrogation. "You want to repay me?"

Grace's tone triggered all Zoey's warning bells. "I do. But I reserve the right to decide if your price is too rich for my blood."

Grace chuckled, leaning against the far locker. "Spill. And please don't insult my intelligence by telling me there's nothing. I don't need my federally trained eye to realize that you're not wearing *your* clothes."

Zoey grimaced, slipping out of the oversized T-shirt and into a silky white blouse. "People noticed?"

"Some people can do a walk of shame without anyone batting an eye, but unfortunately, hon, you're not among them."

Zoey stepped into the pants and slid them up her legs.

She didn't want people passing their shifts trying to fill in the blanks, because what they imagined would no doubt be worse than the real thing—not that she wanted them knowing the truth either.

Grace, contemplative as she folded the discarded T-shirt, dropped her attention to the screen-printed Army insignia on its shoulder. "Holy shit! I am so freaking proud of you! I don't even care that there's an ick factor because it's my cousin. Hold on, I need to sit for a second before I keel over from shock. Seriously? *Knox?*"

"Will you be quiet?" Zoey scanned the room to make sure they were still alone.

"I have to admit that I foresaw something like this happening, but I figured that Liam's a little closer to your temperament, so I—"

"You need to stop. Right there... because *ew*. No."

Zoey wasn't embarrassed that she'd taken a chance in kissing Knox. Because she had, she knew the wicked rush that came with putting your wants and desires out there on the front line. She couldn't be sorry about that. Ever.

But everything that came afterward?

Yeah. She could forever sweep that under the rug and never speak of it again.

But this was Grace. Her honorary sister. Despite their two-year age difference, she'd been privy to a lot of her embarrassing moments growing up, but this was an all-new low that she didn't want to admit to herself, much less someone else.

"Nothing happened," Zoey told a half-truth, "except that I've fulfilled my lifetime embarrassment quota."

Grace snorted her disbelief. "Says the woman who needed a wardrobe change this morning."

Zoey tied off her shoes and finally looked her best friend in the eye. "Okay, fine. There was a kiss—which I instigated. And then I promptly got a speech. *Men like me don't mess around with women like you.* Those were the words he used. So you can save your pride for someone else."

Grace's eyes narrowed into murderous slits. "The bastard!"

"Don't make a big deal out of this." Zoey squeezed her friend's hand. "I want to forget all of it. The pub. My river dance. My apartment. I want to wipe away every single second."

"There was a whole lot of forgetting there, but what happened at your apartment?"

Zoey divulged the sordid details to her best friend, and as Grace's horror grew, so did Zoey's. Up until that moment, she'd done a halfway decent job not picturing a stranger rifling through her belongings.

"I would've felt better if they'd taken my electronics and been on their way."

"Cade didn't pack your bag and offer to pay the fee to break your rental contract?" Grace looked warily impressed. "Huh. Maybe he's mellowing."

Zoey snorted. "Yeah, no. He tried to do just that, and I'm pretty sure my apartment's going to have the same security features as Fort Knox—and I'm not talking about your cousin."

"Then he's definitely mellowing." Grace studied her carefully. "But are you sure you want to turn him down?"

Yes. No. At this point, she barely knew her name. "What would you do if the situation were reversed?"

"Not be as calm as you are, that's for damn sure."

When she'd first stepped into the precinct this morning, she'd been anything but calm. She'd hustled to the bathroom and locked the door seconds before having an old-fashioned freak-out, complete with red-rimmed eyes and flowing snot. But if she didn't hike up her Hear-Me-Roar panties, everyone in her life would go into Fix-It mode.

Her brother.

Knox.

His brothers.

To a certain extent, even Grace, though she wasn't as overbearing as the rest of her family. "I get it. And you're right. I'd probably stick to my guns too...but I sure as hell wouldn't go back until I've bleached every square inch of that place."

"That's already on my agenda. Trust me."

"Good. My room at the Basin isn't the Ritz, but come over for a girl's night, week, whatever you want. We can talk about boys and go shopping. And by boys, I mean you can tell me in explicit detail what happened with Knox."

"I'll accept the room offer but pass on the explicit details." She spun around for Grace's approval. "No longer walk-of-shame fodder?"

Grace gave a nod. "No longer fodder."

Thank God. Getting through the day without reliving the humiliation would be hard enough.

Five minutes later, they squeaked into the task force meeting room just as Captain Trevor demanded everyone's attention.

Chairs screeched as everyone took their seats. Zoey handed out forensic update packets, and as she reached the Assistant District Attorney sitting next to the captain, the last report was unceremoniously ripped from her hands.

"Better late than never." The lithe brunette pivoted in her seat, further dismissing Zoey's presence.

Zoey bit the inside of her cheek to prevent a snarky

retort. Rudeness was Francine Smoke's brand. Her nickname, the Fire-Breathing Dragon, was both a play on her last name and her attitude, and went back to when she'd dated Knox.

Once the handouts were passed around, Zoey took the only open seat, directly across the table from her brother.

"Now that everyone's here, let's get to business." Captain Trevor glanced around the room, his broad stature demanding everyone's attention. "As you can probably guess from the presence of the DA's office, the city's as eager as we are to get the Cupid Killer off the streets. Who's got the rundown on our latest victim?"

Risa Titan, from missing persons, approached the murder board and clipped a picture next to the other eleven. "Confirmed ID is Amanda Middleton. Twenty-five. Doctoral student at Georgetown. When not up to her ears in schoolwork, she worked at the Watering Hole, the college's informal location for student debauchery. Her roommate reported her missing three days ago but admitted to not seeing her for at least a week and a half."

"Nice roomie," someone down the table muttered.

Risa shrugged. "With both of them in doctorate programs it wasn't uncommon for them to go days without seeing each other. The roommate didn't think anything of her absence until she no-showed for a big exam."

"And there's no link to any of the other victims?" Cade bounced his gaze between the board and the thick file in front of him.

"Other than her looks and lifestyle fitting the young,

single professional profile? No. There's no blaring—or even a fuzzy—connection between her and the others."

"There's got to be something we're missing."

"If there is, feel free to find it, because I've been combing over the victims' histories and I can't."

"Boyfriend? Girlfriend?"

"The roomie claims she wasn't a woman-on-the-prowl type, but we have investigators checking out the local hotspots anyway. So far, nothing."

"Maybe she was a woman-surviving-in-the-city type," Zoey murmured.

Heads turned toward her, including Cade's.

Zoey's cheeks pinked. She hadn't meant to be heard. "I'm sorry, I didn't mean—"

"What *did* you mean?" Francine's cool voice held barely veiled hostility. "If you're going to interrupt, the least you could do is explain yourself."

A flash of irritation had her locking gazes with the other woman. "We have twelve victims now and according to their family and friends, none of them embraced the city nightlife. They're professionals, or hope-to-be professionals. All single. All busy. Maybe we shouldn't be looking at bars and clubs."

"What places do you suggest? The Laundromat?" Francine let out a humored snort.

Zoey didn't back down. "That's *exactly* the places we should be looking at. Along with doctors' offices and gyms. Even spas or salons. Like Amanda's roommate said, she was too busy for a romantic relationship. But friendship? *Everyone* could use a friend."

"She could be onto something." Grace aimed a wink

Zoey's way. "I mean, yes, the killer's intentions are linked to romantic circumstances—for example, the dresses and the meticulous primping. But none of the victims have been sexually assaulted. It's as if he's...taken care of them."

Francine rolled her eyes. "Taken care of them? By shackling them up until he injects them with lethal doses of Fentanyl and unceremoniously dumps them in the middle of an alley?"

Grace drilled the other woman with a glare. "There's nothing *unceremonious* about him at all. He's all *about* ceremony. About order. No doubt it's the way he was raised. It could be that his parents were in a field that required an obscene amount of structure—like the military or the medical field. Hell, lawyers. I could easily name at least a dozen occupations right now."

"Fine. He's probably got a stressful job, but to suggest that he takes care of them is utterly ridiculous. He cleans them to wash away any possible DNA."

"And how do you explain the fact that he provides first aid? He stages their resting place to the point that if they'd been lying on a bed, they'd look like they were sleeping."

"So he's the Florence Nightingale of serial killers. Comforting."

Cade slid a quick glance to Zoey. "Zoey's idea has a lot of merit, and we sure as hell haven't gotten any leads on our current course. I'll look into it."

"Then do it." The captain nodded, then gestured toward Mason. "And what does forensics tell us, Lieutenant?"

"Nothing different." Mason frowned, obviously frustrated. "Reports from the lab confirm that he's using the same surgical cleansing agent that he's been using since day one, and it's used at dentist offices, hospitals. It's even sold in drugstores and people are instructed to bathe in it prior to having surgery because it destroys normal bacteria on the body, and unfortunately, evidence. *Anyone* can get their hands on it."

After ensuring everyone was on the same path, Captain Trevor dismissed the meeting and everyone went their own ways. Zoey locked gazes with Grace and the two stepped out of the room and off to the side.

"Is it me, or was the fire-breathing dragon's breath particularly toxic this afternoon?" Grace muttered the moment they were alone. "Most people would feel sorry when a member of their family suffers from a break-up, but when Knox ended things with the Dragon, I had two celebratory glasses of Moscato."

Zoey laughed. "So did I."

"Zoey." At Cade's approach, Grace shifted at her side.

Zoey's hand quickly shot out, looping around her friend's arm. "No you don't. Not this time."

"Liam said he'd have your place locked down by this evening," Cade announced. "But I still think you shouldn't stay there. At least for tonight."

"I'm not. I'm going to stay with Grace and worry about the cleanup tomorrow." Zoey nodded to her friend, but Grace refused to meet Cade's eyes or acknowledge his presence.

"I can have a company come out and handle all that."

Zoey grimaced. "You mean more strangers touching my stuff? No thanks. I got it covered."

His mouth opened and closed no fewer than four times before he turned on his heel with a few mumbled curses.

"Little Zoey Wright cleaning up her own messes? Miracles do exist," Fran's grating voice chided. "What do you do with all your free time if it isn't spent trying to make all the guys around you bend to your will?"

Next to Zoey, Grace's chin lifted in challenge. "If it isn't Francine Smoke. You must have grown extralong talons if you were able to crawl your way out of that slime pit you fell into. How about I show you back there?"

Fran's blood red lips twisted into a sardonic smile. "Careful, Gracie. I'm working in the District Attorney's office now. I'm not exactly someone whose bad side you want to get on. Again."

"Oh. You have a briefcase. How cute." With a small grin, Grace flashed the FBI badge on her hip. "I have a *federal* badge and a gun. So now that we both know that mine is bigger than yours, why don't you go breathe on someone else."

"I'm sure I'll be seeing the two of you again." Francine stalked off on her four-inch heels.

"Am I a horrible person for wishing she'd trip and break her manufactured nose? Or at the least, bloody it a bit?" Zoey asked.

"No. Because if that makes you a horrible person, wishing she'd fall and break her uptight ass would mean I have one foot in hell." Grace rolled her eyes and sighed. "For an observant guy, it sure took Knox a hell of a long time to see through *that*. Personally, I think it was the boobs that blurred his judgment."

As Francine disappeared from the floor, something stabbed Zoey center chest—a sick, pulsing ache that turned her stomach. "I'm as far away from a Fran as it gets."

"Well, I would hope so!"

"You know what I mean, Grace. Even Knox said it. It's obvious he has a type, and I'm not it."

"You mean the soulless fire-breathing-dragon type?" Grace dropped an arm over her shoulder. "If that's what my cousin finds appealing, then count yourself lucky he gave you The Speech. Besides, scales wouldn't go well with your fair complexion—and could you imagine the cost of all that lotion you'd need?"

Zoey's laugh ended on a snort. Grace never ceased to make her see the brighter side of things. "You're right. Who needs a strapping muscle-bound man to bring all your sexual fantasies to life when you're scale-less and have a warm, blood-pumping heart?"

"And have a battery-operated BYOO."

"BYOO? Do I even want to know?"

Grace's smirk turned devilish. "Bring Your Own Orgasm. Now, about replacing your clothes…we need to have a plan of attack. I'm thinking lingerie first, and then we can swing by that cute boutique on Connecticut."

Grinning, Zoey let Grace have her fun. If there was one thing Grace took more seriously than profiling, it was shopping.

* * *

His Heart slowly fluttered from one rack to another, occasionally picking a dress and holding it against Her slender body. She and her FBI friend had already collected a healthy number of bags, and as they stood in front of the cashier of Betty's Boutique, each acquired another two.

It killed him to keep his distance, but he waited until She left to make his approach. The doorbell chimed, signaling a new customer. Him.

"Can I help you?" The attendant who'd plied His Heart with dress after dress smiled.

"I'm hoping you can. I'm looking for something in midnight blue."

"Lovely color." She came out from around the corner. "And a popular one tonight. I just sold a cocktail dress made from the prettiest dark satin."

He smiled. "Really? Do you happen to have another one? I'd love to see it up close."

"Oh, no, hon. We only sell one-of-a-kinds here...but I could probably find you something a lot similar."

"That would be incredible, thank you."

The older woman nearly batted her eyes as she led him toward a corner rack where she found another dark blue dress. "Because we don't deal with mass-manufactured items, finding the correct size can be tricky. But we have an amazing seamstress on staff who does wonders with resizing."

He accepted the dress and refrained—barely—from

caressing it against his cheek. "No, I think this one will be perfect."

"For your girlfriend? Mother? Special...lady friend?"

He found the woman's inquisition unprofessional. "No...this is for My Heart."

CHAPTER
ELEVEN

Knox parked along the curb, his well-loved truck looking like farm equipment next to the sleek Jags and Porsches decorating the Georgetown neighborhood. More than one dog walker shot him and Cade a suspicious look as they climbed out from the pickup.

"I don't think we make enough money to even walk down this street," Cade joked. "Guess we know Roman's guy isn't lying about having money to spare, huh?"

Waiting against one of the swanky gray-stone townhomes, Roman pushed off the wall as they crossed the street. "About time you two showed."

"Considering you gave us a two-hour turnaround time, you're lucky we're here at all," Knox countered.

He'd asked Roman about this meet-up multiple time in the last two days, ever since he'd gotten Cade to agree to it. Each time he'd brought it up, his brother said he was working on it and walked in the opposite direction.

Ro ignored the jibe and led the way up an ornate set of stairs. "Keep in mind that the rest of us need to maintain a working relationship with Wilcox. Bottom line— don't be an ass."

Cade grinned at Knox as they reached the door. "Is

this how the Steeles do wooing? Because I'm not feeling particularly wooed. No wonder none of you have a woman."

Roman muttered a few foul words under his breath and pressed the doorbell. A few seconds later, the door opened, and standing inside a lavishly decorated foyer was an honest-to-God butler.

"Welcome, Mr. Steele. The General has been expecting you. If you care to follow me into the study?"

Roman waved him off. "I know where that is, Charles. Thanks. We'll see ourselves there."

"Very well, sir." Charles hustled away, leaving the three of them standing in front of a grandiose staircase.

Knox glanced at Cade, and the two shared a low chuckle.

"Get it all out of your system now," Roman growled.

Incredulity covered Knox's face. "He makes his staff call him the General?"

"Because he retired as one. Wilcox comes from old money, and as much as he tried shunning it with a stint in the Army, it came back to bite him on the ass—and in the pocketbook." Roman added, "This place may be pretentious, but he's not. He's good people."

Obviously having been here a time or two, Roman led them down the hall. They bypassed no fewer than four rooms, all a hell of a lot bigger than Knox's entire boat.

General Hogan Wilcox sat on a couch, four antique guns spread out on the oversized coffee table in front of him. With a magnifying glass in one hand and a small cleaning brush in another, he examined the chamber of what looked to be Civil War era Smith & Wesson.

Short and meticulous, his gray hair and serious expression identified him as retired military. He glanced up when they entered the room, and stood. "Roman. Good to see you. And you've brought the infamous older brother as well as Detective Wright."

"Thanks for meeting us, sir. I know you're busy."

"I always have time to put minds at ease." Wilcox gestured to some chairs. "Please. Sit. Stand. I just ask that you don't pace the room. I suffer from motion sickness in my old age."

Knox wouldn't call the former Joint Chief of Staff old, and highly doubted the retired officer suffered from sickness of any kind. His wide shoulders and broad chest indicated he worked out probably as hard as he had while on active duty.

Wilcox studied them quietly before taking a seat. "Roman tells me that you have reservations about jumping on board with Steele Ops, Mr. Wright. I have to say, after reading your military history, you don't strike me as the type of man not up for a challenge."

Cade's spine stiffened, and so did Knox's. *Way to start a damn meet and greet.*

"Most of my time with the Army is classified," Cade recovered quickly.

Wilcox grinned. "Not for me."

"Isn't that comforting," Knox muttered.

Cade harrumphed in agreement. "As I told Roman, if it were any other time or place, I'd be all over something like Steele Ops. It's just not what's good for me right now. I'm happy where I am."

Wilcox studied Cade carefully with piercing blue eyes that probably didn't miss a beat. "Are you?"

"What's that supposed to mean?"

"I'm sure you enjoy keeping this city safe, but you strike me as the type of man who needs a little *more* in your life...more action, more challenge...more control. There's an awful lot of restrictions and red tape in law enforcement."

The general's all-knowing attitude finally unsealed Knox's lips. "And you're telling me that you, the man who jimmied open sealed military records, is offering a tape-free environment? Excuse my doubt."

Wilcox slid his attention to Knox. "Sounds like you have a lot of doubt, Mr. Steele...or you would've joined your brothers in DC quite a while ago."

Knox threw a glare at Roman. He stood behind Wilcox, lips pressed into a tight line, and returned Knox's hard look with one of his own.

Wilcox cleared his throat. "We're getting a bit off topic, and I apologize for my lack of social graces. Determined, loyal men of your caliber, and with your skill sets, are few and far between. The difference Steele Ops could make with *one* of you on board is vast. The lives that could be saved with *both* of you? *Limitless.* You'd be damn near unstoppable."

Truth glimmered from the older man's eyes. He believed what he said and said what he thought. No sugarcoating or easing into difficult topics. Knox had more than one commanding officer who'd been the same way.

It took a bit of getting used to, but they were usually always right.

But there was something else Knox couldn't pin. It locked on Cade and spoke through Wilcox's voice. "I understand you have a sister who's struggled with health issues the majority of her life. Am I to assume your need to remain close to home involves her?"

Cade's eyes narrowed in suspicion. "You seem to know a lot already. You tell me."

Wilcox settled back in his seat. "I value family too, Detective Wright, although most of mine are now long gone. I get your need to shelter those you care about. It took me a damn long time to figure out that sometimes on our path to keep them safe, we hurt them more."

One look at Cade's face revealed that the general's words hit home. Hell, they did for Knox too. He snuck a glance at Roman, who now stood less than two feet away. He was either a grumpy ass, or a smart grumpy ass. Knox wasn't sure which.

"I'm not here to apply pressure," Wilcox added, "and the last thing I want to do is push anyone into a decision that's not best for them and their family. But if it's your sister's future that's holding you back, rest assured that I've worked with Roman on a first-class benefits package. I hope we never have reason to execute it, but in the event of an operative loss, loved ones *will* be taken care of…*entirely*. And that's the end of my sales pitch. I hoped I've pleaded my case well enough for the two of you to consider coming on board."

"I'll think about," Cade surprised them all by saying. "No promises."

"Of course not. It's a big decision and it's not without sacrifice." Wilcox stood, and after shaking each of their hands, showed them back out to the foyer. "My door is always open, gentlemen. Feel free to stop by if you have any other questions or concerns. Roman, good seeing you again."

Roman led them outside, waiting until the door closed behind them.

"Well?" he asked the moment they hit the sidewalk.

"He's not what I expected," Knox answered truthfully. Other than that, he didn't know what to feel. He turned to Cade. "What do you think? You're the one he's trying to get on the team."

"He means what he says. He's a straight shooter."

Roman nodded. "The straightest."

Knox knew his brother believed it. Hell, he did too... if it weren't for that little tug of his gut that prevented him from hopping all the way on the Hogan Wilcox fan wagon. It was in the way he watched Cade... in the inflection of his voice when he mentioned Zoey.

His brain wrapped up in deciphering the meeting, it took him an extra second to realize Cade had spoken. "Wait. What?"

His friend threw him a devilish grin. "I said, I met with him. I fulfilled my half of the bargain and now it's time for you to do yours... and it starts tomorrow night."

It took a minute to remember. "Your self-defense class."

"Do yourself a favor and wear long sleeves. And pants. Do you have any Kevlar lying around on that boat?"

"Kevlar to teach grandmas how to gouge out a pair of eyes? Isn't that a bit overkill?"

Roman flat-out laughed. *Laughed!* The sound of it startled both Knox and Cade. "You have Knox taking over at the rec center? Priceless."

"Is there something I should know?" The more he heard about this class, the less he liked the idea of it, and especially now that it seemed to tickle his brother's damn funny bone.

"Cade's been trying to pawn that class off on everyone for months."

Cade's smirk widened. "I knew my efforts would eventually pay off. But seriously? Layers. Those ladies may have a mean age of eighty-two, but their ass pinches are no less lethal. Especially Dottie's. You gotta watch out for Dottie."

Knox climbed into his truck to the chorus of Roman's and Cade's chuckles. His first instinct was to growl about the con job, but seeing a spark of humor in Roman's eyes for the first time since arriving in DC, he clamped his mouth shut.

He'd take the small victories when he could.

Even if they were at his own expense.

* * *

Prematurely shut-off alarm clock. Ice-cold shower. Misplaced jewelry. Add in a thirty-minute late Metro bus, and a re-route to the nearest train station, and it was a sucktastic day from the second the sun peeked over the horizon.

Zoey hustled up the Metro steps and glanced longingly at the corner coffee shop, wishing she could take the gamble. Caffeine was not her friend—or the friend of anyone with a congenital heart defect. A few minutes after taking the first sip, her finicky heart would kick into hyperdrive, and make a solid attempt at bursting through her sternum.

Even *that* was tolerable compared to the heart skips. Nothing freaked Zoey out more than the sensation of her heart stumbling over itself to restart.

With one last longing glance at the coffee shop, she ran into the walking wall exiting though the door. "I'm *so* sorry. Please tell me I didn't make you spill anything."

"Nope. My rocket fuel's safe and sound, sweet pea."

Zoey's head snapped up and she chuckled. "Roman. Do I even want to know how many energy boosts you have in that cup?"

"Probably not. Can I buy you one? Or a java mocha frap something-or-other with extra foam?"

"I wish. But decaf isn't the same. It makes me sad." Zoey stepped to the side to let another customer slip past. "So where you hustling off to this morning?"

"Business meeting for Iron Bars. You?"

"Doctor's appointment at Georgetown."

"Everything okay?" Roman frowned over his coffee.

"Just a checkup. Dr. Samuel's being cautious after last year's surprise surgery. And as much as I hate being poked and prodded, it's worth it if I don't have to go underneath a scalpel again."

"As long as it's nothing serious."

"Nope. All's good here."

"I'm headed that direction if you want company on the walk."

Roman's offer to walk surprised her. Lately he'd been in slink-away mode. Two weeks ago, he'd appeared at the tail end of a joint family dinner, his knuckles split open and the bottom corner of his lip swollen. He'd played it off as an exercise injury, but Zoey didn't know of any heavy bags that punched back.

They walked the few blocks, Roman notably quiet. He'd never been the most vocal of his brothers, but Zoey registered something different, something that she noticed ever since Knox's surprise arrival.

"So Knox is back. All the Steeles are in one geographical location." Zoey finally broke the silence. "That's exciting."

"There a question in there, sweet pea?"

"Nope."

He slid her a sideways glance and sipped his coffee. "One-word answers from you is eerie as shit."

"Now you know how the rest of us feel, Mr. King of the Brood."

His lips twitched, which was no small feat. "King of the Brood?"

She shrugged off his tease with a chuckle. "Whatever. I'm just saying that it's good to have Knox back home."

At Roman's noncommittal grunt, Zoey tugged him to a stop. "Stop speaking caveman and use your *words*, Roman."

"You'll yell at me for the words I want to use."

Not oblivious to the underlying tension the other night at O'Malley's, Zoey frowned.

When Roman returned home after his military discharge, he'd had it rough. Adjusting to life without both legs. Adjusting to life without the *military*. The only thing that seemed to put a spark of excitement in his eye was knowing the reality of Iron Bars was only three brothers away.

Zoey reached for Roman's hand and gave it a squeeze. "Knox being home is a good thing, isn't it? You guys wanted Iron Bars to become a family establishment and now that he's back, it can be."

"He's not *staying*, Zoey. You remember that little fact, right? DC's nothing more than a detour. No point in hoping for things that we have no control over."

"If I lived by that philosophy, I should've just called it quits after my first surgery and been happy living in a plastic bubble."

He guided her into side hug. "That's different. You're meant for a hell of a lot more."

"Maybe Knox needs a little time to realize that he is too."

"You give him more credit than he deserves."

"Maybe. But my mom raised to me look to the positive. Where did yours go wrong with you?" Zoey teased.

Cindy Steele was the world's best mom, second only to Zoey's.

Roman chuckled. "I'll ask her the next time she calls."

"I'm just saying that nothing good comes from expecting failure. All it does is cause a lot of grief and aggravation. And not to mention that if you believe something won't work, it oftentimes doesn't."

"But if you always go around looking on the bright side, disappointment is just around the corner, ready to smack you in the face like a two-by-four."

Roman tore his eyes away from her and focused back on his coffee.

She bit her tongue, barely avoiding asking him who—besides Knox—had disappointed him. The pensive look on his face told her to let it be—for now. "I'd rather suffer a bit of disappointment than walk through life always thinking the worst."

Roman gifted her a gentle smile and dropped an arm over her shoulder. "And that's why we all love you so damn much, sweet pea."

They settled into a comfortable silence as they walked, eventually turning toward Georgetown University Hospital. A grandiose mixture of historic landmarks and modern contemporary, the six-floor hospital had been her home away from home for as long as she could remember.

More times than she could count, she'd missed classmates' birthday parties because of doctors' appointments, and couldn't participate in gym class because of post-operative restrictions. Blending in with your peers was difficult when your limitations made you stand out.

It wasn't until recently that she vowed not to let those limitations define what she could do. It was one of the reasons why she'd kissed Knox.

"Well, this is me." Zoey stopped at the entrance to the cardiology offices.

"What's over there?" Roman's gaze shot down the block. "It looks a little . . ."

"Charred?" Zoey followed his gaze toward the building that could've provided the backdrop for an apocalypse movie set. "The old cancer wing. I don't think you were back in DC yet when the fire happened. They had plans to try and restore it, but it fell through. I'm not sure why."

"That's prime DC real estate."

Zoey chuckled. "Already planning on opening an Iron Bars Two?"

Roman grinned. "You never know. I could make it Liam's pet project and get him out of my hair. That way we'd both come out winners."

"Well, *I* know I'm going to be late if I don't move my rear end." Zoey didn't give him time to escape into the crowd, squeezing him in a tight hug.

Unlike last time, he hugged back, although briefly. "See you around, kiddo."

Zoey watched him disappear around the corner before heading to Dr. Samuel's office. A few tests and bloodwork, and she could get back to disinfecting her entire apartment.

"Zoey! Perfect timing." Lisa, the medical assistant behind the desk, waved her toward the back exam rooms the second she stepped into the office. "You're positively glowing today. It's good to see you."

"You too." Zoey smiled. "Although please don't take offense, but I wish it had been a little longer since I've seen you last."

The young woman laughed and gestured toward the empty room. "None taken. Everyone who steps through these doors feels the same way. You know the drill. Arm out, fist clenched. It's time for me to go vampire."

Lisa drew five vials of blood and after sending the specimens down the pneumatic tube system to the hospital lab, wheeled the mobile EKG machine to the bedside. "Pretty painless visit today. EKG now, and then after Dr. Samuel reads it, he'll do the sonogram to make sure everything's functioning as it should be."

It took more time to put on and take off the EKG leads than it did for Lisa to run a cardiac strip. After getting a good reading, the nurse left Zoey alone to wait for the doctor, and she used the time wisely, checking her voicemails and putting out a few fires for Adam, her replacement in the lab. At a knock, she tucked her phone into her pocket.

Dr. Phillip Samuel's smile flashed her way as he stepped into the room. "If it isn't my favorite patient. I have to admit my morning had gotten off to a pretty abysmal start, but it's looking up now that I'm in your presence."

Zoey snickered. "You say that to all of your patients."

"Yes, but in your case, I mean it." With deep dimples, the thirty-some-year-old cardiologist looked like Paul Walker in *The Fast and the Furious*. His high chiseled cheekbones were covered by blond scuff, which was a new addition since the last time she'd seen him.

"Was it your father who retired or you?" Zoey teased good-naturedly.

It had been Phillip Samuel's father, George, who'd been her cardiologist since her first surgery. Sometimes, with Zoey's mother's approval, the senior doctor left his son in her hospital room while he made patient rounds. They'd played cards, or whatever travel game he'd brought with him that afternoon. Last year, the son took over for the father, both in their cardiology practice and as Zoey's doctor.

Dr. Samuel rubbed his chin as he sat on the wheelie chair. "Trying something new. So far, the majority consensus is that I look more like a surfer than a doc—which of course drives my father crazy."

Zoey lay back on the table as he prepped the sonogram machine. "How's his retirement going? Is it everything he hoped it would be?"

"He claims to love it. It took a few months, but we've finally gone from five hundred phone calls a day to a measly one hundred. He still finds time in between golf games to call in and run the office staff in circles."

Zoey followed the doc's direction, holding her breath for some images and turning on her side for others. Dr. Samuel took pictures of her heart from every angle. Eventually he pulled his gaze off the monitor and flashed her a comforting smile.

"All done. Are you staying active?" he asked, wiping down the equipment.

"I go to the gym three times a week for lightweight exercise and I take a self-defense class Friday nights at the G Street community center. Oh, and sometimes I go for a light jog, nothing too stressful."

"Self-defense, huh?" His attention piqued. "That sounds fun. Is it a women's defense class?"

"Not in the sense that it's *catered* to women. We have a few men who take the class too. And the age range is wide. My brother's the instructor and he does a good job of modifying it to everyone's specific needs."

"G Street isn't too far from my new place, so maybe I'll check it out."

"You should—just make sure you're prepared for female adoration, because there's at least a handful of them that would love a chance to be paired off with a young cardiac surgeon—or a surfer."

He chuckled, revealing his bilateral dimples as he helped her sit up. "If only my life was as glamorous as people thought."

"So what's the verdict, Doc? All good? Because I've been dying to train for the next Marine Corp Marathon, and I figured if I could—"

"Baby steps, Zoey. You'll get there, but I'm not sure you're there quite *yet*."

"It's been a year."

"I know. And all in all, everything looks fairly well. I just don't want you overdoing it too soon and losing all your progress."

Zoey's hands stilled in her lap. "*Fairly* well? Did you see something that kept it from being great?"

"It could be nothing, but there's a bit more regurgitation at the pulmonic valve than was there six months ago. It could also be because your left-sided ejection fraction is slightly diminished." Reading her panicked expression, Dr. Samuel squeezed her arm. "*Slightly*, Zoey. Practically undetectable. Have you been experi-

encing any of the warning signs? Shortness of breath?
Palpitations? Excessive tiredness?"

"No. Not at all."

"*Good*. That's good. I do have one thing I'd like to
try if you're up for it. *Amplify*." He handed her a medication information sheet just like the stack she already
had at home.

Treatment purposes. Side effects. Special precautions.

"This is something new?" she asked, scanning over
all the bullet points.

"So much so that most pharmacies don't yet have
it stocked. I'd like to try adding it to your medication
regimen."

"It won't mess things up? It took us a long time to
get my cocktail right. I'm not so sure I want to mess
with that."

"That's the beauty of Amplify. It's not a cardiac
med. It gives the medications you're currently on a
bit of a boost...helps them be more efficient. Think
of it like a vitamin for meds. No need for close lab
monitoring like with Heparin. No daily injections.
And it may not be readily available to pharmacies
yet, but it's gone through more than adequate regu-
lation trials."

"Sounds too good to be true. Where do I sign up?"

Dr. Samuel grinned. "I knew you'd be up for
it...which is why I made sure to sweet-talk our pharmacy rep into a month's worth of free samples."

He unlocked a medical cabinet and pulled out a
small orange prescription bottle. "One pill twice a day,
and then I want you here for a one-month follow-up.

And you know the drill—any of those nasty symptoms start developing . . . you call."

"Of course," Zoey agreed. She gave the doc an apprehensive smile. "You're sure there's no big problems?"

"No big problems." He helped her off the exam table. "We're doing this as a precautionary measure. That's all."

"Right. I know." She plastered a smile to her face as she said her goodbyes and checked out with the front office.

The abundance of caution angle wouldn't keep her mom and Cade off her back. When her cell phone rang, lighting up with her mom's number, she was still trying to figure out a way to spin her update in a positive way.

"Are you sure you don't have a latent psychic gift?" Zoey asked in lieu of a greeting. "I just stepped out of the office and turned on my phone."

"We were sitting here chatting about you and noticed the time," Gretchen Wright answered.

"And by *we* you mean—"

"Me!" Cindy's Steele's voice came on the line. "Now get with the talking, sweetheart. How did it go?"

"The time? Well, first the thin hand makes a quick sixty-second tick around the clock and then the long black hand moves one small notch," Zoey teased. "And then—"

"Zoey Mae Wright, you know what Cindy was asking."

She chuckled, loving her mom's antics. "I do. And everything's fine. EKG normal. Sono fine. Doc Samuel added a new med to my cocktail and I'm a free bird for another month."

"Why did he put you on something else? Has your cardiac output diminished?" Her mom caught the abnormal quickly.

"Nope. It's not even a cardiac medication," Zoey said truthfully. "It's just something to beef up the performance level of all the other ones."

"Well, you can't fault me for worrying."

"*Us*," Cindy added.

"I don't fault you—either of you. I love you both. Even when you worry for no reason other than to say that you're worried." Zoey smiled, glad neither woman could see her. One look in her eyes and they'd see the truth.

Abundance of caution or not, uncertainty gnawed away at her stomach lining.

Last year, five consecutive years of excellent health had changed with the snap of her fingers... and her mitral valve. It was hard not to be a little wary, but that didn't mean she needed to share that worry with everyone else.

"You had a break-in at your apartment, and you think I worry needlessly?" Her mom sighed on the other end of the phone. "I swear, you and your brother have each had a hand in turning me gray before my time. It's my job—"

"To worry. I know." And it had been one she'd performed enthusiastically since Zoey and Cade had first walked into her house at the ages of five and eight. Gretchen Wright never once made them feel as if they were a responsibility or a state paycheck.

They'd been *family* even before the adoption became official.

"Liam's already installed an awesome alarm system, and Grace and I are clothing shopping *again* tonight to get what we couldn't find yesterday. I'm all set. Really."

"Fine." Her mom didn't sound too convinced. "But before you rush me off the phone, don't forget about the BBQ next weekend. It's been far too long since we've had everyone under the same roof. And remind Grace that her presence is mandatory. No silly excuses because she's afraid to be in the same room with Cade."

Zoey smirked. Grace wouldn't be able to get out of a Gretchen ultimatum no matter how hard she tried. "Maybe I can convince her by reminding her that she can always push him into the river if she gets sick of him."

Her mom chuckled. "Hey, whatever works to get her there."

"And Knox," Cindy chimed from the other end of the phone. "My eldest seems to have woken up and forgotten how to return a text message, so if you could remind him about the BBQ too, that would be great."

Zoey's steps slowed to a halt. "Um…sure. I don't know if I'll be running into him before then, but if I do, I'll say something."

Part of her was upset over the possibility of not seeing him. The other half wanted to retain *some* shred of pride…which meant physical distance. Maybe he'd forget about the family picnic.

In the same second she thought it, she realized it wasn't likely. Just like she'd never do anything to displease Gretchen, he'd never do anything to earn his mother's ire.

An eerie shiver slithered down Zoey's spine. She

scanned the sidewalk for the source, certain someone had to be staring, but there wasn't anyone other than locals hurrying to their morning destinations.

No gawkers. No stragglers.

Zoey pocketed her cell phone and prayed the Metro wasn't still delayed. The last thing that would make that under-a-microscope crawling sensation go away was standing around a sublevel station waiting for a late train.

* * *

Only one thing cured the stress-induced tightness in his chest, so he booted up his laptop and waited, fingers tapping on his thigh, to see Her. He leaned back and enjoyed the weight of the day sliding off his shoulders as one image after another blinked into focus.

His Heart, towel wrapped around Her slender body, padded barefoot from Her bathroom to Her bedroom. Oblivious to his admiration, She stopped in front of Her mirrored dresser, Her back facing him, and dropped the towel.

The sight of a rose-tipped breast pulled a shuddering sigh from his lips. She was exquisite, the soft contours of Her back and bottom nothing short of artistic perfection. Even the dark pigmented line bisecting Her chest didn't detract from Her beauty. If anything, it heightened it, a physical sign of her inner strength.

All too soon, She pulled a long-sleeve top over Her head and hid Her body from view.

From behind him, angry screams and profanities

poured from around the dirty rag shoved into the prostitute's mouth. He'd gagged her an hour ago, unable to tolerate the foulness she oozed from every pore.

"You are nothing like Her." He stood, pointing to the image of Zoey playing on the screen. "You could never be anything remotely close."

Fisting the woman's brittle blond hair, he yanked her off the metal bed, and her legs, unable to bear her body weight, collapsed. He dragged her across the floor. Halfway across the room, her eyes rolled to the back of her head, and her body fell, limp and lifeless, in his hold. He carried her into his plastic-lined Purification Room, where he settled her on the table and checked her pulse.

Nothing.

Soon, her heat-flushed skin would grow cold.

He'd underestimated her resistance to drugs, not factoring in the aged track marks on her arms. Purely his own mistake, and one he wouldn't make again.

This was the part he enjoyed the most.

He pulled gloves onto his hands and prepared his cleansing agent. He didn't need to look it up anymore. Strong enough to dissolve the toughest of impurities, yet gentle enough not to harm the body, it served its purpose well.

Once the distinct odor of chemicals permeated the air, he cut away the woman's bloodied clothes, dumping each piece into a bucket to be burned later. With the dirty work finished, he turned toward his tools, already laid out and ready for use.

Sponge. Grooming pick. File. Brush.

And this time, the necklace.

Its use seemed fitting, a secret between him and His Heart; his promise to Her that no matter how far off Her path She slipped, he'd remain devoted to their future. He didn't care how long it took or how many needed to be sacrificed.

Cleanse and rinse. Clean and care. Starting from the head and traveling to the toes, he washed and bandaged, easily losing himself in the methodical movements he'd become accustomed to.

Finally, it was time.

His hand itched with the need to pick up the scalpel. The second his fingers curled around the handle, a rush of anger flowed through him, and with it, a mental movie reel of His Heart . . .

. . . leaving O'Malley's with Knox Steele.

. . . kissing him on the deck of the boat.

. . . disappearing below deck for a night of debauchery.

He breathed through the pain and brought his hand to the white, pale flesh of the woman on the table. At the first cut, air whooshed from his lungs in a prolonged cleansing breath. On the second, pleasurable tingles rolled down his spine. By the third, he already couldn't wait to do this over again.

Number thirteen would bring His Heart back to him.

As would any others that followed.

CHAPTER TWELVE

Zoey transfixed her gaze on the rear end bent over the sparring equipment and didn't feel one ounce of ickiness—because that was *not* her brother.

Gym shorts hung low on a trim waist, emphasizing the dark hair smattered over thickly muscled legs, and a sleeveless T-shirt visually pronounced that the stranger's shoulders were more than broad enough to toss a woman over...or to prop up an economy-sized van.

"It's a true testament to how much I love you that I agreed to do this instead of hitting another store. This totally goes against my *Watch, Don't Do* exercise philosophy." Grace stepped into the community center gym, wiping the evidence of their burrito stop off the front of her shirt. At the sight of the gym's new addition, she froze. "Oh wow. Never mind. I take back my indignation."

"That's not Cade's ass."

Grace's head whipped away from the mystery butt. "You mean to tell me that you were expecting *Cade* to be here and *you didn't tell me*?"

Zoey slid her friend a coy smirk and shrugged. "I figured I'd worry about keeping you here once you stepped through the doors. But the issue's moot since *that* is not my brother's behind."

Chuckling at Grace's soft mutters, Zoey led the way to her usual spot on the far right side, where they dropped their water bottles and purses. A few people offered hellos, which Zoey returned.

The G Street community center catered to everyone: young adults in the political scene, families, and even residents from the retirement complex a block over—and then there was Tracy Lynn.

The blond pharmaceutical rep stood in a classification all her own, unwilling to hold anything back, which included her cleavage, her intentions, and her words. Right now all three were being directed at the mystery instructor, making Zoey more than a tad bit envious.

Tracy Lynn lived life like Zoey promised herself she'd do.

To the max and without a worry about what others thought.

Zoey retied her left sneaker and was working on its twin when the back of her neck tingled. The longer she ignored it, the stronger it got.

It couldn't be.

Fate couldn't be that cruel.

Grace's throaty chuckle told Zoey that fate really, really could. "I hope you wore the good sports bra."

She followed the heat source to the front of the classroom, where her gaze locked on to Knox's familiar dark eyes. Tracy Lynn shifted close to his side, talking a mile a minute, and pushed her breasts closer. He seemed oblivious, and Tracy, following his line of sight toward Zoey, huffed and stalked away.

It shouldn't have given her a little thrill, but it did. She swallowed the smile that wanted to form and tugged off her oversized sweatshirt. With her hair pulled into a halfhearted ponytail and wearing a commandeered pair of Cade's old basketball shorts, Zoey epitomized functionality, not sexiness. And yet Knox's stare warmed all of her lady bits as if she strutted around in nothing but silk and lace.

"I don't even care that I ogled my cousin's rear end and am now going to need therapy." Grace's murmur barely reached her ears. "You can't pay for this kind of entertainment."

Zoey didn't have time to dwell on Knox's surprise presence before he introduced himself as Cade's replacement. The retirement ladies huddled together. Their leader, Dottie, not a day younger than eighty-eight, muttered about fresh young meat.

Knox took the obvious ogling in stride, giving Dottie a finger wag. "I guess you're the one that Cade warned me about."

Dottie smiled. "He talked about me, did he? I knew I softened him up."

"You were doing something," Knox joked dryly, smirking. "Let's go ahead and do a full five minutes of stretching and then grab your protective gear and break into pairs."

Everyone quickly hustled to their spots. Zoey finished her warm-up first and ignoring Knox, grabbed her and Grace's gear. When she returned, Grace already stood padded—and partnered.

"What are you doing?" Zoey eyed her friend suspiciously.

"You a favor. You'll thank me someday... not today and probably not tomorrow. But you will. Eventually. Besides, Edna's roomie couldn't make it to class today—arthritis flare-up." Grace's mischievous smirk overshadowed the very small speck of truth. "You don't mind, right?"

Zoey scanned the room and quickly realized everyone in the room had a partner—except her. Someone stepped behind her and she didn't need to turn around to know who.

"Lose something, angel?" Knox's voice brushed over her ear.

"Apparently my best friend." She schooled her reaction to his presence as she turned to meet his gaze. "I don't have a partner either, so I'll join another group and make it a trio."

"It'll take too much time to practice. You can be my helper. Some people learn best by seeing what they're not supposed to do."

Did he... ?

The subtle arch of one dark eyebrow confirmed he'd most definitely tossed her a challenge. Zoey swallowed her desire to tell him off and focused. "Does that mean I get to play the victim first?"

"Any way you want to do it."

Grace gave her a double thumbs-up before she and Knox headed toward the front of the room. Once there, she dropped the protective padding at his feet. "Suit up, Steele."

Knox smirked. "I'm not going to need those."

He may as well have added *for you* to the end of his sentence.

She propped her hands on her hips. "You don't put it on, you don't do the moves. Class rule."

"That may have been Cade's rule, but in case you haven't realized, I'm not your brother. Everyone wears padding...except for me."

"You're going to get hurt."

His roaming gaze slid up and down the length of her body, bringing a deep heat to her cheeks. "I'll be fine, angel."

Zoey's shoulders tightened. *Angel.*

He'd given her the nickname a million years ago and other than not knowing what she'd done to earn it, it had never bothered her. But said in *that* tone, it translated into "*little darlin'.*"

She nudged the pads away with her sneaker. "Fine, but when you're crying on the ground, don't go tattling on me to your brothers."

"Wouldn't dream of it."

Zoey wasn't bloodthirsty by nature, but being underestimated got beneath her skin. She waited as Knox went over the basics of escaping a behind-the-back bear hug.

Child's play.

His arms came around her from behind, pushing his chest snugly against her back. "Let's see if you're able to sneak away as easily as you did the other morning," he murmured against her ear.

Zoey sucked in a breath, shocked that he'd even bring up the *really bad idea*. "Don't worry. I learn from my mistakes. I'll never be in a position where I'm forced to sneak out again."

Behind her, Knox's body stiffened. She didn't wait for him to recover. She twisted her torso and tucked a leg behind his right knee. The shifted position threw him off balance and she flung her elbow in what would've been a perfect nose strike if he hadn't jerked backward.

He blinked once, then twice as sporadic laughter rumbled through the room, but he never took his eyes off Zoey. "You could've broken my nose if my reflexes were any slower."

She shrugged. "You should've put on the padding."

Grace's eighty-year-old partner harrumphed. "We're not amateurs. Teach us something that Mr. Sexy hasn't already drilled into our heads."

"What do you ladies want to learn?"

"How about strangulation from behind?" Tracy suggested.

The room went quiet, everyone looking toward the lithe blonde.

Strangulation was the media's unsubstantiated theory of how the Beltway Cupid Killer subdued his victims. Those on the task force knew different. Strangulation left bruises or marks, and none of the victims had so much as a skin rash.

Tracy blustered, propping her hands on her hips. "I can't be the only one who's freaked every time I go outside at night." Her gaze shot to Zoey. "What about you? Your general appearance has to be enough of a similarity to make you nervous, right?"

Zoey could list the ways she didn't fit the Cupid Killer's MO, but as the first one hovered on her lips,

it died. Blonde? Check. Aged twenty-one to thirty-five?
Check. Single professional? Check.

Zoey suddenly wanted to channel her inner Ronda
Rousey and learn *all* the defense techniques.

Knox looked around the class. "Is this something
you all want to learn?"

A dozen or more eager nods answered.

"Then lose the pads and grab a hand towel for each
duo."

Everyone scuttled to grab their sweat towels and
quickly returned to their spots.

Knox's hand cupped Zoey's elbow. "You sure you're
good with this?"

"We're women living in DC right now. I may not like
that we should know this, but we do."

Knox stared at her a split second longer and then gently turned her toward the class. "I want everyone to watch
first. Then we'll go through it together, step by step. Most
assailants will come at you when you're in a forward
motion. That gives them the advantage right from the
start because it throws off your balance. Watch."

Heated bare skin brushed against Zoey's back as
Knox stepped close. She glanced down to see his cotton
shirt brushing against her throat instead of one of the
scratchy gym towels.

"What does your instinct tell you to do?" Knox
asked her. "Don't think about the right self-defense answer. What's the first thing that pops into your head?"

She dipped her chin to her chest and grabbed hold of
his shirt.

"Exactly." He slackened his hold, one hand casually

dropping to her hip as he addressed the class. "Basic human survival instinct tells you to pull away. *Don't.* Once you're in a strangulation position, you have seconds before your attacker renders you unconscious, and let's face it—he picked you because he perceives you as weaker than him. You're not tugging your way out of this."

Everyone watched, enraptured with Knox's lesson, and Zoey had to admit, so was she. "So what do I do? Wiggle out of it?"

Knox gently slid the shirt back across her throat, brushing his knuckles against her skin. "Nope. Turn sideways."

"Turn? You mean face you?"

"Just a quarter step in either direction."

Zoey turned left, seeing Knox's serious expression in her periphery. "Like this?"

"Perfect." Knox fixed his gaze on hers as he stroked the pad of his thumb down the column of her neck. Goose bumps erupted over her skin, making her shiver. "In this position, your attacker can tighten his hold and you'll still have oxygen going to the brain because *this* carotid artery isn't compromised. And it works if he uses a rope or cord, or even an arm. No matter the mode, there's a gap that you can take advantage of."

"What do you do if you don't tug away?" Dottie asked, curious.

"After you twist, you go for the face. Punch it. Rake your fingers down it. Gouge out the eyes. Whatever it takes. Once your attacker's grip loosens, you run like hell and call out for help. Practice."

As everyone turned toward their partners, Knox dropped a hand to Zoey's hip and gently turned her into position. "Let's go again, angel. Don't pull away. Twist and go for the face. No hesitation. No pause."

They worked from the beginning and went through each step. Knox was right. It wasn't easy fighting instinct. It took a solid fifteen minutes before he looked satisfied with her quick attack.

With a glance around the room, and the dozen pairs still struggling against their baser instincts, he turned back to Zoey. "You want to show me what else you have while the class works out their kinks?"

"Sure."

Before Zoey asked what he had in mind, he rushed her from behind, thick arms binding her elbows to her sides. Once he had her in his hold, he hauled her feet off the ground.

Reacting on instinct, she flung her heel back. It cracked against Knox's kneecap, eliciting a low grunt. And then he tumbled them to the ground in a controlled fall, rolling his shoulders to take the brunt of impact.

"What the hell was *that*?" Their bodies less than an inch apart, Knox hovered over her, arms braced on either side of her head.

"You not paying attention...maybe *that's* how I was able to sneak away the other morning."

"So you admit to purposefully trying to evade me. Why?" Something darkened in his eyes—a speck of surprise? Challenge? Maybe a bit of both?

It wasn't a conversation she wanted to have at all,

much less in front of an audience. And a quick glance around them confirmed that the other students had abandoned their practice sessions to watch them closely.

"I'd rather not get into details." Calling on an old lesson on floor escapes, she planted her shoes on his thighs and in one hard shove, pushed herself away. Once her knees locked, she flicked one leg over his head—except she didn't entirely clear it.

Her sneaker smacked into his temple with a loud crack.

Knox teetered sideways, clutching his head. "Shit."

She scrambled to her knees and hustled to his side. "Oh my God. Are you okay? Please tell me I didn't break anything."

"Just my ego," he muttered. "What do you have in your shoes? Lead weights?"

"I wouldn't have kicked you if your head wasn't so swollen. What do you need? A paper towel? Icepack? I can drive you to the hospital—oh wait. No, I can't. I took the Metro here. Name anything else and it's yours."

Knox rubbed his head and grimaced. "That's an awfully dangerous proposition for you to make to someone like me, angel."

At Knox's loaded stare, Zoey's mouth dried, her tongue sticking to the roof. He couldn't mean...

Could he...?

No.

Because it didn't make a damn bit of sense. Heck, he'd said why himself the night on the boat. Not that she hadn't entertained the idea in her wildest dreams. Being with Knox Steele wouldn't be boring, or safe, or forgetful. And if he did sex the way he did everything else in his life, he'd put her girl parts out of commission for anyone else.

No Knox–No Entry. Or at the least, no orgasm.

From across the room, Zoey's cell burst out in an eerie rendition of the *Buffy* theme song. She wanted to kiss whoever was on the other end, but thought better of it after seeing Lieutenant Mason's number. "Mason? What's up?"

"There's been another victim."

Shock froze her vocal cords for a moment as she digested her supervisor's words. "But it's only been a few days. He's never had victims this close together."

"He shifted the tides on us, kid. I need you here to run the on-site collection area."

"You don't want me on scene with you?" Something in his tone put her on alert. Their techs were more than capable of prepping and logging, and maintaining the steady flow between the crime scene and evidence collection.

"Things are different this time, Wright. Avoid the damn doughnuts. And it might be a good idea if you bring a few thermoses of coffee. It's going to be a long night."

"I'll be there as soon as I can."

Grace hustled toward her, her own cell in hand. "I'm guessing we both just got the same call. Can I get a ride with you to the scene?"

"I took the Metro."

"I'll drive the two of you." Carrying his bag on his shoulder, Knox flashed his phone. "Cade called me. Guess he wants a fresh pair of eyes."

"Great," Zoey mumbled, not feeling the least bit thrilled. "Then I guess we'll carpool. Together."

CHAPTER THIRTEEN

Knox took Cade's request for backup seriously. Hanging on the edge of the crime scene, he mentally logged every face that came into, and around, the alley.

He didn't know much about serial killers, but a brief run-in with an arsonist overseas had taught him that criminals sometimes liked returning to the scene to watch the fallout of their handiwork.

He'd already walked the perimeter outside the police tape and snapped pics of the curious onlookers. None wore an obvious sign around their necks that read *Serial Killer Here*, but Liam could run scans through facial recognition if needed.

The downtown alley was amazingly silent for the number of cops and crime scene techs milling about. Those who talked did so with heads bowed, their voices nothing more than murmurs. Unlike the business-as-usual air from the scene a few days ago, tonight felt…different.

Tense.

"Zoey! This damn computer is bugging the hell out again! I can't handle much more of this," someone's voice rose, ending in a screech.

Knox turned toward the other side of the canopied

tent just as Zoey gently ushered a thin twenty-something guy from his chair. Talking to him calmly, she made sure he stepped away and took his place.

The smart thing to do would be to keep his distance and let Zoey do her job. There was a hell of a lot riding on this case. But he'd already proven that when it came to her, he didn't always do the smart thing.

A few hours ago, he'd been inches away from kissing the hell out of her in a room full of people, or at the very least, admitting that he didn't want her running away from him.

He wanted her running *to* him.

He wasn't sure which would've been worse, a kiss or the admission. He had no business doling out either but hadn't cared when she looked at him with her big blue eyes...just like she did now.

As if sensing his stare, she glanced over her shoulder.

Knox's feet moved in her direction before he could stop himself, and by the time he reached her, she'd already corralled the laptop into submission. He braced his hand on the back of her chair, his thumb accidentally brushing against the back of her neck—the first time.

The second time was entirely on purpose.

"You okay? You've given breaks to all your people, but I haven't noticed you taking one."

She shook her head before he even finished talking. "I'm good. The scene needs to be processed and that's not going to happen if everyone who knows what they're doing takes a time-out."

"Those are the pictures Mason's taking right now?"

"Yep." She fidgeted in her seat. Her flowery scent nearly had him taking a deep breath. "We started using the new tech a few months back. As soon as Mason takes the pics, they populate here and download real time. Then it's up to us to file them where we want them to go."

"That's pretty damn cool."

Zoey nodded, her attention riveted to the screen. Exhaustion rolled her neck in a circle and at the faint crack of her neck, she grimaced. "What I wouldn't do for some coffee right now..."

"Wish I could help you out there, angel, but you're not supposed to have caffeine, right?" Knox skated his fingers to her shoulders and kneaded her tight muscles.

Zoey's fingers paused on her keyboard. "You remember my dietary restrictions?"

"I remember a lot of your...stuff." He cleared his throat to cover the sudden awkward silence. "I also remember your penchant for diving into things without scuba gear. Overextending yourself isn't going to do you—or anyone—any good. You need to relax."

"I'll relax when we catch this sicko...which is never going to happen if I don't work." She subtly shifted away from him.

Her brush-off stung, a hell of a lot more than he expected, but she wasn't wrong. He folded his arms in front of him and yanked his head on straight. "How long do these scenes usually take to process?"

"A few hours. An entire day. It all depends on the location and circumstances." She yawned into her elbow. "You don't need to stick around. I can get Mason to give me a ride home."

"If I didn't know any better, I'd say you were eager to get rid of me," he teased.

"Eager? No. Hopeful? Maybe," Knox could've sworn she murmured.

A new image popped up on Zoey's screen, quickly followed by two others. She muttered an un-Zoey-like curse. "He's losing his soft hand."

Knox leaned over her shoulder to better see what she did. "What do you mean?"

She ran her finger along the close-up view of the victim's wound. "The skin here is smooth, and then it puckers as it comes out of the curve. Toward the bottom point of the heart, it's completely agape."

"You lost me."

"It's not one smooth, *even* stroke. He adjusted his pressure and made at least two if not more incisions." Zoey spun her seat toward him. Her abrupt move and his still-crouched posture brought their mouths within inches of touching. Startled, her gaze dropped to his mouth and back. "Oh. Um...hello lips."

He cleared his throat to cover up a smirk, and stood. "Why does the number of cuts make a difference?"

"Because in six months and twelve victims, he hasn't detoured from his execution in the slightest. What happened that made him change it *now*?"

"Exactly what I'm worried about." Grace, unsmiling and pensive, joined them. His cousin looked just as run-down as the rest of them.

"So I'm right to worry? Great. For once I hoped I was wrong."

"Nope. Not wrong. Order is how this guy gets

through a basic day. To make him deviate from that, whatever happened had to be *huge*...at least in his eyes."

Knox knew his cousin well enough to recognize what she wasn't saying. "You think he's deviated in more ways than his penmanship, don't you?"

Grace nodded. "And I think *this* is going to be his new norm."

"An unstable serial killer. Comforting," Zoey mumbled.

"We got an ID." Cade hustled toward them, slamming down a rap sheet that looked about a foot long. "Ginny Monroe."

"You already know who she is?" Knox picked up the background check and whistled. "She definitely wasn't a kindergarten teacher. Drug possession. Solicitation. Assault. And that's just since turning eighteen."

"She's also got sealed juvie records which I bet my truck are just as colorful," Cade added. "I can't even begin to explain how much Ginny Monroe doesn't fit in with all the other victims."

"A copycat?" Shit. The thought of two killers out on the DC streets left him ice cold.

"No." Zoey shook her head. "We've kept all references to the etching purposefully out of the media. To law enforcement he's the Beltway Cupid Killer, but to everyone else he's just the Beltway Killer. Heck, the public erroneously believes that his MO is strangulation, not Fentanyl."

"If he's broadening his requirements, the pool of possible victims just widened to every twenty-something blonde in Washington, DC." Knox slid his gaze to Zoey.

He didn't want to scare her, but he also needed to bring a little reality to the situation.

Smart. Blonde. And with a self-proclaimed stagnant dating life.

With the exception of Ginny Monroe, Zoey matched the profiles of every other Cupid Killer victim.

* * *

Zoey's vision blurred as she fought the exhaustion that had been riding her hard for the last hour. She'd caught herself nodding off no fewer than three times. On the fourth, a lab tech dropped something metallic behind her, and the unexpected crash was the only reason she didn't face-plant on her keyboard.

"Must. Keep. Going." She pinched her cheeks and continued logging images into the data program.

Knox's offhanded insinuation about the Cupid Killer's victim pool made it difficult not to transpose Ginny Monroe's face onto any of her blond-haired, blue-eyed acquaintances—or her own. She expected that had been his intention.

It wasn't the first time her similarities to the victims had been brought up. Cade had pointed it out about seven victims ago, but until that moment, the unfortunate women had been either graduate students or teachers. It wasn't until recently that he extended that MO to nurses...and now Ginny Monroe.

As she shifted her focus back on work, the stack of

evidence dwindled down to one lone bag. "And the light at the end of the tunnel that leads to a nice, warm bed is a... necklace."

Blinking, she adjusted her glasses and brought the evidence closer. Higher on one side than the other, the heart pendant swooped down in an elegant curl, where it melted into a smaller curvature.

Delicate. Memorable. And familiar.

"Are you trying to conjure some kind of latent laser beam power?" Knox's humored voice startled her.

Dropping the bag onto the table, she swung around and glared. "Seriously, Knox! Heart condition here! Stomp or do that annoying throat-clearing thing or yodel. But you don't ninja-walk around a woman at a homicide scene."

"I stomped." His smirk undid most of her annoyance. "Okay, I didn't stomp, but I did drag my feet. Loudly."

"Not loud enough, evidently. If you're still around for the holidays, I know what I'm buying you."

"What's that?"

"A freakin' cowbell."

She hadn't meant to mention the holidays. There was no way he was still going to be around. Iron Bars looked better every day, and once they had the official grand opening, there wasn't a reason for him to stay.

Still, she couldn't help but notice he didn't correct her. And she sure as heck couldn't ignore the roll of flutters that went to her stomach at the idea of him being around months from now.

Knox jutted his chin to the collection bag she held. "What do you have there?"

She mentally scolded herself for daydreaming. *Again.* "The victim's necklace. Which is yet another deviation from the BCK's norm."

"Cade said none of the others wore jewelry, right?"

"None. A few had indentations from rings they'd obviously worn a long time, had tan lines, et cetera, but they'd always been removed. Until this one. It's just..."

"What?"

Part of her wanted to keep her mouth shut. Coincidences happened all the time, and mass production made the chances all the more likely. But her other half was more than a little freaked out.

"You're keeping me in suspense here, angel."

"I'm debating whether I'm going to keep you there," she said honestly, weighing the two possible outcomes against each other.

Reinventing herself as a strong independent woman was difficult to do if she was skittish of all the what-ifs. The other scenario involved an overprotective brother, four Steele bodyguards, and the evaporation of any and all Zoey-alone-time.

Both scenarios sucked.

She took a breath and came clean. "I have a necklace a lot like this one."

Knox's dark-eyed gaze settled on her like an anvil. "Could you repeat that?"

She let out a shaky laugh, already sensing an incoming babble-fest. "I'm pretty sure Georgetown Med buys them in bulk. They hand them out to patients following open-heart surgeries. I have a small collection at home... all slightly different."

Knox's silence had Zoey pushing her glasses to her nose. *Damn her nervous tick*.

"Stay here," Knox ordered abruptly.

She narrowed her eyes, her nerves shifting into annoyance. "You know I'm not a poodle, right?"

"Just stay. *Please*. For one minute." Putting it into request form looked as if it physically pained him.

She rolled her eyes. "I'm sitting. But only because I have to finish *my job*."

He watched her another second before stalking across the alley, no doubt to her brother. She grumbled under her breath as she finished logging the necklace into the database.

"Last one." Zoey handed the bag to her assistant and watched as he locked it up in the case. She stood and stretched out the muscles that had tightened into knots during the course of the last few hours.

"Wright! Give me a hand?" Mason waved her over to help wrap up the scene.

She signed the victim—Ginny—over to the coroner, where she'd be processed and autopsied, and then Zoey and Mason packed up their gear. Once everything was loaded onto two carts, she grabbed the nearer one and lugged it toward the CSI van across the street.

Both the crowd and the cop presence had wound down considerably, someone having already removed the crime scene tape. Trash scraped across the sidewalk like urban tumbleweeds.

Zoey eyed a lone blue sedan a half block away and turned the corner, narrowly avoiding barreling into a pedestrian.

"Holy fudge." Her heart jumped nearly as high as she did. "I didn't run over anything important, did I? I am so sorry."

"Not a problem." The man barely paused his brisk pace as he headed in the opposite direction.

Wearing a dark blue baseball cap pulled low over his eyes and his parka collar tilted up, the man's face was obstructed from her view, but something familiar in the lilt of his voice had her watching him until he turned the corner at the next block.

She just couldn't pin it down, her mind too exhausted to think straight.

"I really need my bed," Zoey muttered.

"Join the club, kid." Lieutenant Mason waited for her a few feet away. "Do you want me to drop you off at your place or are you hitching a ride with Steele?"

As if the name had magical powers, Zoey's cell dinged with a text.

Grace: Where are you?

Knox is buggin' out.

He said he told you to stay put.

Zoey snortled, and replied quickly.

Tell Knox I failed obedience school.

And I'm getting a ride home with Mason.

Not giving Knox's reaction another thought, Zoey accepted Mason's offer and helped him pack the van. She felt slightly bad for evading Knox the way she was, but the eerie shiver that danced down her spine—the second time that day—told her it was probably for the best.

Paranoia wasn't exactly sexy.

She needed to shake it off.

She needed to binge-watch happy Hallmark movies.

She needed to climb into her bed, pull the covers over her head, and sleep for a million years.

CHAPTER FOURTEEN

While parts of Zoey's job would never fully leave her, she'd been decently successful at compartmentalizing her duties. Home life. Work life. Two separate entities. But for the last two days, the image of Ginny Monroe's lifeless body had followed her home and walked straight into her nightmares.

She could blame her new meds, or it being only her second on-site case. Or she could blame the fact that she'd torn her apartment apart—again—to search for the necklace she was positive had been in her destroyed jewelry box.

But blaming others—people or situations—didn't solve anything.

At least that's what her mom told her on days Zoey got down on herself about her health. Surprisingly, it could be used to things other than congenital defects.

"Hey, Liam." Zoey pulled her thoughts away from things she couldn't control and focused on what she could—her designated corner of the Iron Bars lobby. "Did you pick up any miracles when you did your home improvement run? Because I'm pretty sure that's the only thing capable of fixing *this*."

"It can't be that bad." Liam came up next to her and hissed. "Well, hell. Look at that. I guess it can."

"This is going to take more than a dab of spackle and a few coats of eggshell."

"Watch the miracle happen." Liam shot his attention across the room. "Hey, Tank! You got something up your sleeves for a hole that could sink a battleship?"

A low chuckle drifted across the room before the man in question, Hunter Dawson, headed their way. Tall, broad, and with an easy smile and sweet Cajun drawl, Roman's friend from the service had dropped by for a visit and ended up being roped into physical labor.

Liam grinned. "This guy's a one-man construction crew. I'm tempted to see if we can get his discharge papers signed early."

Tank's smirk widened. "And deprive me of knocking around a few more bad-guy heads? Don't you dare, Steele."

"You'll get to knock around more when you join Steele—" Liam's gaze shot awkwardly toward Zoey. He cleared his throat. "I mean, I'm sure they won't be the last heads you knock around. This world's full of assholes who deserve a good beat-down."

Zoey glanced back and forth between the two men. "I will never understand your language."

Liam smirked. "The Language of Awesome?"

"The language of stupidity more like it." Grace sauntered into the room and set two travel cartons of coffees onto the only finished flat surface in the room. "Coffees up. A half dozen black sludges for the Neanderthals. Decaf for their female counterpart. Hot chocolate for me."

Zoey reached for her decaf. "I'm a female Neanderthal?"

Grace gave her a pointed look. "Is that coffee in your cup?"

Zoey peeked inside. "Looks like."

"Is it black? No sugar. No flavored creamer or anything that could remotely make it taste less like battery acid?"

Zoey sniffed her mug. "Smells like it."

"Then yes, you're a female Neanderthal who obviously has a grudge against your stomach lining." Grace sipped her own travel cup. "Mmm. Nothing's. Better. Than chocolate."

"For six-year-olds, and apparently, my cousin." Liam ruffled Grace's hair and dodged away before she could hit him in retaliation.

By the time everyone stopped teasing Grace about her drink of choice, Tank had fixed the hole with a patch and slathered the mat into place. "All good. Let it dry for about an hour, and then you can sand it smooth and paint over it."

"Did you do home improvement before joining the Navy? Helped with a family business or something? You seem to know an awful lot about this stuff."

"The family business?" Tank barked out a laugh. "No, chère. Just learned by reading. A lot."

His response brought up a lot of questions, but she didn't feel right asking.

Ryder called the guys to the other side of the room, leaving Grace and Zoey alone to paint the far wall while the spackle settled.

Grace dipped her roller in the off-white color and grimaced. "Painting the walls this color feels like aiding and abetting. It's boring."

"It's a *distillery*," Liam called out, hearing the complaint. "If we paint it sunflower yellow, every man's ball sack will shrivel the second they walk through the door."

Grace shot him a glare. "It doesn't have to be yellow. There's blue. Or hell, even a soft green."

"Stop moaning and start painting, *Martha*."

Zoey, smirking over her friends' razzing, leaned toward Grace and murmured, "It may be boring, but the cream's going to make the dark hardwood stand out."

Grace's lips twitched. "I think so too, but I'm not telling *him* that he made the right decision. And speaking of decisions...what are you going to do about Delicious Dawson?"

Zoey blinked, unsure what one thing had to do with the other.

"Do not even play coy." Mirth danced in Grace's brown eyes. "Are you going to tell me that you haven't noticed that his attention lingers over here a little too much for it to be casual?"

"I haven't the slightest clue what you're talking about." She shot her gaze to the other side of the room where Roman and Tank, under Liam's guidance, worked in tandem to drop a slab of granite in place over the bar.

Grace rolled her eyes. "You're such a lying sack of poo. I know you're usually oblivious to this kind of thing, but he's not exactly keeping it low-key."

"He's been overseas for months, with mostly other guys for company. It's harmless."

"I'm not so sure everyone sees it that way."

Zoey followed her gaze to where Ryder and Knox carefully installed the glass windows to the antique liquor cabinet. But where Ryder's eyes were focused on the job in front of him, Knox's dark gaze glared toward the bar—and Tank.

Butterflies fluttered in her stomach as she contemplated the possibility—for about two seconds. Knox's game of hot and cold was enough to give a girl whiplash.

Their mind-wiping kiss had been followed up with an epic brush-off. Then there'd been the half-hidden innuendos during self-defense class and his living shadow impersonation at the crime scene. And then nothing.

They hadn't spoken in two days and yet he always seemed to be around. It was more than a little frustrating...and confusing.

"He's on guard duty because he promised Cade he'd keep an eye on me. *Guys like him don't mess around with women like me*. Remember?" Zoey reminded herself as much as Grace.

"I don't know who's denser. Him for saying it, or you for believing it." Grace stepped off the stool and hoisted a lunch cooler into Zoey's hands. "Live-action experiment time. Go hostess and hand out these sandwiches. See what happens."

She knew her friend had more in mind than her acting as waitress. "What are you trying to do?"

"Prove a point. Why are you so hesitant?"

"Because I've known you for a long time and you always have a hidden agenda."

Grace's grin transformed from naughty to downright mischievous. "It's not so hidden, Zo. Serve. Talk. *Smile*. That should be about enough. Go. The boys look famished."

Zoey couldn't believe she was about to cave, but it was close to lunch and her own stomach growled, protesting her skipped breakfast. She took the cooler. "Fine, but only because I'm hungry and it would be rude to eat in front of others."

She ignored Grace's chuckle and went over to where Liam, Roman, and Tank had finished securing the tabletop into place. Sweat poured off them, soaking their shirts.

Roman yanked his off and mopped his head. "This workout is better than hitting the gym."

"You should still hit the gym afterward. You're looking a little soft around the middle." Liam drilled a teasing punch into his brother's stomach.

The idea of Roman needing to amp up his exercise regimen was laughable. The man was one giant slab of hard muscle. Still, his impressive ab display didn't faze Zoey in the least. The only one who would—Knox—had remained fully clothed for the entire day.

She set the cooler by the guys' feet. "It looks like everyone's worked up an appetite. What'll it be? Chicken salad? Roast beef? Or turkey breast?"

"I'm a breast man myself." Ryder grinned, obviously meaning the double entendre as she tossed him his sandwich. "Thanks, Zo."

Liam and Roman dove into the chest, fighting over the same roast beef sandwich despite there being at least three of them.

Tank waited until they finished scuffling and pulled out a chicken salad. "Thanks, chère. Do we have you to thank for these?"

"If you mean that I ordered them from the deli across the street from my place and then picked them up on my way here, then yes. If you mean did I put them together? No. I burn water."

Liam spoke around a mouthful of beef. "She speaks the truth, man. You're probably thinking, no one can burn water, but Zo can—and did. I was there when she had to trash the pot because she couldn't get the black shit off of it."

Zoey smacked him in the chest, making him cough on his sandwich. "See if I ever invite you over for dinner again."

"Thank you. That's the kindest thing you've ever said to me." Liam smirked, dodging another smack.

Tank smiled shyly. "Maybe we can go easy on both our smoke alarms and grab dinner sometime. Together."

Grace's soft chuckle drifted over from the other side of the room. Ryder and Liam chewed their sandwiches, watching unabashedly as their gazes bounced from her to Tank and back. Even Roman looked on with interest.

She should accept, set a date and time, and relish in the fact that a *nice* guy asked her out. She may not have known him long, but it didn't take more than a few seconds to realize Hunter was as far from Scott Reed as it got.

Something stopped her from accepting. Something

that she suspected was connected to the all-too-familiar warmth settling on the back of her neck. "If you keep hanging around this brood chances are high that we'll be sharing meals together pretty often."

Tank smiled, not looking the least bit deterred, or upset. "I hope you're right."

Someone's watch ticked, filling the silence. No one talked. No one moved until Zoey grabbed the nearly empty cooler and tucked it back in the corner, earlier hunger forgotten. "I'm going to look around for any other battleship-sized craters. I'll be back."

Zoey headed toward the doorway connecting the front and back rooms, but she needed to pass Knox to get there. With less than a foot to go before she was in the clear, his stance shifted and his arm brushed hers.

Tingles ran up from the point of contact and zipped to every nerve ending in her body. She glanced up as she passed and immediately wished she hadn't... because if she was confused about him before, she was even more so now.

Knox looked... relieved.

Because she was leaving? Because she'd turned down Tank's offer?

She couldn't shed the question as she walked through the back halls of Iron Bars. Up stairs and then down, making a left, then right, she went deeper into the building than she'd ever gone before, reaching an unfamiliar, slightly ajar iron door.

In contrast to the run-down look everywhere else, the door looked new, a state-of-the-art scanner mounted on the wall next to the handle. She'd heard of extreme measures businesses went to in order to protect family recipes, but this seemed a bit overkill.

Lights, probably on a motion sensor, flickered and then stayed on as she entered the open rotunda. Her eyes widened to anime orbs.

Filled with computers and wall-mounted screens, the room was shaped like a wheel. Doors and corridors branched out like spokes. On the left, a display pen showcased a myriad of weapons from handguns to ones she'd seen in action films. Long, lethal knives and what looked to be throwing stars blinked under the bright overhead lights.

"Didn't know making vanilla-flavored vodka takes a freakin' armory," Zoey murmured.

"It doesn't."

Zoey spun, heart pounding in her chest, and faced Knox. "Didn't anyone ever tell you it's impolite to go around scaring people into massive heart attacks?"

"Didn't anyone tell you that it's impolite to snoop?" Knox leaned against the doorjamb. He didn't look upset, or angry. He didn't look much of anything, his face in that blank emotionless mask she'd come to expect.

"I didn't mean to snoop. The door was open and—"

"It should've been closed and locked. Not your fault."

She glanced around the room. "Either the distillery business is a lot more cutthroat than I thought, or this is something else."

"Definitely something else." Knox brushed against her as he walked past, gesturing to each of the doors. "There's a makeshift barracks down that corridor, and the hall next to it leads to a series of conference rooms.

A workout room is on the left, and that far corner will eventually be a full kitchen."

"A person could live here."

"That's the plan—not living down here, but that we could if we needed to."

"So you can make flavored booze? That's the story you're going with?" Zoey didn't blink away from his intense stare. When he didn't answer, she scoffed. "Glad to see that everyone's still playing the game of Let's Protect Zoey From Everything More Threatening Than a Shadow."

"It's not just you, angel. Even our mom doesn't know about what happens down here."

"And that's supposed to make me feel better?"

"No, it's supposed to make you realize the gravity of the situation." He nodded around the large circular room. "You're standing in the epicenter of Steele Ops. Anti-terrorism. Anti-corruption. Anti-anything that threatens people on a global scale. It's an elite private security firm—emphasis on *private*. The guys aren't going to make many friends outside of a select few military brass. The less who know, the better."

Zoey pretend-zipped her lips and tossed the key before her gaze tracked back to the weapons. "This makes so much more sense than a distillery."

Knox chuckled. "I tell you that my brothers are basically forming their own little army and that's your first comment? The distillery's still a legit business, angel. It's just not the primary venture."

"What about Grace and Cade?"

"What about them?"

"Do they know about this little side venture?"

Zoey saw the answer on his face and tried not to get offended. "I'm going to take a wild guess and say that you've been trying to convince my brother to jump back into his camo and he's told you to take a flying leap."

Knox's lips twitched. "Something like that."

"Don't give up on him yet. He likes working at the DCPD, but it's not what he wants. Not really."

Knox watched her carefully. "And you'd be okay with him jumping on board? It's not a cozy desk job."

Zoey wasn't sure she liked his tone. "Contrary to popular belief—or at least *yours*—I *am* intelligent enough to understand the concept behind a private security firm. Will I miss him when he's not around? Yes. Will I worry? Definitely. But he'll be happy and that's what matters. Lord knows it's about time I supported him for a change."

"Cade hasn't minded looking after you one bit. None of us have."

Zoey's blood pressure spiked, making her vision go wonky. "That's not exactly the point."

"Then what is?" He took a step closer.

"As long as Cade stays with the DCPD, he's always going to sacrifice what he wants to take care of me." An idea struck. "Maybe I should take Tank up on his offer. Maybe seeing me as something other than the little girl you guys had to cart up the hill on your backs will shake Cade's screws back into place."

With renewed determination to get both her life and her brother's back on track, Zoey headed toward the door. She'd barely gone three feet before Knox hooked an arm around her waist and spun her toward him. She collided against his chest with an oomph.

"What are you doing?"

"You're seriously going to accept that date with Tank hoping that Cade will wake up?" Knox demanded. His rough tone threw her off-guard.

"As long as I'm honest with Tank about it, I don't see why I shouldn't. If you have any better ideas, throw them out there. What would it take for *you* to stop seeing me as your best friend's little sister?"

"Nothing. Because I know all too well that you're not a child," Knox growled—and then his mouth dropped onto hers.

On first contact, her body responded, mouth opening to accept the slow swipe of his tongue. Her hands slid over his shoulders and into his hair, dragging him even closer. Knox's touch had had a disastrous effect on her the last time, but it was nothing compared to now.

Her knees buckled, turning to jelly. His arm, wrapped snuggly around her waist, tightened until a telltale firmness pushed against her stomach.

Her body arched against his, and it pulled a low groan from Knox's throat. "Does *that* feel like I don't know you're a woman, angel?"

"No. It feels *incredible.*"

He nibbled her bottom lip. A needy whimper slipped from her throat. Knox, as if reading her mind, skated his hands down her back and over her hips. "Lock your legs around me, Zoey."

He helped guide her legs into position, and the second they locked behind him, he walked them toward the nearest flat surface. Her bum hit the table, and she slipped her hands beneath his shirt, running her palms up the rock-hard planes of his chest.

She half expected him to pull away, to show the remorse she'd seen after the boat kiss. Instead, he kissed what his hands couldn't touch, their mutual greed making her feel more alive than she'd ever felt before.

"Knox." She opened her mouth to let out a moan of encouragement and got cut off by a throat clearing.

"Sorry to interrupt." Roman stood by the door, his lips pressed into a tight line. "Actually, no, I'm not."

Knox ripped his mouth away but didn't move from between her legs. He didn't apologize. He didn't even look away, keeping his gaze on her as he spoke to his brother. "What do you want, Ro?"

Knox's ragged breath matched hers as he waited for an answer.

"Not coming to the Ops Center to find my brother mauling our friend's baby sister would be a good start. Second would be you giving a flying fuck about our livelihoods and wanting to be here. But I feel greedy asking for too much." Roman's hard glare shifted from Knox to Zoey, visibly softening. "You need to be careful, kiddo. He already has one foot out the door."

Knox stalked angrily toward Roman, stopping inches away. "Keep talking and see what happens."

"What? You mean Zoey hearing the truth? Or did you decide to stick around and forget to tell us?" At Knox's strained silence, Roman snorted. "Yeah, I didn't think so. She deserves to know what she's getting into with you, and if you're not going to tell her, then I sure as hell am."

"You don't know a damn thing about me, Ro. Not anymore."

"That's where you're wrong. I probably know you better than you do." Roman stepped back, eerily calm compared to Knox's tense stance. "Both of your absences are getting noticed."

Roman issued Knox another scowl before walking out of the room.

Zoey slipped off the desk and straightened her shirt. Not knowing quite what to do, she approached slowly. "I know this is a stupid question, but are you okay?"

"Never better." His wildly ticking jaw muscle said otherwise.

She gently touched his arm and it tensed, feeling like velvet-covered steel. "I'm not going to push or make some grand speech about you lying your rear end off right now."

"Zoey—"

She shook her head, cutting him off. "I don't need explanations. Just know I have a pretty good set of ears if you need them. Or not," she added when he turned his gaze toward her. "Great. Good talk. If that's all settled, we should probably get back upstairs."

His hand caught hers. "About what he said..."

Zoey glanced down to where their fingers had automatically entwined. "About you not wanting to be here or you having one foot out the door?"

"Both."

"I already knew you weren't planning on staying home, Knox. The only difference is that you're leaving behind more than just the distillery."

"It's not how it sounds." Knox scrubbed a palm over his face. "Or maybe it is. At this point, I don't even fucking know anymore. But he's right, angel. You need to be careful around me."

"I've played it careful my entire life. I'm tired of it." In a rush of moxy, she tugged his mouth down to hers for a short, but impactful kiss.

She pulled away to the sound of his soft groan. "You're killing me here, sweetheart."

"Good. Then my evil plan is working." She flashed him a saucy wink.

Knox muttered under his breath, making her grin widen as she headed for the door.

"Zoey."

She looked back at him still standing in the same spot. "Yeah?"

Excitement tingled down her spine at the lingering heat darkening his eyes. "No more talk about giving Tank *a shot*."

"Is there any reason why I shouldn't?"

Knox stalked toward her with the ease of a predator eyeing his prey. Every step sent a small flutter to her stomach. By the time he breached her personal space, those butterflies turned into pterodactyls. "There are tons of them. As soon as everyone leaves, I'll start listing them out for you . . . one by one."

She scrunched her nose. "I've never been a fan of lists. I much prefer hands-on demonstrations."

Knox's lips twitched with the threat of a smirk. "Be careful what you wish for, angel."

CHAPTER FIFTEEN

An hour after Knox and Zoey headed upstairs to Iron Bars, Knox realized his hands-on demonstration wasn't going to happen—at least not tonight. Roman's foul mood made sure of it. Now, five long hours of manual labor later and with everyone gone, it was time for the inevitable heart-to-heart.

Or ass-kicking.

Knox leaned against the bar top and waited until Roman breached the doorway. Seeing him, he came to an abrupt halt.

"For a man who couldn't be bothered with us for two years, you sure do show up a lot." Roman turned his back and grabbed his car keys from the wall-mounted hook.

"I need you to do me a favor," Knox said.

Roman let out a humorless snort. "That's rich. Excuse me if I don't feel like making *your* life easier."

Knox stepped in Roman's way as he headed for the exit. "Too damn bad. Because Zoey's off limits. If you have a problem with me, you bring it to *me*, and leave her out of it."

Roman looked genuinely surprised—for a second. "You brought her into it the second you shoved your tongue down her throat. What the fuck, man? It's *Zoey*."

"Aren't you the one who said she was a grown-up able to make her own decisions?"

"Yeah, and I meant her job. Where she lives. You? You're not a decision. You're a bad bet. You said it yourself. You're not staying. But while you're here, you're going to what? Get your rocks off with our honorary little sister? That's fucked up."

"I don't know what this thing with Zoey is, but I know it's none of your business." Roman's words hit a little too close for Knox's comfort. He turned to leave, not wanting to hear any more.

Roman followed. "Actually, it *is* my business. Who do you think's going to mop up the mess when you leave her broken? Who *always* cleans up your messes? Who takes over when you drop the ball?"

Knox spun to face him. "What do you want, Ro? Me to leave? You want me to untie my boat and sail the hell away right now?"

"That's what *you* want, isn't it? Why the hell did you even bother coming back?"

"You're pissed I didn't come home. You're pissed I did. You're pissed I made plans to leave. Somehow, Ro, I think you just like being pissed. Because if you're busy being ticked off at the world around you, you don't have to look in the fucking mirror."

"I look in the mirror every damn day. And do you know what I see?" Roman pushed his face within inches of Knox's. "Someone who didn't think you were capable of writing off his entire existence for *two fucking years*.

So you're right. I *am* pissed. *At me.* For being so stupid as to look up to my big brother."

Knox knew it had taken a lot for Roman to admit what he just did. Though part of him wished he'd chosen to throw a punch instead, the other part of him knew this was good. For both of them.

"I wanted to come home. More than you know," Knox admitted gravely.

"Yeah? Did someone tie you up? Keep you hostage in some cabin in the middle of nowhere?" Roman asked snidely.

"My final mission before discharge went sideways. I let my temper get the best of me. Made a bad call. And people got hurt because of it."

Roman waited as if expecting more. "You're not the first one to make a shit call, brother."

"No, but it's the first time it happened to *me*. My body may have gotten off that Boeing two years ago, but my head sure as hell didn't."

"You know what didn't come back with me? My fucking leg. And yet I still managed to make good on my promises...so you can stow your head-shit up your ass." Roman studied him as only a brother could. "What's the real reason you stayed away? Because we both know it's not as simple as a botched call."

"You guys deserve to have someone watching your back who isn't doubting every single decision that runs through his head. Isn't that enough?"

Roman shook his head. "Not buying it. Because you would've told us that you needed time and there isn't a single one of us who wouldn't have understood."

Knox fought to keep his face impassive, but Roman glared hard, practically digging through his head with the power of his stare alone. Creepy-ass Special Forces shit. A clock ticked in the background, the sound like a cannon in the otherwise quiet room.

Finally, Roman gave a noncommittal grunt. "You stayed away because you thought you were protecting us, didn't you?"

"I don't know what you're talking about." Knox turned, but Roman grabbed his arm, hauling him back.

"The hell you don't."

Knox snapped, years of frustration boiling through his veins. "You want the truth? Fine. Yes. I stayed away because everyone was dealing with their own shit, okay? It wasn't right for me to add to it with my own issues."

"I think that's the most ridiculous thing you've ever said, and there's been a lot of stupid shit that's come out of your mouth in thirty-one years."

"Not so ridiculous when you think about it. I got Ma's emails, Ro. It didn't take a genius to figure out she was worried about your sorry ass."

"Me?"

"Problems adjusting to life with your prosthesis? Hitting the bottle a little too hard? Your disappearing acts, and better yet, sudden reappearances looking as if you'd gone a few rounds with Mike Tyson? No way in hell was I about to add onto it with my shit, not if I just needed some time to get my head on right."

"*Two years' time?*" Roman asked, not denying anything he said. "You didn't need more time. You needed a swift kick in the ass, and you didn't come home because you knew I'd be more than happy to give it to you."

"Since you're an underground fighter?"

Roman's dark eyes widened. "How the hell did you—"

"Because I know how your mind works. And I'm not going to tell you to stop because I know it's probably helping you work through stuff, but I am going to remind you that if Ma ever finds out, whatever she does to you is going to be a million times more painful than anything you find in that ring."

"It's not so much a ring as it is a mystery-stained cement floor."

Knox's lips twitched. "Semantics."

Roman grinned, the sight of it momentarily stunning Knox quiet. "Did we just have our own version of a heartfelt conversation?"

"Think so." Knox rubbed his chest, feeling as if a weight had been lifted. "Let's not do it again, okay? That was fucking painful. Thrown punches are definitely the way to go. Hell, it's what I was expecting at the start of this."

"Yeah?" Roman's fist whipped out, the impact propelling Knox into a stack of glasses. "Better?"

"What the hell was that for?" Knox wiped a trail of blood off his bottom lip.

"Didn't want you to walk away without your expectations being met. And for thinking that we'd be better off without you."

"We good now?"

Roman's mouth slid into a half smirk. "Good-ish. But

I reserve the right to change my mind without notice because you're still a jackass. And about the Zoey thing... hurt her, and a single thrown punch is going to be the least of your problems. And I can guaran-damn-tee that I won't be the only one jumping in on the action."

"I have no intentions of hurting Zoey," Knox said truthfully.

"Good intentions doesn't mean it's not going to happen."

This time, Roman's statement didn't drip with animosity. And he wasn't wrong. Bad shit happened with the best of intentions.

There wasn't a minefield in DC. No IEDs buried beneath Pennsylvania Avenue. But no active warfront didn't mean there wouldn't be casualties while he figured out what the hell he was doing with Zoey.

Knox just had to make sure that he'd be the only one.

* * *

Zoey tossed and turned, unable to find a comfortable position. Short of sleeping on her head, she'd tried them all. Most of them at least twice. Eventually, she climbed from bed in a grumpy huff.

Her skin buzzed with the need for... something. And it wasn't ice cream.

It was Knox.

She still couldn't wrap her head around how brazen she'd been in the basement. But whenever she tried excusing her behavior, she realized she didn't want to. She'd liked the woman who'd kissed him first, who'd flashed him a little wink before walking out the door.

That woman was let down that he'd stayed behind at Iron Bars while Liam took her home. It was also why she'd yet to fall asleep at near midnight.

Snuggles jumped off the bed. Mid-stretch, he lifted his rump in the air and yowled.

"You don't need to get up too."

He followed her toward the kitchen, amplifying his annoyance the closer she got to his treat drawer. He pushed his big body between her legs, tripping her. "Okay. Okay. I get the hint. If I'm getting a snack, so are you. Pushy furry thing, aren't you?"

Zoey dolloped a small portion of wet food into his bowl. When he eyed the amount in kitty-disgust, she rolled her eyes. "Take it or leave it."

He took it, devouring it in a few sloppy-sounding seconds.

That done, Zoey glanced around her apartment for something—anything—to do. Nothing would be on TV, and she wasn't in the mood to read the thriller she had sitting on her coffee table. *No thank you.* Real life freaked her out enough.

Opting for a hot bath, she passed her sliding glass doors on the way to the bathroom, when the bottom latch caught her attention. The little knob wasn't fully engaged into the locked position. She turned it around and double-checked it, and every other door and window, for good measure.

At the small window above her sink, she glimpsed a wide-eyed face staring back at her. Her heart jumped into her throat as she teetered backward... and realized the other figure did the same.

Her freakin' reflection.

"Zoey, zero. Paranoia, five thousand." Her heart barely resumed its normal steady thump when an abrupt knock sent it into another sprint.

Only two people had the moxie to stop by this late at night. "I'll let you in if you're carrying a pu pu platter or combination fried rice. Otherwise, go away."

"Sorry, angel. No fried rice. I could probably handle a hot dog from the convenience store around the corner if you give me five minutes."

Zoey's hand froze on the door before she pulled it open.

Wearing the same clothes as earlier, Knox leaned against her doorway. Dark stubble had overrun his jaw since she'd last seen him, but it was his slightly swollen bottom lip that caught her attention.

Her hand reflexively touched it. "What happened?"

"Had a discussion. It went pretty well."

"Good discussions end with fisticuffs?"

"When they happen with my brothers." He ran his hand down her arm and to her fingers.

She hadn't realized she was still touching his mouth, but instead of letting her pull away, he held her hand loosely in his.

"Can I...?" He glanced into her apartment.

"Oh. Sorry. Yes. Come in." She stepped to the side, half expecting him to change his mind. He not only came inside, but crowded her against the wall as he closed and locked the door behind him.

Nerves sent her slinking off to the open living room, and eventually, the kitchen. She grabbed a water and downed half of it, and when she turned, Knox stood in the entryway as if he'd always been a fixture in her place.

"Do you want a water? Or ice for your jaw?" she asked.

"I'm good."

She tried summoning the Zoey from the Iron Bars basement but close quarters and Knox's arrival evidently sent her packing. "So to what do I owe the pleasure of having Knox Steele in my apartment? At almost midnight."

"Couldn't sleep, and I was out driving and happened to see the light on. Thought I'd stop by."

"And of all the condos, you knew which windows were mine? Is this some creepy Steele Ops tactic?"

He didn't grin, his eyes serious. "I'm not part of Steele Ops. At least not technically."

"Is that why you got that?" She gestured to his swollen lip.

"Not for the reason you're probably thinking." Something darkened his eyes before he muttered a curse and headed toward the door.

"Where are you going?" She followed him.

"I shouldn't have come over."

"Then why did you?" She caught his arm, and they both looked down to where their hands touched. "Unless you make a habit of visiting women's apartments late at night, you must've had a reason to stop by."

"The day didn't end like I'd hoped."

Her heart galloped in her chest. "And how did you hope it would end?"

"At the very least? With another kiss like we had at Iron Bars."

"And at the most?" Damn. Was that her breathless voice?

Hello, Basement Zoey, you have returned.

For being a large man, Knox moved gracefully. Cupping her hips, he gently eased her back against the wall. "At the most? With you naked and beneath me . . . or on top. I'm not particular as to which as long as the naked part's the same."

"Oh." Zoey quieted a large gulp.

"Why do you look like you're about to bolt, angel?"

"Because that's a lot of *most*." And a hell of a lot more than she expected. "I don't know what to say. Your mixed signals are a little confusing. What's changed since your speech about not messing with women like me who'd rather binge-watch episodes of *Buffy* than go to nightclubs and shake their bonbons? I mean, *that*, I get. It's not like it's the first time I've heard it, and I'm sure it won't be the last."

The muscle at Knox's temple jumped wildly as he clenched his teeth. "You have no idea how much it pisses me off when you say shit like that."

"Say what? The truth?"

"You're twisting what I said that night out of context."

"I don't think I am. I'm not a Tracy type, Knox. I don't don my underwear and call it my clubbing outfit. Heck, I don't go clubbing—or to bars. Or go much of anywhere that has hordes of drunken, horny people.

And let's not forget that I'm a Wright—the fragile sister of your best friend, the one who needs protecting from anything more challenging than turning oxygen into carbon dioxide." Once her mouth got moving, it couldn't stop.

"You're far from fragile."

Zoey snorted. "Tell that to my brother."

"Can I talk now?" Knox's gaze remained firmly locked on hers.

Forcing a jagged lump back down her throat, Zoey nodded.

Something akin to challenge darkened his eyes. "You're a hell of a lot better than I deserve—and *that's* what I meant before. I fuck things up, sweetheart. My unit. My brothers. You name it, and I'll find a way to screw it all to hell."

"And you're not staying," Zoey added. "You're still planning on doing that bodyguard thing."

"And I'm not staying," he repeated, his face passive. "You deserve a lot more than what I can give you. So you see, it has everything to do with me and not a damn thing to do with you not being a Tracy type. And while we're on that subject, Tracys are a dime a dozen and not the least bit sexy to me. Do you know what is?"

Zoey couldn't speak, so she shook her head.

"A woman who doesn't give a damn about fashion dos or don'ts. She wears cotton shorts for comfort, not realizing how delicious they make her legs look. She wears cartoon-themed T-shirts from her youth, not caring how they perfectly cup her sweet breasts." Knox's gaze slowly slid down her body, coaxing a long trail of goose bumps over her too hot skin. "And at nearly midnight, wearing a tank top and duck shorts, she hasn't the slightest clue how badly I've wanted to strip them off of her since she first opened the door."

Zoey could barely breathe, trying to digest his words and populate his meaning.

The smart thing to do would be thank him for explaining and see him out the door. But the thrill she'd felt at Iron Bars came roaring back. For the first time in her life, she'd made a decision based on what she wanted, not on what she *should* do. That kind of freedom was addictive.

Neither of them had much time for anything serious.

With her working the Cupid Killer case and him helping out with Steele Ops, neither of them would have a lot of free time. And his impending exit put an expiration date on whatever it was they were about to discuss.

"What's going on inside that gorgeous head of yours?" As if realizing where her thoughts migrated, Knox dropped his voice to a husky rumble.

"Truthfully? I don't know. My brain's still processing the fact that you think my duck shorts are sexy."

Knox trailed the backs of his fingers up her sleeveless arm and over her shoulder until he cupped the side of her neck. His thumb, slightly callused, caressed her face in gentle strokes. "There's a hell of a lot more about you that's sexy, angel."

"If you've wanted to toss away my shorts since you walked through the door, why were you about to leave a few minutes ago?"

Knox's Adam's apple bobbed, and for the first time

in forever, he looked nervous as his gaze dropped to her mouth and back. "Because you deserve a guy who's going to be there for you for the long haul. Someone a quick phone call and a skip away."

"I'm a twenty-seven-year-old who's barely had a chance to truly live my life. I'm not ready to start shopping at bridal boutiques. What if what you're offering is exactly what I'm looking for?" Zoey slipped her hand into his hair slowly and guided his mouth down to hers. "I'm tired of letting other people have all the experiences, Knox. I want this. I want *you*. Neither of us have the time—or are in the place—to start anything complicated. I'm working. You're leaving. But there's no reason why two consenting adults can't partake in a mutually agreed upon sexual arrangement."

His lips lifted in a sexy half-crooked smirk. "Mutually agreed upon sexual arrangement?"

"Is your vision of me so clouded that you believe I'm incapable of partaking in a good ole-fashioned booty call? Because I'll have you know, Mr. Sex and Sin, I can be sexually carefree."

A low chuckle rumbled from his chest. "There's isn't a doubt in my mind, angel. But are you sure there isn't one in yours?"

"You're worried that I don't mean what I say?"

"Wouldn't be the first time—and I'm not talking about you. People, as a whole, tend to promise things without knowing if they can follow through."

Something flickered in Knox's eyes when he mentioned promises and she bit her lip to keep from asking if that's why he'd stayed away from DC for so long.

If she and Knox crossed this line, could she keep her word? Could she keep things casual?

She'd always cared about him. A lot. Watching him leave would be painful. Period. But watching him walk away after knowing what life could be like if he stayed?

That could be excruciating.

Zoey prayed she looked more hopeful than she felt. "As long as we both treat it like a carefree adventure, the distraction from the daily grind will probably do our bodies good."

"I'm only willing to be so carefree," Knox admitted, his voice gruff as he nibbled the length of her neck. "I grew up with three brothers and was forced to share my entire life. I won't do it anymore. If we do this, we do it just the two of us."

"Well, duh." Zoey fought to keep the smile off her face. "And we should add some small print."

"Meaning?"

"We keep it simple. If it becomes more than a mutually agreed upon sexual arrangement to either one of us, we end it. No hard feelings going either way. Simple. Clean."

Zoey held her breath waiting for his answer. The little voice in her head urged him to agree, but the one in her heart screamed at him to toss her small print into the fire and burn it to ash.

"Deal." Knox hauled her onto her toes and slanted his mouth over hers. Their tongues collided before he pulled back to nibble her bottom lip. And then he did it again, only retreating when breathing became an issue.

Eventually, he unlatched his mouth and trailed it

down the length of her neck, alternating soft bites with caressing kisses. While his mouth feasted, his palms ran over her hips and beneath her tank top.

Already braless and without constraint, her nipples hardened, throbbing for contact as his hand drifted closer. She pushed her chest toward him, eager for his touch. The second a large palm brushed the lower swell of her breast—less than an inch from her scar—Zoey froze.

It was a testament to how much she wanted this—wanted Knox—that she'd forgotten about it. It was probably the first time in forever, or at least as far back as she had cognizant memory.

But now, his close proximity to those six inches of darkened flesh was all she could think about.

* * *

Sensing the shift from need to panic, Knox immediately stilled his hands beneath Zoey's shirt. Her body, previously lax and molded to his, stiffened. Fear lightened her eyes, widening them to saucer-like disks.

He wouldn't push her into anything, and he didn't want to scare her. In any way. "Talk to me, angel. Do you want to stop?"

When she didn't answer immediately, he ripped his hands away.

Shaking her head, she grabbed them and locked them into position with her own. "No."

"Then tell me what you want to do, sweetheart."

Zoey's throat bobbed as she swallowed. "I want to leave the shirt on."

"Your shirt?" Confusion muddled his brain until she reflexively rubbed the center of her chest. It clicked.

He'd seen her do it before, a mindless action in the same vein as him scratching his jaw. Or hell, cracking his knuckles.

Her scar.

He knew she had one even though it had been close to twelve or more years since he'd seen it. She excelled at keeping it hidden, and last year when he'd visited her in the hospital, layers of gauze had prevented him from catching a glimpse.

Part of Knox wanted to argue the point. That scar was part of her, a symbol of how strong she was. But the other part knew it would take more than a well-written speech to convince her to shed the barrier. He sure as hell had no right to demand transparency.

He released the shirt and slowly slid his hands down the base of her spine. "All right, angel. Shirt on."

For now.

"Is there anything else you don't want me to do?"

She shook her head. "Besides not take too much longer? No."

He nibbled on her lips and, tucking his hands behind her thighs, urged her legs around his waist. "Bedroom?"

"*Please.*"

Knox took them there in record time, easing her onto the edge of the mattress and following her down with a hot, searing kiss that he felt straight to his gut. She rolled her hips, arcing up to his, and brushed her body against his already aching cock.

Afraid he'd shoot off prematurely, he dropped a hand to her waist. "I need to taste you."

Zoey's unfiltered blue eyes, heavy lidded with desire, filled with excitement. "You mean...?"

A naughty smirk twitched his lips. "Hell yeah, *I mean*...unless you changed your mind."

"No. No mind-changing."

She lifted her bottom off the mattress, and they worked in tandem, easing both her duck shorts and silky panties down her legs. His eyes fastened on every inch of her body they revealed together. "You're so fucking gorgeous."

Zoey's chest rose and fell, and when Knox eased her legs over his shoulders, she trembled. "Knox. *Please*."

Brushing his nose along the sensitive flesh of her inner thigh, he relished the sight of her already wet and ready pussy. "Please what, sweetheart?"

"Please don't make me wait." Zoey squirmed as he hovered over her.

Fisting her fingers through his hair, she arched her hips toward his mouth. At first contact, she fell back to the mattress with a pleasure-filled groan. He loved that sound. And as he stroked his tongue through her folds, he heard it again.

"Have mercy." Zoey's eyes drifted closed.

"Eyes on me every step of the way, angel," Knox demanded her attention with little more than a growling whisper.

Their gazes fastened on each other over her mound.

Witnessing Zoey unravel in his hands turned him on like nothing else, and her taste, honey and sweetness, transformed his cock into granite. He tormented them both, skating through the folds of her pussy with long, firm licks before hovering over her hardened clit.

Her blue eyes watched as he caressed the little nub with the tip of his tongue. "Oh, my...that feels...*oh*."

Her breathy moan, a sign that she was close to coming apart in his arms, quickly became an addiction.

Knox pulled her tighter against his mouth and alternated his pace. Slow and then fast. Hard and then feather light. He devoured every ounce of sweetness, doubling his efforts as her hands fisted in his hair.

Her legs, on either side of his head, trembled as she fell into the throes of a powerful climax. "Knox! Oh my God!"

He kissed her body through every gentle quiver, and as the hand in his hair slackened, he dragged his mouth to hers. "You're amazing."

"No, *that* was amazing. Please tell me we're going to do that again."

He gifted her a self-satisfied grin. "That and a lot more, angel."

Propping an arm by her head so he wouldn't crush her into a pancake, he enjoyed the sight of her breathless state and knowing he'd caused it. He couldn't stop touching her, skating his fingers over her bare torso and down her hip.

Zoey took advantage of the small space between them and slipped her hand beneath the band of his pants. His cock jumped as she wrapped her fingers around his girth and squeezed.

He caught her hand, gently pulling it away.

"You don't want me to reciprocate?" Her blue eyes peered at him in uncertainty.

"Fuck yeah I do. There's nothing I'd like better. Trust me. But I want this to last a hell of a lot longer than the two seconds I'd survive with your hand, or your mouth, wrapped around me." Not to mention he wanted her so damn bad. If he let himself go, he was afraid he'd scare her and that was the last thing he wanted to do.

Knox left her lying naked and gorgeous on the bed, and slowly stood. He ripped his shirt off from the back of his neck and quickly tossed it aside. Next, he chucked his pants. With every piece of clothing he removed, Zoey's gaze feasted even more intently.

She licked her lips, nearly making him come on the spot.

"You like what you're seeing, angel?" he asked, voice gruff. His cock jutted out from his body, throbbing with the need to be inside her.

"You would too if you were me."

Knox quickly grabbed his wallet and the condom tucked inside. Gritting his teeth, he rolled it into position and then slowly lowered himself back over Zoey's waiting body.

Despite being sheathed in a T-shirt, her nipples poked against the fabric, searching for attention. He took the left one in his mouth, cotton and all, and when it hardened even more, did the same to its twin.

Zoey squirmed beneath him, shifting her body until her legs anchored around his waist. She swiveled her hips, coating the tip of his erection with her slick heat.

"I don't want to wait anymore, Knox. I don't want slow and soft."

He groaned, dropping his forehead to hers. "I don't want to hurt you, baby."

"You're not going to." She cupped his cheek and stole every ounce of his breath with a slow, leisurely kiss he felt right down to his toes. "Please."

He couldn't deny her. No way in hell. Gently dragging her to the edge of the bed, he planted his feet firmly on the ground, and tightened his hold on her hips. She kept her eyes on him, anticipation dancing in their blue depths.

Her legs tightened around his waist, silently urging him onward.

Knox thrust, and they both groaned together. He'd barely made it two inches when her body flexed around him like a fist. "You're so tight."

Zoey's fingers latched on to his arms and squeezed. "Don't stop."

An expertly executed hip swivel had his dick sinking another three inches.

Knox pulled out and sank back into her wet heat. He didn't stop. He *couldn't* stop. The second his cock slipped into her body, taking his time ceased to be a possibility—and it had nothing to do with living like a monk for the last two years and everything to do with the woman beneath him.

Zoey Wright was addictive—her scent, her breathy moans and little sighs. Knowing that *he'd* caused them spurred him on like nothing else—except the need to hear her scream his name.

Already feeling the telltale throb of his cock, Knox brushed his thumb against the bundle of nerves above her mound. "I'm not coming until you do, angel."

"Knox." Her fingers dug into his ass and tugged him closer, meeting him thrust for thrust.

"That's it, baby. Let go." Thrust and rub, he set a brutal pace that, before long, had them both drenched in sweat.

Knox dropped his mouth to hers, kissing her as if their lives depended on it. That extra contact, the feel of her skin against his, conjured a release that had them each crying out the other's name.

Pleasure rippled through their bodies, Knox nearly losing sight of all time and place...losing sight of everything except Zoey. They stayed locked together, both panting as the last waves of orgasm slowly ebbed.

Knox dropped his mouth to hers in a searing kiss, and when he reluctantly pulled away, Zoey's big blue eyes caught his. Through the heavy desire, he glimpsed the same realization that had come to him before they'd even shed the first article of clothing.

This entire arrangement suddenly got a lot more complicated.

* * *

He couldn't believe it. He couldn't fathom it. Yet the two naked forms on the bed, legs and arms entwined as they writhed together in a lust-filled haze, were crystal clear.

His Heart.

And Knox Steele.

He'd asked around, discreetly, to be told of the circumstances of Steele's absence. Questionable morals, weak familial bonds, and unreliability had been the three characteristics mostly uttered. And now, after years away, he swooped back into Her life, and between Her legs, as if he had the right.

He didn't.

Splinters dug into his hands. His knuckles, wrapped tightly around the edge of his seat, cracked as he battled the urge to throw his computer across the room.

This wasn't how it was supposed to go.

She was supposed to come to him. She was supposed to see him. Instead, She'd drifted further away.

Rage burned his gut as he stood, knocking his chair to the ground, and crossed the room.

To anyone else, the table in front of him was covered in insignificant trinkets. To him, they were treasures, gifts His Heart left for him to find and enjoy: a brush, Her silky tendrils woven through the prongs; an aged photo, taken from the time he first recalled Her entering his life; and the lingerie.

He picked up the blue silken panties and held them to his nose. Her scent temporarily subdued the heat that had started to burn through his veins. His heart rate lowered. His breathing eased. His thoughts, slowly settling, cleared long enough for him to grasp the edges of another plan.

Focus on the goal, and steer toward the path that will get you there. Do whatever needs to be done to make it happen.

His father's advice had never held so much meaning.

His Goal: show His Heart that She has always, and will forever, belong to him.

His Path: clear all obstacles that could hinder projected success.

His Plan: make sure Knox Steele no longer posed a threat to His Heart.

It was already set in motion. Once he dealt with Knox Steele, She'd come to him. She'd ask for his help and he'd be there to give it.

And he'd be the only one who could.

CHAPTER
SIXTEEN

Zoey stood in front of her mom's fireplace and picked up the photo that caught her eye whenever she visited. Zoey and Cade, aged seven and eleven, filled the frame, both with wide smiles despite the dreary hospital background.

Going by the beaming grins, you'd never guess that her mom had taken it three days after pulmonic stenosis sent Zoey to Georgetown Med. That hospitalization had led to her third surgery performed by Dr. Samuel senior, and from what reports said, hadn't been without setbacks.

At the time, she'd been too young to wrap her head around the complexities of Tetralogy of Fallot. All she'd known growing up was that she'd been unable to participate in gym class like most of the other children...that her days revolved around medications and doctors' appointments. That even a slight case of the sniffles was cause for alarm.

Her mom knew. When she'd taken a sick four-year-old and her brother into her home as fosters, she'd been given full transparency of the possible challenges, and hadn't batted an eye. Just like she'd never once, even before formally adopting them, made them feel temporary.

"It's times like this when I wish I had the power to read minds." Her mom stepped up beside her, the only person Zoey knew who was shorter than herself. "I can't tell if these are good thoughts, bad thoughts, or naughty thoughts."

Zoey laughed and leaned her head on her mom's shoulder. "Mostly good. Just thinking how lucky Cade and I were to have you in our lives. If it hadn't been for you, things could've been so different."

Her mom pulled her into a full hug. "Oh, honey. I'm the one that's thankful. That's why I send Maria flowers on the anniversary day of when she brought you to my doorstep. You and your brother gave an old lady a purpose."

"You were not old, Mom."

"Well, not then, but my frequent trips to the salon nowadays say otherwise."

"How did you do it?" Zoey gestured to the long line of family pictures. "How did you do it all by yourself? I mean, the expenses alone would be too much for most people to handle."

Her mom brushed aside a stray lock of hair. "I'm not going to lie, it wasn't at all easy, but I was lucky. Cindy and the boys were right across the street. And our medical angel handled pretty much all of the hospital costs. All I had to do was love you, and *that* I could do. When you have love, nothing's impossible."

Zoey strived to be like her mom every day. Strong. Resilient. *Fierce*. Not afraid of the unknown. It was one of the main reasons why she'd left the lab, a job she'd gotten so used to that she could do it in her sleep, for something that made her heart pound.

Knox almost made her feel the same way...except *more*.

It had been nearly a week since the night at her apartment and their first night together, and she was still riding high. She grinned, thinking about the third—or fourth—sexual romp before he'd left that next morning. She'd lost count.

Her mom studied her a few moments, the scrutiny making Zoey self-conscious. "What are you looking at?"

"You look...different. Lighter." A small smirk pulled up the corners of her mouth. "Almost like you and I should be having a *talk*."

"Gah! No. Please. I barely survived *the talk* the first time. Those stick figures haunt me to this day. Let's just go with *you're right*, I *do* feel a little lighter, and call it a day."

"Just once I would like to hear about my children's love lives. Not details, mind you, but anything that could give an old lady hope for grandchildren someday."

"Cart *way* before the horse, Ma."

"So there *is* a horse?" Mischief perked up her mom's hopeful expression. "Is he a...*stud*?"

Zoey laughed so hard tears came to her eyes.

She and Knox hadn't sat down and talked particulars, but they both knew whatever was happening between them had a shelf life. He had no intentions of staying in DC, and this was her home. There would be no Wright-Steele babies popping out anytime soon. Or ever...unless Cade and Grace got their act together.

"The cavalry is here!" Loud laughter and the opening of the front door saved Zoey from an embarrassing sex talk. Cindy Steele strutted her stuff, filling the simple one-level ranch house with her short stature and big personality. "I already sent the boys around back to fire up the grill...and keep them out of our hair for a bit."

Grace lagged behind her aunt, glancing around as if expecting a clown to pop out at any second. Zoey couldn't help but chuckle.

"He's not here. *Yet*," she murmured to her best friend.

Grace gave her a defeated look. "I tried everything to get out of this. I begged. I bartered. I bribed. My aunt could've had a lucrative career as a spy because she'd never crack under pressure."

"Sorry, my friend. But I figure you have an hour or so of freedom. Cade got stuck at work and said he'd be by a little later."

"Zoey, sweetheart. You look beautiful as always." Cindy gave her a loud kiss on the cheek, her hands filled with bowls. "I have meatballs and something chocolate. We need to get these out of the boys' line of sight *pronto* because I've had a time and a half keeping their fingers out of them."

Zoey took one of the bowls off her hands and led the way into the kitchen. She busied herself rearranging the fridge. "You'd think we were feeding an army instead of less than ten people."

"Each of the boys counts as three regular humans. Right, Knox?"

"At least." Knox's voice sent a wave of heat down Zoey's spine.

They'd talked and texted since the night at her apartment, but she hadn't laid eyes on him in six long days. She made up for it now.

His arms rippled when he moved, showcased by his fitted tee and reminding her of how easily he'd picked her up and taken her to her bed. His hair, slightly damp, looked as if he'd stepped out of the shower a short time ago and combed his fingers through it in lieu of using an actual comb.

In short, he looked good. Edible. *Distracting*.

Zoey caught herself nibbling her bottom lip, and so did Knox.

He smirked. "Angel. You're lookin' good this afternoon."

Zoey gave her throat a nervous clear. "You too."

Cindy's gaze bounced back and forth between them before she shooed her eldest away with her hands. "Go with Gretchen and make sure your brothers don't burn down her backyard. Grace, you're on pyrotechnic watch. And for goodness' sake, do *not* let Liam anywhere near that kerosene. He nearly scorched his eyebrows off last time."

"On it, Aunt Cindy." Grace gave a little wave before steering Knox outside.

Zoey grinned. Cindy spoke about her boys as if they were barely out of training diapers rather than grown men who fought for their country. There wasn't a single one of them who balked at a challenge, but one stern look from their mother and they caved.

Finally alone, Cindy turned her full-blown attention to Zoey. "You look glowing, hon. If I didn't know any better I'd say you were pregnant...or in love."

On her way to pull the sodas out of the pantry, Zoey tripped over her own two feet. "Uh, yeah. No to both. Must be good sleep."

Cindy smiled mischievously. "Uh-huh. Lying to an old woman's a sin."

"So's trying to fish for information when there isn't any."

Cindy laughed, the sound so much like Liam's hearty bellow. With dark hair turning gray at the temples, the Steele matriarch was still a beautiful, formidable woman who'd raised four boys after the death of her husband.

That's why she and Gretchen had gotten close. Left alone to raise their families, they counted on their own determination and each other to get through the difficult times. And because of Zoey's health, her mom had experienced a lot of them.

Cindy Steele had been a rock. She ruled with an iron fist, loved just as hard, and Zoey considered herself lucky to be circled into their loop. Two families for the price of one.

"Are you sure you don't want to divulge anything? I've been told I'm a great listener," Cindy prodded.

"And also a great gossip. Words would no sooner pass my lips than you'd be pulling my mom off to the side."

"So that means there *is* something to tell."

"You're incorrigible."

Cindy gave up the Great Interrogation when she heard Grace's voice scold Liam for unsafe kerosene practice. "I'd better go play firefighter."

"I'm pretty sure Mom got a replacement extinguisher specifically for today's occasion. It's taped underneath the picnic table for easy access."

"Of course she did." The older woman laughed harder as she walked toward the commotion.

Zoey stayed indoors, pulling out plates and setting out utensils and other odds and ends they'd need once the guys got the fire roaring. Soon, laughter and jokes filled the backyard and someone flipped on the radio. Through the screen door, Zoey heard her mom direct the guys on how to arrange the patio table and chairs.

She glanced around at the island and surveyed her collection. "One more thing and we're all set."

Eyeing the object of her desire, she contemplated how to get the glass decanter from its precarious position above the cabinets. It wasn't *her* desire. It was her mom's, who claimed the crystal lemonade pitcher needed to be used for every backyard barbecue from now until eternity.

She dragged the stepstool from the pantry, and after carefully climbing to the highest rung, still stood a good three inches short. "Extra boost, here I come."

She kicked off her shoes for better traction and stepped onto the counter. Her fingers brushed against the pitcher's handle, and her heart, with its sucky timing, missed a beat. Zoey gasped, taken by surprise, and lost her balance.

She grappled for anything with a handhold and instead, felt two warm, firm hands planted on her hips. Half turning, she peered down into Knox's eyes. From their different vantage points, his head came to a few inches above her belly button.

"Impeccable timing." Her heart still thundered out a few staccato beats before finally getting with the program.

"Glad I could be of service, angel. Now can I ask why the hell you're table-dancing?"

"Technically, it's counter-dancing. And it's not a bar-becue without the Wright family lemonade picture." She nodded to the decanter inches from her reach. "Trust me, I wouldn't be up here otherwise."

Knox eased her off the counter. She slid against him on her way to the floor, making every inch of her body come alive with the contact. Even when her feet touched down, his arm remained firmly tucked around her waist, a dangerous position since anyone could walk into the kitchen at any moment.

"Thanks for the save, but I still need that pitcher."

"This one?" He stepped onto the lowest step-rung and easily plucked the decanter off the shelf.

"Show-off."

He smirked. "Glad I get to show you *something* these last few days."

Her cheeks heated at his not-so-hidden innuendo.

They'd attempted to meet up no fewer than three times and each one, something had come up either with her work or an unforeseen situation at the distillery. Today she had a rare day off, and with Knox and his brothers here, she'd been hopeful for something hap-pening tonight.

"Before the horde descends on us again, I was hop-ing we could talk." Knox immediately squashed those hopes with one simple sentence.

Here it comes.

Her pessimistic side had been half expecting this conversation. She just hadn't thought it would happen with their family less than ten feet away.

"You don't need to do this." Pulling away, she turned to the ice tub on the counter and dropped in the sodas from the pantry. "I'd rather you didn't."

"Do what?"

"Explain."

Behind her, Knox went quiet. She would've thought he'd left if it weren't for that tingle at the base of her neck. It intensified right before a wall of heat bracketed her back. Knox's hands settled low on her hips, gently tugging her into the cradle of his pelvis.

"What do you believe I'm here to do, angel?" Knox's mouth murmured against her ear.

Zoey cleared her Saharan dry throat. "To initiate that small-print clause. To end . . . *this*."

He eased her into a spin and tipped her chin up until she met his gaze. "That's definitely not what I came in here for."

And judging by the flash of heat radiating from his eyes, it was the truth. She was just a little apprehensive to let herself believe it.

"Usually when a guy says that he wants to talk it means—"

The screen door opened. Cade, followed by a steady stream of Steeles, stalked into the kitchen. Her mom, Cindy, and Grace followed behind them, and looked no less happy.

"What's up?" Knox took a small step back but stayed close to her side.

Zoey chuckled nervously at everyone's dour expressions. "Wow. If I didn't know any better, I'd say that this was an intervention or something."

"We need to talk." Cade said grimly.

"Obviously since you guys have thoroughly blocked all exits. About what?"

"That silver necklace. At the Monroe crime scene."

"What about it?"

"When was the last time you saw it?"

Zoey stared at her brother, confused. "The evidence bag? I locked it in with—"

"No. *Your* necklace. The one you told Knox about."

"Why?" Knox scooted closer until she felt his arm brush against hers. "What are you getting at?"

Cade reached for her hand and gestured toward the living room. "Let's sit and talk about this."

"Why don't you pull up your big-boy boxers and spill it already?" She tugged away. The use of her brother's Detective Tone ticked her off. "Why are you asking me about a necklace that I rarely ever wear?"

"Because your former lab tech got two DNA hits from the crime scene necklace. Our victim's. And *yours*."

CHAPTER SEVENTEEN

Knox watched Zoey hustle outside and fought the urge to immediately go after her. She needed to process what this could mean. Hell, he did too, and none of what went through his head was pleasant.

His gaze drifted through the patio doors. Zoey, fingers with a death grip on the porch railing, stared over the Potomac. Her shoulders heaved, either from losing her shit or trying to keep it together.

He'd stayed away long enough.

He and Cade moved toward the back door at the same time.

"I'll go," Knox insisted.

"She needs to take this fucking seriously."

"I get that. I'll get her to come back inside. Just give us a few minutes."

Cade looked like he wanted to argue. His gaze bounced outside and back before he nodded. "Five minutes."

"We'll come back in whenever she's good and ready."

When Knox closed the patio door behind him, Zoey stiffened. Eyes closed, she didn't even turn toward him as he tucked her hair behind her shoulder.

"What are the chances that it's a coincidence?" She

pried her eyes open to meet his. "Ginny had a record, right? What if she was the one who broke into my place? She could've taken the necklace and—"

"And nothing else?" Knox interjected. "Trust me, angel, I wish it were one big coincidence, but my gut won't let me. It fits. *You* fit. You're a young, attractive, single professional."

Zoey shook her head, refusing to go along with his train of thought. "But we've never gotten evidence that he's fixated on a target beforehand. Why would he start now?"

"Why would he target someone so soon after the previous? Why would he butcher her when he was previously all about control? Why would he clean everything except the damn necklace?" Knox's voice rose in small increments. He took his own calming breath and counted to five. Twice. "I don't have the answers and I don't know what's in the bastard's sick head. But I do know it's probably best if you transfer off this case."

Zoey snapped her gaze to his. "What? Why?"

"Because for all we know, the sick fuck's keeping tabs on everyone involved in it, and that includes you."

"But we already knew that was a possibility. He's a sociopath. It's part of his game."

"And now he's changing the rules."

Zoey's fear turned to anger. "Only if we let him. We can't play into it and reassign everyone on the damn case!"

"You're the one he's potentially fixated on right now!" Knox gripped her arms and dragged her closer. He'd never felt more helpless than he did at that very moment. "*You're* the one who fits his type. *You're* the one in danger if we let this drag on any longer, and I'll be damned if I'm going to let anything happen to you!"

Knox saw the moment she shut down. Jaw clenched, she switched her anger to determination. The more he pushed, the more resolved she'd be to tell him to fuck off.

"Let's get one thing straight right now, Knox Steele. Just because we had a single night together does not mean that you get to go all alpha on me. Do it again, and I'll take that caveman club and tuck it so far up your backside that you feel it tickle your tonsils. We clear?"

A throat clearing turned both their attentions to where Grace and Roman stood outside the kitchen door. Grace's mouth was agape while Roman remained eerily still.

"The two of you should come into the house," Roman said, way too calm to be good.

"Great. Because it suddenly got too darn stuffy out here." Zoey drilled Knox with a glare as she stalked toward the back door.

Grace quickly followed, but Roman hung back, waiting for Knox. "Remember what I said back at Iron Bars?"

"That you love me?" Knox joked dryly.

"Don't make me kick your ass, Knox."

He nodded and slipped inside, receiving two icy glares for the price of one—from Zoey and his cousin.

He'd kick himself in the ass if he could. He'd lost his temper, and that fuck-up now put him squarely on

Zoey's shit list, a bullet point that usually consisted of one name. Her brother's.

For the next hour, everyone talked, most at the same time, as they debated and argued. As expected, Cade's protectiveness descended like a vengeance, quickly followed by those of Knox's brothers and their mothers. Even Grace chimed in with suggestions, and sometimes got everyone back on track.

Zoey sat, noticeably quiet in the loud room, and stared straight ahead. She'd stopped voicing her objections fifteen minutes ago when Cade bellowed about protective custody and armed guards. When his friend mentioned it, Knox had thought it was a great fucking idea. Now, watching Zoey's blank face, his perspective changed.

Ignoring everyone around him, he stood and focused solely on Zoey. He stopped in front of her, silently holding out his hand.

She looked at it as if it were a snake prepped to strike.

"Please," he murmured.

Her blue eyes, filled with unspent tears, flickered to his.

He knew this was the right thing to do. "Let's get out of here."

He waited with bated breath until she took his hand and followed him out to the patio. The sun had already dropped over the river, and the wind picked up, whipping Zoey's hair across her cheek.

"Thank you," she murmured softly.

"You don't need to thank me. All that talking was

giving me a damn headache." His lighthearted response didn't even garner him a lip twitch.

He kept himself a good three feet away. "What do you want to do?"

"Why are you asking me? Shouldn't you be telling me what I'm doing like the others? You said earlier that I should recuse myself from the case. It sounds like that's an opinion supported by everyone inside."

He didn't like her defeated tone. "Do I think you should have Mason transfer you off the case, at least temporarily? Yes. But I'm also not so delusional to believe that you'd go along with it."

She slid her gaze toward him. "And the *going into hiding*? Where was it that Liam suggested? Timbuktu?"

Knox snorted. "That's a little overkill."

"Cade seemed to like the idea fine."

"It's because he cares." At her sharp glare, he lifted his hands in mock surrender. "I'm not saying it's not stupid. I'm saying that all the arguing happening in there is because everyone's worried."

"It's a necklace, and it could be a huge coincidence. I live within a few blocks of some of the other victims. He could've intercepted the necklace from whoever broke into my apartment."

Knox knew she wanted to believe that. And like him, she also knew those chances were pretty damn slim.

Zoey pushed off the railing, building a good steam as she stalked closer to him. "I'm not taking a leave of absence from work, and there's no way in hell I'm moving in with my brother. I have an apartment, which, thanks to Liam, is now more secure than most military bases, and I'll be damned if I'm going to leave it! Heck, it's probably safer there than here in the burbs."

"You're probably right."

"Damn straight I'm right. And you're not going to talk me out of—"

Knox captured her face between his hands and dropped a hard, quick kiss on her lips. "I said you were right, angel. You need to take a deep breath."

Her shoulders slumped and her forehead dropped onto his chest. She stayed there for a minute until her breathing returned to normal. "I'm just so tired, Knox. I'm tired of all the talking. I'm tired of all the debating, and I'm tired because I haven't slept through the night since... well, since the other night."

"We have that in common." Knox made a decision right there despite knowing it wouldn't be a popular one. "Do you want to get out of here?"

She gifted him a hopeful look that increased his determination. "You think they'll let us leave?"

"If you ignore the yelling and keep your eyes on the exit, they won't have a choice. Let me be your bulldozer."

"Then yes. *Please*."

Knox threaded his fingers through hers, not dwelling on the fact it had come—and felt—as natural as breathing, and weaved their way back through the house. Grace saw them first, her gaze navigating to their joined hands. Cade was next.

"Where the hell are the two of you going?" Cade's demand turned a handful of stares their way.

"Someplace that isn't here."

Cade stepped into his path. "Like hell. We haven't decided the best-case scenario for her yet, and until we do, Zoey stays."

"The best place is anywhere she doesn't have to listen to you lot making decisions like she's not a grown-ass woman." Knox met his best friend glare for glare. He stepped closer, nearly going nose to nose. "You want to throw ideas around and make decisions. Fine. Do what you feel you need to, but Zoey doesn't need to sit here and listen to the people she cares about making decisions on her behalf. She's coming with me, and all you have to know is that she's safe for the night."

Red-faced and a second from spewing smoke, Cade opened his mouth to argue when Grace stepped up to his side, squeezing his arm. "He's right, Cade. It's been a long day for everyone. Just let her go."

Cade's blue eyes locked on Knox. "I'm entrusting my baby sister to you, Steele. You know what will happen to you if she gets so much as a scratch while in your custody."

"Custody?" Zoey's temper flared as she stepped toward her brother. "Wait a—"

Knox nodded, holding her back. "I'm not going to let anything happen to her."

He led the way to his truck, the task more difficult due to the glare she threw over her shoulder to a watching Cade.

When he opened the passenger side of his pickup, her scowl deepened. "What about my car? Or will this *custody* arrangement just be a different form of house arrest?"

"This *custody* arrangement can be as stifling or as

freeing as you make it, angel. What's it going to be?" At her continued silence, he easily hoisted her into the passenger seat and buckled her belt. "Stifling wins. Hope what you said is true and that you like my place."

She looked at him, surprised. "You're taking me to the boat?"

"Did you want to go somewhere else?"

She shrugged, her indignation a bit depleted. "No. I like your place—at least until I fell into the water."

Less than five minutes into the commute from Alexandria to DC, Zoey's yawns turned into a soft purring snore. Her complaint about no sleep wasn't an exaggeration, because she didn't wake when he pulled into his spot at the marina, or when he carried her to his bed.

A warmth had settled in his chest when she admitted she liked his boat. He liked the fact that she was here, in his bed. There wasn't anywhere else he wanted her to be.

Timbuktu? Fuck no.

Some rat-infested hole in the wall, guarded by two ego-inflated retired cops with guns? Not on his watch.

Everyone back at Gretchen's could debate and vote all they wanted, but Knox wouldn't accept any location that didn't involve his presence. That assertion alone brought on at least a half dozen problems…

Pissing off his best friend didn't even come close to the top of the list.

* * *

Voices dragged Zoey's eyes open. She blinked, focusing on the sliver of sunlight escaping from the bottom of the blackout curtains as memories of Knox bringing her to the marina slowly came back to her.

She'd only woken up one time that she remembered. Surrounded by the warmth of Knox's arms, she'd tucked herself deeper into his embrace and promptly felt right back to sleep. Until now.

She headed to the bathroom, hearing the voices that had woken her up. Her brother's baritone was difficult to miss, and so she detoured upstairs.

Cade glanced her way as she stepped on deck, and immediately guided her into a sheepish hug. "Hey, little bit. You doing okay?"

"As well as to be expected. Unless you're here to whisk me away to some undisclosed location. In which case, I'll be fine once I toss you overboard."

"I'm sorry to disappoint you, but my feet are staying firmly on the ground, er, the boat."

Knox, sporting old sweats and a holey DC United T-shirt, grinned at her from over the rim of his coffee mug. The secret moment sent a series of flutters to her stomach.

"Cade came with good-ish news," Knox interjected into her thoughts. "Your necklace being at the crime scene may have been a coincidence after all."

"Really?" She turned to her brother.

"*Maybe*." Cade leaned his rear end against the side rail. "Ginny cozied around with a guy named Rick Stuart. Turns out he's the lead suspect in a burglary ring that's been hitting condos in—surprise, surprise—your neck of the woods."

"He broke into my apartment and stole the necklace, and what? Gave it to Ginny?"

"That's my theory. Right now, Stuart's in the wind. It's the reason I dropped by the boat." Cade glanced to Knox. "Figured you'd want in on a little domestic action."

"Sure thing. Give me thirty and I'll meet you back at the station. Just got to get dressed and drop off some special cargo over at Iron Bars."

Zoey caught their silent exchange and she folded her arms, annoyed. "Let me guess...I'm the special cargo? So what you're saying is that you're handing me over to your brothers to babysit?"

"Good call."

Laughing, Cade punched Knox in the arm. "Good luck getting her there with all your appendages intact. Give me a shout when you get to the precinct."

Knox nodded, but kept his eyes on Zoey as Cade left.

Zoey continued glaring. "Guess I should be thankful that whole what *I* want lasted for a few hours, huh? I mean, I wasn't conscious for it, but still...I consider myself fortunate."

Knox eased her into his arms, and palming her cheek, brushed his thumb over her bottom lip. The intimate gesture nearly melted all her annoyance. *Almost*, but not quite. "You think you're going to seduce me into complacency?"

Knox's full mouth twitched with a threatening grin. "Will that work?"

"No. Maybe. But it would only be temporary."

"All we need to do is get Stuart to implicate himself in the burglaries and admit to giving Ginny the goods.

Once we can verify his part in all this, you're a free woman."

Zoey wasn't stupid. She may not like that he was right, but he was. "Can I at least shower before you drop me off at the sitters'?"

"I'll even grab you a change of clothes."

After she showered and changed into another set of Knox's gym clothes, they headed back across the river. The second Knox came to a complete stop in front of Iron Bars, she headed upstairs.

He caught up to her at the door, holding it open. "Zo—"

She lifted her hand to silence him, and only allowed herself a small glimpse of the concern in his eyes. "I understand why we're doing this. Just let me have my pouty moment. I'm tired. I'm grumpy. And I can't stay mad if you're going to be all reasonable, okay?"

"Shutting down my reasoning."

"Good."

Knox navigated them downstairs and this time, the security pad outside the iron door worked. He scanned his eye and typed in a series of numbers. Finally, the door clicked open with a heavy *thunk*. Liam and Roman, sitting behind two computers, glanced up as they entered.

"So which cell is mine?" Zoey couldn't help herself. "I'd really like a corner to optimize privacy—anything with natural light will do."

Knox and his brothers exchanged silent looks. "She's not exactly happy about this."

Zoey snorted. "But *she* still has the ability to speak

for herself, and no, I'm not happy about missing an entire day of work because of a freak occurrence."

Liam cleared his throat. "Well, I, for one, am glad you're here, because when Roman gets in one of his moods, it's like I'm speaking to myself. Which I usually am because he goes all mute and broody and shit."

"Maybe you talk too much," Roman muttered.

"Talk. Don't talk," Knox grumbled. "I don't care what you do as long as it involves keeping an eye on Zoey. Don't let her out of your sight."

"What do you want us to do? Put a leash on her?"

The two brothers glared at each other before Knox relented, gently pulling her aside. "When I get back, we're having a talk."

"Goody. Can't wait."

Dark eyes narrowing on her, he trapped her chin between his fingers and tugged her gaze upward. "I know you don't like this, but it's for the best. For now."

"I know. I'm just...I know," she repeated her sentiments from upstairs. "You and Cade better look for this Stuart *really* hard. I don't care if you have to flip over rocks in every park from Northeast to Southwest. Got me?"

"Got you, angel." He looked torn, his gaze dropping to her mouth.

She waited with bated breath to see what he'd do. Kiss her? Not? Part of her wished he'd lay one on her that brought her leg up in that rom-com toe-pop she always saw in movies. In the end, she swallowed her disappointment when he left without another word.

She had no right to be disappointed and yet it was there, festering in her chest like a bad case of pneumonia. She turned toward Liam and Roman, who'd been watching the entire exchange. "Do you have a little bell that you need me to wear? Oh, wait. That's probably not advanced enough for you guys. Want to insert a GPS chip under my skin?"

Liam fidgeted in his seat. "I'd settle for a compromise. You leave my balls intact and I'll make a coffeehouse run and get you that chocolate chip crème thing you love."

Zoey's anger leaked out of her body. This entire situation sucked, but it was no one's fault—except the Cupid Killer's. "You got a deal."

Unless this babysitting gig lasted more than a day.

Then it was every woman for herself.

CHAPTER
EIGHTEEN

Knox eyed the line of townhomes, one more run-down than the next. Colorful graffiti sprawled across the brick walls and front sidewalks. Most windows that hadn't already been boarded sported yellow police tape. And then there was the health code warning stuck to the front of Rick Stuart's door.

"Stuart's obviously not hitting the right places if he can't improve his living situation any." Knox followed Cade out of his car and onto the sidewalk.

Cade looked at the address on his phone. "Never claimed the guy was smart, just greedy. This is it. A neighbor confirmed she saw him slink inside less than an hour ago. How do you want to do this? Split the bill?"

Using their old Ranger terminology brought back fond memories. To curb insurgents piggybacking onto their frequencies and using their lingo to stay one step ahead, his operating base had created a new dictionary of often raunchy military slang.

Some of that slang obviously stayed with Cade even in civilian life.

"I'd be more than happy to take the back exit so you can pound on the door and do your *DC Police* bellow," Knox offered. "I'm magnanimous that way."

"You're not magnanimous. You're hoping that he makes a run for it and runs smack into your ugly mug."

He grinned. That very scenario happened all the time when they'd cleared villages out in Kandahar. "You know me well."

"I do. Which is how I know that bodyguard thing isn't going to pan out. I give you two months. *Tops*. And only because quitting is the ultimate sin in your eyes."

"Two whole months, huh?"

"Yep. Then you'll be back begging for a job at Steele Ops, and I'm going to tell you to pound sand."

"You?" Knox caught his friend's slip. "As if you're going to be in charge of hiring or something? You'd have to be a member of the unit to do that, my friend."

Cade shook his head and chuckled. "I'm *thinking* about it."

Knox sealed his lips, not wanting to push. If Cade admitted to thinking about it, he wasn't about to give him a reason to say no.

They split, Knox heading around the back. A one-lane alleyway abutted the rear end of each house, shared from the row on the next block. Stuart's yard wasn't much more than a six-by-six patch of browned grass, fenced in with a mesh wire that had seen better days.

Cade texted.

Reaching the door now. Look alive.

Knox hopped the back gate and looked around, keeping his eyes open as he took position at the base of the steps.

"DCPD! Open up!" Cade's voice echoed around the building.

Frantic footsteps pounded within the house seconds before Stuart burst through the back door. He barreled down the stairs, jeans half undone, and screeched to a halt the second he spotted Knox.

Stuart sprinted left, vaulting over the chain-link fence like a damn ninja. And with a panicked glance over his shoulder, he scrambled away like an alley rat.

Knox took off after him. "He's on the move! Heading east!"

Adrenaline burst through Knox's veins as he pumped his arms and legs. Stuart was faster than he looked, booking it down a private alley. He passed a metal garbage can and flung it behind him. Knox dodged around it with inches to spare before it collided with his head.

In the distance, music and laughter broke through the sounds of city traffic. He knew that was where Stuart was heading before he even veered right, and he didn't disappoint, hurdling over another mesh fence and into a private yard.

"Knox!" Cade shouted from two yards away.

"Go east! Go east!" Knox sailed over the fence and landed smack in the thick of a family party.

Heads swiveled his way, two of which belonged to a pair of ten-year-olds who looked about to piss their pants. A grandma type came flying at him with a piñata stick. "Get out of here before I crack you open! Did you hear me? Get the hell out of my backyard!"

"Sorry, ma'am. I didn't mean to—" He dodged a swing to his head and slowly backed away. "I'm leaving. I'm leaving."

"He went that way." A young twenty-something kid nodded over yet another damn fence.

"I don't get paid enough for this shit," Knox muttered dryly. *He wasn't getting paid for this at all.*

He hurdled over a second fence and into another back alley. This one, as narrow as the one before, looked empty. He scanned left and right, listening for movement. The quick bastard could've gone in either direction, hiding behind the stack of empty boxes tossed out by the pharmacy or ducked into any of the back exits.

He shot off a one-handed text to Cade with his location, and picked left. Fifteen yards from the main street, the distinct smell of urine and rotting garbage filled his nose. Muffled conversations spilled out from the broken window on his right, but there wasn't any sign of Stuart.

Knox stepped lightly, listening for anything that didn't belong. It finally came in the form of metal scraping against asphalt. Knox spun around seconds before white-hot pain ripped through his shoulder.

He'd heard enough gunfire in his lifetime to recognize the difference between a rifle shot and a car backfiring. And if he hadn't, the blood running down his left arm clued him in real damn quick.

* * *

Zoey glanced at the clock on the wall to verify what she already knew.

Wizards and Warlocks was the game that *never* ended.

As she pushed away from the table, Liam lifted his

eyes from the board for the first time in what felt like hours. "Where you going?"

"I'm calling it, Liam. You've conquered the world, slayed all my dragons, and defeated me in that Magic Cup Olympics thing. You win."

"No, no, no. You can't withdraw," Liam protested. "That's like winning by default, and I do not win by default."

"Then fast-forward a few thousand hours and claim your victory, because I cannot sit in this chair a second longer. I'm developing a bed sore on my rear end. And no"—she cut him off as he opened his mouth—"you can't see it."

"You don't know how to have fun."

"Maybe not, but I'm pretty sure it's not by playing this." She laughed when he stuck out his tongue at her and packed up the game pieces. "So, where can I venture to and where can I not?"

Liam glanced up and nodded his chin. "Go anywhere you want... but know that wherever it is, you're not going to have even half as much fun."

Zoey snort-laughed. "Let's hope so."

Using eeny, meeny, miny, moe, she chose the corridor off to the left of the rotunda and just walked. She passed bedrooms still too empty to even be called spartan, and something that looked like the situation room you always saw on television shows.

She was about to turn around and investigate another hall when she heard a *thunk*. Six in a row, followed by a short pause, and then it started again. With nothing better to do, she followed the noise until she found it—and Roman—in a gym the size of a basketball court.

He stood with his back toward her and a table full of shiny knives on his left. Taking a deep breath, he picked three up, flipped one in his palm, and hurled them in quick succession toward the life-sized dummy fifteen yards away.

Thunk. Thunk. Thunk.

"Remind me to never piss you off," Zoey said, announcing her presence.

Roman didn't so much as flinch and tossed another three knives, even quicker than the last set. Of course he would've known she was there. "Who won the game?"

"I withdrew."

Roman shot her a knowing glance. "Did Liam start whining about winning by default?"

"Yep. But I couldn't sit there for another minute. How long have you trained to be able to do that?" She gestured to where a half dozen knives stuck out of the training dummy.

"Truthfully? I lost count. You find a hell of a lot of time when your ass is confined to a bed for months." He wore exercise clothes, his prosthetic on display as he stalked toward the dummy.

Zoey noticed a slight limp, something that showed when he pushed himself too hard. Roman wasn't the type to take it easy, not before the IED explosion and not after.

"I guess you're eager to get Steele Ops up and running, huh?" Zoey stated off-handedly.

"It'll be good to feel useful again." He slid her a side

eye. "But you were trying to lead into something else, weren't you, sweetheart?"

"No," Zoey lied. "Okay, maybe. I'd have to be, well, a man, if I didn't sense a little...discord between you and Knox."

"Discord?" He snorted. "That's one way to put it. But you don't have to worry about me and him. We're big boys."

"Meaning what? You've kissed and made up?"

His lip twitched. "Something like that."

"You were the reason for the sore jaw, weren't you?"

Roman lined his knives back on the table. "It was sore? Good. Bastard deserved it. But you can wipe that frown off your face, sweet pea. He and I agree to disagree. Until he does something else that's stupid, the two of us are good."

Liam barged into the room, no whining or joking smile in sight. "Knox was shot."

Zoey took a moment to mentally connect those three little words.

Next to her, Roman didn't need time. "What the fuck are you talking about?"

"Cade called. They were out trying to wrangle that Stuart guy and Knox was shot in the process."

"Stuart *shot* him?" Her panic raised the pitch of her voice. The two brothers quickly hustled down the corridor, Zoey hot on their heels.

"That's what they think. Cade has him in custody now, but Knox was taken to Georgetown. Mom and everyone are meeting us at the hospital."

This time, Zoey didn't wait for Liam and Roman to lead.

She rushed past them on the steps leading to Iron Bars. The first one upstairs, she grabbed the nearest set of keys—Roman's—and burst into a full run toward his pickup.

She'd already pulled away from the curb when the two brothers stepped outside. Roman, flashing his beloved truck a quick worried glance, waved her off as they headed toward Liam's car.

Knox had been on multiple tours of duty, in one of the most demanding military units around, and he'd come out unscathed. A few weeks home and he'd been shot. Zoey tried not reading into it or letting her mind wander to dangerous territory. But as she weaved Roman's truck through yellow lights and cut people off in yield lanes, it couldn't be helped.

Cade's defensive driving lessons put her at Georgetown's drop-off zone in less than fifteen minutes. She'd barely thrown the truck into park before she barreled through the sliding glass doors and to the registration desk. "Knox Steele. He was brought in a while ago . . . a gunshot?"

The attendant clacked on her computer without glancing up. "Are you family?"

"Yes, she is." Mouth set into a grim line, Grace didn't look like a woman about to spring good news. When she reached Zoey, she pulled her into a hug, reading her panic. "It's okay. He's okay."

"Liam said he was shot."

"Lucky jerk only has a small chunk missing out of his shoulder. They've already stitched him up, although they refused to stitch his mouth closed—I've asked. He's finishing up his statement to the police."

"What happened? How—?"

"Don't know. All I got from Cade before he went to the station to interrogate Stuart was that Knox chased him to some alley. He didn't *see* him fire the weapon."

"Forensics will paint the entire picture." Zoey focused on what she knew rather than all the questions up in the air.

She pushed her hair from her face, realizing as she brushed her cheeks that they were wet. Not slightly damp. Not just an errant tear. She'd conjured Niagara Falls from her tear ducts and Grace, the good friend she was, simply handed her a fistful of tissues.

She'd barely finished mopping up the mess when Liam and Roman entered the emergency room.

"How is he? Have you heard anything?" Roman's earlier annoyance had been replaced by worry.

"He'll live to piss you off another day," Grace quipped. "Come on. I'll take you to his room."

Grace led them through the back halls of the emergency department, and the whole way, Zoey imagined Knox, attached to tubes and wires, pale and plastic-looking from blood loss. He hated hospitals nearly as much as she did, so any kind of hospitalization would be nothing short of torture.

Two uniformed cops stepped out from a corner room, one of them her friend Nat. Seeing Zoey, she walked over. "Now I know why you were running away from Steele the other day. He's…intense. And a pain in the ass. Patients like him make me thankful that I became a cop instead of a nurse."

"Sounds about right," Roman muttered, pushing Knox's room door open.

"Thank you, Nat," Zoey squeezed her friend's hand and followed Roman, Grace, and Liam into Knox's room.

He sat at the edge of the bed, shirtless, a white bandage slapped over his left shoulder. Cindy fussed at his side, and everyone talked over one another, stating concerns, or in Liam's case, joking about turning himself in for the botched assassination attempt.

Zoey remained behind a rolling chair, fighting the desperate urge to push everyone away and climb into Knox's arms. She didn't want to get in the way of a family moment, and definitely didn't want to make this moment about her.

Knox's dark eyes caught hers from over Grace's head. He'd been the one shot, and yet worry deepened his frown the longer his gaze remained locked on her. Zoey couldn't ignore the escalating tremble in her heart anymore.

She covered a breathless gasp by a fake cough and left the room with a softly muttered apology. The second she reached the hallway, a new onslaught of tears appeared. This time, she didn't wipe them away, leaning heavily against the wall.

She'd come way too close to losing Knox.

Already.

She'd reminded herself a million times daily that it was going to happen eventually. But there was nothing quite like reality smacking you in the face. And watching him walk out of her life was a hell of a lot different from him being ripped from it.

It left her more than a bit shaken.

"Zoey? I thought that was you." Dr. Samuel approached, concern etched over his face. "Are you okay? No one paged me that you were here."

She wiped her dampened cheeks and straightened. "Oh, no. I'm okay. I'm not here for me. A friend of mine was brought in."

Dr. Samuel's gaze strayed to Knox's door. "I hope your friend's okay. Who's the attending? Maybe I could check on things and see if they need a second pair of eyes."

"Thanks for the offer, but that's not necessary. He's okay." Which was why she should be inside the room with everyone else, rejoicing, instead of in the hall cowering.

"You sure?"

"Positive, but thank you."

"Then I guess I'll see you at your follow-up . . . which you've yet to schedule with the office."

Zoey tried to laugh at his obvious warning, but it fell a bit flat. "I'll do that first thing in the morning. Cross my heart."

A harried nurse hustled over to him, asking questions about a patient, and Zoey and Dr. Samuel parted ways. Knox's door whipped open and the entire Steele lineup filed out.

Liam saw her first. "We're being kicked out by the patient—which means he's back to his old self. You want a ride home?"

Crap. Roman's truck, if it hadn't already been towed, still sat out front.

Roman must have read her sudden panic. "I moved

my truck to the emergency room lot so Knox can drive his own ass home."

A nurse slipped past them and into Knox's room. Before the door even closed, his adamant protests filtered into the hall. All Zoey heard was *overdue* and *injection*, so she imagined the nurse wanted to give him a tetanus shot.

"One way to cut hospital costs is to have as many nurses as possible take care of Knox. They'd all quit right after." Ryder's comment earned him a head biff from his mother.

"Talk nice about your brother. He was *shot*." Cindy Steele drilled her middle son with a warning glare.

"In the arm, Ma," Liam interjected. "It's not like he got hit anywhere important—like his ass, where he does most of his thinking. And talking."

Cindy reached out to smack Liam's arm, but he scooted away, chuckling. The nurse who'd just entered Knox's room stormed out, stopping short at the sight of them. "Which of you is Zoey?"

Everyone's eyes slid to her.

Zoey hesitantly raised her hand. "That would be me, although I'm not sure by your face that I should admit to it."

"Good luck with that one, honey. You're going to need it, because he's asking for you."

After declining a ride home, Zoey said goodbye to the rest of the Steeles and stood in front of Knox's door a solid three minutes before stepping inside.

Still sitting shirtless, he glanced up from the paperwork in his hand, something that almost looked like relief dropping his shoulders. "I thought you left."

"Nope. Still here."

He tossed the papers on the gurney and crooked his finger. "Come here."

"I'm okay where I am." Zoey pushed her glasses higher onto the bridge of her nose and mentally cursed at the tear remnants dotting the lenses.

Evidence that she'd more than lost her cool out in the hallway.

Knox's gaze remained fastened on her. "Well, *I'm* not okay where you are. You going to make an injured man get up and drag you over here?"

"It's your shoulder that's the problem, not your legs."

He fought back a smile and crooked his finger again. "Angel."

She fought a losing battle, because she'd wanted to run to him the second Liam burst into the gym with news of the shooting.

Lifting her chin, she took a wary first step, and then a second. After the third, she couldn't hold back. She sprinted the rest of the way. Knox's good arm hauled her between his spread thighs and flush against his body.

"Are you okay? Really?" Her hands automatically drifted to his shoulders, and he sucked in a hiss. "Oh crap. Sorry. I should come with my own orange caution cones."

She stepped back, but Knox caged her against him with both arms, pulling her nearly nose to nose. "I like living dangerously. Why'd you hightail it out of here earlier?"

"I ... forgot to turn off my phone."

Knox searched her entire face before zoning in on her eyes. If he was half-good at his job, he'd see the truth staring back at him, plain as the nose on her face. And he wasn't just good.

He was great.

"Zoey."

She shook her head, silently pleading with him not to continue. Barely hanging on to her wits as it was, she'd break if he called her out. Or worse, wanted answers. Half of the emotions going through her head she didn't understand herself.

"Roman left his truck here." Zoey cleared her throat and pushed through the awkward silence. "So I can drop you at the marina ... or we could go to my place. You don't have to stay if you don't want," she added quickly. "If you're up to driving, you could drop me off."

His heated gaze lingered on her lips, making her throat dry.

"Aren't you going to say something? Anything?"

Knox stood, reaching for a clean shirt she hadn't seen with one hand and held her close to him with the other. "I have plenty to say, angel. But I'm saving it for later."

With discharge papers in hand, he linked their fingers and led the way to the parking lot. By the time they'd reached Roman's truck, she had a vise grip on his hand.

"Sorry." She released it, embarrassed.

"Don't be." Knox opened the passenger door and waited for her to buckle up before getting into the driver's side. A second after flipping the ignition, he entwined their hands again and pulled hers gently into his lap.

Where he planned to lay his head tonight shouldn't matter, but it did. Her need to touch him had grown more in the last few hours, and if he went back to his boat, there wasn't a doubt in her mind that she'd have another sleepless night.

Now, as Knox walked her to her door, she held her breath.

"Is that offer to stay still good?" Knox rubbed his thumb along the back of her hand, but it felt as if he touched her entire body. Warmth slipped into her cheeks and to parts beyond. "I can head home if you'd rather be alone."

"No," Zoey blurted out.

"No? No the offer isn't any good, or no you'd rather not be alone."

"You can stay. I'd like it if you stayed." She took a deep breath. "I think I kind of need you to stay, if I'm being truthful right now."

A small smile tugged up the corner of his mouth, nearly melting her on the spot. "I was *really* hoping you'd say that, angel, because I think I kind of need to stay with you too."

Cupping Zoey's cheeks, Knox leaned in for a slow, gentle kiss that she felt down to her toes. She carefully gripped his shirt and held him close, content to finally be *in* his arms. Her concern shifted away from alleyway shootings and raging serial killers and even the possibility of her jewelry being involved in a homicide.

All Zoey could think about was that she'd only fully embraced her live-free lifestyle weeks ago and she was already having a difficult time envisioning Knox not being part of it.

* * *

With one hand, he overturned the table in front of him. Its surface hit the wall, scattering debris to every corner of the room...and he wasn't done.

He ripped...crashed...destroyed. Nothing in his path was safe as his scream tore from his throat, coating the back of his tongue in blood.

He'd fucked up.

He'd had his chance, one that had taken hours of careful planning, of stalking and studying, and he'd squandered it in the blink of an eye. The second he'd pulled the trigger, he'd known he'd missed his mark.

Instead of a bullet between the eyes, Steele had spun to the ground, crimson blood darkening his shoulder. HIS SHOULDER. His own inadequacy meant he hadn't gotten a second chance.

The price for his failure was watching His Heart, Her blue eyes wide with concern, run into the hospital.

To Steele.

He ripped the calendar off the wall, anger only barely held at bay at seeing the countdown. It had already begun. He'd made certain of it. With every red X, his goal came closer. He no longer relied on luck or happenstance, instead trusting actualities.

It would happen.

By holding his course, His Heart would come to him.

And then Steele would be inconsequential.

CHAPTER NINETEEN

The only thing more difficult than prying himself from Zoey's bed this morning—with news she had to spend yet another day with his brothers   was watching Cade do things his way.

The *slow* way.

It wasn't that he wasn't effective. Cade knew his shit and they'd already gotten bits and pieces about what made the kid tick. But cops couldn't *force* people to talk. Hogan Wilcox had been right on the money when he said that there was a lot of red tape in law enforcement.

Knox watched from the observer side of the two-way mirror while his friend interrogated Rick Stuart for the third time that day.

"I told you. I didn't do anything. I've been keeping my nose clean." Stuart sniffed as if thinking about his nose turned the damn thing on.

"Innocent people don't flee when the cops knock on their door, Rick. And you weren't fleeing. You were flying like a bat out of hell," Cade reminded, kicking his feet onto the desk in front of them.

"Yeah, well. I don't like cops. No offense."

Cade smirked. "None taken. I'm not particularly

fond of thieves. Or attempted murderers. And I really hate serial killers."

Stuart's eyes widened. "Attempted murder? Serial killer? What? No way, man. I may have stolen some shit, but I ain't never tried to kill anyone!"

"The hole in my buddy's arm says otherwise."

Stuart was already shaking his head. "Not me. I don't know who shot your guy, but it sure as hell wasn't me."

"And why should I believe you? Two minutes ago you swore up and down that you keep your nose clean and now you say that you stole some shit." Cade dropped his feet to the floor and leaned on the table, hands clasped casually. "I got news for you, man. I know you stole some shit. Your place was stacked with hot items taken from the Kingsbrooke burglaries as far back as last November. The question in front of us now is if we add murder onto the charge list. Where were you the night of April eighth?"

"Fuck. I don't know." Stuart shifted in his chair. Rivulets of sweat poured down his forehead and into his eyes. "I was flying hi—I mean, I don't know. But I know I didn't kill nobody."

"You were high? Is that what you were going to say? Look, I don't care about whatever habit you got that's melting away brain cells. What I *do* care about is finding a killer."

Cade slid a photograph toward Stuart, and judging by the guy's ashen face, it wasn't a nice image. "Gin's...dead? Who—who did this?"

"Figured you'd be able to tell us."

"Me? No way, man. I l-loved her. I mean, we had our issues, but I treated her like gold. I'd never hurt her."

"What about the necklace around her neck. You recognize it?"

Stuart studied the image again. "No, man. I've never seen it before."

"You didn't give it to her? Maybe from one of your hauls?"

Stuart went quiet before shrugging. "I mean, yeah, I lifted a shit-ton of jewelry, but I grab and go. I don't inspect the loot. I always gave Gin first crack at it, let her pick out anything she wants before I hock it. Keeps her happy and makes her feel special. But who gives a damn about a fucking necklace. Someone killed my girlfriend!"

"Why don't you tell us what you think, Stuart? Who could've done this to her?"

"You're the fucking cops. It's *your* job to find out. Or maybe you don't care because she wasn't a pillar of the damn community."

"We're doing everything we can, but sometimes we need a little bit of help."

"I can't tell you what I don't know. It's been days since I've seen her. She's been working a lot, trying to save some cash."

It continued for another thirty minutes before Cade nodded to the guard in the corner and they hauled away a visibly distraught Stuart. Ten minutes later, Cade stalked into the observation room. "What does your gut tell you?"

"That your job would be a hell of a lot easier if all criminals were as dumb as Stuart. But I also think that necklace was a coincidence," Knox admitted.

Cade sunk into a nearby chair. "Thank fuck. As pissed as I am that we've hit another road block, I'm glad Zoey's in the clear."

Knox too.

Last night, he'd lain awake, too wired and too *everything* to fall asleep. He'd thought about the shooting, and about the chase through the alley. But his mind always drifted to the hesitant way Zoey had walked into his hospital room.

He'd wanted nothing more than to lay eyes on her for hours and there she'd stood, looking as if the slightest noise would send her bolting away. It was a good thing the doctor hadn't been listening to his lungs right then, because he hadn't breathed until she sprinted into his arms. The only reason he'd let her go was because he hadn't wanted to stay in that damn hospital another second.

He knew she hated them. And hell, he couldn't blame her.

But the real reason was that he'd just needed to hold her. He'd told her the truth. He would've dropped her home and gone back to the boat if she wanted to be alone, but he was damn glad that wasn't the option she chose.

Everything seemed easier when it involved Zoey. Breathing. Sleeping. *Living.* Around her, he didn't feel like the colossal fuck-up who'd disappointed his entire family.

Knox pulled his cell from his pocket, and got eyed by Cade. "I'm calling your sister to give her her Get Out of Jail Free card. Unless you want to do the honors."

"Nah." Cade shook his head. "You were the poor bastard who had to tell her she had to spend another day with your brothers. You need the bonus points more than I do."

Tallying up bonus points should be the last thing on Knox's mind. He wasn't going to be around long enough to collect any amount that would give him what he truly wanted.

* * *

Zoey thought after Knox's phone call and the ending of an agonizingly long game of chess with Liam, her headache would disappear, but she had no such luck.

Massaging her temple with one hand, she reached into her desk drawer with the other, blindly searching for the bulk bottle of Tylenol she'd stashed in there last week.

"Are you trying to communicate with someone telepathically? Because you know we have interoffice mail. More paperwork but less headaches." Lieutenant Mason leaned a hip on her desk and looked down on her in fatherly concern.

"I hear the words coming from your lips, but I can't quite string them together." Her fingers bumped into the bottle. "Aha! Jackpot! My head's echoing like a tom-tom drum and it brought orchestra friends."

Zoey popped two pills into her mouth and, realizing

she'd forgotten her cardiac meds, shuffled through her purse and added them to the tally. "Did you come over to make bad jokes or did you need something?"

"Someone said they saw you come in and I needed to see for myself. Didn't you take the day off?"

Zoey quietly returned her meds to her purse. "No, I was *directed* to take it off by a certain big brother and four obnoxiously large Steele men."

Mason nodded in understanding. "The necklace thing."

"You know about it too? Oh, wait. Of course you do. Thank God it turned out to be a coincidence or I'd still be on lockdown."

"And instead of enjoying the rest of the day and night, you came into work. You young people seriously have your work ethic screwed up."

Zoey laughed at his sarcasm. "I had paperwork to finish before the next task force meeting. And yes, I realize how pathetic that sounds. You don't need to rub it in."

He stuck out his hand. "Give it to me. I'll finish. You go."

"It's my job as the grunt to get this done."

"And it's my job to make sure that I don't scare off my future replacement." Mason grinned. "If I scare you off before you take over, I don't get to retire and, kid, I need to retire . . . to somewhere with a beach and a hammock that my ass doesn't have to get out of except to take a piss."

Zoey's headache melted away her stubbornness. "Okay, I relent. The test report on top is the only one that needs to be interpreted. All the others are already done. And then we need to make copies for—"

"This was my job until they approved for me to have my own servant—I mean, protégé."

Zoey chuckled, pushing her glasses onto her nose. "Point taken. I'm going to clean my desk and head out."

"Sounds like a plan." He winked and left, leaving Zoey to straighten up the mess left behind. Once she was able to see the dented metal surface, she'd pulled her purse from her drawer.

The phone rang, nearly splitting her head in half. A quick glance at the caller ID, and she knew she couldn't ignore it.

"Adam," she said in lieu of a greeting because only one person in the lab worked this late on a weekend, "please keep in mind before you say anything that it's been a long day and my vocabulary pretty much consists of fire-bad, puppy-cute."

"I need you to come down here," Adam hissed. "Pronto."

Zoey swallowed a sigh. Her former assistant was as smart as they came, but he didn't take unexpected stress well. "Whatever it is, you got this. You're—"

"Locked in the lab and he's probably leaving freakin' fist indents on the other side."

"I'm sorry, *what*?"

"Will you please come and fix this?"

"I'm on my way."

She grabbed her things and bypassed the slow elevator in favor of the stairs.

Located in the precinct basement, the district lab was

called the Dungeon for a reason, because except for small half windows that were even with the DC sidewalk, there wasn't much natural light.

The Dungeon consisted, in total, of three rooms. The smaller, outer room off the hall looked like any other office space with desks and computers. Techs typed up reports and sent them upstairs to the appropriate detectives.

Purgatory was the middle room. A window-encased clean-prep area tucked between the actual lab and office, it was where staff donned their gowns and gloves before heading into the glass-protected lab—the third room—on the other side.

Scott Reed stood in Purgatory, shouting a string of curses at the man in the lab, already gowned, gloved, and wearing his favorite Minion operating cap.

Through the slit between his cap and his mask, Adam's eyes caught Zoey's.

Zoey prepped herself for contact and cleared her throat. "Is there something that I can get for you, Officer Reed?"

"What are you—?" Scott spun around, shooting Adam a death glare through the window. "Seriously, you little pipsqueak? You called *her*?"

"Hell yeah I called *her*. No one will protect this place quite like the Mother of Dungeons." Adam's muffled statement would have made Zoey grin if she hadn't been standing face-to-face with Reed.

"He's right," Zoey agreed. "I may not be in the lab anymore, but I worked damn hard to get it to the point it is now. What can we do for you?"

"I tried finding out from this little pip what was taking so damn long with this fucking Cupid case. I mean it's been six months and nothing? I find that hard to believe...unless there's a moron running the ship."

"I assure you that Adam's far from a moron. He probably has as many letters behind his name as are in the alphabet."

"Which makes it even harder to believe that we've got jack shit to fucking go on." He took a small step closer and Zoey inched to the left, farther behind the desk...and closer to the panic alarm if needed.

If Reed didn't like *her* presence, he *really* wouldn't like the slew of officers that alarm would bring. But no way would she let him compromise the lab's integrity and all the testing happening inside either. "I must have missed your name on the task force roster. When did you transfer onto the team?"

His face hardened as he shifted on his feet, a subtle but noticeable move. "You think I can't get on that team? I'm waiting for the official word, and then you better believe that things will move along."

"Just a little bit of advice. Harassing the lab manager to the point that he locks himself in the lab isn't how you go about moving things along. It's a good way to increase the likelihood that something happens to irreplaceable evidence."

Scott snorted. "What-the-fuck-ever. Forget it. I'm not going to be part of a team that doesn't know the difference between their ass and their elbow."

Scott stormed out through the main office, slamming the door behind him.

Adam buzzed himself back into Purgatory, and immediately wrapped her in a bone-crushing hug. "I can't thank you enough."

"What the hell was that about?" Zoey shook out her hands, not realizing until now just how bad she'd been shaking through that entire sideshow. "I knew he was a hothead, but *cheese and crackers*."

"Damned if I know. He came strolling into Purgatory like he owned the place and tried badging into the lab. He could've ruined six months' worth of results. *Prick*." Adam glared at the door before his cheeks reddened. "Sorry, I know you had a temporary moment of insanity with him."

Zoey tugged his cap off his head and smacked him with it, making him laugh. "Seriously, am I ever going to live that down?"

"Not until you have something juicier that I can use against you." Zoey clamped her mouth shut, and Adam immediately latched on to her silence. "Oh, man. I know that face. That's an I-know-something-that-would-be-gossip-fodder-for-the-entire-precinct-for-a-year-but-I'm-not-saying-anything face."

"You think too much of my faces."

He chuckled. "Fine. Be close-mouthed. You're going to tell me eventually. Or Grace will let it slip after I ply her with a pitcher of margaritas and some good ol' Cade bashing."

"You are pure evil."

He grinned. "Even got the horns, baby."

Zoey scanned the room. "You're okay now? You're not going to lock yourself in the freezer or anything if I leave, are you?"

"Heading to a secret rendezvous?" Adam teased.

"Yes, my secret rendezvous with my very comfortable bed." A bed in which she hoped to find a very sexy—and naked—former Ranger. But he didn't need to know that.

Adam glanced at the door through which Scott had left. "You know what? I'm heading out too. Walk up with me?"

"Sure thing."

Zoey helped lock up the lab, and then they headed up to the main floor. Low voices echoed from the direction of the cubicles, one of which never ceased to send warm tingles of excitement through her.

Adam, standing next to her, grinned. "No secret rendezvous my cute rear end."

At Adam's tease, Knox and Mason glanced their way.

She hadn't seen Knox since this morning, and she admittedly hadn't been in the best mood. The second he'd left to meet up with Cade, she'd felt bad for taking her frustrations out on him.

It wasn't Knox's fault that someone broke into her apartment, or that the Cupid Killer decided her necklace was a good way to deviate from his normal pattern. Sometimes in her quest to stand on her own two feet, she experienced a little...tunnel vision.

"Angel." Knox's eyes devoured every inch of her as she walked closer, his mouth curling into a naughty smirk. "When most people get a Get Out of Jail Free card, they usually do something fun. Not head into work."

"Exactly what I said," Mason chuckled.

"Are you offering to take me somewhere fun now?" Zoey ignored the older officer and kept her gaze on Knox.

Next to her, Adam coughed. She ignored him, matching Knox's grin with one of her own.

She really hoped his answer was going to be yes.

CHAPTER TWENTY

It was hard to believe it had been over a week since Zoey and Knox crossed that line from simple friendship...to something else. As happy as she was to be out of her comfort zone, being in uncharted territory wasn't all it was cracked up to be.

For one, she couldn't begin to guess what was going through his mind. They'd said goodbye to Mason and Adam and walked to the rear lot, not one word spoken. It would've made her paranoid if it weren't for the fact that he'd found some way to touch her the entire time.

In front of Mason and Adam, it had been his palm on the small of her back. Now it was the firm curl of his fingers around her hand.

After unlocking her car, she tossed her things into the passenger seat. Across the street, a green sports car peeled away from the curb, leaving behind the stench of burnt rubble. "Sometimes I think Roman's antisocial ways are the way to go."

Knox smiled, slowly easing his arms around her waist. "That...makes me feel a little paranoid, I'm not going to lie."

Zoey laughed. "Not you. Scott." She nodded toward

the now empty parking spot. "The jerk was in the lab giving Adam a hard time."

"About?"

"He *claimed* because things weren't moving along on the Cupid Killer case."

"Is he on the task force?"

"Nope. But he doesn't care. For as long as I've known him, which, unfortunately, has been since we were kids, he's always pranced around like he gets special privileges because his father's a state senator."

"And yet you went to the movies together." Knox leaned his rear end against her car and tugged her into the cradle of his pelvis.

Zoey threw her hands in the air, exasperated. "You'd think that I took out a billboard ad or something."

"I'm teasing you, angel. Trust me, I have no room to rag on you about bad dating choices."

"Because of FBD?" The second she said the words, she slapped a hand over her mouth.

"FBD?" He chuckled, prying her hand from her over her lips. "You're not getting tight-lipped on me now, are you? Come on now. Spill. What, or who, is FBD?"

"FBD." She grimaced. "Fire-Breathing Dragon. *Francine*. It sorta came natural. I mean, her last name's Smoke, and she has the temperament of a dragon."

"You're right. It's . . . suitably fitting." Knox laughed.

"Grace and I thought so."

Zoey's finger traced the edge of the white bandage peeking out from beneath Knox's shirt sleeve. "How's your shoulder? You haven't done a lot of resting since last night."

"If I say horrible, will you come to my place and play nursemaid?"

"I don't think you want me playing nurse. I'd be more likely to create fresh wounds than help them heal."

"I think we'd both manage." Smirking, Knox slid his hands from her hips to just beneath the hem of her shirt. "But I'm not going to lie. I have a few ulterior motives, and they're not all innocent in nature."

Both the course of his hands and the heat in his eyes gave her hope. "Yeah? Maybe it's something close to what I imagined."

He held his mouth a hairsbreadth away from hers. "In your imagination, do we end up naked in my bed, passed out from sexual exhaustion, and waking up to do it all over again?"

"It's like you were in my head."

Zoey sighed as Knox caressed his mouth over the curve of her neck.

He chuckled. "If we're both thinking it, then I guess it's meant to be."

After a few long, drugging kisses and her adamancy that she wasn't leaving her car at the precinct to be stranded in the morning, she and Knox parted ways long enough to meet back at the marina.

This time, she managed both the gangway and the stairs leading below deck without incident. Knox's military upbringing showed not just in his uncluttered space, but in the way he reacted. The things he said. The passion he showed.

They kissed their way across the small living room,

Zoey's legs bumping against the back of the couch. She stumbled onto the cushion, chuckling at her own klutziness. "Guess I'll take a seat."

"I was about to ask you to take one anyway." Knox's mouth arched into a sexy half grin. Keeping his hot gaze focused on her, he eased onto the sofa and glided her legs over his thighs until she sat astride his lap.

"Right here?" She wiggled, pulling a groan from his throat.

"No place better." Palms braced on her hips, he shifted her closer, and tugged her mouth down to his. "You have no idea how bad I want you right now."

"Probably as bad as I do you," Zoey flirted brazenly. His confession sent a warm thrill through her. "But you were shot twenty-four hours ago. As much as I want this, maybe we should take a breather."

"It's nothing more than a scratch. Trust me, I've had worse."

She didn't doubt it, but he also couldn't hide his pain. Not from her, a verifiable expert on glossing over physical discomfort. She'd had a lifetime experience of masking it. "Knox."

"Angel. I'm fine." He trailed his mouth up the curve of her neck, making her sigh. "But I could be fanfucking-tastic if we stopped talking and started doing."

Zoey chuckled. Days without his hands on her body, and her skin ached to feel him again too. Grinning, she slid off his lap and gently pulled him to his feet. "Then we're going to do this my way."

"This just keeps getting better and better." Knox dropped his hands to his sides and watched her shove his jeans and boxers down his legs. When they hit his ankles, he kicked them away.

"Sit." She gently pushed him back onto the couch. "And behave."

"Do I have to?" Knox smirked.

Taking charge felt odd at first, but then it just felt...right. She knelt on the floor in front of him, spreading his knees wide enough to fit her shoulders.

Knox swallowed a curse as she wrapped her fingers around his hard shaft and squeezed. "Fuck. You don't have to do this, angel."

"I know I don't. I want to." More than anything.

She flicked away a clear drop of fluid with the tip of her tongue. Knox groaned, sliding his hand into her hair. "You're killing me here."

"Killing you softly?"

"Yeah. Not so soft."

Fueled by his pleasure, Zoey wrapped her mouth around his shaft and slowly slid her mouth down his entire length, inch by inch. His cock nearly hit the back of her throat, and she swallowed, her muscles contracting around his girth.

"I love your mouth, baby." Eyes hooded with desire, Knox watched her, his face softening from raging lust to pure bliss.

She couldn't tear her eyes away from his as she tightened her lips around him and set a slow, firm pace. Knox gently bumped his hips up to meet her mouth. The taste of his pre-come seeped onto her tongue, coaxing her faster.

She tightened her lips and felt his body respond. His

breath, the only other sound on the boat other than the wet slide of her mouth, grew louder.

On the next upswing, he pulled her off his cock. "I want that sweet pussy of yours wrapped around me when I come."

"Condom?"

He tore through his wallet, distracted by her shimmying out of her pants and underwear. "Shit. You're so damn gorgeous."

She left her shirt on, and he didn't say a thing or look the least bit deterred.

"Come here, baby." Having already donned the latex, he gripped her hips and eased her onto his lap. His fingers slid through the wetness between her legs, making her groan.

"This is *so* not fair," Zoey panted, her fingers digging into his good shoulder for support.

"Just making sure you're ready for me." He smirked.

"I'm more than ready." Even though his touch was pleasant torture, she moved his hand out of her way and took his entire shaft in one slow drop.

They groaned in unison.

Zoey braced her forehead against his and rotated her hips. Every swivel sent him even deeper, a delicious torture that she wished could last forever. "Please tell me if I hurt you."

"Could never happen." Knox cupped her hips, and together they worked their two bodies into sync. A slow grind turned into a frantic coupling that creaked the couch beneath them.

"Knox." Zoey tossed her head back, her body beginning to quake.

"It's all you, baby. Take it. Take *me*. You have no idea how much I've wanted this." Knox guided her hips, keeping up with her frantic pace. He palmed a breast, and flicking a hardened cloth-covered nipple with his thumb, sent her over the edge. "God, Zoey. You have no idea how much I've wanted you."

His words could've meant anything.

Right now. The last twenty-four hours.

As Zoey's orgasm tightened her body, Knox grew even harder inside of her with his own release. Grabbing her hips, he anchored her to him as wave after wave of pleasure crashed through them, one immediately on top of the other until they were both breathless and panting.

A casual, no-strings sexual arrangement sounded great in theory.

But that theory had never been applied to Knox Steele.

* * *

He'd verified his timeline, again and again, not about to squander another opportunity. Everything was in clear working order, running smoothly just as he planned.

There was no turning back. There was no backpedaling. There was no second-guessing.

All that was left to do...was prepare.

He'd get to see Her again.

Soon.

Much sooner than even he expected.

CHAPTER
TWENTY-ONE

Knox prided himself on sticking to his guns. No one could talk him into anything if he didn't have half his mind already made to do it. Except, apparently, Roman. Forcing him into attending the DC Police Gala was just one in a string of ways that Ro used Knox's lingering guilt to his advantage.

His tactics wouldn't last forever. He wished they hadn't worked *this* time.

Knox didn't schmooze. Or gloat. And he sure as hell didn't have spare money to throw into the DCPD.

There wasn't a single person in the room who wasn't dressed to the nines. A mellow song filtered through the speakers, echoing off the high walls and steep glass-covered ceiling. In the background, voices droned and silverware clinked as people enjoyed the lavish spread in front of them.

Knox navigated himself through the crowd, wishing more and more with each step that he was with Zoey rather than here. A night wasted in his eyes. And with them numbered, he wanted to take advantage of every one that he got.

Thinking about her small-print, mutual sexual arrangement was enough to curl his stomach into knots. But thinking about leaving DC took those damn knots and set them on fire.

Across the way, Cade stood with Hogan Wilcox, the old man no doubt using the event to once again convince his friend to jump on board with Steele Ops. He'd almost glanced over them. But Cade's head snapping up at something Wilcox said put Knox on alert.

He'd seen his friend wear that face before. It was the one that showed up seconds before he lost his shit—which didn't happen often. The two men argued heatedly, Cade's hands flying around, before both stalked out the door. Together.

Knox followed his gut…and Cade.

He'd no sooner stepped onto the empty patio when Cade's low growl reached his ears.

Knox followed the sound, turning the bend to find his friend mere inches from Wilcox's face.

He didn't know whom to defend—the older man about to get his ass kicked, or his friend who was about to do the kicking.

"Am I interrupting something?" Knox shoved his hands into his pockets, ready to intervene if necessary.

Wilcox released a small sigh, but it wasn't relief. "We're okay, Mr. Steele."

"We are so fucking far from okay," Cade snarled.

Knox's presence did what he'd hoped. His friend took a small step back, but still remained within punching distance. "Do you know who this asshole is? You're going to get a real kick out of it. Why don't you go ahead and take a guess?"

"You mean other than a former Joint Chief of

Staff?" His answer was meant to make Cade *think* before reacting. Wilcox wasn't someone you wanted to piss off.

Cade's burst of laughter didn't hold a single ounce of humor. He shot a glare at Wilcox. "Do you want to reintroduce yourself or should I? No? Fine. Then I'll do the honors. Knox, I want to introduce my bastard of a father who left his sick four-year-old daughter and eight-year-old son with strangers rather than fess up to fatherhood."

Not much shocked Knox, but this did. "I don't—"

"Understand? Yeah, neither did I until Hogan here used a phrase I remembered from forever ago...one my dear old dad used right before he walked out the door and never came back."

Fists clenched at his side, Cade looked about to blow his top. "You took a big chance meeting me the other day, didn't you, *Dad*? Did you cross your fingers and hope that my eight-year-old memory sucked? Well, congrats. It did.

"You want to know the twisted shit?" Cade glanced to Knox. "He'd *kept tabs on us*. Those were his words. He'd made sure we got the best possible caregiver— Gretchen—and was even the anonymous source that paid all Zoey's medical bills. Wasn't that nice of him, Knox? To make sure his daughter wasn't bogged down with unsightly debt?"

"It's not how you're making it sound," Wilcox said in his own defense.

"I don't give a shit about your *my family didn't approve* excuse. You left your children. *Alone*. And then you have the fucking gall to say that you provided for them behind the scenes. Screw. You."

Cade pushed Wilcox out of the way and stalked toward the hotel.

"I only wanted the best for you and Zoey," Wilcox called after him.

Cade wasn't the only one who stopped. Hearing the jerk mention Zoey's name rose Knox's hackles. "You cared so much that you left her to rely on strangers? Handpicking Gretchen or not, that's exactly what you did."

Cade's nostrils flared. "You just go ahead and keep your distance from Zoey. Do you hear me? We've made it this far without you, we'll make it the rest of the way."

"Cade, maybe you should—"

"No. The bastard doesn't get to fuck up her head. She's finally in a good spot. She's the happiest I've ever seen her. *Ever*. I'm not telling her, or letting this bastard tell her, that he cared enough to fork over money, but he just didn't care enough to introduce himself in person."

Cade stormed away, leaving Knox alone with a now silent Wilcox.

"He has a right to be angry," Wilcox began.

"Damn right he does. If Cade was any less of a man, you'd be using all that money of yours to find someone to reattach your jaw."

"I know." Wilcox glanced at his feet, a telling sight for an Army general.

"I don't think you do. Cade sacrificed a lot to be there for Zoey when she was little—sacrifices that he'd make again. There isn't a single one of us who wouldn't do anything for her."

Something lit up in Wilcox's eyes. For the first time, Knox saw his best friend lying in their depths. "You care about her. My daughter."

More than Knox had ever said aloud. And he sure as hell wasn't saying it to *him*. "I may not agree with Cade's decision to keep you from Zoey, but I agree to not letting you mess with her head. Tread carefully, Wilcox, or next time, I'm going to let Cade off his leash and Roman's just going to have to deal."

Knox returned to the ballroom but unsurprisingly, didn't see Cade anywhere. Wanting to be here even less than he did before, he tugged his cell from his jacket and brought Roman's name up on his contact list.

Before he shot off a text announcing that he was leaving, a swatch of midnight blue caught his attention. Knox spotted Zoey immediately.

Her dress molded to her curves like a well-fitted glove, blue waves of fabric falling from the delicate clasp around her neck to the floor. But where her dress embraced the extra folds in front, it made up for it with its entirely backless rear.

Laughing at something Grace said, Zoey's face lit up. The delicate strength of her body made him stop and pause. But that smile?

That smile stopped his breathing.

* * *

Zoey had tried everything in her power—and Cade's—to get out of attending the police gala, but the commissioner's department memo had been adamant. *For everyone working on the Beltway Cupid Killer case, attendance is mandatory.*

At least that meant she had Grace to commiserate with.

A woman clutching the arm of her older escort passed them by and looked down her sloped nose. Her gaze drifted from Zoey to Grace before silently labeling them as inconsequential and moving onward.

"I feel underdressed," Zoey complained, gesturing to the golf-ball-sized pendant hanging around the woman's neck.

"I'd rather be underdressed than look like I have a severe case of constipation. I mean look at her. All that weight must be locking her colon down nice and tight," Grace murmured at Zoey's side.

Zoey burst into laughter, earning them both a glare from the woman in question.

"What was the captain's answer when you asked him about this attendance nonsense?" Grace questioned.

"He wanted a *united front*...and for the public to *be able to put faces to the names of those striving to make our city safe.*" Zoey pushed her glasses onto the bridge of her nose. "He went on, but I stopped listening after he said formal attire. The point he *didn't* say, is that we're to try and impress the people with fat wallets to let the moths out and put money into the DCPD."

"Great." Grace plastered a fake smile to her face. "So if someone comes up to me and asks what my roll with the DCPD is, I guess I shouldn't say that I'm the federal agent who can't get an accurate read on this bastard."

Zoey tugged on her friend's arm. "You're human, Grace. Not a magician. Did you seriously expect to be able to point us in the right direction within five minutes?"

"Truthfully? Yeah. I didn't think I'd be stuck here for *weeks*." At Zoey's diminished smile, she added, "You know what I mean, Zo. I love you. I love my cousins and Cindy. I even love DC. But unfortunately, those aren't the memories that are the loudest in my head when I'm here."

"I know." Zoey pulled Grace into a hug, avoiding a collision of their champagne glasses. "And once we nab our guy, you'll be off to nail the next sicko."

"From your mouth to my supervisor's ears." Grace blew out a breath and scanned the room. She subtly jabbed her in the side. "Isn't that your doctor?"

Zoey followed her gaze and immediately recognized Dr. Samuel. He'd shed his surfer look and doctor's coat and donned a smart black tux much like the other men in attendance. And he wasn't alone.

Knox's ex dropped a flirty hand onto his arm and laughed at something he said.

"Wasn't he some kind of child prodigy? It seems to me that a genius would see right through the scales." Grace released a little sigh. "Why can't I be attracted to sweet, wholesome doctors? Or predictable insurance brokers? Or intelligent college professors?"

Zoey chuckled. "Because you're allergic to sweet,

steady, and reliable. It's why you can't get Cade out of your system."

"Freakin' allergies," Grace mumbled.

"You need a tissue, Gracie?" Knox's voice teased over their shoulders.

Zoey spun around just in time to witness Knox's gaze sliding over her in a casual caress. "What are you doing here?"

He smirked. "Hello to you, angel. You look gorgeous tonight."

From him, the words weren't a social nicety. She bit her lip before telling him the same. Knox in jeans and a T-shirt was enough to make her drool. Knox in a tux, his dark hair brushing his collar, threw fuel into every woman's billionaire fantasy.

"What *are* you doing here?" Grace asked. "This isn't exactly your kind of scene."

"Tell me about it. This is just Roman's new tactic to torture me." He tossed a quick look around the room. "He's here somewhere...unless he ditched my ass, which wouldn't surprise me in the least."

"You don't strike me as someone who's easily taken by surprise at all, Mr. Steele." An older man came up on Knox's left. He stuck out his hand, first to Grace, then to her. "Judging by the beauty in this corner of the room, the two of you must be Grace Steele and Zoey Wright."

If Zoey wasn't her brother's sister, she would've missed Knox stiffening as she shook the new arrival's hand. "Have we met before?"

"Only in passing conversations, my dear. But I have

met your brother, and may I say that you're infinitely more pleasant." He held on to Zoey's hand a little longer before introducing himself. "Hogan Wilcox."

"Do you know Cade from the Army?"

Hogan Wilcox looked a little surprised. "You pegged me as an Army man? What gave it away? The short hair? I keep telling myself I'm going to let it grow, and yet I'm back at the barber shop every four weeks."

"It was a hunch. You remind me of my brother. And Knox. And all of the Steeles. It's something about the way you fill a room. It's not bad."

"I didn't take it as such." Hogan Wilcox smiled, which compared to some of the others flashing around the room, seemed sincere.

Knox stepped close and tipped his chin toward the dance floor. "Want to take a spin?"

Zoey startled at the abrupt switch in conversation, and his sudden dark tone. "You want to dance? Now? *Here?*"

"Is that a yes?"

She contemplated telling him no, not until he worked on his people skills. But something in his eyes and the way he refused to look at the man next to him had her swallowing her words.

"Guess I'm dancing. Do you mind?" She handed her champagne flute to Grace.

Knox took Zoey's hand and led her onto the middle of the floor. He slid his arms around her waist and tucked her snugly against him. "That's much better. I'd rather be alone and holding you, but this is a close second."

The hard look he'd worn a few seconds ago was gone, replaced by the man she'd gotten to know better these last few weeks. He rocked their bodies into a slow sway that couldn't exactly be considered dancing. His hand, resting low on her bare back, gently caressed her skin. The touch sparked a slow burning heat and sent her hands up the length of his chest until she felt his heart beating steadily beneath her palms.

"Since when do you dance?" She peered up at him, and easily lost herself to the dark twinkle in his eyes.

"Since I get to do it with a beautiful woman in my arms."

"Riiiiiight. And it didn't have anything to do with Mr. Wilcox?"

Knox's jaw flexed.

"Ah. So it does have something to do with him. What's wrong? He seems like a nice enough guy."

"Don't know him too well."

"But enough to look as though you wanted to send a fist through his face." Zoey waited for him to say something.

"He's the wallet that Roman used to help start up Steele Ops."

"So if he's one of the good guys, why break out your caveman club?"

He smirked. "I want to dance with you and you call me a caveman? I'm hurt."

"Somehow I think your feelings will remain intact. Evade all you want, Knox Steele. But I call bullshit." His brow cocked up at her word choice, making her chuckle.

"Careful now, Miss Wright. Keep swearing like a sailor the way you have been and I'm going to start thinking that you're not the sweet, innocent woman that I once believed you were."

She opened her mouth to make a very un-innocent retort, but he took her in a quick spin. Head tilting back, she laughed as butterflies swarmed her stomach. "Your brothers lift me up. You make my head twirl. You Steeles like living dangerously."

"Some things are worth the little bit of danger." Knox grinned. "So I make your head twirl, huh? I hope that's a good thing."

"Definitely." But when they came to a slow stop, Zoey's head continued to spin. Her fingers latched tightly on to Knox's arms.

He held her flush against his chest. "Whoa there, angel. You okay?"

She took a few deep breaths in an attempt to shrug it off. "Yeah. No. I'm fine. Just a little light-headed there for a second."

He didn't look convinced. "You look a little pale."

"*I'm fine*. Honest." The longer they remained still, the better she felt. "But I am going to use the ladies' room."

He took a step as if to follow.

She patted him apologetically on the chest. "Sorry, big guy, but a girl's got to do this business on her own."

"I'll be right here when you're done."

She nodded and left him standing to the side of the dance floor. The tingle on the back of her neck told her he watched her until she left the ballroom.

Surprisingly, there wasn't a line for the restroom. She slipped inside, glad to find it empty, and wetted a paper towel. She'd pressed it to her forehead as the door opened.

Francine, decked out in a slinky gold dress and heels that could probably pierce a man's heart, stepped inside.

"Well, well, well. If it isn't the hometown sweetheart," Francine said in a singsong voice. "Out playing dress-up with the adults tonight?"

"Hello, Fran. And goodbye." Zoey reached the door.

"You think you're something special, don't you?"

Francine's question turned her back around. "Excuse me?"

"I suppose it's not entirely your fault. You've been doted on your entire life."

"I don't know what you're talking about, and honestly, I don't care to. So if you don't mind, I'm leaving."

"I get it," Francine's tone altered. With no sign of her usual snarl, she actually looked *human*.

"You get what?"

"Knox. On the outside, he's a real tempting package. He's got enough alpha to make a woman swoon, and bad boy to fulfill her wildest dreams. But trust me, honey, it's not all it's cracked up to be."

"And why should I listen to you?"

Francine's mouth twisted into a sardonic smile. "Because I saw that look on your face out on the dance floor. Hell, I wore that look. So I'm going to do you a favor, woman to woman."

"Other than leave?" Zoey summoned her inner fire.

Francine coated her lips in another layer of vivid

red and dropped the tube in her purse. "And *that* little spark... the one wishing you could disintegrate me with a bat of those pretty blue eyes? *That's* why you and Knox will never work.

"Knox is a *fixer*," Fran added. "He's the hero. Put someone in front of him that needs to be protected, and he'd walk through bullets to keep them safe. But once that woman shows she's not without a little bit of Kevlar in her spine? It's party over. At least for the woman. Knox, however, will pick up where he left off... with someone else who needs a little saving."

Zoey forced her gaze to hold Francine's, wanting to blame her words on catty jealously, but there was a grain of truth emanating from her tone. Even if it wasn't true, Fran believed that it was.

Zoey summoned her brother's mask of indifference. "Is that all?"

"That's all." Francine brushed past her on her way to the door. "I felt it was my duty to warn you. Now it's up to you what you do with the information."

Zoey stood alone in the bathroom and fought through the round of nausea turning her stomach. Despite her desire to shrug off Francine's words, she couldn't. Not entirely. She'd seen Knox's protective streak more times than she could count.

Was his interest in her that simple?

When they were alone, and naked, he didn't treat her as a breakable object, but that didn't mean it wasn't how he viewed her. That was the risk she took in getting involved with someone who'd seen her past firsthand. Two weeks was hardly enough time to shed a stigma that'd followed you around for your entire life.

The longer Zoey tried making sense of it all, the fiercer the pounding headache behind her eyes became.

No longer in the mood to deal with anyone, much less a room full of pretentious strangers, she called for a Lyft, and once she was waiting at the hotel's entrance, fired off a quick text to Grace, and an even shorter one to Knox telling them she didn't feel well and was going home.

She needed time alone. With no distractions. With no one's thoughts and opinions other than her own. Thankfully, her ride came quickly. No sooner was the driver pulling away from the curb than the hotel's front door swung open.

Knox stepped onto the sidewalk, his head swiveling as if looking for someone.

For her.

His gaze locked on to the car pulling away, and despite the dark hour and the tint of the back window, it felt as if he stared straight into her soul. Tears welled in Zoey's eyes as she mourned the loss of something that had never been hers for the taking.

* * *

Standing in the shadows, oblivious to the activity around him, he drew in a deep breath and shivered as Her flowery scent wrapped around him like a warm hug.

So close.

It had taken every ounce of restraint he owned not to act impulsively... and he'd reaped the reward.

It was happening.

He'd witnessed the signs with his own two eyes.

It was only a matter of time now.

There was just the small matter of his current distraction...

He couldn't lump this one with the others. From first glance, he'd known that this one was nothing more than a means to bring Her back. He'd proven it with the foul creature before. The second he disposed of the body, She would be called. His Heart would return, and he'd be there to watch.

He opened the door to his home, returning the woman's hopeful smile with one of his own, and gestured inside. "This is me."

"It's gorgeous." Her greedy eyes flickered from the professionally hung artwork to the elaborately decorated library. "I have to admit something. I didn't run into you by accident. I made sure it happened."

"And why would you do that?"

"Because I always go after what I want. No sense in waiting for something to happen when you can speed the process along. Am I right?"

"I couldn't agree more."

CHAPTER TWENTY-TWO

Sweat superglued Zoey's back to the gym mat. Moving meant losing the first layer of skin. Not that she could move. She'd lost feeling in all her extremities about ten minutes ago and couldn't push herself to her feet, much less remain standing.

"When I die, make sure I'm buried with all seven seasons of *Buffy*." Her lungs worked overtime to haul in fresh doses of oxygen.

Grace's chuckle ended with a breathless pant. "What about your Angel collection?"

"Donate them—except for the *Angel-Buffy* crossover episodes. Tuck those by my feet. Just make sure my shoes don't smudge the covers."

"Anything else before I read you your last rites?"

"Yeah. Don't let my brother dress me in that horrific cherry-print dress he bought me for my last birthday. I will *not* spend eternity dressed as a fruit salad." They laughed as Zoey struggled into a sitting position. "I'd hate to think how I'd feel right now if I hadn't taken a nap earlier."

"It doesn't constitute as a nap when it's over two hours." Grace tossed Zoey her water bottle and threw a critical glare to the other side of the room. "That class was punishment because he's not getting any."

Zoey choked on her water and coughed. "What?"

Grace's mouth lifted in a coy smirk. "I'm a walking people-reader, and I can spot sexual frustration from miles away. It resembles drug withdrawal."

"Sex withdrawal? Seriously?"

"It's a thing. Which brings us to the question *Why is Knox withdrawing?* And from whom?"

Zoey took a large drink to avoid answering. Grace chuckled and threw a towel at her head. "Keep your secrets. Lord knows you deserve to have a few skeletons in your closet. Just know that they have a habit of popping out when you least expect."

"I'm not so sure the skeleton's big enough to pop out."

Grace's smirk widened. "So there *is* a skeleton."

"I don't know *what* there is," Zoey muttered under her breath. "Or if it's going to continue."

Which was why she hadn't wanted to go to self-defense tonight. She needed time to get her thoughts in order. But Grace had shown up on her doorstep, gym bag in hand, and strong-armed her off her couch and out the door. And why not? It was a Cade-free zone.

Zoey wasn't as lucky.

She'd spent the better part of the last three days avoiding Knox because seeing him confused her more. She couldn't quite meld Francine's words at the gala with the man who looked at her as if he couldn't wait to strip away her clothes.

"Is the sex that bad?" Grace's question pulled Zoey away from her internal struggle. Immediately contemplating her words, her friend held out a hand. "Never mind. Don't tell me. Hearing about my cousin's sex life has way too high of an ick factor. Just tell me the important details."

"I don't want to be *that* woman, Gracie. I've spent my entire life trying not to be *that* woman."

"You're going to have to be a little more specific."

"Someone to be fixed. Someone to be stuffed in a box and marked up with red *fragile* tape."

"Who the hell is stuffing you in a box?" Grace looked about ready to knock heads together.

"You know what I mean. My past makes me an obvious target for hero types." Zoey's gaze automatically drifted to where Knox stood across the room talking to Dottie. "And there are no bigger Mr. Fix-Its than your cousins. Especially Knox."

Realization dawned all over Grace's face. "I'm going to go out on a limb here and say that whoever gave you that ridiculous idea likes talking out of their ass. And now I'm going to go exactly where I said I didn't want to go."

Face contorted into a look of pain, Grace released a long breath. "With as few details as possible, *please*, on a scale of one to ten...one being something *you* could sleep through and ten being something people in the neighboring county *couldn't* sleep through...how would you rate your sexual experiences with Knox?"

"Grace!" Zoey threw her towel back in her friend's face.

"Trust me, this topic of conversation is *not* bringing me any joy. But seriously, Zo. When you're together, has he taken off your clothes and broken out the bubble wrap?"

"You're being ridiculous."

"One of us is, but it's not me, my friend. Men don't usually visually and physically devour women they think are fragile little daylilies."

"So you're saying Knox isn't protective?"

Grace snort-chuckled. "That's not what I'm saying at all. Of course he is. All my cousins are. But there's a huge difference between someone who thrives on the adrenaline associated with saving the world, and one who simply wants to keep the people they care about safe. And just so there's no misunderstanding, Knox is the latter."

A shadow fell over Zoey, pulling her attention up.

The man himself, his shirt dampened with sweat, stopped inches shy of her sneakers. His gaze bounced between his cousin and her, lingering over Zoey. "Looks like an intense conversation over here. You two aren't plotting to overthrow the teacher, are you?"

"It would serve you right if we were." Grace got to her feet, wincing. "This is self-defense class. I'm not supposed to feel like I'm training for the Olympics."

"If you don't like it, the front door's right behind you, cuz," Knox challenged.

"And leave your sadistic self alone with my best friend? No freakin' way."

Zoey got to her feet. The second she stood, someone—or some*thing*—stole the breath from her lungs. She sucked in a gasp and felt Knox's arm immediately at her elbow. "You okay?"

"Yeah. Just . . . got a little winded there for a second. I'm fine now." And it was the truth—mostly. She took a deep breath and fought off the slight swirl of her head.

She eased from Knox's arms only for him to sweep her up into a princess carry. "What are you doing? Knox! Put me down!"

He deposited her into a chair and hovered so close she had no choice but to stay seated. "Sit. Breathe."

Clenching her teeth, she growled, "I'm. *Fine*."

"People who are fine don't go around collapsing."

Zoey's head could've been on a merry-go-round and she would've stood up just to wipe that hear-man-speak tone from Knox's voice. She edged her seat backward far enough to stand her ground.

His hand shot toward her elbow, but she slid it away. "Plant my ass in a chair as if I'm a preschooler again, and you're going to be the one that's not *fine*."

Knox's eyes darkened in silent challenge, but she refused to back down. Francine's words echoed in her head on a repetitive wheel, making her more determined to stand on her own two feet.

Literally.

Finally, Knox lifted his hands in a sign of defeat and stepped back, but he didn't go far. His mouth, already frowning, pinched tight as Grace hustled over, another person in tow.

"Look who I found walking through the door."

Wearing basketball shorts and a T-shirt, Dr. Samuel followed quickly on her heels. "What's wrong?"

"Zoey nearly collapsed," Grace tattled.

"I didn't *nearly* collapse. I got a little winded, but it's over now," Zoey protested the fuss, fully aware of the attention they'd drawn as Dr. Samuel guided her back into her seat.

That standing on her own two feet was pretty short-lived.

"This is overkill," she complained.

"I say it's not-enough-kill. And the only reason you didn't drop was because I caught you." Knox didn't flinch at her sharp glare. "Narrow those pretty eyes at me all you want, angel, but I'm not going to lie to the one person you may actually listen to."

"Grace sounds as if she's sucking in oxygen through a straw and no one's making a fuss over her right now."

"Hey, leave me out of it!" Grace hid a smirk.

"As far as I know, your friend isn't a cardiac patient." Dr. Samuel reached for her wrist and checked her pulse. "Get my gym bag. The black one with the silver handles? My stethoscope's in there and I need to take a quick listen."

Dr. Samuel looked toward Knox, signifying that the order had been meant for him. The two men locked gazes before Knox reluctantly left to go in search of the doctor's bag.

When he dropped it next to them, Doc Samuel didn't waste any time. "You know the drill, Zoey. In and out."

Zoey turned her deep breath into a heavy sigh, earning a chuckle from the cardiologist. He listened at every pivotal position around her heart, both front and back. "Everything still in its proper place?"

Dr. Samuel linked his stethoscope around his neck. "Is this the first time you've felt this way? Have you been having any other symptoms? Palpitations? Excessive fatigue?"

"First time. And no, no, and no."

"Zoey," Grace warned.

Her face heated as she snuck a glance at Knox. If he already saw her as needing a few layers of bubble wrap, this wasn't exactly the way to get him to strip it away. "I guess I have been a little more tired than usual lately, but in my defense, work has been crazy intense. And then when I'm not on duty, I'm..." She snuck another look at Knox. "...my schedule has just been a little hectic."

Dr. Samuel helped her up to her feet. "Hectic or not, you're coming into the office. *Tomorrow*. Don't even bother calling to make an appointment. I'll tell Lisa when I get in and we'll make it happen. We'll do an echo and check your labs...see if we need to change your meds again."

Zoey resigned herself to her fate. "Sure."

"And you should put the brakes on the self-defense classes for the time being—at least until we get a good grasp on what's going on. You need to be your own patient advocate, Zoey, especially if your instructors aren't going to do it."

Silence hung in the air, tense and expanding by the second, and judging by Knox's tight expression, about to explode.

Dr. Samuel packed his things and stood. "Do you need a ride home?"

"She has one," Knox growled.

Before long, Zoey and Knox had walked Grace to her car, and the awkward silence from inside the gym returned. By the time they reached Knox's truck, the tension snapped.

He held the passenger door open but snagged her elbow before she climbed inside. "Are you okay? No dizziness? No shortness of breath?" Knox asked, voice gruff.

Annoyance pulled Zoey's arm from his grip. "Yes, I'm sure. Do you want to check my oxygen saturation?"

"No. I want to do *this*." Knox caged her against the door and dropped his mouth onto hers in a mind-numbing kiss. There was no easy buildup. The second his tongue slipped between her lips, her body melted. She forgot they stood on a DC sidewalk, forgot they were keeping their relationship on the down-low and that anyone could walk by and see them.

She damn near forgot her name by the time he slowly pulled away.

Zoey touched her kiss-swollen lips. "Just when I think kissing you can't get any better."

"Is that why you've been avoiding me for three days?"

"I haven't—" She couldn't even deny it. "Okay, yeah. I have. I needed to think about a few things."

His eyes roamed her face as if trying to pull an explanation directly from her mind. "And were any of these things brought up by Francine by any chance?" At her stunned expression, he added, "I saw her walk out of the gala ballroom right after you. I put two and two together."

Zoey still struggled to wrap her head around her feelings. What Grace had said inside made sense, but it didn't make her fear any less real. Or debilitating.

Knox, misconstruing her silence for defiance, added

gruffly, "If you're going to let whatever Francine said chase you away, then the least you could do is tell me why you're running."

Zoey frowned at the insinuation that she'd gone on the run—even though she had. "Am I just a notch on your Save-o-Meter?"

"What the hell are you talking about?" Genuine confusion clouded his dark eyes.

His gaze dropped to where she nervously bit her bottom lip, and he freed it with his thumb. "Is that what's been going through your head for the last few days? You think that I see you as a way to get my hero on?"

"When you say it like that, it sounds stupid," Zoey muttered, rolling her eyes.

"It's not stupid if it kept us apart for three days and nights." Knox gently pinched her chin between his fingers, holding her attention hostage. "It's not stupid if you believe that it's the reason I'm with you right now. Do I want to keep you from harm? Yes. Shout at me if you want, but I'm not going to apologize for caring about you."

Zoey's breath hitched. "You care?"

"Of course I do." Knox's hands edged along the inch of bare skin between her exercise pants and tank top. He gently lifted her into the seat, and leaned close. "If I saw you as a notch on my Save-o-Meter, or as some kind of delicate flower," he said, using her own words, "I wouldn't be standing here right now debating how long it would take me to get to the boat, strip off your clothes, and slide inside you."

Heat zipped through Zoey's body, intensifying as she

sunk her fingers through the back of his hair. "That's a good point."

"It is." He nibbled her bottom lip.

"We should test it out."

The corner of his mouth tilted up in a sexy smirk. "You think so, huh?"

"Without a doubt. *Next* time. Right now, we should see how long it takes to get to my place. It *is* closer."

Knox hoisted her farther back in her seat, eliciting a small yelp. "I like the way your mind works, Wright. Break out your stopwatch. We're on the clock."

CHAPTER
TWENTY-THREE

Zoey swore the clock moved in reverse, making every tick of the second hand seem as though an hour had passed. Doctor visits ramped up her blood pressure, a physiological memory from a childhood spent in the hospital, and today's was no exception.

The difference was that this one required physical labor.

She eyed the treadmill, already loathing everything it stood for. Ever since she'd been able to get back to a more active life, she'd done everything in her power to make sure that happened outdoors...or around people. Running in place didn't meet that criteria.

The door opened and Dr. Samuel entered. "Hello, favorite patient."

"Hello, favorite doctor," Zoey quipped.

Instead of his usual suit and white lab coat, Dr. Samuel wore jeans and a polo shirt, making him look less like the well-known cardiac surgeon that he was.

"That's practically your pj's compared with what you normally wear," she teased. "Or is it dress-down day at the office?"

Dr. Samuel chuckled. "I try to be a little more laid-back on lab days. I've been told that it makes the patients feel comfortable."

"Gotcha." Zoey tugged on her own baggy T-shirt and well-loved yoga pants.

"You wore your running shoes?"

She flexed her feet and showed off her almost-new Converse. "I did, and I'm ready to get this show on the road."

He chuckled, easily reading her. "Eager for freedom?"

"Eager to be anywhere that isn't here—no offense."

"None taken. All right, have a seat first and let's go ahead and get our pre-exercise echocardiography shots. Once we got what we need, we'll jump on the treadmill for about fifteen minutes."

Zoey sat on the exam table. "Oh, *we'll* jump on the treadmill?"

He grinned. "Okay, you'll jump on the treadmill and I will lazily kick back and watch the monitors...but I'll try to look exhausted while doing it. How does that sound?"

"You got yourself a deal."

The sonogram tech came into the room, and with the suggestions made by Dr. Samuel, took no fewer than a thousand images of her heart. What felt like years later, it was time to sweat. The test itself wasn't an issue. Light jogs no longer left her winded.

It was the boredom, mixed with Dr. Samuel's focus on the EKG machine, that made her want to run screaming.

After a brisk fifteen minutes on the treadmill, it was back to the pretty images that flashed red and blue, outlining Zoey's cardiac function. This time as Dr. Samuel walked the tech through the images he wanted, the picture count went from a thousand to a million.

Zoey aged twenty years by the time Doc Samuel said she could get dressed back into her street clothes. Ten minutes after that, they sat in the result room, and his smile had yet to return.

"I'm not going to lie to you, Zoey. There are changes that I'm not thrilled with, but I won't know how extensive they are until I study the feed a bit more. And I know I'm risking my favorite doctor status, but we also need to schedule you for a cardiac catheterization."

"You're right. You're not my favorite anymore." Although now a routine procedure, lying on a hard, sterile slab and holding still while someone shoved a camera through your heart was not a fun night out on the town. "The changes are that bad? It's really necessary?"

"After last year's event, I'm not willing to chance it and you shouldn't either. I'm not saying that it needs to be done tomorrow, but it needs to be scheduled for sometime within the next two weeks."

Zoey swallowed her disappointment. "Okay. And the Amplify that you put me on?"

"Keep taking it. When you're two days from running out, give me a call."

Zoey agreed and hustled into the fresh air, pulling her jacket close. She hunted for the Metro schedule stashed in her purse and headed toward the nearest train station.

The twenty-minute ride from Georgetown to Alexandria passed quickly, and from there, she hoofed it the three blocks to Iron Bars.

Picnic tables had been set out in what was soon to be the beer garden. Zoey liked the idea. Beer. Drinks.

Food. Music. All in an outdoor garden setting that brushed alongside the Potomac. At the first sign of warm weather, people would flock here in droves.

As she reached the back door, it crashed open. A young redhead, her bag clutched to her chest, nearly knocked her down the steps. Her attention shot to Zoey. "Do yourself a favor and turn around. No job is worth having to deal with the king of assholes."

Zoey watched the redhead stalk around the side of the building before stepping into the distillery. She peeked around the corner, looking to see which Steele brother had earned the asshole title. Roman stood behind the bar, muttering under his breath.

"I knew you were a talented fighter, but I didn't know you were royalty. You're so down to earth." Zoey flashed Roman a teasing smirk. "King of Assholes, I think is your title."

He stopped unpacking a carton of bottles. "You forgot to mention my incredible sense of humor. Why do people always forget the humor?"

"Is that what happened with the redhead? She didn't appreciate Roman Steele's comedic talents?"

Roman dropped another crate of bottles next to the first. "She wouldn't recognize the difference between an aged lager and a golden ale if it were written out in bold letters on the damn bottle."

"*I* don't know the difference between an aged lager and a golden ale—although I could if the bottles were labeled."

"You're not applying to run a beer garden. It was evident in the first five minutes that she didn't know a damn thing. Hell, five *seconds*. But she made sure to demand every weekend off so she could *have a social life*. And did I mention the free booze she thought she'd get?"

Liam poked his head around the corner and, seeing Zoey, came all the way inside. "Did Roman scare off another one?"

Zoey smirked. "If you mean a prospective manager, then yes."

"I doubt she could even manage her own checkbook, much less an entire business," Roman defended himself. "No, thank you. We need someone out front that's competent and knows what the hell they're doing."

Liam snickered. "If you don't give the Roman Stamp of Approval to someone, *you're* going to be the one managing the business...which means no blow-things-up assignments for you. The big boys will be off playing and you'll be stuck minding the home front."

"Fuck-and-you, Liam," Roman grumbled, but the twitch on his lips belied the lack of heat behind the words.

Zoey shook her head at the brothers' bickering when Knox walked into the room. Their gazes immediately locked.

She didn't know what to say, or why she came. After a doctor's appointment, she usually headed home to bury her sorrow in a pint of chocolate fudge ice cream.

With how this one ended, she would've polished off the entire damn container and then gone to the store to buy another.

Knox ignored his brothers' curious expressions. "Do

you want to come upstairs? I have some paperwork that needs finishing, and Liam's responsible for making sure Roman doesn't scare away another prospective manager."

"Too late for that," Liam teased.

Roman released a string of colorful curses, and Knox chuckled. Palming the small of Zoey's back, he guided her up the stairs.

"So you have an office now?" Zoey glanced around on the way up in an attempt to distract herself, and grimaced. Her hopeful distraction ended up sounding simply *hopeful*.

He led her through an open doorway and closed the door behind them. "It's Roman's office, but they'll all have Iron Bar offices on the third floor to be close to the distillery. The basement's entirely Steele Ops. No merging of the two."

Tan walls complemented the stark white molding. A massive bookshelf that covered one length of the wall and a desk tucked into the corner were both a rich, dark mahogany. It might have been Roman's office, but it reminded her more of Knox.

Zoey expected him to sit, but he leaned his rear end against the desk and gestured for her to come closer. She wanted to. Her body practically propelled herself forward, but she veered left, opting for the plush leather couch positioned beneath the bay window.

Her doctor's appointment messed with her emotions. All the uncertainty. The questions. The unknowns and the possibilities. Being that raw and vulnerable wasn't a good thing when in close proximity to Knox. It made falling into his arms way too comfortable—and tempting.

Especially lately.

"What brings you out here today, angel?" Knox's stance looked casual, but Zoey knew different. He waited. He observed. And the fact she'd shoved her glasses up her nose twice in less than a minute didn't escape his notice.

"I haven't been out here in a few days and I was curious to see how far you'd gotten. I'm guessing pretty far if you're already hiring staff for the distillery."

Knox folded his arms across his chest. "It's pulling together a lot easier than I thought, which means the other shoe's about to drop. Hopefully it'll be on Liam's head. I know Roman would like that scenario best."

Zoey's smile melted away as Knox's gaze dropped to where her fingers fidgeted with her purse strap. She forced herself to stop.

Feeling ridiculous, she jumped to her feet and slinked toward the door. "I think I'm going to head out now. I'm not really looking for company. I'm not even sure why I came."

"Zoey." Knox pushed off the desk.

His slow, steady pace gave her more than enough time to make her escape. But her feet rooted themselves to the floor. Never once taking his eyes off her, he eased his arms around her waist and tucked her intimately against his chest.

"Talk to me. What's wrong? You came here with a purpose. I can see it written all over your face."

"Then maybe you can tell me what that is."

He stared straight into her eyes with an intensity that nearly made her squirm. "You had a doctor's appointment today, and I'm guessing you got news you didn't want to hear."

Zoey swallowed the lump from her dry throat and eased away from his arms. She immediately wanted to go back. "It wasn't *bad* in the sense that I need to rush into surgery, but it wasn't good either."

"So it's *bad* good news and not *bad* bad news?"

"Exactly."

"Sweetheart, bad anything isn't necessarily good." Knox scrubbed a hand over his face. "Liam gave me a headache this morning, so my brain's functioning on half power. You need to spell this out for me, angel."

Zoey peered through the window that overlooked the beer garden. Right now, it was a sea of picnic tables and budding flower beds. In another week, the entire yard would be an oasis of flowers, food, and friends.

Realization dawned on Zoey.

That's why she crossed the river.

She didn't need sexy, orgasm proficient Knox. She didn't need alpha, protective Knox.

She needed *friend* Knox.

She needed the Knox who listened and didn't offer anecdotes. Who didn't push or force her to meet his gaze so he could tell her everything would be fine— words that often came up seconds before people went into fix-it mode.

From behind, Knox's arms wrapped around her waist. Resting his chin on the curve of her shoulder, he held her and gave her the chance to pull both her thoughts and herself together.

Zoey settled her hands over his and sunk into the embrace. "Even though I didn't show any outward symptoms, my stress test didn't produce stellar results. Dr. Samuel wants me to have a cardiac catheterization sometime within the next few weeks."

His cheek brushed the side of her head. "You've had those before, right? They've become pretty routine."

"They are, and he wouldn't order one if it weren't necessary. I hate this. All of it. I hate that I have to worry about any of it, that hospitals make me break out into hives, and that every time I leave the house, I have to make sure my meds are with me. And yes, I know I sound like a petulant child, but—"

"Hey." Knox's arms squeezed her in a gentle hug. "You're far from petulant or a child. You're an amazingly strong woman, and you'll get through this like you've gotten through everything else that's been tossed your way. With ease."

"You think any of this has been easy?" Zoey turned around but was unable to meet his eyes until his finger cupped her chin.

"Not at all. You make it *look* easy. But have no fear. If you get stuck, I'm here to drag you out of the rough patch."

Until he wasn't.

The closer that Steele Ops got to opening its doors, the sooner he'd leave to start the next chapter in his life. Away from DC. Away from *her*. Relying on him when their time clock had already started its final countdown wasn't smart.

But it didn't change the fact that it felt good to voice her concerns and be heard. Knox listened, not diminishing her worries, and more importantly...

He didn't try to *solve* them.

Zoey slid her hands up his chest and kissed his cheek. "Thank you."

"For what? I literally didn't do a damn thing."

"Exactly."

Chuckling, Knox ran his hand up her back and into her hair. "I think that's the first time I've been thanked for doing nothing."

"You didn't do nothing. You did *everything*." She knew he didn't get it. Not quite.

He tucked a callused palm against her cheek, the tender touch freezing her breath. "Whatever I did do or didn't, I'm just happy that it put that look in your eye. And I hope I can keep it there."

Knox dropped a feather-soft kiss to her lips.

There was no tongue-on-tongue-I-want-to-eat-you-alive devouring. No burning need to rip off each other's clothes. Slow and gentle, the delicateness of their embrace reached deep into her core, affecting her more than any of their hottest, out-of-control kisses.

Zoey groaned in protest when he pulled his mouth from hers, failing to hide a dopey, happy smile. "Are you ever going to tell me where you got the nickname *angel*?"

His gaze locked onto her eyes in a deep, heated stare that left goose bumps on her arms. "Someday...when I'm ready."

"Ready for what?"

He shrugged. "To let someone else in on my little secret."

Secrets.

Standing in the middle of the Iron Bars offices, with Knox's arms wrapped around her, Zoey realized that she had one whopper of a secret herself.

She was at least halfway to falling in love with him, and sinking deeper every day that they spent together.

CHAPTER
TWENTY-FOUR

Zoey stared into her nearly empty fridge, contemplating the fine dining option of ketchup and questionable fried chicken leftovers from the week before, or maybe it was two weeks ago. The dark speckles on the crispy coating could either be Italian seasoning or the cure for cancer.

At the queasy roll of her stomach, she pitched the entire package into the garbage and closed the fridge with a heavy sigh. "Well, now what are we going to do, Snuggles?"

A night home alone had sounded like heaven when she declined a movie date with Grace and opted for her fuzzy duck pajamas and slippers. Now she was bored. She contemplated calling Knox to see what he was up to, but she was still a little off kilter from their earlier conversation at Iron Bars.

A little distance was probably best.

Snuggles sat in the living room, golden eyes locked on the air vent. As the furnace growled to life, his long hair wafted in the breeze. When it stopped, he pounced, claws scraping against the grates. He did it no fewer than three times before biting something off with his teeth and carrying it to his corner bed.

"If it's edible, are you willing to share?" Zoey joked. She glanced back at the vent and squinted.

Bundled in a dark, plastic, snake-like shell, a group of frayed wires stuck out from the grate Snuggles had been playing with.

"Wires! Do not eat whatever you have!" Zoey wrestled Snuggles's new toy from his paws and got swat at in the process. "Go ahead. Be grumpy. But I'm not letting you turn into Robo Cat."

She inspected the plastic knob in the palm of her hand. See-through and no larger than her pinky nail, it almost looked like a button except there wasn't a hole in which to pass any thread.

She took it to the grate and crouched, tugging on the remaining cord. It gave an inch and then something larger behind the vent smashed against the back side. Five minutes and four screws later, Zoey's bad feeling turned into a strong roll of nausea.

A camera.

She'd seen the things on television. Heck, working in the lab, she'd downloaded the surveillance images taken from police versions of this very device. But she wasn't under investigation, and no one had been in her apartment.

"Do *not* touch that thing," Zoey scolded Snuggles as she left the remnants on the floor and searched for her cell.

She dialed the only person who'd been charged with turning her apartment into a fortress. Liam answered on the third ring.

"What's up, Zo?" Loud music and banging sounded in the background. Roman's distinct growl caused a loud bark of laughter. "Excuse my asshole brothers.

They're being particularly obnoxious. I'd say it was the paint fumes flying high here at Iron Bars, but they're always like this."

"Did you put cameras in my apartment?" Zoey had to ask even though she knew the answer.

"Hold on, Zo. Let me go somewhere I can hear you." He muttered to someone else, and Zoey was pretty certain she heard Knox. Suddenly, it was a lot quieter. "Okay, now ask me that again. Did I put what in your apartment? A kick-ass alarm system? Yes, yes I did."

"And did that come with cameras...oh, say, tucked into my heating vents?" Liam's abrupt silence answered her question. "Liam?"

Soft mumbles preceded the clacking of the phone changing hands.

"What are you talking about, angel?" Knox asked.

"I'm talking about Snuggles pulling a camera snake out from the freakin' heating vent...that's what I'm talking about." The longer Zoey stayed on the line, the more freaked out she became. *Talk about delayed reaction.* "Why is there a camera in my freakin' air vent, Knox? Why?"

"Babe, relax. Breathe. Maybe it's not—"

"I know what a camera looks like! Do not tell me to relax!"

"Stay on the line." Knox muttered to someone on his end, and then it was quiet again for another minute until she heard the low rumble of his truck. "You have the camera there?"

She eyed it across the room, where Snuggles currently prepped to pounce on it. "It's on the floor."

"Leave it there and go into the bathroom."

"And how do I know there's not one in the bath-room?" A thought struck, and with it a rise of bile. "Oh. My. God. Knox, what if there's one in my *bedroom*? What if whoever is on the other end saw us—"

"Angel?"

"Yeah?"

"You may want to curb your details."

Zoey closed her eyes and prayed for the earth to swallow her whole. Realization dawned. "Who?"

Please don't be Cade.

Roman cleared his throat. "Are you in the bathroom yet, sweet pea?"

"Almost." Zoey nudged the camera aside with her toe, barely resisting the urge to stomp it into little pieces, and picked up a displeased Snuggles. "I'm on the way now."

"Stay put until we get there, okay?"

She wasn't about to argue. On the chance there were more, she didn't want to give whoever was responsible the thrill of watching her panic.

Zoey closed herself and Snuggles into her small bathroom, and paced. Highly unlike himself, Roman kept her talking for the next thirty minutes before an-nouncing that they pulled into the lot.

Zoey hustled to open the door for them and was met with a quartet of grim faces, and for once, Knox out-scowled his younger brothers, even Roman.

"You guys moving in?" Zoey joked sarcastically, nodding to the duffels Ryder and Liam carried.

"We're egg-hunting." Knox eased her aside as his

brothers entered and got right down to work. Ryder immediately went to the kitchen while Liam took the main room. Roman, Zoey noted, headed straight to her bedroom.

"How did this happen with the system Liam installed?" Zoey asked.

Knox kept his face impassive. "The cameras were more than likely here longer than your alarm system. The question is how long?"

"Cameras? *Plural?* How do you know that there's—"

"Found one!" Ryder exploded the last of her hope.

"In here too," Roman's voice echoed from the bedroom.

"I'm going to be sick." Clutching her stomach, Zoey ran to the bathroom and promptly heaved what little contents hadn't yet been digested through the day.

That violated feeling from the break-in came back tenfold. Every time she thought about someone watching her every move, she released a new wave of vomit. Eventually, her heaves turned to dry retches.

Five minutes after the last one, she scrubbed her face and brushed her teeth, and stepped into her living room to see Liam packing no less than four cameras just like the one she'd found in her vent.

"I should've stayed in the bathroom," she muttered.

Knox gave her shoulder a gentle squeeze. "Liam's going to try and get a read on the hardware used . . . see if it leads us to any specific makers."

"What about what's been recorded on it?"

Liam shook his head. "I didn't see any recording mechanisms, which means whoever's on the other end is acquiring the signal digitally."

"So they could be recording everything remotely?"

Liam nodded, face grim. "Yeah, I guess that's what I'm saying. But we got them all, Zo. Your place is clean."

Zoey would never feel *clean* standing in this apartment again. "Thank you, guys. For coming over."

They all nodded, each taking time to wrap her in a hug before heading out. Knox stayed behind, notably quiet as he enveloped her in a tight embrace. "I'm not even going to ask you if you're okay. You've had one hell of a day, sweetheart."

"Tell me about it."

His hand slid to her nape, massaging the tight knot that had formed there since finding the first camera. "Come back to the boat with me. And hear me out before you say no. I know this is your place, but a change of scenery would make us both feel—"

"Okay." Knox's raised eyebrows made her chuckle. "You weren't expecting me to agree so quickly?"

"Or at all."

"Guess there's something about being an unofficial member of the *Big Brother* cast that makes me more agreeable." She'd meant it as a halfhearted joke, but didn't get a smile. "Can you wait a few minutes while I grab some things?"

"I'll wait as long as you need me to."

Zoey didn't look at what she tossed in her bag. She could've had four sets of underwear, no bras, and one pair of socks. It didn't make sense considering her apartment was nearly three times bigger than Knox's boat, but it suddenly felt as if it were the size of a postage stamp, and she needed to get out of there.

By the time she came out from the bedroom, Knox had somehow—miraculously—coaxed Snuggles into his carrier. With the crate and a bag of what looked to be Snug's necessities tucked under one arm, he reached for her hand with his free one. "Ready to go?"

"More than."

Zoey breathed easier twenty minutes later. Twinkling boat lights reflected off the river, looking like magical particles floating on a black canvas. They parked and climbed out from his truck, and then without a word, they climbed onto the *Angel Eyes*.

Knox took her things—and Snuggles—below deck and returned empty-handed. "I let Snuggles roam around the main room downstairs. Figured that would piss him off less than penning him up in my room."

"Great. Thanks."

"Do you want to go to bed? Get some rest?"

She leaned her elbows on the railing and tilted her face to the star-lit sky. "I want to stay here for a bit." When he didn't move from his spot three feet away, she added, "You're more than welcome to join me."

He slipped her a small smile and closed the distance. "I thought you'd want a little time alone."

"I want a little time with you more." As she waited for him, she closed her eyes and inhaled the soft spring air.

The scent of cherry blossoms drifted down the river, a far superior smell to even her mom's snickerdoodles. It surpassed everything except Knox's piney musk, which thankfully wrapped around her at the same time his arms did.

His chin, scratchy with stubble, brushed her neck.

"I get why you love it out here," Zoey admitted, looking out over the floating lights. "It's your own little world, separate from anything and anyone."

"Except you." His lips brushed over her ear. "I like it even more when you're here with me."

His admission jumped her heart. She turned in his arms, carefully sliding her own around his shoulders. "And I like being here with you."

His gaze zipped from her eyes to her mouth and back, desire written on every line of his face. His fingers flexed around her hips and stroked up the length of her back. "That's a dangerous thing to say to me, sweetheart."

"Why's that?"

"Because I'm trying damn hard not to kiss you right now."

"Why's that?"

"Because it's been one hell of a night, and I'm not the kind of guy who takes advantage." Something else flashed across his face. Regret, or something similar. "And we need to talk, Zoey."

Zoey. Not angel. Not sweetheart.

"That doesn't sound pleasant, and as you pointed out, I've already had my fair share of unpleasant tonight."

"It may not be pleasant, but it's got to be said. It's about your—"

"If you say *brother* while I'm standing here, asking you with my eyes to take me downstairs and make love to me, I will kick you in the solar plexus." Zoey slipped one hand into his hair and savored the stark difference between the locks in her fingers and the sharp stubble on his chin. "I can't take any more reveals tonight, Knox. I really can't."

She hated admitting it, but it was the truth. Both her mind and body were physically drained, unable to tell up from down, or left from right. All that was still perfectly clear was Knox.

In their short period of time together, she'd experienced a wide range of emotions. Fear. Nervousness. Excitement. Strength. She even celebrated the feelings that scared her because it meant she'd *experienced* them.

And she wanted to experience *everything*.

With Knox.

Zoey lifted the hem of her shirt.

Knox's hand stopped her halfway, his dark eyes narrowed in concern. "What are you doing, angel?"

"*All* of me wants *all* of you."

She didn't know what she was doing, or how it would end, but it didn't matter. Something changed. Something shifted in her, and she suddenly didn't care about the past, or the future...

Just the now.

CHAPTER TWENTY-FIVE

The shift in the air, in the friction between Knox's and Zoey's bodies, and even more, deep in his chest, caught Knox off-guard. He couldn't take his eyes off hers, peering up at him with a sexy coyness that drove him insane.

In offering to strip off her shirt, she offered him more than her body. She offered her fear and her strength, and everything that made her uniquely Zoey.

And his greedy bastard self wanted it all—and more. For the first time in two years, he didn't feel like a fuckup. Her strength fueled his. His heart beat for hers.

No way in hell would he destroy this feeling by being anything less than truthful. "Angel, I know it may not be pleasant, but we need to talk about—"

"Nope." She lifted to her toes, her soft mouth silencing his. "Right now, the only thing we need to talk about is you taking me downstairs. *Please.*"

Any restraint he had blew off the damn boat with her soft plea.

He hiked her legs around his hips and walked them downstairs. They bypassed Snuggles sleeping on the couch and headed to his bedroom.

Zoey nibbled and kissed him across his jaw and down his neck. Her body, so much smaller than his, squirmed against the erection throbbing behind his zipper. By the time he dropped her feet to the floor, he was one hip swivel away from coming in his pants like a randy teenager.

He couldn't stop touching her, dragging his mouth over the sensitive column of her neck.

She sighed, clutching his shoulders and throwing her head back. "I love it when you touch me there."

"I love it when I touch you anywhere." He nibbled her shoulder and got a shiver in response.

At some point, her hands slipped beneath his shirt. Knox broke their kiss long enough to tug it over his head and toss it away. His hands gripped her soft duck flannels, and at her small nod, he eased both her pants and her panties down her slender legs.

Crouched on the floor, he peered up at her, and the sight of her eyes, hooded in desire, took his breath away.

She watched as he trailed both his mouth and his hands back up the length of her now exposed body. "Knox."

"I can't get enough of you, angel. It's not possible for me to ever get enough." He dragged his mouth over her shirt-covered breasts, able to tell she wasn't wearing a bra. He ached to strip her bare, to feast on every inch of her flesh, but he wanted to be the one to shed his layers first.

Clothes.

And everything else—all the feelings. All the fear.

Knox reached for the first button on his jeans, enjoying the way she eyed him pulling them down and shucking them aside. His cock stood hard and proud out in front of him, not making a secret of how much he wanted her.

And he wanted *all* of her.

Zoey subconsciously licked her plush lips, and Knox stepped forward, his erection rubbing against her belly as he took her in his arms. He slowly slipped his hand beneath her shirt and edged it up in the back, giving her all the time in the world to pull away.

He stopped as the hem reached mid-torso level.

"Don't." Zoey trembled in his arms. Her throat bobbed as she swallowed, a storm of emotions swirling in her big blue eyes. "Don't stop. T-take it off."

"Baby, we don't have to rush this. I can work my way around the shirt and still taste every inch of your body."

Her voice, barely audible, shook. "No. I want to feel you... *all* of you. It's just that it's been a long time since I've... since I've taken it off during... sex. The last time didn't go well."

Anger at what she must've experienced before rushed through him, but he dampened it, gentling his fingers as he caught her chin and maneuvered her gaze back to his. "Do you seriously think I care about a little scar?"

"It's not little. Or pretty."

"But it's a part of you. It's your badge of courage. It's visual proof of how damn strong you are. You shouldn't hide it, especially from me."

Knox hated the trepidation in her eyes. He wanted a dark alley and time alone with the bastard who'd made her feel self-conscious about it. He knew this was hard for her. By taking off her shirt, she was exposing more than her scar.

By letting him see all of her, she was baring her *fears*. No way was he taking that lightly.

He brushed his thumb across her lower lip. "You're perfection. Do you know that?"

He glided his knuckles along the dip of her waist...

He caressed the curve of her torso...

Moonlight slipped through the slats of his bedroom window, casting her body in a sensuous display of light and dark. Knox kissed her exposed belly button before trailing a path toward the bottom swell of her breasts.

Zoey's breathing hitched.

"Breathe, angel."

"I am." She lifted her arms and he slipped her shirt over her head and onto their pile of clothes.

"Liar." They shared a small grin as he guided her flush against him, and took her mouth in a slow, drugging kiss.

Sparks ignited at every point of contact, warming his blood. The sound of her soft moan against his lips spurred him on. He palmed a breast, the perfect size to fit into his hand, and thumbed an already firm nipple.

Zoey arched her back, pushing her breasts closer to where he worshipped every inch of luscious skin before slowly migrating to the valley between. Despite the dim light, her scar was still visible. Slightly darker and more raised than the skin around, it marred her flesh. But he hadn't lied. She was still gorgeous, with or without.

Knox dropped his mouth to the top edge, and slowly kissed his way down the six puckered inches. "You're gorgeous, angel."

Beneath him, Zoey trembled.

"Beautiful." Another soft kiss. Another inch.

"You're perfect. You're strong. And you're resilient." He skated his way to the bottom.

Tears welled in her eyes, but she didn't let them fall. "Please make love to me? No more waiting. No more anything...just *you*. Now."

"Baby, you don't even need to ask."

He'd wanted to take his time. To taste her. Touch her. And he still would...all night long if she was up for it. But his body practically vibrated with needing her.

He grabbed a condom from the end table and quickly sheathed himself. He'd no sooner slipped it onto the base than she gripped his ass and lowered them to the mattress. On impact, she arched her hips and with her body already wet and warm, his cock slipped inches deep on the first half thrust.

Knox quickly withdrew and sunk home again, this time stretching her body to take him to the hilt. She wrapped around him perfectly.

He'd been deluding himself into thinking he wouldn't get attached...and that he hadn't already been attached for years. He hadn't kept his distance for the last two for fear of failing his brothers, or Cade, or anyone else in his life.

He'd kept his distance for fear of failing *Zoey*.

Because even back then he'd known how important she *had been*...

How important she *was*...

And how important she always *would be*...

Knox dropped his forehead to hers as warm, tingling pleasure rolled through them both. He'd never felt anything like it before. He was pretty damn sure he never would again.

Unless he was with Zoey.

This could never get old. That heat. That excitement every time he touched her. Instead of claiming a new piece of *her* every time they were together, Zoey Wright, without a doubt, claimed a small piece of him.

* * *

Zoey stuck her head beneath the hot spray of water and hummed the tune "Happy." Her feet had barely touched the ground since she'd climbed out of bed.

Knox's bed.

A few weeks ago, she wouldn't have dreamed that she'd be able to shed all her insecurities, and least of all with Knox Steele. But not only had she stripped herself bare—both emotionally and literally—she didn't have a single regret.

Not a damn one.

Waking up to Knox worshipping her breasts with his mouth had had a big hand in her good mood. Her body still hummed. And it hadn't been *sex*, at least not that first time. Not the second. Maybe by the third, but by then she'd been too high on endorphins to much care about anything except his body on hers.

Still singing, she shut off the water and towel-dried, quickly realizing she'd forgotten her clothes in the bedroom. She opted for Knox's T-shirt that she'd slipped into after their third round of lovemaking, and padded barefoot into the living room to get dressed.

Raised voices from above stopped her in front of the bedroom door. She counted at least two, and possibly more. Definitely her brother's. His low bellow wasn't one anyone could miss—or ignore.

She'd hoped to have at least one cup of decaf in her system before she had to face the reality of the day— and last evening. But fate had other plans.

Forgetting her clothes, she climbed the stairs.

"How the fucking hell am I supposed to make sense of everything?" Cade demanded angrily, his tone abrasive. "I asked *you* to look out for her...and then *this* happens?"

"You need to calm down," Knox urged in a low tone.

"I will not calm down! It's all shades of fucked up! It's—"

Zoey stepped onto the deck and finished his statement her way: "None of your business."

Cade's eyes, a lot like her own, widened before slowly dropping to her bare legs and obviously wet hair. His anger slowly dissolved and turned to something akin to shock. Zoey recognized it right away. Whatever they'd been arguing about hadn't been about her and Knox.

Crap on a cracker.

Cade's glare shot from Zoey to Knox. "First someone slinks into her apartment and makes her a part of the *Big* fucking *Brother* club and now *this*? You care to fucking explain *this* to me too?"

Cade didn't wait for an explanation. Face twisted into a feral snarl, he charged Knox.

"Cade, stop!" Zoey stepped between the two men.

This wasn't what she'd wanted. She'd wanted Knox,

yes, but she didn't want to cause a rift between the two longtime friends.

"Move, little bit."

"No. Let me explain—"

"I get the picture pretty loud and clear, Zo. You're standing in the middle of my best friend's boat with a wet head and no clothes. Strike that—you're wearing *his* fucking clothes."

A large hand landed on Cade's shoulder. "Take a deep breath, son."

Cade shrugged off the touch and turned his glare on its owner. "Don't you dare call me *son*. I told you about the damn cameras for one reason, and one reason only. Because you claimed you could help. Don't make me regret it."

For the first time, Zoey noticed Cade and Knox weren't alone on deck.

Hogan Wilcox stood nearly nose to nose with her brother, his scowl nearly matching Cade's. "You may have let me come along, but I'm not about to let you do something you're going to regret."

"No way in hell am I going to regret pounding Knox to a bloody pulp. He knows my baby sister is off limits."

Behind her, Knox tensed. "In case you haven't noticed, she's not a baby anymore."

Cade lurched forward. Zoey pushed on her brother's chest to keep them separated. "Stop it! Or I'm going to douse you both with...something."

"Stay out of this, Zoey," Cade ordered. "This is between me and the asshole."

Either one of them could've tucked her aside without

much effort, but they glared at each other from over the top of her head.

Zoey jabbed Cade hard in the stomach to get his attention. "Actually, unless you've been sleeping with him too, it's between *me* and Knox. It has nothing to do with you."

"When my best friend and baby sister are fucking behind my back, it sure as hell does."

"Don't talk to her like that." Knox's voice dropped, eerily calm and deadly low. "If you want to go a round with me, let's have at it, but leave Zoey out of it."

Zoey tossed her hands in the air. "I'm a grown woman with her own mind and body—which, just so you know, I happen to own all the rights to. *Mine*."

"Yours," Cade agreed with a scowl, "and apparently his. Isn't that right?"

"We're not doing anything wrong."

"Yeah? Then why haven't you come out in the open with whatever the fuck *this* is?" Cade challenged.

Partly for this reason, and Zoey had to admit, keeping it under wraps meant not having to explain things to people when it ended. Breakups were always difficult. Having her insides ripped out and set on fire would tickle compared to what she'd feel when she and Knox parted ways.

"That's what I thought." Cade took her silence as a point in his favor.

She ignored the slight tremble in her chest. "None of it's what you thought because you're wrong."

"Because he's *the one*?" Cade snorted. "Pardon me if I don't believe that."

"Because he treats me—and *believes*—that I'm more than capable of making my own decisions. That's probably a difficult concept for you to grasp considering you're so damn used to trying to make them *for* me."

Something glinted in her brother's eyes as his gaze shifted from her, to Knox, and back. "He doesn't make decisions for you? Are you sure about that, sis?"

Knox stepped up next to Zoey, his jaw clenched. "Maybe now's not the best time."

Cade let out a humorless chuckle. "It's the perfect time, Knox. I mean, *come on*."

"Time for what?" Zoey demanded.

"Cade. Not like this," Hogan Wilcox added.

Frustration knotted Zoey's hands at her side. "What does everyone know that I don't? I swear, if someone doesn't spill it soon I'm going to—"

"Meet our dear old dad, Zo," Cade interjected. He shot a scowl at the older man. "*Dad*, meet the daughter whose life you gambled with by watching from the sidelines...the one whose hospital bills you paid *anonymously* because you didn't want to ruin your esteemed family's reputation."

Zoey's heart tripped a beat before stumbling back into its normal rhythm. Her brain struggled to catch up. "What?"

Wilcox shifted on his feet, looking uncomfortable. "There's a lot more to it than that."

"Is there? Really?" Cade shook his head. "Everything can be boiled down to those simple facts."

Zoey heard the truth in Cade's voice. She saw it on his face...and on Hogan Wilcox's.

A rush of feelings bombarded her, and she couldn't wrap her head around a single one. Even being blessed with a mother as wonderful as Gretchen, a foster child always—at least once—thought about the *what-ifs*. It couldn't be helped.

Except...

Zoey turned toward Knox. In his eyes, she saw concern, worry...and knowledge.

Her voice sounded breathless as she worked around speaking through the forming lump. "You told Cade that *now wasn't the best time*. You...*knew*? About my...Wilcox?"

"Angel." He reached out to her, and she stepped back.

Shaking her head, she barely withheld tears. "Why? Why didn't you tell me?"

"I tried. Last night, I told you that we needed to talk. I didn't know long." Knox cursed, scrubbing a hand over his face. "I know that doesn't make it any easier to hear, but—"

"But *you knew*. Before you took me downstairs and let me bare myself to you, *you knew*. Before we made love, *you knew*. And you didn't think that maybe that would be something that *I'd* want to know...that I *deserved* to know?"

Knox looked tenser than she had ever seen him. "I was going to tell you."

"But you didn't. Why?" Zoey held her breath and mentally prepared herself for the answer. Her gut already told her why. "*Why*, Knox?"

"Because I knew it would hurt you. I wanted..."

Knox's throat bobbed with the force of his swallow. For the first time in forever, he looked uncomfortable.

Good.

"I wanted to protect you," he admitted gruffly, voice barely audible. "From getting hurt."

"Because I couldn't handle hearing the truth?"

"*No*." Knox grasped her arms. "Zoey, *no*. You're the strongest person I know."

"Except, evidently, when it comes to miraculously reappearing father figures."

She pulled away, and with every step that separated them, a pain pierced through the center of her chest. Tears blurred her vision. "I can't be around any of you right now."

"Zoey. Don't do anything foolish." Cade took a step closer, but she warned him off with a glare.

"Foolish?" She laughed, the sound hollow even to her own ears. "You mean like lie to someone I supposedly care about? No, I'll leave that to the three of you." She tossed a harsh look toward Hogan Wilcox. "Well, *two* of you. Because you, *Dad*, are a stranger to me."

Suddenly, the open space of the river was too stifling. She went below deck and fired off a mayday text to Grace, who answered right away.

Fifteen minutes.

Zoey changed back into her clothes and collected her things. Soon after fifteen minutes passed, she went topside. Hogan Wilcox, Cade, and Knox stood on separate ends of the boat. All pissed. All glaring.

They could push one another overboard for all she cared.

"Did I miss the party?" Grace stopped mid-gangway and muttered a round of expletives under her breath. "Evidently I did."

"Thanks for coming to get me."

"No problem." She glanced around at the stern faces, but said nothing.

Knox's hand reached out as she walked past. "Angel."

She whirled around, angry and close to tears. "You can stop calling me that anytime now. You can stop calling me *period*."

"That's not going to happen, sweetheart. Because there's still the matter of those cameras."

"And I'll handle it...with Liam. And Roman. And Ryder. *Steele Ops*. That way, you're free to head out to California anytime you want." She turned to a concerned Grace. "Let's go."

"Are you sure you don't—"

"Yes." At the crack of Zoey's voice, her friend nodded and led the way.

Knox called over the boat, "Don't leave like this. *Please*."

The pain in his voice made her own ten times worse. "One of us was always going to leave, Knox. I just happen to be doing it first."

Last night, she'd opened herself like she'd never done with anyone before. She'd exposed everything, every last fear and need, every last desire. And instead of handing it back or ignoring it, Knox had taken it with both hands and did what it had taken her until that very moment to do.

Embrace it.

Accept it.

Love it.

She hustled toward Grace's rental, more tears pouring down her cheeks with every step. She couldn't look back toward the boat. She couldn't look back—period.

If she did, she'd see her heart lying in front of Knox's feet.

In pieces.

CHAPTER
TWENTY-SIX

Knox whaled on the heavy bag in front of him, taking out the frustrations of the day on his fists. His knuckles, one of which he may have knocked out of its socket a time or two, had cracked open twenty minutes ago, but he didn't care.

He deserved all that and a hell of a lot more.

He'd been punishing his body for the last two hours and still hadn't come close to the pain of watching Zoey walk away. That had dug deep...far deeper than anything he could've imagined.

And he didn't have anyone to blame but himself.

Every last bit of her anger was justified. She'd laid her trust in him and he'd taken it for a fucking joyride. Good intentions or not, he'd done exactly what he knew she hated.

He'd taken her decisions away from her.

He should've insisted on talking, on telling her about Wilcox, and then have been there for her during the fallout. It wouldn't have been easy for either of them, but at least they'd still be on his boat and wound together like two vines.

Maybe.

"If this isn't the sight of a guy who screwed up, I

don't know what is." Roman's voice echoed through the room.

"Enlightening. Now go the fuck away." Knox hooked a severe left jab into the bag and winced when something cracked.

"The cool thing about being boss is that I go where I want. You're in my gym, man."

"Fine. Then *I'll* go." Knox gave the bag one last punch and pushed his way toward his stuff.

"You're leaving? Just like that?"

"You said it yourself, Ro. I'm not needed here. You guys are what? A week from opening Iron Bars? All you have to do at Steele Ops is hire a few more bodies and you'll be well on your way to having enough of a team to start taking assignments. You don't need me here *using your gym*."

"That's a pretty asshole thing to say...even for you."

Knox whipped around, fists clenched at his sides. "What the hell do you want from me, Roman? You've been chomping at the bit to have me out of your hair. Well, congratulations. You got what you wanted."

"*Expected*, not wanted."

Knox let out a humorless snort. "Not a big difference there."

"Actually, it's huge. Just like the empty area in your back where your spine should be."

Knox tossed his towel aside and got right in Roman's face. "Care to say that again? Be warned though, because this time, I'll punch back."

"At least you'll be fighting for something that's important to you." His younger brother didn't move, or flinch, staring him dead in the eye. "Hey, I get it. It's a hell of a lot easier to run than deal with shit. Or drink. Or fuck. Or punch the shit out of things until your knuckles bleed. I. Get. It. Which means I'm going to be real with you for a second."

"Can't wait to hear Roman's Words of Wisdom."

"You admitted before that you stayed away to protect all of us from your issues, and that may be. But dig a bit deeper and you'll realize that it's not the only reason. You stayed away for *you*."

"For me?"

"Why are you taking a job three thousand miles away? One that we both know you're going to hate with a fiery passion?" Roman shook his head, cutting off Knox's retort. "Because if you don't care, you don't get invested. And then it doesn't hurt if things go to hell."

"Yeah? So why didn't I just stay away? Why did I even bother coming back to DC?"

"Because you either thought we'd do your dirty work for you and tell you to stay lost...or that we'd drill some common sense into you and convince you to stay where you belong. *Here*."

Suddenly bone-tired and unwilling to argue anymore, Knox dropped to the nearby bench. "What makes you so sure this is where I belong?"

"Because it's where your family is, asshole. And not to mention the woman you're in love with." Roman followed, sitting next to him, and stretched out his legs.

"I don't think I ever said that I was in love with her."

"And yet you knew exactly who I was talking about." Roman smirked.

Knox's chest constricted, unable to disagree. Despite their years apart, Roman could still read him like an open book. "It's not that simple."

"Seems pretty damn basic to me. Girl loves guy. Guy loves girl. Guy does something stupid to piss off girl. Guy gets his grovel on. It's pretty universal from what I hear."

"You didn't see her face when she walked away."

"No, but I got an earful about it from Cade and Grace." Roman gave him a pointed look. "By the way, do yourself a favor and stay clear of both of them for a bit. After Gracie's fourth call, I started believing she really did hex your man-bits."

Knox released a deep sigh. "If I thought dropping to Zoey's feet and groveling an apology would work, I would. But it won't."

"Not that alone, but it's a start. If you're lucky, it could pave the way for a hell of a lot more. But you'll never know unless you take your head out of your ass."

Knox shook his head, grinning. *Love*.

Roman mentioned it so casually, and despite not saying the word aloud, Knox knew it was true. He loved Zoey. He was *in* love with her. Yeah, he screwed up, and knowing him, it wouldn't be the last time.

This thing with her had been different from the get-go. He'd known it the second he'd laid eyes on her in that alley, dressed head to toe in disposable coveralls. And every time since, without trying, she reminded him that he didn't want to head off someplace where people wouldn't give him a swift kick in the ass if he deserved it.

He wanted attitudes, not platitudes. He wanted daily arguments from his brothers, hexes from Grace, and one-glance guilt trips from his mother.

He wanted *DC*. Steele Ops. His family.

Zoey.

Because Roman was right. He loved her... with everything he had. "There's one small problem with your plan."

"And what's that?"

"Even if Zoey forgives me for the Wilcox thing, we made an agreement to end things if it got too complicated. Falling in love with her would be the ultimate complication."

Roman shrugged. "Agreements were meant to be adapted."

"And if Zoey doesn't want to adapt?"

"Guess you won't know until you ask her."

* * *

Zoey hadn't known where she'd end up when she'd slid into Grace's passenger side seat. Her only idea had been the community center where she could vent at least a few of the emotions burning through her chest. As much as Grace loathed physical exertion, she hadn't said a word as she'd signed them up for the next available Zumba class.

With it now done, Zoey, desperate for fresh air instead of the center's musty gym stench, fanned herself with a flyer. She hadn't even pushed herself and she'd worked up a sweat.

"I'm going to get us waters before you continue the torture." Grace lifted her heavy dark hair off her neck and crinkled her nose. "I can't even stand my own smell right now."

"That just means you were doing it right." Zoey's smile felt sadly hollow.

"Then I wish I'd done it wrong." Grace rolled her eyes and disappeared around the corner in her quest to rehydrate.

She'd tried getting Zoey to talk about what happened, but she couldn't do it. Every time she tried, her throat swelled.

Multiple surgeries. Invasive tests. Shattered hopes and crushing setbacks. After each one of them, she'd stood straight, dried her tears, and kept moving forward. This wasn't one of those times. The next time the tears came, she wasn't so sure she'd be able to stop them.

The worst of it wasn't learning about her father. Or that both Cade and Knox had known. Did it piss her off that neither saw fit to tell her? *Definitely*. No way would she dole out forgiveness easily. But eventually, she'd forgive and figure out what it meant for next steps.

What destroyed her the most was realizing Knox would never see her as an equal.

He hadn't told her about Wilcox to *protect* her.

Although a noble intent, it wouldn't work if hiding things from her was his go-to reaction. *They* wouldn't work.

The breath in Zoey's lungs stalled. In desperate search of fresh air, she left a message for Grace with the front desk that she'd gone for a quick walk, and hustled outside. The second her feet hit the sidewalk, she realized it wasn't enough.

Zoey turned left and walked without a destination in mind. Slow and deep, she pulled fresh air into her lungs and released it with a heavy sigh. The tightness in her chest abated the more she focused…the more she walked.

Before she realized it, she'd gone three blocks and stood in front of her own neighborhood deli.

Mr. Cohen waved at her from behind the counter. Arm raised, she returned it and was rewarded with a sharp stab of pain. Wrenching its way beneath her sternum, it doubled her over.

"Miss Zoey! Are you okay?" Mr. Cohen's alarmed voice preceded his gentle hands. He helped her stand upright. "Do you want me to call for help?"

"I…" Zoey's chest constricted more with every attempt to inhale. A coughing fit wracked her body as she dropped her hands to her knees. "…just need a minute."

Another deep breath immediately threw her into another coughing fit. This one left her more winded than the first. *Maybe she needed more than a minute.*

"Zoey? I thought that was you. Are you okay?" Strong hands replaced those of Mr. Cohen.

"Should I call 911, Dr. Samuel?" Mr. Cohen asked, his tone worried.

"No, I got this, Ira. Thanks."

Dr. Samuel kneeled in front of her, concern etched on every line of his face. "Please tell me you weren't out running."

"Just clearing my head with a walk." She sucked in

another breath. "And I may have taken a Zumba class. But I...I didn't overdo it."

At his disbelieving look, she changed tactics. "You said it was still safe to exercise."

"I did. In careful moderation. We need to get you off your feet." Dr. Samuel nodded toward the red brick brownstone three doors down. "That's me right there. I'd like it if you let me take a listen. I don't like the sound of that wheezing one bit."

"I'm..." She heard the loud-pitched inhale too. "Okay. Yeah."

Dr. Samuel thanked Mr. Cohen and with one hand on her elbow, guided her toward his front door. Dressed in shorts and a sweat-wicking shirt, he looked as if he'd been out running.

"Come inside and let's get you comfortable." He dropped his keys on the small antique table just inside the foyer.

Unlike her place, which had been built in the back half of this century, Dr. Samuel's house had seen a lot of history. Although updated with a modern flare, the room-to-room layout had a turn-of-the-century feel, with a long, single hall that led to a rear kitchen and rooms on either side.

"This place is gorgeous," Zoey huffed, still a little breathless, but better.

He threw a grin back at her. "Thank you, but I can't claim to be the one behind it. It came fully furnished, but when I saw it, I loved it. I'm around sterile environments all the time at work, so when I come home, I want to be in a space that feels lived in."

"I get it. I still can't clean my apartment with bleach. It reminds me too much of the hospital."

"And I get *that*. Okay, let's get you situated."

He guided her into the room on the left, where a dark brown sofa and chair complemented stucco white walls and dark wood bookcases. He had *a lot* of bookcases, with every space filled with either aged classics or framed photographs.

He eased her onto the couch. "Sit here while I run upstairs and grab my stethoscope."

"I'm already feeling better," she said truthfully. "Still winded, but not like I'm sucking air through a straw."

"You do look better, but I want to make sure." He saw her hesitancy and smiled. "If you're fine, I promise I'll drive you home, but—"

"If I'm not, I'm going in for tests, and probably that cardiac cath—ahead of schedule," she finished.

"That's why you're my favorite patient. Pretty *and* smart." He handed her a bottle of water. "Drink this. *Slowly*. Small sips. And stay put. No jogging around the room."

She snorted and watched him take the old jigsaw staircase two steps at a time.

Feeling an itchy tingle in her limbs from the abrupt cease of movement, she stood and stretched. Although no longer feeling like she'd knocked on death's door with both her fists, she mentally prepared herself for a trip to the hospital.

Zoey scanned the myriad of photographs interspersed on the bookshelves. A few were of Dr. Samuel as a child, wide-smiled and dimpled, standing next to his parents in various exotic locations.

Down the line, the images changed from locations to people, most in hospital settings. Phillip Samuel with his patients.

His father had done the same thing, taking "team" pictures with patients days after a successful operation. She'd posed for four through the years, and smiled for one with the younger Samuel last year.

"Guess I'm not the favorite after all," Zoey quipped, noting her face wasn't displayed with the others.

An abrupt wave of light-headedness forced her back to the sofa, where she grabbed the water bottle with a shaking hand.

Two sips in, she dropped its contents all over the expensive looking leather sofa. "*Crap.*"

She dabbed the dripping trail of water with her shirt, and grimaced at the obvious wet spot left behind. "If it works for the guys..."

Zoey tugged on the offending cushion, prepared to make her indiscretion disappear by flipping it upside down, and found a gold-letter-embossed photo album wedged between the cushion and the sofa frame. Cover torn and edges bent, it looked as though someone flipped through it repeatedly, and had done so for a long time.

She shouldn't snoop. People who hid things did so for a reason. Still, she wanted to make sure she hadn't ruined it with her clumsiness. At least that's what she told herself as she eased the album onto her lap and flipped it open.

Taking the entire first eight-by-ten page was the image missing from the bookshelf: her and the younger Dr. Samuel, post-surgery, smiling into the camera and celebrating a valve restoration that would hopefully be her last.

Zoey turned to the next page and on the left was greeted by another eight-by-ten image, but not one for which she'd posed.

The photo was carefully cropped to cut out the person to whom she'd been talking, but Zoey recognized the unflattering purple dress as one she'd been coerced into wearing to a coworker's wedding seven months ago.

Zoey's nausea ratcheted upward three pegs, but soared a dozen more when she glanced at the images on the right.

In a similar purple dress, another woman was the focus of a series of collaged pictures.

One focused on the satiny texture of the purple dress. Another showcased meticulously brushed golden hair. A pale shoulder. Bruised—and bandaged—wrists. A close-up of a face, eyes closed as if sleeping.

And a sickening familiar heart etching.

Unlike the crime scene photos that migrated across Zoey's desk, these images had been taken with great care and carefully arranged. They'd been displayed by someone proud of what they'd done.

Zoey turned the pages, and each time, she was met with another collection: a full-sized photo of her on the left, and a collage of a different woman on the right.

A young, blond woman.

"Oh my God."

Zoey jumped to her feet. The book fell open at her feet.

Above her head, the ceiling creaked as Dr. Samuel— the Cupid Killer—headed toward the stairs. The old-fashioned brownstone layout meant one way into the room and one way out. She'd never beat him to the front door.

She shoved the photo album back beneath the cushion, making sure she angled it exactly as she'd found it. She'd no sooner planted her butt on the other end than Dr. Samuel came into the room, his stethoscope in his hand.

"Sorry it took so long, but I was so tired after my last on-call shift that I tossed my bag aside. I had to go hunting for this."

"Not a problem." Zoey focused on keeping her voice even—and not throwing up.

As he sat next to her, she choked back rising bile. He'd listened to her heart and lungs a million times, and as she recalled each and every one, her nausea worsened.

"Breathe deep for me and hold it," Dr. Samuel ordered, his voice deceivingly gentle.

Every time he touched his stethoscope in a different position, Zoey fought against jolting away. She needed a plan, and she needed one quick. Even if given an opening to escape, she couldn't outrun him. Not in her still breathless condition.

"I hate to say it, but we need those tests." He flung his scope around his neck and stood, handing her the water she'd sat on the table. "I'm hearing a lot more regurgitation around your valve and I'm afraid it's because your heart's not handling the increased load. If we don't nip this in the bud, fluid will start backing into your lungs."

She forced her head into a nod. "Okay. I'll go back to my place, change my clothes, and meet you at the hospital."

His smile remained friendly as he helped her to her feet. "Nonsense. I'll drive you straight there myself. This isn't something we want to postpone."

Oh yes it was, especially the part where she'd be in close confines with him—the *Cupid Killer*.

It all clicked...the MOs, the victim histories, the sharp, pristine condition of the crime scenes. It took a smart person to get away with so much and for so long.

"Are you sure you're okay?" Dr. Samuel studied her carefully.

"I'm fine." Her voice cracked.

His eyes eased around their surroundings...and slowly dropped to the cushion. If her gaze hadn't been locked on him, she would've missed the slight flaring of his nose.

He knew.

Dr. Samuel transformed into a different person before her eyes—stance, facial expressions. Hell, even his voice changed.

He solidly inserted himself between her and the only exit to the room, an eerie smile melting into place on his face. "I can't tell you how relieved I am that it's finally out in the open, Zoey."

He stepped forward and she jumped back, keeping the arm of the sofa in between them. "You're happy that I know?"

"You must be so disappointed in me."

"*Disappointed?* That you killed all those women?"

"Disappointed that I even entertained the idea that they could take your place." Dr. Samuel pulled the album from its hiding spot, and after thumbing through the pages, tossed it onto the couch with a heavy sigh. "They couldn't. I tried, and tried again, hoping each time that the next would be different. But it wasn't. Because you're irreplaceable."

Nausea rolled into a sharp, piercing pain through her stomach. Her head spun, gaining momentum by the second. This wasn't panic. This wasn't her heart. This wasn't *normal.*

"W-what did you do?" She stumbled into the back of the couch, hands scrambling to hold herself upright.

"What was needed to keep you safe."

She looked at the water. "You drugged me."

"In time, you'll see that I had no choice."

"No choice?" Equilibrium lost, she crashed into an end table, knocking over a lamp in her attempt to remain standing. "No one forced you to do this...*any* of it."

"*You* did, Zoey. Every life that walks this earth is frail, but yours? Yours needs extra protection. Yours needs *me.* I knew it from the moment my father came home talking about the blond-haired little girl who'd been rushed into his operating room."

Samuel's smile went in and out of focus.

Zoey blinked, her periphery darkening by the second. Shadows closed in all around her until the only thing she could see was a small point of light...and Phillip Samuel's nearby face.

"You'd been his responsibility all those years ago, but last year, you became mine. You became my miracle, Zoey Wright. You became *My Heart*."

Zoey's tongue turned into an uncooperative mass of muscles in her mouth. Her legs buckled, and this time, she couldn't conjure one more ounce of energy.

She dropped, hard.

The last thing she did consciously was cry out Knox's name.

CHAPTER
TWENTY-SEVEN

For the first time in a hell of a long time, Knox saw his future clearly.

It involved DC. His family. And it involved him and Zoey. Together.

How to make that last part happen was a little less obvious. A simple apology wouldn't hack it. Hell, regular *words* wouldn't do the trick. In her eyes, he'd viewed her as a weak, defenseless slip of a woman who couldn't possibly take care of herself.

Somehow, he needed to force her to look through *his* eyes and see the strength, beauty, and resilience that had captured his heart. But it wasn't about to happen at Steele Ops.

Throwing on clean clothes, Knox left the locker room and followed the shouts to Ops Command. He'd no sooner taken one step into the room than Cade was in his face.

"This is your fucking fault."

Grace, her eyes rimmed in red as if she'd been crying, gently tugged on her ex's arm. "It's not. It's mine. I'm the one who left her alone."

"But she wouldn't have needed *fresh air* if it weren't for him."

"How about instead of playing the blame game, someone tells me what the hell's going on." Knox looked around the room, noting that everyone wore matching grim expressions.

And he did mean everyone. His brothers. Tank, who'd yet to rejoin his unit. Hell, even Hogan Wilcox stood off to the side, hands speared into his pants pockets.

Only one face was distinctly missing.

"Where's Zoey? She shouldn't be off on her own until we figure out who's responsible for the cameras at her apartment."

No one offered an answer, and Ryder even shifted his gaze away.

"Someone better start talking," Knox warned, his voice growing louder. "*Now.*"

"Zoey's missing," Roman said.

"What the fuck do you mean she's missing?"

Grace shifted uneasily, mercilessly biting her lower lip. "I went to get us water at the gym, and when I got back, she'd left a note at the main desk saying she was taking a quick walk around the block. I waited twenty minutes, thinking she'd be back any second. But she wasn't."

"What about her phone? Did anyone try calling her?"

Grace smacked her palm to her forehead. "My God! *Why the hell didn't I think of that? You're a damn genius, Knox!*"

"All calls go to voicemail." Liam sat behind one of the Steele Ops computers. "And I can't get a ping on it, which means that it's turned off."

If it was even with her.

Knox took a deep breath and tried to think rationally. But damn, it was hard. His first instinct was to haul ass to the gym and look for her himself, no matter that it would be a colossal waste of time.

"How long has it been since she's been gone?" Knox forced his voice calm.

Grace glanced at her watch. "About two hours now...give or take."

"Then let's stop talking and start doing." Jumping into action, Knox stalked around Liam's desk to see his brother's fingers already flying at breakneck speed. "I know you can't ping her phone, but what about its last location? It might give us some idea of where she'd go."

"Are you sure she wouldn't have gone back to her place? Or to Gretchen's?" Wilcox asked from the sidelines. "She was upset earlier. She could've just wanted something familiar."

Knox threw his glare across the room. "You're part of the damn reason she was *upset*."

"The way I see it, I wasn't the only one," Wilcox growled back.

Cade stepped into the line of fire. "Shut the fuck up. Both of you. All three of us have a hand in this, but we can't fix it until we find my sister."

Grace's whistle pierced the air. All arguments immediately stopped as every single pair of eyes turned her way. No nibbling. No shifty feet.

FBI Special Agent Grace Steele had pushed her way to the surface. "None of this whining shit is going to get us to Zoey any faster, and I'm going to throw a little bit of reality your way because obviously someone has to. Zoey's out there, *alone*, while DC's resident psycho could be looking for his next Ginny Monroe."

Knox's stomach twisted. "It's been days since the Monroe murder."

"And prior to her it had been *four*. If our Cupid Killer has fallen off the rails like we suspect, it's a matter time before he picks out his next victim...if he hasn't already. And I don't know about you, but Zoey fits the outside package a little too much for my comfort."

Grace was right. They couldn't let their own issues get in the way of what was important, and that was finding Zoey. Once he had her safely in his arms, Knox wasn't letting her go until she heard him out.

Completely.

He'd bare his heart and soul, and if she still wanted him gone, he'd leave. But he'd come back and try again. And again.

Ryder got off his cell and stuffed it into his front pocket. "She still hasn't been by Gretchen's or Ma's. And she hasn't been back to her place because Liam's alarm system would've clocked in an entry."

Knox's gut churned with a bad feeling. "Then where the hell is she?"

Liam's computer dinged with a hit. "I got something."

Knox immediately lasered in on the ping. "George Washington Park."

Cade's head snapped up. "That's right around the corner from the gym."

"Does the park have a digital signature? Security cams? Red-phoned emergency stations?"

Liam grimaced as he continued working his magic. "That area's been slated for camera replacements for a while now but it hasn't been approved yet. I'm pretty sure there are a few mounted traffic cameras, though. I can hack my way into the DMV feeds without much fuss and see if I can spot her."

"Do it." Knox clapped him on the shoulder. "And text me the coordinates of that last ping. I can't sit here and just wait. I'm going to see if I can find her."

"I'm going with you," Cade offered.

They headed out immediately, jumping into Cade's truck since it was the closest.

Knox didn't expect a friendly chat, and that was okay with him. The longer he went without seeing Zoey, the more her unexplained absence twisted his guts into knots.

She wouldn't let the people she cared about worry, even in protest. Not in a perfect world and not with the Cupid Killer investigation on high alert.

The second Knox and Cade reached Washington Park, they split, searching every damn trail twice before tag-teaming the walking loop that she would've taken around the gym.

"Nothing?" Knox asked the second Cade stepped out from the community center.

"Not a damn thing. Last anyone saw of her was when she'd been in the lobby with Grace."

"Fucking hell." Knox punched a nearby mailbox, the impact feeling like nothing more than a feather. "I shouldn't have let her leave upset. I should have made her stay and talk it out."

Cade let out a strained snort. "We both know that you could've talked until you went blue in the face, but unless she was *willing* to listen, she wasn't going to hear a damn thing you said. And trust me, my friend, she wasn't in a listening mood this morning."

"And what about you?" Knox went there. Hell, he didn't have anything to lose.

"What about me?"

"I'm going to make something clear right now, and it isn't up for debate. I don't give a shit how it makes you feel. I love your sister. I'm *in* love with Zoey. And barring her kicking my ass to the fucking curb, I'm prepared to spend the rest of my life proving to her just how much she means to me. Don't like it? Too damn bad. Because that's how it is."

"You know Zoey's not leaving DC, right?" Cade's question didn't hold the malice Knox expected. "Hard to play house from three thousand miles away."

"I don't intend on being that far away."

A slow smile slid onto Cade's face. "You're joining Steele Ops."

"I haven't said anything to Ro yet because Zoey comes first, *always*, but yeah." Saying the words took at least one weight off his chest. "Maybe you should take your head out of your ass too. And I'm not just talking about Steele Ops."

"One thing at a time, brother. Zoey first. Then job. Then I'll work on your cousin."

Knox's phone rang, and he immediately put it on speaker. "Yeah?"

"I found Zoey walking north on M Street about

an hour and a half ago...three blocks down from the community center," Liam's voice rang out, "but I don't see her on any other traffic cams after that...which means—"

"That she never left that three-block radius."

Knox and Cade moved in unison. They each earned a few glares as they pushed their way past commuters and tourists alike, eventually stopping dead center in the 300 block of M Street.

"I don't see her." Knox snapped his head left and right. "Even if she'd been here a while ago, she's not here now. *Fuck*."

Cade's phone rang, and seeing the station's number, answered with a "It's not a good time right now, Adam."

As Cade tried rushing Zoey's lab friend off the phone, Knox spotted the deli owner flashing them a curious glance from behind his counter.

Knox stepped through the doors and got a friendly, although reserved, smile. "What can I do for you, young man?"

"I'm looking for a missing friend of mine, and I was wondering if you've seen her around any time within the last two hours or so." Knox pulled up a photo of Zoey from his phone and showed the older business owner.

"Oh. Zoey." He smiled. "She's such a sweetheart, that one."

Knox's heart skipped a beat. "You know her?"

"Of course, she drops in every week. I get the feeling she's not much of a cook."

The older man's smile slowly melted. "You said she's missing? Oh. Dear. I . . . I hope nothing happened."

"That's what we're trying to find out."

"Maybe Dr. Samuel will be able to tell you more. I offered to call 911, but Doc said he had it under control. Smart guy. Great job. Good-looking too, although my wife keeps insisting that something must be wrong with him. Says no man that perfect wouldn't have a steady woman in his life by now."

Knox's internal alarm blared to DEFCON 1.

He kept his shit together—barely—so as not to scare the eighty-some-year-old. "You saw her with Dr. Samuel? When was this?"

He rubbed a whiskered chin. "Well, I guess it was about an hour ago. I'd been filling a catering order when I saw her stop outside the deli. The poor thing looked ready to keel over, almost called my wife out to help. But then Doc showed up."

"She was sick?"

"Honestly, I don't know what was wrong, but Doc sure looked worried enough."

"But not enough to let you call the paramedics."

"I guess he figured he could assess her as easily as they could. Took her down to his place. It's possible he called the EMTs from there. I didn't hear any lights or sirens, but my hearing isn't the greatest these days."

"Is his place nearby?"

"Sure is. It's the gray brownstone three doors down. The one with the red door."

Cade stormed into the deli, his cell clutched tightly in his hand. "We've got a huge fucking problem.

There's a partial print on the bullet that sliced your shoulder."

"I don't give a rat's ass about Stuart right now. We have a *real* problem here." With single-minded focus, Knox pushed past his friend.

"This *is* fucking real because the prints didn't belong to him."

That damn sick feeling brought Knox to a stop. "Who did they belong to?"

"Phillip Samuel. Zoey's *doctor*."

Knox's head snapped toward the brownstone three doors down. Heart pounding in his ears, it took a few seconds for him to remember how to fucking walk much less run. Then he took off.

Cade's grip spun him around a split second before he kicked down Samuel's front door. "Do you want to tell me what the fuck this is about and why you're about to commit a B and E?"

"Less than an hour ago, Zoey stood outside that deli. *Sick*. And with *Samuel*."

"Shit." Cade pinched the bridge of his nose. "Okay...calm down and let's think about this before we do something we can't take back. I know where your mind's going, but shooting your sorry ass doesn't equal serial killer."

"*Why* me, Cade?" Knox demanded angrily.

"Why did he shoot you? What? Because you're so lovable all the damn time?"

"I met the man once at the community center, and way after the Great Stuart chase." Knox's gaze shifted to the brownstone. "Think about it. The BCK followed his own set of rules for six months. Then out of nowhere, he changes them. He changes them around the time *I* came into Zoey's life."

"But how would he...fuck." Cade's face went still. "The cameras."

"And her break-in? Her necklace? What if Ginny Monroe having it wasn't a fucking coincidence? Stuart may be responsible for a shit ton of other robberies, but there's nothing linking him to Zoey's place, is there?" Knox wanted to hit his friend over the head. "For fuck's sake, Cade, tack Zoey's picture onto the murder board and she'd fit right in with the thirteen other Cupid blondes!"

"Do *not* fucking move," Cade warned him, still cursing as he called in backup. He hung up and called another number. From what Knox could tell, it was to an on-call judge to get the verbal go-ahead to search the premises.

Waiting went against everything Knox stood for. His body ached with the need to break down the fucking door and get to Zoey. The only reason he didn't right then was the light-flashing squad car that came to a squealing stop right in front of them.

Knox wasn't waiting another damn second. If that Samuel bastard was behind Zoey's disappearance...if he touched a hair on her head, Knox would make sure that he needed a surgeon himself.

CHAPTER TWENTY-EIGHT

Zoey pried her eyes open. Her brain, once in a deep, foggy blackness, slowly blinked her world back into focus. No longer in Dr. Samuel's apartment, she lay sprawled over a mattress, her arms bound to a metal bed frame.

Six feet away, a single light bulb flickered off charred remains of an already dank room. The place looked as if it had been burnt to a crisp and only half rebuilt before being abandoned entirely.

She craned her neck to catch a glimpse of something—or someone—and slowly realized the tickle beneath her nose came from the oxygen cannula fastened to her face.

"You're up." Dr. Samuel walked into the room from a door on the left.

Dressed in the same T-shirt and shorts he'd been in at his place, he smiled at her as he did whenever she stepped into his office, and looked a mile away from the part of killer doctor.

"I have to apologize, Zoey." He looked almost sincere. "In the excitement of the moment, I dosed you with Fentanyl before taking your diminished cardiac output into account. But you have nothing to fear. I'll be more careful in the future. The last thing I want is to harm you in any way."

Zoey almost laughed at how absurd he sounded. She wiggled her numbing fingers. "You don't want to hurt me and yet I'm tied to a bed?"

"I'll release the bindings in time." He sat on a nearby stool and looked at her intently, his eyes glittering. He leaned over to stroke her cheek and she flinched away, the move pulling his smile into a frown. "I've waited for this moment for so long, suffered so many failures and setbacks. You finally being here hardly feels real to me."

Zoey swallowed around the dozen rusty nails lodged in her throat. "Where exactly is here?"

Dr. Samuel returned to his feet and moved to a small side table. One by one, he pulled a set of syringes from his black bag and set them aside. "At the start of our new life. I'm going to make sure you have everything you want...everything you deserve. Happiness. Health."

Zoey twisted her hand, testing the binding on her wrists. "Do I deserve to be free?"

He paused, glancing at her from over his shoulder. "Of course. And like I said, it'll happen. In time. First, we need to get you healthy again. I hated messing with your medications, but it was a necessary evil."

"You messed with my meds?"

"I needed you to need me."

He said it so simply, so matter-of-factly, that Zoey blinked. "But how? I was on the same meds as...*Amplify*."

He flashed her an eerily proud smile. "You've always

had such a sharp mind. I knew it from the moment I first laid eyes on you."

"Is it even a real medication?"

"Oh, yes. It was on the market for a short period of time...about long enough to have an official medication data sheet. Unfortunately, it had unexpected side effects."

"Wh-what kind of side effects?" She almost didn't want to know.

"Decreasing the threshold of certain cardiac meds."

Looking back, Zoey wanted to kick herself in the ass. At some point, her regular, everyday life had changed, and she'd glazed over it without realizing. *Not that it would've done her any good.*

Her *doctor* had been the one to cause the change.

"I usually research new meds, but—"

Tears welled in his eyes. "But you *trusted* me...as you did with our last few dosage changes. That's a good thing. All successful relationships are based on *trust*."

Zoey was stuck between wanting to laugh and cry.

Dr. Samuel flicked the tip of a syringe and discarded an air bubble. She redoubled her efforts to pull her arms free.

"This is only Lasix. To manage your increased fluid load." Samuel pushed the clear liquid into the IV line embedded in her left forearm. "I know this all must seem a little severe, but you have to believe that I did this for the greater good. For *our* greater good."

"Drugging me. Kidnapping me. Murdering all those innocent women was for the greater good?"

"They were not innocent!" Dr. Samuel threw the used syringe across the room.

Zoey jumped, startled by his abrupt change in mood.

In the snap of his fingers, his eyes went from placid to wild. Ripping his hand through his hair, he paced. "They *lied*. They *manipulated*. They wove me into their twisted games and then they had the gall to think there wouldn't be repercussions. I tried so hard to give them a chance, but they *just weren't you*."

"You killed them because they weren't *me*?"

"I'm sorry, Zoey." In another dizzying switch, Dr. Samuel softened his voice. He dropped to his knees and gripped tightly on to the fingers of her bound left hand. "I'm *so* sorry that I ever thought that I could replace you."

He was sorry...

Not for killing thirteen women.

He regretted that none of them had measured up to *her*.

Guilt attacked Zoey in the form of rising vomit, a sensation worsened by Dr. Samuel caressing a knuckle over her cheek. "From the first time I listened to my father talk about you, I knew you were special. My father did too. I saw it in his eyes, in the way he dropped everything to rush to your side at a moment's notice... by the number of times he missed special occasions to make sure you got what you needed."

"I'm sorry."

"Don't be sorry. I'm not. Because when he retired, he entrusted your well-being to *me*, and it's a job that I'll honor until my last breath. Your life is mine, Zoey. Your *heart's* mine... and mine is yours."

She pulled her face away from him as far she could. "My heart's *mine*. And I sure as hell don't want yours."

Dr. Samuel blinked as if smacked. He stood, flaring nostrils distorting his once-handsome features. "That's not you talking. That's *him*. I tried dealing with him before his poison touched you too severely, but I failed. I failed to protect you from Steele, but I won't fail again. I'll make things right. I'll make sure nothing comes between the two of us again."

Realization would've dumped her from the bed if she hadn't been tied down. "You're the one who shot Knox."

"He's an obstacle. Obstacles are meant to be overcome, and once we do, we'll finally get the life that we deserve."

Zoey didn't need Grace's psychology degree to know that talking sense into Dr. Samuel wouldn't work.

She shifted, hand bumping into something sharp. The bed frame. As she inspected the jagged edge, warm wetness coated her right index finger. With one eye on a now pacing Samuel, she stretched her arm and did it again, this time on purpose, and this time with the nylon rope binding her wrist.

Pain laced into her hand as she occasionally missed her target, but she didn't stop, slowly sawing away while Dr. Samuel stared into the distance.

"Things had been perfect after your surgery. You *came* to me." Eyes hollow and unfocused, he didn't seem to see her anymore. "You *counted* on me. Seeing you in my office was the highlight of my day, and then in the blink of an eye, you were gone. You moved on. Without me."

Zoey winced as she missed her mark, the bed cutting deep into her palm. "The surgery fixed what was wrong. Y-you fixed me."

She nearly gagged playing along, but she needed to distract him long enough to free her arms. And then she'd figure out the rest.

Dr. Samuel shook his head. "I made you too strong... *too* independent."

A muffled shout whipped Zoey's attention to the metal door across the room. "What was that?"

"Just another way to bring you to me... a mistake... but I didn't have time to take care of it before you practically showed up on my doorstep." He slowly stalked closer, hovering as he stared down on her with a bone-chilling smile. "You're not to worry about it. I'm going to handle it like I did the others... and then I'm going to heal you like I did before."

Zoey chiseled her tongue off the roof of her mouth. "And then?"

"We're going to start the rest of our lives... *My Heart*."

Zoey's heart rate ratcheted up about five hundred beats. If there was ever a time she wished her brother and Knox had implanted that GPS tracking chip under her skin, it was now.

* * *

Knox's skin buzzed as he stood on Phillip Samuel's front stoop, waiting for Cade to finish doling out instructions to Officers Natasha James and her partner, Deacon Black. The two beat cops hustled around back.

"Get your head in the game," Cade warned, joining him on the steps. "Going in there half-cocked isn't going to do anything but create problems."

"So you want me to what? Hold Samuel's hand and get him a glass of water while I patiently wait for him to share what he knows? That may be the cop style, but it's not mine."

Cade drilled him with a glare. "The cop style means we'll get the bastard and make sure he pays. Your method increases the likelihood that the sicko gets off on technicalities. Think *smart*, Knox, or I'll make your ass stand on the sidewalk."

"Like hell." Knox cracked his knuckles. "The only thing I can think about right now is Zoey."

Cade dropped an understanding hand on his shoulder. "Me too. And if this bastard had anything to do with her going MIA, we'll make sure he experiences a world of hurt. The *right* way."

Knox hated that his friend was right.

He removed his gun from its holster, and Cade did the same before radioing to the officers in the rear.

"On three," Cade announced. He counted down, nodding at Knox to kick in the front door.

The heavy wood caved on impact, smacking against the wall behind.

They breached the residence in one fluid motion, immediately falling back on their Ranger training as they cleared the first few rooms. Officer James and her partner could be heard doing the same to the back end before they all met in the center hall.

"Clear the entire residence first, then go back and assess," Cade ordered.

James nodded, and they immediately split again, she and her partner heading toward the basement while

Cade and Knox took the stairs to the second level. With every room that came up empty, Knox's agitation grew.

James's voice crackled on the radio. "Basement. Now."

Knox stopped breathing as he and Cade raced down the two flights. He reached the sublevel first, and what he saw ignited a curse reel that would've had his mother smacking the back of his head.

Though the room was mostly unfurnished, a small corner cot and desk stood out, as did the three powered-up laptops. The murmur of noises echoed off the walls, and it took him a minute to realize the sounds came from the speakers... and from the images playing out on the computer screens.

He didn't need to step closer to recognize him and Zoey, naked in her bed, their bodies entwined. Their love-making... their first... played on a repetitive loop.

"There's a ton of videos like this." James gestured to a large stack of CDs. "And judging by the titles, all of Zoey."

"Fucking hell." Cade looked ill as he shot a quick look to Knox. "You were right."

"It's fucking worse than a bunch of damn videos!" James's partner shouted down the stairs. "Get your asses up here!"

Knox wasn't sure how much worse it could get, but he was clued in the second he glimpsed the album on the floor.

On one side, there was a glossy image of a starry-eyed Zoey, head tossed back in laugher.

On the other, was an image collection from the Cupid Killer's last victim.

Ginny Monroe.

CHAPTER TWENTY-NINE

Red and blue lights bounced off plain-clothed and uniformed police as they navigated the crime scene. Some ran interference with gathering news crews, while others walked door to door in an attempt to reassure curious residents.

Cade directed them all, growling orders to anyone stupid enough to sit around doing nothing. He'd long since divided his DCPD crew into teams, one inspecting the rest of Samuel's house, and the other sent to the hospital in the hopes that the sick fuck showed up to work.

Knox stood by the back of the ops van and fought not to raise his voice. "You've got to give me something to work with, Grace. I know you're trying, but—"

"I know. I know." His cousin thunked her head against the back of the truck in a repetitive beat. "We're missing something. *I'm* missing something."

"Grace..."

"*Yes!*" Grace jumped into the back of the van and hovered over Liam's shoulder. "Bring up Samuel's personal timeline again."

Liam clicked a few keys, and Phillip Samuel's background popped onto the laptop.

Grace ran her finger over the info, eyes scanning.

"Normal childhood. Normal childhood. College grad. Medical school. Yadda, yadda, yadda."

Liam scoffed, "I'm bored even listening to it. None of this screams *I'm-a-freakin'-serial-killer-who-likes-to-etch-hearts-into-the-chests-of-my-victims*."

"And nothing will. If a girl thinks the guy who's asking her out for coffee is acting like a deranged killer, she's not about to say yes. They hide it. Hell, a lot of time, serial killers have full-blown families who know nothing about their twisted little hobby."

Liam shuddered. "Stuff of fucking nightmares."

"Bring up Zoey's timeline. *There*..." Grace smacked her finger into the screen, bouncing the image. "What the hell just happened?"

"Touch-screen. Hands off the merch. Literally."

Grace pointed to Zoey's surgery last year and glanced to Knox. "*There's* your hot point."

"When Samuel performed her surgery."

"With his degree of obsession, it's quite possible that he's harbored feelings even before that. Hell, maybe even when his father took care of her. But performing that surgery ignited something in him that once let out, he wasn't about to pack up and put away."

"Except he did." Roman, listening closely, leaned onto the bumper.

Ryder and Tank stood next to him, carefully observing.

"What do you mean?" Knox asked his brother.

"The surgery may have been a rough one, but it got the job done. It was successful. She walked out of that hospital on her own two feet and didn't go back."

Knox suddenly realized what Grace meant. "But she

did go back. For follow-ups. For physicals. Typical open-heart patients return monthly until about six months post-op."

All eyes turned to him. Knox didn't even bother getting defensive.

"He's right," Grace agreed. "There's about six months of regular visits and then *bam*—it's once, or sometimes twice a year. When you overlay Samuel's and Zoey's timelines, matching up that one significant event…"

"The Cupid Killer's first victim coincides with Zoey's last follow-up."

Roman cursed. "He missed her."

"He wanted to *replace* her," Grace corrected Ro. "But it wasn't right. And so he tried again, and again, until everything finally crashes around him. He hit his breaking point."

She regretfully slid her gaze Knox's way.

"With me." Knox knew what she wasn't saying. "He'd been keeping tabs on Zoey and when she and I…"

"I'm sorry, Knox. But yeah. Your relationship with her triggered something in him. It threw him. It veered him off course and made him make up another one. And you can bet that he won't be happy about it. A man like Samuel doesn't like failure, and he's going to be extremely territorial of what he perceives as his property."

Roman leaned against the van bumper. "Then why weren't his victims…more messed up? I mean yeah, I get that he deviated some, but overall not much."

"Because as unstable as he is, that's not him. It's why

he dresses their wounds. What we need to ask ourselves is where would a doctor care for his patients?"

"The hospital," Knox realized. "But someone would realize that a serial killer's using the surgical suites as a torture ground."

"Unless they were using an abandoned hospital building." Roman ripped the DC map off the wall of the van and smacked his hand on a familiar DC block. "The burned-out wing of Georgetown Med. I saw it when I bumped into Zoey downtown. The rest of the campus was swarming with people, but no one spared it a second glance. Hell, it had caution signs all over the place."

Knox's body stiffened, ready for action. "Smart fucking bastard. Using a condemned building means no one would bother him, and he'd be close enough to access whatever supplies he needed from the main hospital."

Liam brought up comparison-image floor plans of the old hospital wing and what stood today. He pointed to the south end, lower level. "Here. It's far enough from the main hospital that no one would stumble on him by accident, and has easy, out-of-the-way access from the rear loading dock. Perfect for a twisted psycho lair."

Knox tossed a look onto the street. "Cade? You hearing this?"

"Already sending a team to the hospital to clear out the building next door, and I'm prepping SWAT to go in as backup," Cade confirmed.

"Backup?"

Cade stared him dead in the eye. "Fuck yeah. I'm not putting Zoey's life in anybody's hands but the best."

Liam smirked. "Just to make that clear, you mean us, right?"

"Damn straight."

Knox nodded. "And you realize you lumped yourself in there with us."

Cade snorted. "Yep. We'll start job offer negotiations once my sister's safe and sound."

Knox slapped him on the shoulder. Getting Zoey back where she belonged was the only option, and his brothers and Cade were the only people he trusted to get it done too. He'd been kidding himself even contemplating that damn bodyguard job.

DC was where he was meant to be. Steele Ops was where he was meant to work. And Zoey was the woman he was meant to love. Now that he finally realized it, he wasn't about to let any of it go...especially Zoey.

She made him better. She made him feel. She made him *whole*.

* * *

Zoey forced her lungs' cooperation through another breath, but with every inhalation, her quickly depleting energy sunk lower. In another few minutes, picking her head up would be next to impossible.

Dr. Samuel emerged from the far door, his face a mask of barely withheld contempt, which Zoey suspected had something to do with the muffled shout that had followed him. He hadn't yet *fixed his mistake*.

That meant both Zoey and the woman in the other room had time.

Keeping an eye on a muttering Samuel, Zoey continued sawing away at her rope-bound hands. Centimeter by centimeter, the tie loosened, until with a final tug, her right arm came free.

"Time for another round of meds," Dr. Samuel announced.

Zoey grabbed on to the railing and faked being tied. "Tell me why I should take anything from you."

He blinked, taken aback by her tone. "Because I would never do anything to harm you in any way, My Heart."

"Except mess with my meds. Kidnap me. Keep me tied like a Thanksgiving turkey."

He shook his head as he slowly approached. "I told you. This is for the best. As for the restraints, I can't have you disappearing and getting into trouble."

Zoey's eyes shot to the three filled syringes he carried on a small metal tray. "I'm not one of your victims that you can drug and toss away. You said I was different."

"You *are*, sweetheart. Two of these are to improve your cardiac function."

"And the third?" A lump knotted in Zoey's throat.

"To relax you. Your breathing's become more labored. It'll relax your chest muscles, make it easier to inhale deeply. I know this isn't an ideal situation, but things will all work out in the end. I promise."

"What about for the woman in the room next door?"

The eerie calm in his voice dissipated. "*She* will get what she deserves as well. But you're not to worry yourself about her. Doctor's order."

Zoey counted down as he approached. At three steps

from the bed, she took as deep a breath as her lungs allowed, bunching her fingers into a tight fist. At one, she rolled.

Using her free hand, she smashed his tray up into his face. Samuel doubled over, giving her a prime target in which to aim a kick. Her sneaker impacted his temple with a thud, and Samuel went down hard.

Zoey attacked her bindings with blood-coated fingers. She lost her grip three times before she realized it wasn't going to work. Behind her, Dr. Samuel groaned, straining to his knees.

"Suck it up, Zoey." She gritted her teeth, and tugged.

A sharp stab of pain zipped up from her disjointed thumb and up her arm, but it worked. Her wrist came free, and a second later, she ripped the IV from her arm and sprinted for the back door.

"Zoey! Stop!" Samuel shouted.

Rusted with age and disuse, the door felt heavier than it looked. She yanked it open with a power-yell Cade would've been proud of, and quickly slipped through the crack. It slammed shut behind her, and she smacked the deadbolt into place, praying it would hold.

Muffled screams stole her attention to the other side of the room.

Although a gag hid half her face, Samuel's *mistake* was impossible not to recognize. "Francine."

Knox's ex screamed, her orders muffled and panicked, and spurring Zoey into action.

"Let me find something to cut you loose." She rifled through a dozen drawers and cabinets before her fingers bumped against a blunt-tipped file that looked about as threatening as a paperclip. "This is going to have to do."

She attacked Fran's ties with a vengeance, sweat breaking out across her forehead by the time the other woman's first hand broke free.

Francine ripped away her gag. "I have never been so happy to see you in my fucking life. We need to get the hell out of here...although I don't know where *here* is."

Zoey freed her other hand and moved to her legs. "I recognize the floor tiles. Sure spent enough time staring at them through the years. I think we're in the old Georgetown cancer wing, which means that we have a long way before we run into someone."

"Then let's get moving before that psycho gets back." Barefoot and dirtied, and wearing a ripped version of her gala cocktail dress, Francine sprung from the bed.

From the other room, Dr. Samuel bellowed, "Zoey! You don't want to do this! You can't leave!"

Fran backed away from the door, her eyes widening. "I don't know what the hell happened. He seemed normal when he asked me out. Charming even. And then we went back to his place and—*holy crap*. I almost let him get me *naked*!"

"Probably good you didn't...because he's the killer you've been chomping at the bit to prosecute."

Francine's face paled. "Are you shitting me?"

"Wish I was." Zoey shoved the file into her pants.

Dr. Samuel pounded on the rusted door. "Please! You're *My Heart*, Zoey! You're my *everything*!"

"You're my living nightmare," Zoey muttered, and frantically scanned the room. A free-standing supply closet, cocked at an odd angle, blocked what she hoped was a second exit. "Help me move this thing."

Francine didn't argue. They worked together, nudging the metal unit across the cement floor an inch at a time until they revealed the sagging archway behind.

The second the gap became large enough to fit a person, Zoey barked, "Go. Go."

Francine squeezed through the one-foot space, and she followed.

"Which way?" Francine asked.

Zoey took a second to collect her bearings, and then grabbing the other woman's hand, tugged her left down the empty corridor. "This one."

Her chest constricted with the physical effort it took to keep pace with Francine, but there was no way in hell she was about to give up.

They no sooner made it to the far end than Dr. Samuel burst through the second door behind them. He stalked toward them at a slow trot. "Give me more time, My Heart. That's all I ask. More time to prove that we're meant to be!"

"Through here! Go!" Zoey pushed Francine into a fire exit stairwell. "We need to get up to the first floor."

Francine stood on the first landing before Zoey even reached the third step. "What's taking you so long? *Hurry!*"

"I...can't." Zoey careened into the railing.

Francine came back, concern shining in her eyes. "Did he already drug you? I'm pretty sure that's what he planned to do to me."

Zoey wheezed. "H-he messed with my meds. My lungs...I can't keep running. L-leave me. Get help."

Muttering under her breath, Francine slipped her

shoulder beneath Zoey's arm. "I'm too self-sacrificing for my own damn good. I may not like you much, but I can't leave you to a psycho who's been etching hearts into women's chests."

Zoey half smiled. "That was...nice."

"Don't get used to it."

Using both the railing and Fran's support, Zoey climbed the flight of stairs one excruciating step at a time. Behind them, Samuel's shouts echoed off the walls, getting closer.

"Do *not* make me carry you," Francine warned.

As they reached the first-floor landing, Samuel threw open the door below them, hot on their heels.

"There." Zoey gasped, pointing toward the old loading dock doors a good thirty yards away.

Zoey's feet, weighted like anchors, refused to lift higher than an inch. Francine panted, redoubling her efforts to propel them down the hall.

Twenty-five yards to freedom.

Twenty.

At fifteen, strong hands ripped Zoey from Francine's hold.

"I told you once, and I'll tell you again." Dr. Samuel's mouth scraped against her ear. "You. Are. My. Heart. You're not going anywhere."

At this point, Zoey knew that was true.

Colorful dots swam across her vision. Sounds muted. And all her focus was narrowed into one small, but very important act.

Breathing.

CHAPTER THIRTY

Parked on the utility road bisecting the old and new parts of the Georgetown medical campus, Hogan Wilcox manned Liam's pride and joy, an infrared drone equipped with a magnifying camera and state-of-the-art listening capabilities. The tech-toy now hovered over Knox's head, and the charred remains of the old cancer building, acting as their eyes and ears.

Knox's palms sweat as he sat hunched behind a forgotten dumpster outside the old dock. He'd been on countless high-stress missions, but none as important as this one.

Roman crouched next to him, his hand dropping onto his shoulder. "We're going to get her back safe."

Knox flexed his fist, his fingers cracking under the pressure. "I won't accept anything else." He took a slow breath before finally admitting, "You were right."

"I usually am. Which time are you talking about?"

"I stayed away because it was the easier path. No bumps. No surprises. No having to look in anyone's eyes and see their regret staring back at me." He slid his gaze to his brother.

"Easy way to live," Roman mumbled.

"Not fulfilling either. It also means I don't get to see their joy staring back at me...*or* their love."

Of the four Steele brothers, Roman had always kept his emotions close to his chest...and inside his head. His run-in with the IED and everything following made it more so. But now something flashed in Roman's eyes that Knox hadn't seen in a long time.

Hope.

"I'm staying, Ro. Whether you let me in on Steele Ops is up to you, but I'm not going anywhere. I love you guys. I love Zoey. And I'm not about to let anything—including myself—keep me away from all of you."

Roman stared him dead in the eye. "Good."

Knox waited for more, but he didn't expect it. He didn't need it. For now. Staying in DC, he'd have time to work on his stubborn-ass younger brother.

Wilcox's voice came online via their comm links. "We have three heat signatures less than fifteen yards from that loading dock. Two huddled on the far south end, and one on the north, closest to the door."

"SWAT Command's telling me that there's three points of entry," Cade announced. "The main door, which puts you smack in the middle, and then two side entrances that are used for in-processing and outgoing shipments. Both lead to the main corridor from opposite ends."

Roman grunted. "That's more than enough entry points."

Knox agreed, but his stomach knotted. "We don't know who's making up those heat signatures, so we need to tread carefully and not go in guns blazing.

Chances are high that Samuel's one of the two huddled close...and Zoey's the other."

"Then who's the third?"

"Guess we'll find out soon enough. I'm on the main door."

Roman cleared his throat, temporarily nabbing his attention. "You think that's a good idea? Samuel already tried taking you out once. Who's to say he won't try again?"

"Part of me hopes the bastard does." Knox readied his weapon. "Zoey's in there, and I'll be damned if I'm not the first one through that door. I need to lay eyes on her, Ro. I need to make sure she believes that we're getting her out of this."

Roman waited a beat before tipping his chin in a grim nod. "Then I'll ride on your six. Cade, you and Tank come in via the left. Ryder and Liam, you go right. General, make sure SWAT's on our asses prepped to intervene if this goes sideways."

"Got it," Wilcox affirmed. "Get our girl back safely, boys."

Knox recited a mental countdown...and then one aloud. "On my three. One. Two. Three."

Roman tugged open the main door and dropped to a knee, providing Knox immediate cover. "Go. Go."

Knox breached the building first, not knowing what he was about to see. He sure as hell hadn't expected Francine to be the single heat signature closest to the door, and in an obvious stand-off with Phillip Samuel—and Zoey.

"Ro," Knox growled.

"Got her." His brother hauled Fran backward, and quickly out the door. Her colorful string of profanities could still be heard when the door clicked closed.

"One hostage freed," Knox murmured into his comm. "Ryder. Change course to the south."

"Got it."

Knox locked his gun sight directly on Samuel and forced himself still. Cade and Tank emerged from the left. Ryder and Liam, detoured around the back, silently approached Samuel and Zoey from the rear.

Only when his team was in position did Knox slide his attention to the woman who meant the world to him.

His heart immediately stalled.

With blood-soaked fingers, Zoey clutched the arm throttling her bare neck. The dark red, in varying stages of freshness, was the only color on her pale skin. "Zoey."

"Do not say her name! You don't have the right!" Samuel tightened his grip around her neck, his eyes skating around the hall like a penned animal. "She's not yours! She's mine! *Mine!*"

Knox dragged his gaze back to Samuel. "Is that how you treat what's yours?"

"Jesus, Knox," Grace's voice chimed in from the tactical van. "Do *not* piss him off. You need to placate him. Make him think you understand. Use his name. *Sympathize.*"

"How good of an actor do you think I am?" Knox murmured. But hell, she was right. "Look, Samuel, we all want everyone to walk away from this safely, right?"

Samuel dragged Zoey back a step, deeper into the corridor. "Then let us go."

"You're not leaving with her."

"You've done nothing but taint the precious life that *I've* given her," Samuel hissed, spittle flying from his mouth. "But *I* can make her happy. *I* can make her healthy."

"Take a look at her, Samuel. Does she seem happy and healthy to you?"

His steps faltered. "I did it once and I'll do it again."

Zoey let out a soft moan.

Knox whipped his attention toward her.

Lips parted, she audibly struggled for each breath. Her complexion had morphed from sickly pale to gray-tinged in the seconds since he'd first laid eyes on her, and it darkened the longer this took.

"We need an ambulance on standby. Now," Knox murmured into his mic. Oblivious to Liam and Ryder approaching cautiously from the rear, Samuel locked all his attention and hatred on Knox.

And that was fine by him.

"Angel." Knox prayed she was coherent enough to hear him.

Zoey's eyes drifted close. Her chest, in a series of labored rises and falls, worked overtime.

"*Zoey*," Knox softly called her. "Baby, please look at me."

Her pretty blue eyes flickered open, and he immediately registered the knowledge glinting in their depths. *They didn't have much time.*

She dropped her eyes to her feet, drawing his attention to the slight widening of her stance. Her shoulders relaxed, and she dropped her grip on Samuel's arm. *No way. No way could she do what he thought...*

"Get ready to move," Knox murmured to the team.

Wilcox, watching from the body cams, growled, "What the hell is she doing?"

"Giving us the opening we need to take him down." *By taking herself out of the equation.*

Zoey's eyes flashed to Knox, and then she pivoted left. The abrupt move freed up the left side of her neck, and not pausing a beat, she went for Samuel's eyes. Startled, he pushed her back. She dropped to the ground and quickly rolled out of the way, giving them room.

"Move! Move! Move!" Knox shouted.

The team quickly locked the bastard in on all four corners.

"You have nowhere to go, Samuel," Knox warned.

"You won't get away with this." He took a step back. "You're not cops." Another step. "You have no authority over me!"

Samuel backed right into Cade.

His best friend face-planted the sick bastard into the wall. The satisfying crunch of a breaking nose echoed along with Samuel's screams.

"*This* is my authority, asshole." Cade drilled his weapon into the back of the bastard's head. "You're under arrest. Liam? Ties?"

"With pleasure." Liam yanked Samuel's arms behind his back.

"I'll kill you for this, Steele," Samuel howled. "And I

won't miss this time! She's *mine*! She needs *me*! I'm the only one that can help her! *Me!*"

Roman took over pushing his face into the wall. "The only thing that's yours, asshole, is a four-by-four cell in a maximum security prison."

"You got this?" Knox asked.

"Go."

Three feet away, Zoey lay on the ground, face ashen and chest barely moving. He sprinted to her side and dropped to his knees. "Where the hell are those paramedics?"

"They're already on their way inside," Wilcox assured. "How's our girl, Steele?"

"I don't know." He held her clammy hand against his cheek. "Come on, angel. You need to stay with me. Please, baby."

A swell of emotion made it difficult to talk. He couldn't lose her. Not now. Not after he'd finally gotten out of his own way. Not after she'd helped him see that happiness was his for the taking.

Her eyes fluttered as she struggled to open them. "Can't . . . br—"

He brushed a lock of hair from her eyes. "I know, angel. I know. Help's coming."

Two paramedics rushed through the side door and lasered in on Zoey immediately.

"Hurry!" Knox growled. "She's having problems breathing!"

"We'll take it from here," the first one said, ushering Knox to the side.

"She has heart issues."

"We know. We got a rundown on our way in. The hospital's already on alert." The paramedic put an oxygen mask over her face while his partner inserted an intravenous line.

Knox stood by, helpless, as the duo worked in tandem strapping her onto a gurney.

He stayed on their heels until the EMT stopped him at the waiting ambulance. "I'm sorry sir, but we can't allow—"

"You're not taking her anywhere without me." Knox ignored Cade and Roman at his side, ready to pull him back.

"Look, normally I'd let it slide. But we need the extra room to . . . move."

Or use extreme measures to save her life.

Knox didn't need to hear the words to know that was what he meant. As they closed the ambulance doors, a little piece of Knox's heart split apart. "Go. Just help her. *Please.*"

"Where are you taking her?" Roman asked.

"Next door. Georgetown."

Roman held his hands out to Knox. "Give me your weapons and go."

He didn't need to be told twice. The second he unloaded, Knox took off in a sprint. People threw him curious looks as he navigated the medical campus, detouring through footpaths that would get him to the ER a hell of a lot faster than jumping in a truck.

Fuck keeping his distance. Fuck his damn insecurities. Fuck everything that didn't revolve around Zoey and never leaving her side again.

Knox spotted the ambulance bay and burst through the double doors.

"Zoey Wright," he barked at the volunteer behind the counter. "She was brought in...hell, I don't know when they got here."

Behind him, the bay doors flew open. Medical staff ran to meet the two familiar EMTs, one of which sat astride the gurney in an unmistakable attempt at CPR.

"Oh my God." Knox's knees buckled.

Roman appeared at his side, keeping him on his feet. "Think positive. Zoey's strong. She's defied the odds her entire life. She's not about to stop now."

Knox prayed he was right.

Knox prayed he'd gotten to her in time.

Knox closed his eyes and just prayed.

* * *

He paced, unable to sit on his ass another minute. Four hours into Zoey's surgery and they hadn't heard a damn thing. No news. No updates. Knox was one second-hand tick away from losing his mind.

"Honey, why don't you go with Roman to get some coffee?" his mother, her tone concerned, asked for the third time in as many minutes. "Or some herbal tea."

"I don't want to relax, Ma."

"Then go with the boys and get *me* some tea."

He stopped pacing. "Ma, I appreciate what you're trying to do, but I'm not going anywhere until we hear something, and even then, I'm not moving a damn inch."

She digested his words and nodded. Next to her, Gretchen clutched tightly to a rosary, and the General, standing alone in the far corner, looked about as good as Knox felt. No one moved, because no one was about to go anywhere.

The door opened and a tall, middle-aged man in green surgical scrubs stepped into the waiting room. He glanced around, taking note of the filled room. "Are you all Zoey Wright's family?"

"Yes," Cade answered, stepping next to Knox. "How's my sister?"

"I'm Dr. Benedict, the cardiac surgeon called in to evaluate Zoey. Your sister is one lucky woman."

"So she's okay?" Knox asked, breathless.

"I'm not going to lie. There were a few moments it was touch-and-go. Acute congestive heart failure is no small thing."

"*Heart failure?*" Knox needed to sit down after all. He plunked into the nearest seat and kept his eyes on the doctor. "Isn't she on meds to prevent that from happening?"

"She is. And I believe that if her medical records were correct, we wouldn't be here today."

Cade caught on to his statement too. "You think her records have been altered? By Samuel?"

"Zoey's bloodwork indicates that she'd been taking a medication that's been recently pulled from the market, but there's no record of her ever having been prescribed it."

"Why was it taken off the market?" Knox asked.

Grim-faced, the surgeon answered, "It has been

proven to decrease the effectiveness of certain cardiac medications. With a decrease in cardiac function, and an overload of fluid to her heart, Zoey's replaced valve couldn't keep pace with the demand."

Knox's fists bunched at his side. "Samuel knew this med could equal a death sentence for her, and yet he put her on it. So she'd be forced to go back to his office."

"It would appear that way, yes."

Nausea churned Knox's gut. "I wish I would've shot him."

"You and me both," Cade said, furious. "So what happens with Zoey now?"

Benedict nodded. "The fact she'd been healthy before Amplify, and the relatively short period of time she'd been subjected to it, works in her favor. With proper monitoring and careful post-operative care, she'll make a full recovery."

Knox leaped from his seat. "Can we see her?"

Asking was just a formality because he'd find his way to her regardless.

"Once she's finished with her recovery and taken to the Cardiac Care Unit, you can see her in groups of two. For a *limited amount of time*. But I need to warn you, we're keeping her intubated and in a medically induced coma for the night."

"Why?" Knox questioned. "If the surgery went well, why not let her wake up?"

"We want to make sure she can maintain a sufficient cardiac output while the vent does a large percentage of her respiratory work. Taking her off too soon could erase all the progress we've achieved to this point."

Gretchen wrapped the doctor in a bone-crushing hug, and immediately following, Knox's mother did the same.

Dr. Benedict smiled for the first time since entering the room. "I'll be around if any of you should have any other questions."

As everyone around him cried and hugged, Knox dropped his head to his hands and didn't bother to hide his overwhelming tears of relief.

CHAPTER
THIRTY-ONE

Bright overhead lights seared Zoey's retinas as she blinked her vision into focus. Stark white walls surrounded her, one of which consisted entirely of clear glass. Nurses hustled up and down a long corridor, some alone, some in pairs, and some with purple-gowned patients.

Georgetown Med.

Zoey registered the sound of her cardiac monitor just as her door opened. A young nurse with a stethoscope around her neck cleaned her hands with wall-mounted foam, and glanced up.

Zoey recognized her immediately as one of the nurses who'd taken care of her last year. "Nickie."

"You're awake! That means those meds are working." She hustled to the monitor and adjusted the settings. "Your oxygen level's near one hundred percent. How are you feeling? Any residual shortness of breath? Do you want to see if we can ween you a bit?"

"That would be great." Zoey sat up, making it halfway before a sharp pain ice-picked through her chest. She sucked in a quick gasp. "What happened?"

The nurse shifted her gaze to the monitors. "I have

some pain medicine for you, and then I'll tell the doctor that you're up. And that sweet friend of yours from last time around should be back any second."

"You're not going to tell me what happened, huh? Then I guess it's not exactly good news." Zoey tried un-fogging her memory, but every attempt left her even more confused.

The nurse smiled compassionately. "What's important is that you're exactly where you need to be. Now, how about those pain meds?"

Zoey nodded and watched her push the medication into her IV. A minute later, she lost the battle against her droopy eyelids, and when she cracked them open again, the lights had been dimmed and noticeably fewer people roamed the hall outside her room.

Something flexed around her right hand.

Knox sat hunched in a chair pulled close to her bed, his head resting next to their entwined hands. *Asleep.*

The sight of him brought a rush of emotions—and tears—to her eyes. She tried sniffing them away but it didn't work.

Knox jolted upright. His startled gaze fastened on hers before a rush of emotions flickered over his face. "You're awake."

Zoey smiled tiredly. "I am . . . unless I'm dreaming."

Knox brushed away an errant tear with his thumb. "Not dreaming. How are you feeling, angel?"

"Like an elephant used my sternum as a foot rest." She grimaced as she shifted in bed. "Or maybe a parade of elephants. A circus? Is the circus in town and I didn't know it?"

"I'll call the nurse for more pain meds." Knox reached for the call bell.

She dropped her hand over his. "No. No more meds. That's why I slept for . . . how long has it been since I was last awake?"

He glanced at his watch. "Nickie said you were up briefly around four o'clock, but when I came back five minutes later, you were fast asleep. But that's okay. You need your rest."

"What happened?" She gestured to the bulky bandage beneath her patient gown. "I mean, other than the obvious."

"All you need to know is that it's over. We can talk about the rest once you're feeling better."

"Knox." Zoey squeezed his hand. "*Please*. I keep saying to myself that what I remember couldn't possibly be right . . . that Dr. Samuel couldn't have been the Cupid Killer."

He blew out a heavy sigh. "Well, he was. The question we couldn't answer was how you found out, and why you were at his place."

There wasn't any accusation in his voice. Just concern. Zoey rewound time until her memory finally came back into focus. Her walk. His house. The album. Zoey spilled it all, noting that not much seemed a surprise to him.

"And he's the one who took a shot at you . . . because of *me*," it pained Zoey to admit. " . . . and all those innocent women. It's all my fault."

Tears took over Zoey's voice.

"Hey." Knox sat on her bed and gently eased her

into his side. "None of that is on you, baby. Do you hear me? No way in hell are you responsible for his actions. None of them."

"It doesn't change what happened."

"But it can change how we move forward from here." Knox cupped her cheek and gently tilted her face toward his. "I'm so sorry, angel. I should've told you about Wilcox as soon as I found out who he was."

"And why didn't you?"

There was no judgment in her voice. No anger. Knox swallowed his emotions—or tried to—and was honest. "Because I knew hearing about Wilcox would hurt you, and since I was doing such a piss poor job of protecting you from myself, I needed to protect you from something. It was fucked up, I know."

Zoey clutched his hand tight. "You don't need to save me from you."

"Obviously I do. I pissed you off so much that you stalked away from me and got caught in a killer's web. I'm a hazard if I ever saw one." His gaze flickered over her face. "But I'm a selfish bastard because I still don't want to let you go. I love you, Zoey. *So damn much*. And I was a coward not to say anything earlier."

Zoey's monitor picked up its pace. "Wh-what did you say?"

"That I'm a hazard?"

"After that."

"That I'm a selfish bastard?"

"Even after that."

Knox's gaze dropped to their entwined hands. He brought them up to his mouth and brushed his lips softly against her knuckles. "You mean about loving you?"

"You love me?" Zoey whispered.

Knox's hand firmed around hers. "You're passing over an opportunity to call me a selfish bastard?"

"I'll get back to that...later." The sight of a grin on Knox's tired face made Zoey's heart flip...for a good reason.

"You reminded me that home is where my heart is...Steele Ops, my family, my friends...you. *You're* my home, Zoey. I love you with everything that I have and all that I am."

An outpouring of happiness bubbled from Zoey's chest in the form of tears. "Will you do me a favor?"

"Anything, baby. You name it."

"Will you tell me why you've always called me angel?"

His unfiltered smile tugged up Zoey's own lips. "You haven't figured it out yet?"

"No."

"When I first laid eyes on you, strutting up from the riverbank, the sun setting behind you, there was this golden halo all around you. You looked like an earthbound angel. A guardian angel. *My* angel. Calling you anything else didn't seem right."

The throbbing ache in her chest was slowly replaced by an all-encompassing warmth.

Love.

"I love you, Knox Steele. So much. I know we both made some mistakes along the way, but I'm willing to go all-in. I want you to be the Angel to my Buffy—

but with a happily ever after ending. I want to be your everything."

Knox brushed his mouth against hers. "You already are, Zoey."

Bulky bandage be damned, she caught his cheeks between her palms and pulled his mouths to hers. She kissed him until her cardiac monitor squealed, and nurse Nickie came running.

Something the other woman said when she'd first woken up clicked into place. *Your sweet friend from the last time around.*

Zoey propped her forehead against his and felt the ghost of a smile slip onto her face. "Last year. You came. You were here."

His thumb caressed her bottom lip. "I'll *always* be here for you, angel."

EPILOGUE

Zoey stuck her head out of Knox's truck window and inhaled the scent of lilacs. "This is the best thing I've ever smelled. And I'm not just saying that because for the first time in weeks, I'm not surrounded by bleach."

Knox came around to the passenger side and opened her door, grinning. "Wait until I get you around back. Between the blooming flower beds and the river, your cute little nose is going to be in heaven."

He scooped her into a princess carry, making her laugh. "My heart malfunctioned on me, Knox, not my legs. I can walk around to the garden."

"My time as your Knight in Shining Kevlar has a shelf life, so let me get my time in while I can, woman."

Zoey rolled her eyes and chuckled. During the course of her hospitalization, they'd had a long-overdue talk. About everything. Them. Their families. Her condition. Even Samuel, may his ass rot in jail forever.

She'd agreed to let Knox hover until she was cleared to go back to work, and then it was Neanderthal caveman only *part* of the time, within reason, and she retained full authority to tell him to leave her alone and suck it up.

For now, she enjoyed the special treatment.

They cleared the back corner of Iron Bars and were immediately greeted by a loud *Welcome Home*. All Zoey's favorite people stood on the patio, soft music playing in the background as they waited for their arrival.

Knox gently returned her to her feet and dropped a soft kiss onto her lips. "Visit. Rest. And do *not* overdo it. Knox's order."

"Trying to get those in there while you can?" Zoey teased.

"I'm not one to waste opportunities, sweetheart."

Liam cleared his throat and inserted himself between them. "Seriously, man. You've been hogging her for weeks. Step aside."

"Just...be careful," Knox warned, making Zoey's eyes roll.

She wrapped Liam in a hug, and then quickly did the same to everyone else.

Cade, looking uneasy, approached last.

"What's wrong, big brother?" She hugged him close and then held on a bit longer.

"You know I love you, right, little bit?"

"And I love you."

"You know I'd do anything for you."

"Same here."

She pulled back, noticing her brother's preoccupation. "You're starting to freak me out."

"Mom made me invite him. I didn't want to, but..." He gestured to their left.

Zoey's gaze slid over to the back steps of Iron Bars. Hogan Wilcox stood apart from everyone else, hands shoved deep in his pockets.

She and Knox had talked about her father too.

Beneath the shock his presence had caused was a wide range of emotions, some good, some not. But they were there, and they weren't about to go away.

She looked back to her brother to see unveiled anger simmering beneath the surface. "I don't like what he did."

"Nope."

"I don't like his reasoning for doing it."

"Me neither."

"But..."

Cade looked at her expectantly. "But?"

"We've all learned that there aren't any guarantees in life. I don't want to live—or die—with any regrets. And I suspect that Hogan...our dad...doesn't either."

Cade cursed. "I hate it when you break out the common sense."

Knox's warm arms wrapped around her from behind. His mouth dropped on her neck in a series of gentle kisses. "Frowning isn't allowed, angel."

"I'm not frowning. I'm discussing." Zoey slid an evil smirk toward Cade. "And I was about to tell my brother that my common sense can be used for a wide range of scenarios. Work. Family. *And* love."

On cue, Grace's laughter drifted toward them from where she talked to Tank and Roman less than twelve feet away.

"I adore you, sis, but please do *not* give me love advice," Cade pleaded.

Liam called for some assistance manning the grill, giving her brother a reason to escape.

Zoey chuckled as Knox turned her toward him. "You're a menace, Wright."

She wrapped her arms around his waist and clung to the back of his shirt. "I'm not a menace. I just want to see the people I care about happy."

"And you think Grace would make Cade happy."

"I don't think it. I know it. Cade and Grace know it too. They just need a bit of time to come to terms with it."

Chuckling, Knox picked her up into another princess carry and stalked toward the *Angel Eyes*, tied to the Iron Bars' recently renovated dock.

"Where are we going?" Zoey asked, hopeful.

"We're going to sit out on the deck and watch the stars...and if I fall asleep holding you in my arms, good."

"What about the party?"

"They'll get us...or we'll hear the shouts when Liam burns off his eyebrows."

Zoey laughed all the way to the boat, her cheek pressed against Knox's chest. Love warmed every inch of her body, and beneath her sternum, her heart fell into perfect sync with his.

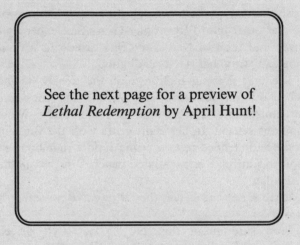

See the next page for a preview of
Lethal Redemption by April Hunt!

CHAPTER
ONE

Trash skidded across the street, the only inhabitant of the pier other than FBI profiler Grace Steele, her Lyft driver, and the two New York City–sized rats scrambling away from her ride's headlights.

The tall, arching buildings of the urban skyline etched out the lowering sun, putting the dock-side warehouse into close running for World's Most Ominous setting. In her eight years with the Bureau, Grace hadn't once read a crime report that boasted about beautiful, overpopulated beaches in the middle of the day.

Three times out of ten, they showcased a scene just like this one.

"You sure about this, lady?" Her Lyft driver, Anthony, glanced at the building in front of them, and frowned. "My ma always claimed I couldn't spot a bad idea if it stared me dead in the eye, but I can see that isn't a place you should walk in daylight, much less this late at night. I can take you back—no charge."

Grace bit her tongue to keep from accepting the offer, and read her boss's text message for the third time in as many minutes: *321 Pier Six. Be there. Nine o'clock. No excuses!*

Correct address. Correct time. And loaded with an invisible warning that to defy the FBI Director's explicit demand would mean severe consequences. Still, she'd never wanted to disobey orders so bad in her life—except when Aunt Cindy forbade her from buying a prom dress she considered "light-years too short for a grown woman, much less a sixteen-year-old girl."

Thwarting Aunt Cindy's edict had gotten her laundry duty, which was no small punishment living with four overgrown male cousins. But disregarding a direct order from Director Vance would get her fired.

She was already on the director's shit-list and couldn't afford a second ding.

Not that the first one was her fault. Misogyny had no place in the Bureau, and she'd gladly sit through another Resolving Conflict seminar for the chance to tell her former regional supervisor where he could stuff his sexist comments.

Side note: *It would've involved heavy-duty spelunking equipment and an industrial-lit flashlight.*

But her notorious Steele temper flare-up last month was the reason why she couldn't disobey orders now.

Grace tucked her phone into her back pocket and climbed out of the car. "Thanks for the offer, but I'm sure."

"It's your life, lady . . . but I may hang around a bit to be on the safe side."

It hovered on her lips to tell him that it wasn't needed, but she swallowed the words at the last minute. "Thanks."

Grace turned toward the ramshackle building and

cursed. Windows not boarded up were broken, revealing the dark abyss beyond. No lights. No sounds. The entire place looked as if it hadn't seen a caretaker in close to a decade.

If it wasn't December, and if the text hadn't come from Vance herself, she'd think this was an office April Fool's prank. But the director didn't joke, or smile, or make second requests.

Grace tugged her coat collar up to protect from the chilling wind whipping in from the Hudson. "Maybe this is her new way to weed out subpar agents."

She didn't believe that either.

In eight years with the Bureau, she'd made a name for herself, partly because she was damn good at what she did, and also because she did it *a lot*. Vacations weren't her thing, and so she had a lot of time to perfect her craft.

She dissected people—*psychologically*. A criminal profiler, she picked away at people's thought processes, examined their motives, what made them tick, and why they did the things they did with the hope of stopping them before they did it again.

Though trained like any field agent, she spent most of her time behind a desk, or across an interview table...which made her even more wary about why she'd been directed to make a Cloak and Dagger appearance down at the docks.

"And you're not going to find out standing here like a statue." Grace's smart business heels clacked on the broken asphalt as she steadily headed to the rusted iron doors.

Three feet away, two men stepped out from behind a stack of crates.

"You can stop right there, ma'am." The one on her left, focused and unsmiling, aimed his gun toward her chest.

The second one stepped forward, holstering his weapon. "Special Agent Steele."

"You seem to have one up on me. You know who I am."

Clean-shaven with dark, close-cropped hair, and a fit, lean physique, he couldn't have been much older than herself. His long, confident stride and that little glint in his eye identified him as law enforcement right away.

Grace's eyes flickered down to the pin attached to his left suit lapel.

Secret-freakin'-Service.

"Agent Jake Carelli. Secret Service. Are you carrying a weapon, ma'am?"

At barely thirty years old, she considered herself a few years away from *ma'am*. But with one gun still aimed in her direction, she swallowed her smart retort. "In this neighborhood? Yeah, I have my service weapon."

"You'll need to relinquish it to me." Agent Carelli held out his hand expectantly.

Grace laughed . . . and realized she was the only one. "Oh wait. You're serious? Yeah, sorry, but that's not happening."

"Sorry, ma'am, but it is."

Again with the damn ma'am crap. Releasing a heavy sigh, she carefully reached beneath her jacket and unhooked Magdalena, her trusty Magnum .22, from her holster and placed it in Agent Carelli's hand. "Only God can help you if something happens to her. You hear me?"

"Loud and clear, ma'am." The Secret Service agent's lips twitched. "I'll take good care of her."

"Good. And while you're at it, you can stop the *ma'am* business anytime."

"Noted...*Special Agent Steele*." He smirked, the move showcasing an impressive set of dimples.

Once upon a time, the handsome, cocky type had been her catnip. But teenager Grace had gotten a first-hand crash course on all the epic ways for that to smack you in the face. It was fun at first, but reality had a way of waking you up. The only way to ensure a happily ever after was to make it yourself.

Agent Carelli tapped the communication device hooked around his left ear. "Special Agent Steele has arrived and is on her way inside."

The door behind him opened with a heavy *thunk*.

"And where exactly am I going once I'm inside?" Grace asked.

"You'll see."

"Great. I just love surprises that lurk in dark warehouses," Grace muttered, her sarcasm earning her a small chuckle from the agent.

With a final warning glare at Carelli, still holding Magdalena hostage, she stepped through the doorway and was instantly greeted by two more Secret Service agents, one of whom blocked her entry into the main room.

"Arms and legs out, ma'am."

Grace sighed, but did as requested. The second agent ran a metal detector baton over her body, and once satisfied, nodded to his cohort, who ushered her through a second set of double doors and into the large, and obviously unused, old sewing factory.

The second she spotted the lone figure standing center stage, her curiosity turned into a lead weight that dropped her stomach to her feet.

Pierce Brandt.

Vice President of the United States.

Deemed too pretty for government work while on the campaign trail, the former senator sported a full head of salt-and-pepper hair and broad shoulders that remained from his days in the military. Both his smile and his general youth had been media fodder before he'd taken office... but neither was in the room.

Dark circles framed his once brilliant green eyes, and his well-known smile had been replaced by a tight-lipped grimace. He looked a far cry and a few decades away from the man on the news who effortlessly charmed foreign dignitaries.

This Brandt, with his shoulders slouched, looked more like a man defeated.

"Special Agent Grace Steele. Finally, we meet." He held out a hand in greeting. "I've heard many great things about you from Director Vance, and I can see that my presence is a shock, which means the director abided my wishes and didn't tell you anything about this meeting."

Grace sucked down her nerves. "Not a thing, sir."

"Good. Good. I really am sorry for all the secrecy, but I'm afraid it was a necessary evil. I needed to make sure this conversation remained private."

"Because the White House isn't secure... sir?"

He chuckled at her brazen question. "Secure? Most definitely. Private? No. I've asked you here as a personal favor because for a litany of reasons, I can't involve local law enforcement or federal resources."

And the surprises kept coming. She cleared her throat. "You do realize that I'm a *federal* agent, right?"

He smiled, the act never reaching his eyes. "I know many things about you, Special Agent Steele. I also know that you've worked with a private security firm in the very recent past—although I believe there was a small technicality."

"The technicality being that it was actually the DCPD with whom I was consulting on the Beltway Cupid Killer case."

Brandt leaned against the lone table, crossing his arms across his broad chest. "Very true. But it was Steele Ops that played a key role in the apprehension of the Cupid Killer, as well as in the rescue of your friend Zoey Wright."

Grace bit the inside of her cheek.

She knew whom she'd worked with, and how everything played out six months ago. She'd had a first-row seat to the Cupid Killer horror show. The image of medics straddling her best friend's near lifeless body in an attempt to restart her heart would forever haunt her nightmares.

"Sir..." Grace treaded carefully, holding back the

snark her aunt said would get her into trouble one day. "I'm not one for playing games. You obviously know that Steele Ops is run by my cousins, so if we could get to the reason why we're here, that would be great."

"I like your brash, unapologetic tenacity, Special Agent Steele." Pierce Brandt's gaze slid over her left shoulder. "You weren't lying, Mr. Wright. She's perfect for this assignment. I don't think I could've chosen better myself."

Grace froze.

Wright.

A common name. Thousands of people had it in New York alone, but only one possessed the power to raise her body temperature a good few hundred degrees. Right now, she was dangerously close to finding out how hot a human had to be before bursting into flames.

This didn't make sense. This was New York, not DC, where her cousins had been deep in the throes of wooing him into the family business.

Steeling her spine, Grace turned, and came face-to-face with the last man on which she ever wanted to lay eyes—or anything except a strong right hook.

Cade Wright leaned against the far wall, looking better than he had any right to in worn blue jeans and a long-sleeved dark Henley that molded to his broad shoulders. Dirty-blond hair brushed against his collar, and a few days' worth of stubble covered the old scar on his chin, but it was there.

She'd been the one to give it to him what felt like a million years ago.

"What the hell are you doing here?" Grace forced her gaze off his body and up to his eyes.

Those cobalt-blue eyes had helped him get away with murder more times than she could count, and had been a key factor not only in gifting him her virginity, but played a role in her lapse of judgment—and shedding of clothes—six months ago.

Grace fisted her hands at her side, barely resisting the urge to throw the nearest object at his overinflated head. Probably a good thing, since that thing happened to be Vice President Brandt.

"Grace. It's good to see you too." Cade's mouth twitched as he pushed off the wall and slowly approached.

Not a day went by that she didn't wonder how her sweet best friend shared an entire genepool with the cocky ass.

Grace ripped her gaze—and her ire—away from her best friend's brother and turned to Brandt. "I'm sorry, sir, but no. I can't help you."

Brandt's eyebrows rose into his hairline. "You can't help me? I haven't even told you what the job entails."

"I know, but it's not possible. If it's a criminal profiler you need, I can give you the names of a few colleagues who I'm sure will do a fantastic job."

"I'm afraid you don't understand, Special Agent Steele. *Your* name is the one that's been recommended—not only by the director herself, but by the security firm that I've hired to handle this personal matter." The vice president's tone didn't leave room for debate. "This involves my family...my only child...which means I need the best. And you, along with Mr. Wright and Steele Ops, are the best in your fields. I'm not taking any chances with the life of my daughter, Agent Steele."

Grace sputtered, unable to think of an argument. "Isn't your daughter studying art abroad?"

"That was the public excuse we gave for her absence. I'm afraid my daughter's been conned into leaving everything and everyone she loves."

"Conned by who?"

"A group I believe that you're familiar with. The Order of the New Dawn."

Grace's blood froze in her veins.

Not much shocked her. Diving into the disturbed minds of criminals was how she made her living. But that name. *That group.*

Pierce Brandt's description of the OND made them sound like a binge-drinking fraternity rather than the mind-wiping cult she knew them to be...

And she knew because from the age of five to thirteen, Grace Steele had been considered a Child of the New Dawn.

She'd spent most of her childhood in a cult.

And as far as she knew, she was the only one who'd ever gotten out.

* * *

Intervening now, regardless of how much Cade wanted to, risked not only getting on the vice president's bad side, but jeopardized his jaw's mobility when Grace threw a punch . . . which she would the second he opened his mouth.

It's why he'd volunteered to represent Steele Ops at this meeting. She already hated him, and it kept her cousins, the Steele behind Steele Ops, in her somewhat amiable good graces. They'd talk sense into her—if he could get her back to DC.

Grace straightened her spine and turned her golden brown gaze back to Brandt. "Mr. Vice President . . . sir. I'm sorry about your daughter. New Dawn sinks their claws in deep, and from what I've heard about them since, that hold has gotten progressively tighter."

"Which is why I need *you*. Steele Ops has been working tirelessly to get into Teague Rossbach's inner circle, but it's proven more difficult than expected. I believe *you* are the missing link, Special Agent Steele. Both your training and your history with the group could be the key factor in bringing my daughter home."

Jake Carelli stepped up to Brandt, clearing his throat. "Sir, we need to be moving along."

The vice president locked Grace in his sights and gestured to a manila envelope on the table. "That's everything we have on Sarah's new boyfriend, including a timeline of their relationship and their days leading up to her disappearance. Mr. Wright and his colleagues already have the updated information on the OND. Thank you, Special Agent Steele. This means a great deal to me and to my family."

Grace remained statue-still, moving only to take her firearm from Carelli, and watched Brandt's team leave the warehouse.

Cade braced for impact. "Grace—"

"*Don't*." One word, weighted with a steep warning.

She grabbed the manila folder and stalked angrily toward the exit. Sighing, he followed.

Quiet-Grace was more dangerous than her fly-off-the-handle counterpart. Quiet-Grace meant more time to dwell and stew. Quiet-Grace plotted retributions that made grown men cry and call out for their mamas.

"I should've let Liam come out here instead," Cade muttered to himself.

They'd barely cleared the front door when Grace whirled around. His hand automatically shot out to steady her as she teetered on her feet.

"Touch me only if you want to lose that hand." Grace skewered him with her golden-eyed glare.

"Gracie."

"It's *Grace*," she corrected through gritted teeth. "Don't you dare try that wounded look on me, Cade Wright. Seriously? *An ambush?*"

"Ambush is going a little too far, don't you think?"

"No, I don't. DC is the capital of the free world. They don't have working telephones? Or hell, email? You let me walk into this freakin' blind!"

Cade's hackles rose. He crossed his arms across his chest, going on the defensive. "It's not like we didn't try to get hold of you. Knox, Roman, *and* Ryder. Liam was five seconds away from attempting carrier pigeon. We even roped Zoey into the coordinated effort, but surprise, surprise, all voicemails, texts, and emails went unreturned."

"If I didn't get back to you, then there was a good reason. Oh, say, my *job*!"

"For what it's worth, I was against it."

Grace released an unladylike snort. "It's worth nothing."

With a low growl, she stalked away, even the clack of her heels telling him to fuck himself.

Cade couldn't help but watch. Tall and curvy, she filled out her suit in a way that was meant to be business-smart, but instead, fueled every naughty librarian fantasy he'd had as a horny teenager.

Headlights flashed in the distance. Cade's attention ripped away from Grace's ass and on to the approaching sedan. "Where are you going?"

"Home. Which is where you should go."

Cade spotted the Lyft sticker on the car window, and the scowling man sitting behind the steering wheel. "There's no reason for you to pay for a ride. I'm parked around the corner."

Grace stopped cold, aiming her glare his way. "Why would you think that I'd get in a car with *you*?"

"Because unless your views on commercial flying have changed, I'm your ticket to the Steele Ops jet. Or we can drive down to DC. Eight hours. You and me. Side by side. We'd have a hell of a lot time to catch up."

He smirked.

She hated flying coach, and booking a flight this out of the blue guaranteed her a seat within toilet-sniffing distance. Close quarters on the jet, or closer quarters in his rental car. Either option was a win for him, although the masochist in him hoped she picked the car ride. Eight hours of jibes and strewn insults sounded like fun.

She smiled sweetly, and the sight of it dissolved his own. "I'll see you in DC."

Without another glance, she slipped into the back seat of the waiting car, leaving him to stare after her like some kind of abandoned lover...which coincidentally, was close to what he'd done to her thirteen years earlier.

ABOUT THE AUTHOR

April blames her incurable chocolate addiction on growing up in rural Pennsylvania, way too close to America's chocolate capital, Hershey. She now lives in Virginia with her college sweetheart husband, two young children, and a cat who thinks she's a human-dog hybrid. On those rare occasions she's not donning the cape of her children's personal chauffer, April's either planning, plotting, or writing about her next alpha hero and the woman he never knew he needed, but now can't live without.

To learn more, visit:
AprilHuntBooks.com
Twitter @AprilHuntBooks
Facebook.com/AprilHuntBooks